RONDO

Kazimierz Brandys

RONDO

Translated by Jaroslaw Anders

Europa
editions

Europa Editions
116 East 16th Street
New York, N.Y. 10003
www.europaeditions.com
info@europaeditions.com

Library of Congress Cataloging in Publication Data is available
ISBN 978-1-60945-004-5

Brandys, Kazimierz
Rondo

Book design by Emanuele Ragnisco
www.mekkanografici.com
Cover photo © Hulton Archive/Getty Images

Prepress by Grafica Punto Print – Rome

Printed in Canada

RONDO

If someone whose name means nothing sends a letter to a magazine, he can neither expect a reply nor be certain his remarks will ever see print. There are times, however, when writing such a letter is a necessity. That's how it is in my case.

Having read the article "A Chapter in the History of Struggle" by Professor W. Janota, published in issue No. 11 of your quarterly, I am taking the liberty of sending you some of my comments and reminiscences concerning the Rondo organization, whose activities in 1942-44 are the subject of Professor Janota's study. I am quite aware you may consider my contribution unprintable, at the very least for two reasons: excessive length and the rather personal character of my testimony. There also may be the third reason—the highly improbable nature of the events I wish to present. If I have decided, nevertheless, to submit these pages to you, I have done it less for the sake of publication than out of respect for objective truth. My only wish is to share this truth with someone interested in contemporary history, someone who will ponder my remarks for a time and, instead of throwing them into a wastebasket, will place them in some file in his archive.

I have chosen you as my trustee. I shall not deny that the immediate reason was the publication of "A Chapter in the History of Struggle" in your quarterly. I hope you will find my statements interesting, at least insofar as they call into question the thesis of the article accepted by you for publication. I also believe the task of your periodical is not only publishing but collecting truthful materials from the war years. That is why I decided to write to you.

Let me start with some essential "facts" mentioned by the author of the article. I should stress that the events I am going to talk about, as well as many others, were the subject of repeated interrogations to which I was subjected by the security forces shortly after the war. My written testimonies of that time, as well as transcripts of the hearings, agree in general outline with the following explanations provided here in a more elaborate form.

Professor W. Janota claims that (1) Rondo was founded in May 1942; (2) it was established by people smuggled in secretly from London; (3) its activities included extensive infiltration of the Wehrmacht and SS circles as well as surveillance of German strategic objectives. (4) While discussing the leadership of the group the author mentions unverified rumors circulating even up to the present day that the real commander of Rondo was an undercover plenipotentiary of the Supreme Command in London, a mysterious person of "legendary origins," to use the author's expression. Professor Janota dismisses these rumors as "probably unfounded." And finally, (5) the author remarks that the most important operations of Rondo were carried out by the IR section (Intelligence and Reconnaissance), headed by Professor Janota himself. Among his collaborators of that time he includes Tola Mohoczy, a Warsaw actress of the interwar period. I shall try to demonstrate that all the above claims except the first are dubious in nature and imprecise. First, however, I shall concentrate on the most fundamental issue, or rather a question: Did Rondo really exist?

I beg your patience. I cannot provide a decisive yes or no answer, but I can assure you that in the initial stage Rondo did not exist. What is more important, it was conceived expressly for the purpose of nonexistence. If I can still ask for your patience and attention—I am not a maniac, I do not suffer from hallucinations, and I have never sent letters to magazines before. I would not trouble myself with this scribbling if its subject did not concern—as you shall see soon enough—the most dramatic issue of my life. I was the founder of Rondo, or, to be more precise, its inventor. At least one item mentioned in "A Chapter in the History of Struggle" is absolutely correct—the date: May 1942.

I was twenty-eight. I was born in 1913 in Krakow, where my father was a high school teacher. In the first years of the Independence my parents moved to the western part of the country—to Wielkopolska, where my father became the principal of a local Gymnasium in a provincial town formerly occupied under the Prussian partition. I spent my early youth there. Upon matriculation I completed my army training in a military college in Wlodzimierz Wolynski, and I later joined the Department of Law at Warsaw University. I shall have to dwell on that period a little longer since it included certain decisive events of my life.

I spent my first months in Warsaw walking the streets. I had plenty of time. Lectures were usually scheduled in the morning and I had whole afternoons for myself. Nobody knew me in that city. I did not expect adventure and I would have been truly astonished if I had been told my life would be anything but a sequence of days filled with simple activities lived in semi-resignation and not so desperate boredom. Resignation and boredom experienced without comment, almost as a natural fact of life—that is how I reacted at that time to my immediate surroundings, such as city traffic, snowstorms, passing streetcars, store windows, and the faces of women in the streets. I could say without exaggeration that even my attitude toward myself was devoid of any strong emotion and marked by the proper indifference of a servant. I made myself coffee, polished my shoes, and washed my hands as if assisting someone else. I did not expect any unusual events or changes in my routine and I lived in a quiet certainty that this was exactly how human life should be. Only one thing sometimes unsettled the course of my existence: the thought of my hair. The fact that it was red seemed to separate me from my environment and to portend certain irregularities in my destiny. I inherited the color of my hair from my mother.

While reading "A Chapter in the History of Struggle" I came across several remarks concerning my person that stressed this particular detail. Professor Janota writes that I used to appear with "blazing hair cut to a stubble," which was a "characteristic element of the local scene." He usually puts me at the very end: ". . . and finally Tom [followed by my real name and surname]—silent, reliable, with his solid provincial elegance and a mane of fiery hair." I close the pageant: red-haired, superfluous, odd. This picture, however, does not offend me since I consider myself a typical outsider. I was and I am an outsider in the theater as well. If it were not for a certain invitation to dinner, and everything that followed, today I would probably be working as a legal counselor to some housing cooperative.

I must make a small correction, however, in reference to Professor Janota's article. I never used my pseudonym Tom in Rondo. I used it in the Home Army, and Professor Janota could have learned of it only after the war.

I wish you could understand me. I am probably writing more for myself than for you. I am getting involved in my own past. Memory is a warm morass; one sinks in deeper and deeper . . .

After the clean provinces of Wielkopolska, Warsaw made an unfavorable impression on me, and during the first period of my stay I could not understand what that city of drafts and speeding streetcars was really about. There were more palaces than in Poznan, a city I knew quite well, but the local tenement houses with their flat, soot-covered façades seemed rather poor and unkempt. The dominant colors were dirty sand and tallow gray. What struck me about the façades was the absence of granite or ashlar facing. Burnt brick, so typical of the towns of the Prussian partition, was practically nowhere to be found. Sometimes I thought the local tenements must have been modeled after one-story brick village houses. Several such houses, placed one on top of the other, made a tenement house, like those that filled sprawling and poorly integrated sections of the city. One could hardly "walk around" Warsaw. Main streets led directly to ugly suburbs, which suddenly turned into fields. The river seemed to flow too low and too wide. I had to take a streetcar to get to a park. I was surprised to see urinals hidden among trees in downtown areas. The passersby, who did not notice these curiosities, seemed to be preoccupied. When I left the station and walked with my suitcase to the nearest street corner, I asked somebody how to get to the center of the city. It turned out that I was in the center, at its most central point. It was an intersection of streetcar rails. Streetcars were coming from four directions, people were getting off and on, and streetcars were leaving in four directions. The railway station, with its clock tower, resembled municipal buildings, yet there was no sign of a central square, a cathedral, a palace, or an opera house—only tall buildings covered with signboards, a tangle of power lines, and rows of streetlamps stretching in the same four directions. And yet I was standing in the very center of the capital, in the most important place in the whole country, so to speak. I took a horse cab and asked the driver to take me to the Belvedere Palace. After a quarter of an hour of shaking and clattering I came upon a country manor house with a colonnade and surrounded by a fence. Farther on, the street plunged downhill, evidently leaving the city.

I had my reasons for going directly from the station to the Belvedere. My mother had died several years earlier, but before World War I, when my parents were still living in Krakow, their home was frequently visited by Marshal Pilsudski. I did not know the facts, but a legend concerning my origins survived until the Independence. Once, during a school recess, two of my classmates informed me that I was the natural son of the Marshal. The gossip must have followed us all the way from Krakow, for I soon learned to recognize its effects in the way my teachers looked at me when calling me to the blackboard. I suppose the rumor must have upset my father's life, because less than two years after my mother's death he wedded a nurse from the local hospital—many years his junior—and shortly after my return from the military college he sent me off to Warsaw to study law.

All this not only explains my urge to see the Belvedere upon my arrival in Warsaw but also sheds some light on other circumstances that played a prominent role in my life. After a couple of months in Warsaw, while walking along Krucza Street I came upon one of my old classmates, Wladek Sznej, a student of the humanities, who supplemented his budget by working as an extra in a theater. He invited me to come the next day to see him rush onstage in Act III with a halberd in his hand. Just before we parted I reached into my pocketbook for my calling card and handed it to him—just in case, to stay in touch. Before putting it into his pocket he glanced briefly at my printed name and address. It was only a second, but I guessed he must have been visited at that moment by certain doubts as to whether he had treated me with sufficient respect and courtesy. I could not have misinterpreted the glimmer of memory in his eyes when he said, "Till tomorrow evening, then," and departed in his light—one could say, subtle—stride.

For the sake of clarity, let me explain that he was one of the two classmates who revealed to me, in the school corridor, my alleged origin. Even before that incident, however, I always approached him with mixed feelings. Before and after. I hear that his recent literary essays are innovative in certain respects, but for me Wladek Sznej remains the least desirable companion of my adventures.

The next day, reluctant to give up my afternoon stroll, I left as early as five. I had put on the darker of my two suits and a white shirt with a stiff collar. Instead of a regular tie I had chosen a cherry-red bow, and in addition to a hat and a cane I had brought along my gloves. I held the gloves in my left hand and the cane in the right. Dress requirements at that time were less liberal than today, but even if I had appeared in the theater without a hat, a cane, and gloves, nobody would have paid much attention. Only the ushers would have recognized me as a student trying to save some pennies on the cloakroom.

On Napoleon Square I was caught in a storm. I waited out the downpour at the Postal Building, and around seven o'clock the sky started to clear. I leisurely crossed the street and walked toward the public restroom. Raindrops rattled down from wet branches. I placed my gloves in the left pocket of my jacket, hung my cane on my shoulder, and held my breath to avoid the smell of ammonia. After a minute I was back on the street. I almost bumped into a tall, stately man who was leaving the restroom at the same moment. He must have been in a hurry, since he did not seem to notice me, despite my apologies. A moment later I saw him on the corner of Warecka Street getting into a cab drawn by a stalwart gray horse. His posture and appearance seemed to me uncommon, and I thought I must have known him from a portrait or a photograph. His face was not of the kind one encounters every day, and the wide, upward-bent brim of his hat gave it the look of faces from the remote past. I was also struck by yet another distinctive feature of that face, which I shall try to explain later.

I had the most unusual feeling when a couple of minutes after the curtain I saw the same man dashing onstage. I recognized him immediately even though his features were hidden beneath a traveler's hood. The casual and lordly fashion in which he folded the hood above his forehead was unmistakable. Apart from him, the characters consisted of three women. The author, Herman Fey, whom I did not know at that time, placed the action at the turn of the thirteenth century in a feudal castle, probably in Flanders. The title of the play was *The Dove*, and it was one of numerous variations of the story of Don Juan. This time Don Juan was married. During the intermission I bought the program. The main male part was played by a famous actor, Karol Cezarewicz, whose face I must have remembered from photographs. Wladek Sznej appeared—just as he told me—only in the third act, as one of the halberd-carrying guards. When the wise and forgiving wife stabs her husband with a dagger to save him from the ax, the guards freeze in horror. I noticed the way my friend, motionless like the rest of them, looked at the murderess. His gaze astonished me. Wladek Sznej gazed at that woman with the pretty, shapely head with a kind of hungry fascination. His eyes glittered with the same indecent temptation as during a school recess when he could not resist uttering a couple of perfidious words, after which I slapped his face.

It was a loathsome memory—the only time I actually slapped a man, who groaned and covered his cheek with his hand. I noticed that he was afraid, not of another blow (he could have been certain that it would not be repeated), but of a new situation. I had hit him as the alleged Marshal's son. He obviously thought that I would seek revenge in this dangerous and unpredictable capacity.

After the performance I waited in line for a long time at the cloakroom. When I finally handed my ticket to the attendant, she at first could not find my things, and then, after a while, produced a crumpled beige hat. I returned it, explaining that my hat was dark gray and accompanied by a cane and a pair of gloves. She asked me to wait until the cloakroom emptied, when she was sure to find my belongings. I stepped aside, lit a cigarette, and tried to think of nothing in particular, because the consideration of my friend's glance recalled the memory of my slapping his face. I felt myself blush. I blush at the thought to the present day, even though many years have passed since that time and the incident itself seems insignificant when compared with events I would experience later. Besides, we made up shortly afterward and even—in a certain sense—became close friends. I cannot fully understand the phenomenon, though perhaps the age at which one experiences something is more important than the event itself. At the time of that incident I was sixteen years old.

When the foyer emptied I returned to the cloakroom to ask about my things, but a woman there explained that the attendant had already left and she was only a cleaning lady. There was no trace of my hat, my cane, or my gloves. At that time I remembered the only man to whom I could turn for assistance. The cleaning lady led me through the empty theater to a small door above three steps. I hoped the extras had not managed to change and leave yet. There was a dark passage behind the stage sets and more steps leading to a narrow corridor with a row of doors. I passed them without meeting anybody. The corridor ended in a landing decorated with theater posters. There were more stairs leading down. I found myself back in the empty foyer. I turned and found the same corridor I passed a moment earlier. There were sounds of conversation coming from behind the doors on both sides, but I was too embarrassed to knock. I stopped in front of the fourth door. It was ajar. I heard a man's voice. In fact, it was a shrill and piercing shout immediately interrupted by a woman's laughter and a short reply. I was struck by the discrepancy between the tone and what was said. The man shouted, "Everything will be all right, you'll see!" Yet his voice was full of desperation. The woman replied in a tone of forbearing mockery, "No, never,

never," and burst out laughing. Before I had time to think, the door was flung open. For a moment we stood face to face, our chests almost touching. Then she stepped back, saying, "You'd look better with a mustache." I mumbled some apology and quickly left. The door behind me was slammed shut.

I recognized her, of course, but not instantly. She must have removed her makeup, but I recognized her small, shapely head. The bright light from the dressing room shrouded her. Truly, her eyes pierced me with an amused hatred—that is how I would describe it. I could not even guess who the man was, since everything lasted only a second, and apart from her glance nothing reached my consciousness. When I stumbled back to the cloakroom, I realized that I had already heard the words they exchanged. Yes, I had heard them from the stage, though in a different way. But I could not identify the difference, the change. Was it only the intonation? I wasn't listening carefully when the cleaning lady explained that my things had been found on a shelf under the counter. While I was thanking her, I strained my memory to discover what was so intriguing, so special and different in the way the lines were spoken: "Everything will be all right, you'll see!" . . . "No, never, never." But at that time I could not find the answer.

I took my hat, my cane, and my gloves and started looking for the exit. Suddenly I heard my name and my classmate-halberdier appeared in front of me. He said he had been looking for me in the theater "for an hour." Wladek Sznej, whom I had already managed to forget, seemed to me unpleasantly real with his parted hair, his intelligently glittering glasses, his white shirt open at the neck. I rejected as absurd the thought that anything might have existed between that woman and him.

Why since that day did I start going every evening to the Actors' Theater to see *The Dove*? I do not remember. Perhaps it was due to an excess of free time. I still felt lonely in Warsaw, my studies at the Department of Law were limited, as before, to morning lectures, and the prospect of examinations did not bother me at all. My brain was sharp enough. Besides, my almost daily meetings with Wladek Sznej became a habit that gave me no pleasure yet one that I was unable to break. He was my only close associate in the capital, and we shared the history of our provincial youth. He irritated me—that is true— yet loneliness often contents itself with somebody's irritating or boring presence. We could at least talk about our school years. I also have to admit that my friend was well read and well informed. I often used his eloquence—too speculative for my taste and too prone to jumping from one subject to another— as a substitute for reading and also for firsthand observations. He knew Warsaw much better than I, he had information about government circles, and while discussing literary or artistic trends, he liked to drop names: Kaden, Nalkowska, Miriam, Boy. After a performance I usually waited for him in front of the theater. At first he used to arrange a free pass for me. Later, when I started to hide my addiction from him, I bought a student ticket with my university card.

I knew Herman Fey's play by heart. It was by no means a masterpiece, and I doubt whether any theater staged it after the war. Yet each time Jorgens, accompanied by his wife, entered the castle gallery saying, "Heaven and hell! Damned horses! Am I the only one in the whole world who doesn't tire on his journey?" a warm draft of joy filled me and flowed down to my legs. From that moment on my eyes never left the actress with the small head who played Jorgens's wife. She seemed younger onstage than when I saw her in the doorway where our glances first met. I watched with rapture her gestures and mimicry. I experienced with her the feelings of a woman who forgives the infidelities of a man she pities.

Let me briefly summarize the plot.

The horses are tired. The Jorgenses, who are on their way to France, are invited to spend the night at the castle of widow de Rijs. The gentle yet perceptive wife instantly notices a flash of mutual bedazzlement: her husband's eyes reflect the desire of the young widow—and vice versa. "A dove?" the wife asks, smiling, when they are left alone. This is their intimate code name for women who stir Jorgens's passion. The wise companion knows how to wait out the bouts of her husband's lust. This time, however, fate piles on unexpected complications. Madame de Rijs has a fourteen-year-old daughter, Uth. The enamored glances the girl casts at Jorgens intimate a tragedy. The mother is given a sleeping potion, and the daughter appears in her stead at the appointed place. Jorgens does not recognize her—everything happens in the darkness. The catastrophe is not slow in coming.

The dialogue I overheard in the corridor takes place toward the very end of the drama—but in a different sequence. I have pondered for a long time why the pair behind the door chose to change the tone and the order of their lines and, what is more, why they swapped roles. In order to explain that, I have to return once more to the plot of the play.

Having fallen into the trap, Jorgens assures his wife that she is his only love. He is telling the truth. They both love each other and are bound by the deepest mutual understanding of their natures. With unwitting cynicism Jorgens describes the essence of their marital union: "I shall never leave you. You will never betray me." That scene—perhaps the best in the whole play—takes place in a prison cell. Little Uth avenges the night that left her nothing but bloodstained linen. She tells her mother that Jorgens has raped her. Then it is Madame de Rijs's turn to take her revenge as the offended mother and rejected lover. She accuses him before the bishop's tribunal. The verdict: beheading by the ax. When Jorgens's wife spends the last night with him in the prison cell, all she wants is to rescue him from the terror of awaiting death. His plea for mercy, she tells him, will certainly be heard. His punishment will be commuted to five years in the tower. She swears: "You'll endure all. Five years will soon pass. Later—we shall always be together." Bringing him a cup of wine, she repeats with a smile: "You will never leave me. I shall never betray you." The sun shines through the bars. They stand embracing by the window. A young girl with blond hair crosses the bishop's garden carrying a jug. The steps of the guards can be heard behind the stage. The wife points to the girl. "Look, a dove . . ." Watching her swaying hips, Jorgens does not notice the dagger, has no time to feel the terror of death. At that moment the halberdiers enter the stage.

The two mentioned lines are uttered during that last scene. The man prefers death to five years in prison. ("No, never, never.") The woman consoles him in a motherly way. ("Everything will be all right, you'll see!") Thus the words spoken onstage by the man were uttered behind the door by the woman. The woman's lines were spoken by the man. A different stress and tone gave each line a different meaning.

By the end of the third performance, through close observation of both actors, I had a hunch. My suspicions were confirmed one week later by Wladek Sznej on the day he saw me leaving the Belvedere.

I was arrested at half past four in the afternoon on May 13. A sergeant of the gendarmerie and a man in a winter coat approached me from both sides when I was walking with my hat and my cane along the fence watching a navy-blue car parked inside. I remember the date, the hour, and many other details because on the same day, late in the evening, an event of predominant importance in my life took place. I was led through the court of the Belvedere to the guardhouse, where I was interrogated by an officer with a black beard and a yellow cord hanging from his shoulder across his chest. My only identification was my university card, but my sober answers seemed to make a good impression. The officer asked about my nationality and political affiliations. He was especially interested in whether I was Ukrainian. He asked me three times why I had been "hanging around" the Belvedere for a whole week. I replied that I was interested in historical sites. The officer said nothing. He was turning my university card in his hands, and though he was not looking at me, I am sure he was bothered by the color of my hair. I prepared to leave, but he asked me to stay. He went to the adjacent room and I heard him speaking on the phone. After a quarter of an hour I heard the jingling of spurs behind the door and somebody's voice demanded loudly, "So where is that redhead?" A major of the cavalry entered the room. From that moment on events moved very quickly. He looked briefly at my card and me and explained that there had been a misunderstanding. While shaking my hand he gave his rank and name. Then he returned my card, asking politely whether anybody from my family had served in the Legions. I gave a rather vague reply. The sergeant was ordered to walk me to the gate. At the guard booth he saluted me, and the man in the winter coat handed me my hat and my cane. At the same moment a streetcar turned from Bagatela Street into Ujazdowskie Avenue. A pair of glittering glasses was aimed at me from the platform.

My father used to say that clashing doctrines are nothing but a battle of letters, and that extremist worldviews rush above the world in the form of contradictory axioms. Real life quietly flows below. To the mind overpowered by doctrine man is always an abstraction because doctrines do not recognize nature or fate. They perceive reality only as a reflection of thought. A doctrine may call, for example, for the erection of a new city in place of an old one. If we embrace the idea and give it our support, we shall not anticipate the tragedy of the inhabitants of the old city that must be demolished, nor shall we experience their pain. We shall suffer only when confronted by an adverse opinion and to us the main threat comes from people who claim that cities should not be destroyed. Thus an essential difference of opinion turns into a clash of slogans—a "battle of letters," as my father used to say, or a "polarization of signs," as it would be called today. Life, on the other hand, continues through the power of nature.

Sometimes I asked myself secretly how it really was. Does anything depend on people? Does it depend on them whether the city is left alone or whether it is destroyed and built anew? And I told myself that the city changes and people's views probably change too.

For the twentieth century that was a moderately optimistic philosophy. Indirectly I owed it to my father—a man who possessed the qualities of a provincial thinker. He was popular among his students precisely because of his skepticism toward all human reality—including his duties as principal. He treated me with reserve. I often felt his critical look from behind his glasses. Yet I seemed to interest him. He knew I had been secretly using his library, and our first serious conversation concerned Darwin's theory. To my surprise, he made light of it. He said that history "devours" theories, it chews systems, programs, and theories, and then defecates them. Looking at me with a touch of malice, he said, "Humanity can swallow even a hedgehog." I remembered these words a dozen or so years later, when my father—having escaped from the Reich—lived in the Zoliborz section of Warsaw, where I used to visit him.

During my walks along the fence at the Belvedere I hoped, in fact, to see the Marshal. I had heard about his frequent walks between the palace and the General Inspectorate of the Armed Forces, located several hundred meters from the old Military College. I wanted to see the man whose blood was said to run in my veins. I was fascinated by the theory, although I rejected it as incredible. Besides, I wished to see with my own eyes the leader who was said to stand above party divisions. His famous disdain for political theories was similar to my father's views. That was something that fascinated me more than anything else. Did they discuss the ways the world should be arranged? That was quite possible. Perhaps it was he who convinced my father in Krakow before World War I and later my father handed his views down to me. How much in my own upbringing was the result of the suggestive powers and indirect influence of his personality? My mother, working as a courier, rendered important service to the Legions. Her admiration for the Marshal bordered on religious worship. The Grandpa, the Commander, the Brigadier, Victor, Ziuk—his names, titles, and pseudonyms were mentioned in my presence from my earliest years, probably more frequently than my father's doctor's degree. His face looked at me from postcards, photographs, and commemorative medals. During my matriculation exam he stared at me from a portrait above the heads of the examination board, his hands resting on the hilt of his saber. Even a passing thought that this elderly man might be my real father was an unusual sensation.

Wladek Sznej saw me from the platform of a passing streetcar exactly at the moment when the man in civilian clothes was handing me my hat and cane and the sergeant was saluting with two fingers at the visor of his cap. My friend got off at the next stop.

A moment later I saw him walking in my direction. We met near the Botanical Gardens. He must have been deeply impressed by the scene he witnessed from the streetcar, and his reaction could best be described as solemn silence. He broke it only when we reached the Lobzowianka café. He suggested a cup of coffee, and he must have mentioned the Ritz. After a few steps we both hesitated. The Ritz was an elegant café with a flower garden where waiters who balanced their trays on their palms bustled around under the eye of a gray-haired maître d' in a jacket with epaulets. It was impossible to catch the glances of women whose faces were shaded by wide-brimmed hats. Thus we settled for the Lobzowianka. We sat down at a round wooden table. You can well imagine that I was slightly off balance after my strange adventure. While stirring his coffee Wladek Sznej declared he was in love, and someone loved him too, but not the same woman. Suddenly he jumped to his feet, knocking against the table. Several people did the same. I lifted my eyes from a dog lying under the next table and heard somebody cry, "He just drove by!" My friend explained that the Marshal had just passed our café in an open navy-blue Cadillac. He was apparently wearing motoring goggles and his chauffeur in a cavalry cap was sitting in the passenger seat. I did not react. I sipped my coffee and tried to maintain the appearance of total composure. From the side, Wladek Sznej's voice was coming through the hum of the promenade. The woman he loved was the actress playing Jorgens's wife. I listened with my brows slightly raised, since I imagined this was how a man should listen to the confessions of another man. Yet I was distracted by my own daze and embarrassment. That afternoon I seemed superfluous to myself. Everything came at the wrong time and without purpose. The avenue was full of people who walked around without overcoats. Smiling, blushing, warm faces passed me by. I saw lips moving in conversation I could not hear but the sense of which I could easily guess: a smiling girl with luxuriant hair and a bunch of lilacs stood between two students in fraternity caps. I suddenly thought that life was rushing by within my reach but that I lacked the courage to jump in.

I listened more attentively when Wladek started to talk about the feud that was going on offstage between the pair of actors who played the Jorgenses. In his opinion she was right to stick to her concept of a mother-wife full of compassion for the immature man. I became interested and asked if he was really sure about that. Yes, he had absolutely no doubts. I learned that Jorgens's wife acted with deliberation in spite of her partner and that, in order to humiliate him, she treated him onstage as though he were a frightened boy. He in turn tried to impose upon her—even during rehearsals—the role of a female blindly in love with her partner, overwhelmed by her admiration. The prison scene—Wladek explained—contained some of the most heated lines of the whole play, and in these scenes, in his opinion, the woman always wins. He asked me whether I noticed that, and repeated several times the sentences I knew so well. I did not interrupt when he elaborated on their different meanings in both interpretations. I had no need or intention to interrupt, because the story was interesting. I smiled to myself, comprehending the change of roles in the dressing room when in their quarrel they used the lines from their roles. Apparently the man was showing his partner how she should act, and she quoted casually a couple of words from his earlier part as if mocking the sense he seemed to impose upon her. Wladek claimed that the woman was fascinating, and secretly I could hardly disagree with him. I had not forgotten her narrow, small head and her slightly concave eyes, which seemed to be dark brown as they pierced me with amused irritation (it seemed I could even pick up the scent of her décolletage), and her remark about the mustache also impressed itself in my memory. When my friend asked me, however, whether he should play *va banque*—that is the expression he used—I could hardly give him any advice. As if not trusting my knowledge of French, he quickly added that he was hesitating whether to accept the full risk, including the possibility of failure and other consequences.

Again I had to conceal a smile. At the same time I had an unpleasant sensation, as if catching myself in some insincerity or deception. I did not wish him luck with the woman. And I did not believe he could succeed. But I also suspected I might be wrong. It was a mysterious domain. Trying to maintain the attitude of a loyal friend, I clenched my jaws and tightened my fingers around the knob of my cane.

Over the years my opinion of Wladek Sznej often changed. In fact, even now I am unable to describe him with any accuracy. My attitude toward him changed because he also changed—and more easily than I. I see this inconstancy as a part of his nature. The changes were perhaps gratuitous, or at least unconscious, like the changes of fur or hue in some animals. Yet I never considered him an evil man. An evil man—in my understanding—is someone who considers all people evil and whose wrongdoings are the result of anticipation or defense against that supposed universal evil. I doubt whether Wladek Sznej had such inclinations.

I watched him over the knob of my cane. I could see his profile and his left eye uncovered by his glasses. It was dark blue, serious, and somehow childish in its unwitting nakedness. Feeling like a voyeur, I fixed my eyes on the gravel under the table, trying to pay attention to his story of Jorgens's attempt to establish his superiority. Suddenly my friend said that he had an appointment after the theater and asked whether I would like to accompany them to the Savoy restaurant. The invitation was quite unexpected. At first I searched for an excuse. I wanted to say that I was also engaged for the evening. I do not know whether I already heard her steps from afar, but if I had said something at that time, my life would have taken a different course. Before I managed to utter a word, however, Wladek said that it would be only the three of us, and I felt my face flush.

I owe you an explanation. I did not intend to get in my friend's way. Yet I wanted to meet Jorgens's beautiful wife. I wanted to meet again her dark, golden glance, and to see the hand that executed the sharp strike of the dagger. It is true that I did not regard Wladek's chances as very good, yet it never occurred to me—even for a moment—that mine would be better. If at that time I saw any merit in myself, it was a sense of dignity rather than any other quality. With my external self-control and composure I was shy, and my twenty years weighed on me like twenty burdens, or rather like a schoolbag or a soldier's pack on my shoulders. No, I definitely did not anticipate a romantic adventure. The most I could expect was that I would fall in love. But with whom, for God's sake? With a famous actress whose name was featured on the poster right under the title of the play! I lacked the courage, hope, and persuasiveness. I didn't even have the desire. All I wanted was to see her, to touch her hand, to hear some words said to me, to leave in one piece and without blame.

We agreed I would come to the theater after the performance and wait for them at the entrance. Wladek left immediately, evidently planning to change his shirt at home and to put on a better suit. I saw him climb on a streetcar, nod in my direction, and take out his monthly ticket. The car moved on, and his glasses flashed at me again from the platform. I stayed at the table alone. I bought a newspaper offered me by a newsboy who was shouting out the latest headlines about the trial of a woman accused of murder in Krakow and about the parliamentary speech of the Prime Minister. I started an article about a train crash near Rogow. After a moment I realized that we had not finished our conversation. Wladek had still to tell me about the woman who was in love with him. I stayed in the café for a while trying to sort out everything we had been talking about. I soon realized, however, that I was not really thinking, but glancing at couples in the street and anticipating my meeting with Jorgens's wife. I was confusing the actors with characters from Fey's play. In about an hour Jorgens would appear in the gallery cursing the tired horses, and she would laugh and rest her hand on his shoulder. Three hours later a dagger would flash in her hand and Wladek Sznej, armed with a halberd, would run onstage. Later the three of us would go to the Savoy in Nowy Swiat. When a gray-haired stranger asked me with old-fashioned politeness whether he might use the other chair, I looked instinctively at my watch. Half an hour later, I excused myself, got up, and left, leaving the newspaper rolled on the table.

Wladek Sznej would be surprised to know that I was at the performance. I kept the secret and did not say a word even when he was telling me later about that unusual evening. I do not know whether the audience noticed that Jorgens, entering the gallery, had to lean against one of the columns. I noticed it immediately from my seat in the next-to-the-last row in the upper circle. I saw him lean against a column and stagger. I also saw fear in her eyes. She put her hand on his lips sooner than usual, and I knew why: he had forgotten his line. He said "Damn horses" twice and staggered again. The audience might have begun to suspect something, and I was afraid it would all end in a scandal. Throughout the performance I felt growing tension and anxiety onstage and I waited impatiently for the last scene, when the dagger flashes in her hand and everything is done and finished. I thought she must have waited for that too. During the prison dialogue he clung to the window bars, and several times I seemed to hear suppressed sobbing through his words. The house was absolutely quiet, but I had no illusions. The audience certainly reacted to his every trick and every mistake, and someone might have started giggling at any time. Suddenly I stirred. I heard his voice. Was it a moan, or a laugh? I was certain that nobody except me could understand these half-spoken words: "No, never, never," interrupted by her scream, which sounded desperate in spite of the text: "Everything will be all right, you'll see!!!" Again I was the only one to guess that Jorgens's wife had lost control over her role. When, struck by the dagger, he fell, I gave a sigh of relief. I noticed the desperation of the blow. I was sweating from excitement. Jorgens-Cezarewicz was lying on his back with outstretched hands. Then, to my amazement, the house thundered with applause. Some people next to me jumped to their feet. I had never witnessed such an ovation, such a triumph by an actor. When, a quarter of an hour later, standing at the theater door, I noticed a couple walking arm in arm in my direction, my astonishment, instead of intensifying, began to subside. Should I not expect that my next ludicrous adventure that evening would involve the Savoy restaurant, Wladek Sznej, and an unknown pale girl in a bonnet—a girl he had probably forgotten to tell me about. It was only later, when we were walking together toward the Savoy, that I realized she was the young actress who played little Uth. That is how I made my acquaintance with Tola Mohoczy.

I should explain that the evening in the Savoy was a date rather than an experience. Objectively speaking, it was the turning point in my biography, although I was not aware of it at that time. Soon came the examination period at the university, and the nights spent studying overshadowed the evening at the Savoy. Only several months later did the event, which I regarded at first as rather accidental and even slightly ridiculous (especially the problem with the check!), start to appear to me in a more narrative context. In other words, on that particular evening I felt mostly embarrassed and ill at ease, but after a year I was able to tell its story to myself. Its significance, however, was retrospective—it was an introduction to something that happened later, and, following the pattern of traditional narration, I tried to find in it the seeds of future events.

At the Savoy I felt rather bored. We were sitting at a table covered with white linen, at the end of a large, almost empty room. I avoided the eyes of that girl. If there was anything in her that could appear to me as interesting, it was the mystery of her emotion toward Wladek Sznej. Later, when I was struggling with the phenomenological interpretation of the law, and tried to recall all images and thoughts unrelated to the text, so that I would not fall asleep, her face never appeared in my mind. I suppose I would have been unable to remember her features. All that came to my mind was the skinniness of her arms and her husky voice when she asked for *bigos* and a beer. It was something else, though, that struck me. After a couple of minutes I was absolutely sure that Wladek was wrong. I could not explain the reason for my conviction, but it was clear to me that she was not in love with him. I soon realized that I was privy to a mystification carefully arranged by one of the parties and accepted without protest—even with some patronizing nonchalance—by the other. Wladek Sznej did not seem to show the girl much passionate attention, and after we had ordered three *bigos* and three beers, he continued the brilliant monologue he had begun on our way to the restaurant. He was talking about what happened that evening at the theater. In his opinion Jorgens's wife had finally lost. She was defeated the moment she felt threatened, when she realized the performance might be ruined. That fear was the reason for her failure, since from that moment on she was at odds with her own concept of her role and unwittingly, inevitably, became the slave of her partner.

Evidently I was not the most perceptive listener, since I asked how I should understand that last statement. Wladek stared at me for a moment. When he was speaking and thinking at the same time—that is, when he was searching for the right word and the right thought—his eyes took on an azure hue and he peered from behind his glasses in a somehow bedazzled way. He said that I should picture the Jorgenses in real life and note that we were talking about a real couple—a marriage that had gone dry, most probably through her own fault.

What can a man do if his wife shows him nothing but tender indulgence and he does not want to accept that state of affairs? He can only go mad—to win her respect through madness. That was exactly what he did that evening—of course, within the bounds of what was possible. He got drunk in order to frighten her. He had been drinking for a long time, but he never came drunk to the theater. That evening, however, he got drunk deliberately. He forced her into a different role—that of a wife whose husband is losing his mind. Finally he conjured up the role he desired: the helpless rage and desperation of a woman who loves a doomed man. That evening she killed Jorgens out of fear of his madness, not in motherly compassion. He had won for the first time. He was a born actor. He knew how to break the resistance of his partners.

Wladek Sznej was choosing his words carefully, and I noticed the satisfaction with which he emphasized some of them. I was slightly surprised. His comments seemed to indicate that events were taking a course unfavorable to him. If he had ever had a chance, he must have realized now how slight it was. And yet he seemed calm, one could say intellectually fulfilled. I started to think that I had taken his declaration of affection too literally. Perhaps he was more excited by the thought of falling in love with a famous actress than by a hopeless love affair. Eating my *bigos* slowly and sipping my beer, I watched him with some curiosity, while a motionless red spot remained in the corner of my eye. It was the bonnet which the girl did not care to take off. During Wladek's explanations she watched the next table—occupied by a family with sleepy children. They had come there for a late supper directly from the station; judging by their accent, they must have been landowners from Wolyn. When Wladek was saying, "You'll see, Cezar will finish himself off with that drinking," the girl suddenly got up, and the boy at the next table started vomiting. Seeing my confusion, Wladek explained casually, "She went to help the mother," and continued his speech. I turned slightly in my chair and saw them both leading the crying boy toward the restroom as directed by a waiter. From a distance the girl seemed taller than I had thought. I also noticed her slender, straight neck, and I was struck by her walk: quick and confident, but also careless—as if scornful of everything around her. I wondered why she left the table. I was almost sure the boy started vomiting a moment after she had got up. I remember I was a bit surprised. I noticed a change that was difficult to describe: an angry sparkle in her eyes, or rather in one of her eyes, since I saw her in profile. It occurred to me that something in our conversation—at least the last couple of words— must have touched her very deeply. Wladek did not seem to pay much attention to all that, but he must have noticed my confusion, for he shrugged his shoulders. "She is very sensitive and kind," he said. "She will be right back." Yet I thought he was wrong again, although what he said proved to be true.

She came back after ten minutes. I heard her laughter behind my back and saw her bending over the boy, who had stopped crying. She turned up the tip of her nose with her finger, and the boy started laughing. His mother was thanking her and blushing, from either embarrassment or gratitude. When she returned to our table, I glanced at her warmly, quite taken by the simplicity of her behavior. I also liked the way she excused herself briefly without commenting on the episode. At the same moment I met her eyes. It seemed she was looking at my hair and I felt a touch of irritation. Soon, however, her glance shifted to my lips—slowly and with a kind of arrogant deliberation— and I felt for a moment that I was under inspection. I wanted to pick up the interrupted conversation and to direct her attention somewhere else, yet I had no time to open my mouth. She announced she was hungry and summoned the waiter by drumming her nails against her glass. Before I had managed to overcome my confusion, she had ordered veal steaks with assorted vegetables, three peach desserts, and coffee.

She ordered all that despite our assurances that we were not hungry. When the waiter left, I looked at Wladek. He gave me an unpleasant signal, and I understood I could expect little support from him. Before we had left the Lobzowianka earlier that day we had counted our assets and Wladek had assured me we had enough money. I was thinking now about what we would do if the check surpassed our means. It occurred to me that my Swiss watch could perhaps save us from an unpleasant situation. I kept my savings account book in my linen closet and I would be able to pay the check the next morning. Our position, however, was most embarrassing, and we were totally at the waiter's mercy. What is more, while serving our table, he was always looking in my direction, evidently taking me—God knows why—for the host. I decided that I would ask him for the check, and if I found that we were short of money, I would try to discuss the matter discreetly with the manager. Despite the late hour the room filled with guests. A party at a nearby table was drinking vodka. I noticed several men staring at us—they had probably seen Fey's play at the Actors' Theater—and I wanted by all means to avoid a compromising scene.

Besides, I started to doubt the sanity of our companion. Looking through the corner of my eye at her long, knotty fingers manipulating her knife and fork, I seemed to notice something like a lack of coordination in her movements. I was also alarmed by her sudden animation: she was laughing for no apparent reason and talking with her mouth full while looking at Wladek Sznej. Each time, however, her eyes were clearly avoiding me. Wladek, in turn, accepted all her attention with calm indifference. When bringing a piece of veal to her mouth she said, "Ah, I am sure about you. Nothing will ever finish you off." He only smiled and said nothing. There was no doubt he was counting on me. Not so much on my financial resources, the scarcity of which he knew all too well, as on my character. He knew I surpassed him in stature, and not only physically, and that seemed to make him quite self-confident in a situation whose weight rested on my shoulders. For a moment I nourished the thought that he might have brought some money with him after all. I knew that he went home to change and now, in his polished collar and dark tie, he presented himself—hard to deny it—quite well. Yet his lack of interest soon robbed me of any hope. I could count only on myself.

I trust, however, that I had not let the others see my anxiety. My quiet correctness was identical to my reticence at the beginning of the evening. One could come to the conclusion that I was merely bored. In fact, from that time on I was bored in a certain peculiar way. She must have noticed it soon enough and decided I should be bored no more. When the waiter put coffee cups and glittering pots in front of us, she shook ash from her cigarette, ordered three liqueurs, and addressed me directly: "A wonderful evening! Is there anything bothering you?" It was an attack launched with piercing eyes—left brow slightly raised. I answered that as a rule I was not very talkative and that the evening was in fact very interesting. And I added: "That is mostly because of you." She nodded her head and unexpectedly took off her bonnet. She did it very quickly in a gesture resembling a magician's trick. Her ruffled hair fell in all directions simultaneously—upon her forehead, her neck, her cheeks and temples. I looked at her in astonishment because I had never seen anybody change that much in such a short time. She now resembled the boy from the colorful covers of the Tarzan series. She made a face in her little mirror and mumbled something unpleasant about her looks. "You have a sore throat," Wladek said. "You must have caught another cold." She agreed without paying much attention. "Yes, it must have been that night on the Vistula." And without turning away from her mirror she added: "I must have fallen asleep in the willows." Wladek laughed, and I took her answer for a joke. Later I learned that her jokes were to be taken seriously.

Our waiter disappeared. Trying to catch his eye, I did not notice her leave our table again. I used her absence to ask Wladek quietly whether he had any money. He did not. I asked him again to count everything he had in his purse. He told me what it came to. I then told him what I would do. When the waiter came, I would ask him for the check and see how much we were short. While I was doing this, he was expected to engage the girl in a conversation. Having accepted the check, I would send the waiter away and then look for the manager. I drew back my cuff to show Wladek my watch. He understood. He started to apologize while wiping his glasses. Apparently, she had never indulged in such excesses before. He found an explanation in the complexes of the beginning actress—it was her first year on the stage after drama school. And maybe—he hesitated for a moment—yes, maybe he was misled by her appearance. I did not respond. I knew nothing about her, and I preferred to keep my silence. The unpleasant moment was coming. Our waiter was still nowhere to be seen. I thought it would be better if he appeared before she came back. I wished for that. The gambit with my watch might not work and I considered the possibility of a scandalous scene including a written report for the police. I reached the conclusion that I should arrange for them to leave the restaurant before my encounter with the manager. I was about to tell Wladek about my plan when I suddenly heard her hoarse voice behind me. "They both died! One at Tannenberg and the other also during the Czar's days. He was beaten to death by drunken soldiers!" It took me some time to understand whom she was talking about. She was speaking of the sons of the old lady who worked as an attendant in the ladies' restroom. The girl sat down at the table and murmured, "She pities more the one who was beaten . . ." At that moment our waiter materialized. He was standing with a napkin hanging over his arm. When I gestured to him, he eagerly stuck out his neck. I asked for the check. He smiled and whispered that the check had been paid in full.

After we had left the Savoy, Wladek stopped at the corner of Ordynacka Street and said, "You must be crazy!" I was sure they would start quarreling. I stepped aside and waited for the insanity of our unfortunate meeting to end. I resolved to keep silent. In that ridiculous situation, completely out of place in my life, every gesture seemed funny. I did not notice the street-car coming. There was some tussle between Wladek and the girl. He insisted on seeing her home. I heard him shout, "You idiot! Why?" and her sharp voice: "Because I don't want to." She quickly crossed the street with a lit cigarette and managed to get on the second car. As it left from the stop at Warecka Street, I saw her standing with her hand in the leather strap, and it seemed, at that moment, that she turned, in her red bonnet, in my direction. At that time I could hardly have anticipated the course of earthly, human, and mortal events—or perhaps unearthly, superhuman, and immortal ones—that would bond our lives into one integral whole.

Wladek and I said goodbye quickly and departed in separate directions.

Examinations were set for the end of June. I had five weeks to prepare myself in four subjects: I had to demonstrate some fifteen hundred pages of knowledge within a couple of hours. On Monday I went to the florist's. I attached my calling card to seven red roses, and under my printed name I scribbled: "For an undeserved treat at the Savoy." I arranged for the flowers to be delivered to her at the theater. I thought I had settled the matter in a decent way, and I did not expect any reply. In fact, no reply came. I did what the ever-present witness of my acts, my words, and my loneliness demanded—the immaterial being born with me, whose name I do not know, yet who has guided my actions in every situation.

We were taking the examinations in groups of three or four

students. I was quite well prepared. I answered my questions calmly, each after a short pause, which impressed the professors. By noon I had passed Roman law, the history of the Polish political system, and the history of judiciary procedures. Groups of students clustered in the hallway waiting for their turn. After each exam I was asked to repeat my questions and my colleagues jotted them down on slips of paper. The atmosphere was anxious and thick with cigarette smoke. The janitors were sweeping away the butts. I decided to get some air and went into the university courtyard. I had still to take an exam on the theory of law.

I had been walking for about ten minutes in front of the library when I heard the patter of feet and shouts. Somebody was lying on the round and covering his head with his hands. At the same time I was passed by two students. One of them was wearing knee boots and carrying a heavy cane. A moment later, when I was helping the man to his feet, I felt a dull pain at the base of my skull, and I must have passed out for a couple of seconds, since I do not remember whether I managed to return to the examination room on my own. Neither do I remember the questions. All I know is that after the last one I fell from my chair, though not before giving some kind of an answer. When I was lifted up the professor declared, "You have passed, despite the evident signs of exhaustion." With these words in my mind I woke up the next morning in the Holy Infant Hospital with a concussion, caused by a blow with a blunt object.

The incident had no serious consequences as far as my health was concerned, nor did it interfere with my studies. As soon as I was discharged from the hospital one week later, I reported to the university to learn the results of my examinations. I had passed with the equivalent of a B. Yet the blow to my head was disconcerting. I was beaten because I tried to help a man lying on the ground. It was a paradox I found quite difficult to understand. I had acted according to a rule accepted by any society. My behavior was ordinary—neither cowardly nor heroic. And because of this behavior somebody had hit me over the head. I did not know what to think. I had been witness to several brawls in the university courtyard, yet I never imagined that the slogans shouted on such occasions applied also to bystanders—people not belonging to any political organization and not advocating any particular ideology; people like me, guided by a simple sense of decency and common sense, who no doubt constituted the majority of the country's population. If at that point I had started analyzing the meaning of decency and common sense and through some ready-made philosophy arrived at the relativity of both these old-fashioned notions, I would have probably lost the firm ground I was standing on and become susceptible material for history. Luckily, I was not brilliant enough.

In early July one of my friends invited me to visit his family's estate in the Poznan district. I spent two weeks playing tennis and riding. Later I went to see my father. There were lakes and forests near his house and I spent the next month walking in the country. I would return at dusk and by dinner I usually felt quite sleepy. In a half-conscious state I would hit the sack and sleep soundly until the next morning. One day at breakfast, over coffee and crescent buns, my father asked me whether I knew that I moaned in my sleep. I said it was probably because of mental fatigue. I did not tell him about my adventure in the university courtyard, although I mentioned campus brawls and rallies. He stared at me for a moment, but we changed the subject. It was a predictable reaction. He would behave in exactly the same way if I told him about somebody's gambling loss, or the questionable conduct of a certain woman. Ten days later I remembered this conversation when I saw a newsreel showing the black-and-white silhouette of a man in battle shirt and riding boots prancing on a stage with his right arm outstretched. He was surrounded by a crowd of people with bulging eyes and faces swollen from shouting. The image lasted only a couple of seconds, while the commentator's voice informed us about the victory of some political party in Germany. Later there were pictures of dog races near London. A longhaired hound was being decorated by a lady in a light sports hat.

I hope you will excuse all these details and long-winded reminiscences, which only now bring me to the point where the main part of my narrative begins. Without these digressions, however, I might not be able to sufficiently explain the circumstances in which Rondo was born and address the contentions of Professor Janota's article. You may certainly ask what an old newsreel seen before the war in the Stylowy Theater has to do with my subject. The point is, however, that I did not leave the cinema alone. It turned out that we were sitting in the darkness only a couple of seats apart, and after the show I saw her directly in front of me. I recognized her red bonnet. I am speaking, of course, about the woman to whom I have devoted my whole life.

Tola Mohoczy was at that time on the threshold of her acting career. I was able to boast only of the exams qualifying me for the second year at the Department of Law. What was the force that drew us together? The only answer seems to be fate. I am using this word quite consciously, though I anticipate your smile. But let us think about it for a minute. Of all the accidental meetings that took place on this particular day, in the streets, movie theaters, or cafés, only one was marked by a sense of logical necessity. Only one led to unavoidable consequences. By pure coincidence, in a cinema, a young man meets a young woman he has met before: this alone certainly does not amount to much. But if this man is lonely and dreams of meeting a woman, and if the woman he meets is an egocentric in love with another man, and if she confides in the young man, speaking of her hopeless passion and her suicidal thoughts—the coincidence is much more potent in possibilities. If we add his gallantry—his selflessness and eagerness for sacrifice—and her passionate femininity—her wounded quality, her need for support—such a meeting can be considered a mathematical formula for destiny. None of the several possible solutions will be totally random or accidental.

We walked through the noisy, hot streets until late at night. Warsaw did not empty out in August. Restaurant gardens and cafés were full till midnight, and Jerozolimskie Avenue, between Marszalkowska Street and Nowy Swiat, resembled a minor Paris boulevard. We walked back and forth, turning many times at Nowy Swiat and Marszalkowska in a crowd drowsy with heat and fatigue but still looking for adventure. She spoke about herself. She spoke with irony and furious bitterness, yet I knew she wanted me to listen and needed my presence. I cannot describe her voice. Years later, when its throbbing melody and strange, fervent accent became famous, not a single reviewer could describe or define it accurately. Today, if asked, I would say that it expressed some relentless, blind conviction about herself. It resounded with a strength of illusion and stubbornness capable of the wildest extravagance. I also sensed the most important feature of that voice, the secret of its success and power over audiences: contempt.

Even in the years just before the war, when her name was pronounced like that of a precious stone ("Mohoczy plays . . ." "Mohoczy was superb"), and when her first name was eliminated by fame, I never considered her a good actress. As you shall see, I was destined to get acquainted with the actors' circle quite intimately, and not only as a spectator. In my opinion, the art of an actor consists in the lack of personality. I shall even venture to say that it consists in the lack of courage.

Personality is nothing more than the courage to expose oneself to certain risks, like that of ridicule. This is something a born actor is totally incapable of. He possesses an opposite quality: he identifies with others out of fear of being himself. He is always ready to mimic, to adjust, to assume somebody else's appearance. He fulfills himself onstage by magnifying this flaw of his character. While onstage, he is not allowed to be himself. His defect becomes his profession. He has to measure himself against life—but not his own. He identifies not with people, but with characters. Instead of somebody's appearance, he assumes a mask. Acting, in my opinion, reaches its pinnacle when the actor loses his natural fear of being human and transforms himself into his own synthetic creation. At this point his roles become his personality. Tola Mohoczy seemed to be just the opposite case—as if she had chosen herself at the moment of her birth. Such an overwhelming certainty of being—of being someone in particular—must have demolished all other forms of being. She did not respect her roles. She trampled her Electras and Violas. Her every performance was an act of usurpation which rendered the audience breathless in awe and fear. I watched her triumphs fascinated and horrified at the same time, as one watches a great murderess, and I felt half- or sub-consciously that the time would come when her victims would rise from their graves.

Yet all that was still ahead of her on that August evening when she tried to convince me she was really insane, when she told me of her lonely nights on the bank of the Vistula. She told me about a new role in a play that was going into rehearsal in September: she should have been mad with joy, but in fact she could not sleep from despair. She grabbed my arm and giggled: "Someday somebody will strangle me in these willows." For a moment I felt uneasy, though I was perceptive enough to associate her sleeplessness with something that appeared to me at the Savoy. I knew the man she was suffering for, and I realized that the evening at the Savoy must have been especially difficult for her. The conversation was devoted almost exclusively to that person. I felt pity for her when she said gloomily, "He is married." She asked me suddenly if I was surprised she was telling me all this. It was hard to make anything out of my silence. "It's because you are a wise person," she said. "After ten minutes in the restaurant you knew more about me than your friend has learned in ten months." I was not mistaken, therefore, about her and Wladek. I looked at her out of the corner of my eye. A small, shapely ear was visible from under her bonnet. I stood head and shoulders above her. I turned away, but after a moment I looked again, this time at her neck. From the side I saw the opaque shadow of her nape. She told me she did not like my name. "Why do you keep silent? You must talk to me." She fixed her eyes on me. They were very light, almost transparent. She squinted from time to time.

How, in your opinion, could such an August evening end? In seeing her to her house and saying goodbye at her door? It could have happened late in the night, perhaps in the morning, but still it should have been goodbye. I thought the same—that is, I thought nothing. I can assure you, I felt the physical calm of a well-rested body and the happy astonishment of unexpected adventure. I was free of the passionate anxiety that usually accompanies the very notion of adventure. I was calm, strong, and sympathetic. There was a pause in my loneliness. That evening somebody weaker than I had chosen to trust me. I learned of somebody else's pain. I felt a slender, nervous hand on my arm, and I became even stronger and more trustworthy. Later, when I thought about that evening, I concluded that it was not the sequence of events, not the words spoken, not the facts and the bodies that were decisive. The solution was within me, in the first movement of my thought—before I started to desire and before I raised my eyes.

If, instead of asking me on the Savior's Square to see her home, and later, on Topolowa Street, instead of asking me to come up for a cup of tea, if, rather, she had told me she wanted to spend the night with me, I would have been shocked. I would have been shocked if she had told me—in this round, dimly lit square, and later in front of her house, where we stopped in the shadows under the trees—that she was afraid to sleep alone, or that it was her private revenge on a man who at that moment was lying at the side of another woman, or that such nights happened to her often. I would have been even more shocked if I learned that she was interested in me because she liked red-haired men, or because she had not yet had a lover in whose veins (according to the information provided, no doubt, by my intelligent friend) coursed the blood of the Marshal. I can hardly imagine my reaction to such a proposition, but in any case I would have woken the next day with a different consciousness.

Yet she invited me up for a cup of tea. I became her lover only in the morning, and I felt responsible for what had happened. One can certainly smile at my naïveté, yet it is necessary to keep in mind my provincial background, and the cult of women—deriving probably from the cult of the Virgin Mary—in which I was brought up. It was a superficial cult. I have often heard stories about my great-grandfather on my mother's side, who—upon arriving at a ball in his sleigh—used to throw his fur in the mud for my great-grandmother to step on. I suspect that amid the trials of everyday life this adoration somehow disappeared, to be replaced by family tyranny and bedroom aggression. I was, however, imbued with the national literature, national poetry and novels, in which martyrs in crowns, virgin daughters of castellans, and female knights appeared in their lily-white majesty. Feminine psychology? I knew as much about it as any good Boy Scout. I cannot say, however, that I regret it. The idealization of the woman is in my opinion a less dangerous thing than the cult of masculinity, although it may seem that the two usually go together. Far from it. Dreams of providential leaders of the herd and dreams of despotic prophets usually take root in societies where women are not idealized, where the naïveté of notions of gender has been unsettled, and the feminine myth has lost its maiden appearance. Femininity was idealized by husbands and sons of quiet virtues, solid convictions, and a deep sense of the continuity of their social existence—people who had no need for the mystic authority of the Male. The search for the Relentless and Visionary Leader who would substitute for conscience and reason begins when values and ideas are in ruins and when spiritual emptiness has set in. If I had to express it in the shortest possible way, I would say that real men need a woman-saint. The dream of the Great Leader belongs to those who are not their own masters.

I should also explain that the apartment was empty, because the owners had left on vacation. A rather large main room filled with light furniture resembled the little "salons" from the time of the Duchy of Warsaw. She told me it was left over from her mother's maiden years. A birch-wood sofa and three matching chairs with backs in the shape of trefoils have miraculously survived until this day. Tola's portrait, painted by Witkacy in 1937, hangs now above the sofa. The daybed was situated in an alcove. That August morning, when we lay naked in the receding darkness, and I moved rhythmically within her, was for her a quite familiar situation. For me, however, it was a kind of metaphysical distinction, which I testified to with my gasping breath and silent moans. Thus the terms of our relationship were established.

So was my name, since on that night, in the darkness, she called me Tom for the first time. Later it became my underground pseudonym. There are still people alive who call me by this name.

*

It seems that what I have said so far resembles the beginning of a detective novel: a gradual introduction, a description of the days preceding the event—for instance, a murder. In any case, it has little to do with my polemic against Professor Janota's article "A Chapter in the History of Struggle," and I wonder whether I should destroy these pages. However—since I have mentioned a murder—Professor Janota must be familiar with the dissertation "Art and Crime." My friend Wladek Sznej worked on it during the war and he showed me some excerpts. I must admit that I found them exciting—especially the chapter on "malice and the novel." As I remember, it discussed the similarities between fabulation and the structure of illusion created by a perpetrator of premeditated crime. I am unable to repeat his striking argument. As far as I know, the idea that every artist has criminal potential is far from original, yet Sznej did not base his study on comparative psychology, but demonstrated correspondences in the very process of creation. Famous poisoners plotted their murders just like great writers conceive the plots of their novels: in both cases the ultimate goal is the triumph of fiction achieved through the perfection and invisibility of means, turning the attention away from the real perpetrator—the artist or the murderer. To illustrate his thesis Sznej used the works of Dostoyevsky, especially *The Brothers Karamazov*, which he called a brilliant conjectural prosecution. His study appeared not long ago in a collection of critical works on Dostoyevsky published—as far as I remember—on the 150th anniversary of his birth.

My account, therefore, could be seen as an imitation of a certain mechanism, or as a technique of fiction. First a biographical exposition, then a hot August night when the real action begins, then one or two cliff-hangers, the psychological background—and the machine is set in motion. From now on the structure of illusion functions on its own. As an author I could fulfill my task according to this plan. This, however, would be contrary to my basic assumption: in fact nobody planned the course of events. If I were to ask who created this plot, I would have to risk a hypothesis on the unsettling resemblance, not between crime and art, but between crime and life. I would have to conclude that an analogy exists between the schemes of fortune and criminal intent. But I would have ventured too far. Besides, for a variety of reasons I do not feel up to such speculations.

Let us return, therefore, to the main subject. Having read my short biography, you may wonder that a man of less than passionate nature and rather practical disposition lost his head so easily. You will be even more surprised to learn that from the very beginning I received certain warning signs. I have nobody to blame but myself. I could have recovered after that first night. Flight was urged upon me. I was stripped of any hopes and delusions. It all happened in the Turecka café one hour after we both woke up. You may not remember the location of the Turecka in prewar Warsaw. It was on Marszalkowska Street, not far from the railway station, in the area now covered with cubical apartment houses.

She told me that we had to part immediately. "What happened has absolutely no meaning." "How is that possible?" I asked. "Just this morning you were saying something very different." She looked at me with acerbic pity and said that she was an erotomaniac incapable of any fidelity, and besides, she was obsessed with another man. "Try to understand!" she exclaimed. "His least gesture would be enough to make me cut off your head and sell it to the butcher." Squinting at the marble tabletop, she kept repeating, "Tom, go away, don't think about me, run."

A girl selling my severed head to the butcher . . . I did not expect to inspire anybody with such a vivid vision. Everything she was saying impressed me deeply, but contrary to her intentions. I did not feel like carrying my dear head away. I wanted to lose my head and stay. I was being warned about all the dangers and torments that awaited me, yet strangely enough it was I who felt pity. I did not interrupt her admonitions, but I was absolutely sure that everything would be different and that my hands, which rested on the table, were strong enough to bear the burden of my duty. I would not be able to explain my duty exactly, but I knew that from that time on I had a duty to fulfill. You may believe me or not, but if after three weeks I started to work as an extra in *The Dove*, it was not because I was unable to bear the separation—self-discipline and common decency would prevent me from any such desperate gesture. Led by a prophetic instinct, I agreed to replace Wladek Sznej. I was certain that the fate of Tola Mohoczy would become my life.

These were the last triumphs of the play before the change of repertoire. On the day of my first performance—exactly twenty days after our parting in the Turecka—I was standing in a narrow corridor behind the stage. I was dressed in a helmet and greaves, and I was waiting with a wooden halberd at the steps leading to the backstage area. She saw me from behind on her way from the dressing room and probably did not recognize me at first. Perhaps she was simply interested in the strange tall halberdier. I must add that I was taller than the other members of the bishop's guard. She stopped. I turned around. She looked at me without a word, sadly and carefully. Then she went away. I also said nothing. There was a bell for the end of the intermission. A prop man passed by carrying a jug and a cup needed in the next scenes. I knew I might appear comical to her—my cardboard greaves, my lonely promptness (other guards were still getting dressed), not to mention my grotesque appearance in the theater as one of the help. It was an embarrassing moment and yet I did not feel bad at all. I could even say that I felt a certain satisfaction at the thought of having suddenly and voluntarily gone astray. Astray? For the first time in my life I was in the right place. True, it was a mere walk-on, but through it I had jumped, on the run, into the midst of my own life, which until then was always passing me by. Yet I would like to elaborate a little on the motives and circumstances of my decision.

Wladek Sznej, darkened from the sun, returned from his vacation at the beginning of September. During such excited reunions—joyful and noisy—one can usually detect a touch of melancholy beneath the shield of soldierly gruffness. We were returning suntanned and hungry for life, yet each return was a measure of passing time; we were beginning again something which had been finished earlier, something which would be started and finished again a year from now. On such occasions, when the end of summer blends with the beginning of fall, we seem to be slightly embarrassed by this affinity between beginnings and endings—a phenomenon ingrained not only in nature. We were masking our annual anxiety at the process of transition with boisterous chatter. Although the leaves had not turned yet, the air was purified after the summer doldrums. It had the transparency of glass. Shadows were sharper now. On one such day I made an appointment with Wladek Sznej, who had spent part of July kayaking and all of August traveling in the Polesie area. I was intrigued not so much by what he told me as by a subtle change in his behavior. I do not mean any change in his attitude toward me. I wish to make this perfectly clear. There were no personal insinuations, although, as you can imagine, I had reasons to expect something of this sort. And yet something had happened. There was a change in the way he looked, in the tone of his voice, in the meditative pauses in the midst of his narrative. It was a deeper, more fundamental change than I thought. I have already mentioned that he spent the whole of August in Polesie. If I hadn't known him for such a long time, I could have thought he was deeply affected by what he saw there: the incredible poverty of the region which he described to me as we entered the Zacheta gallery not far from the Warsaw Lutheran Church. I do not mean to suggest that I knew him to be insensitive to social deprivation. I mean simply to point out that I had known him long enough to guess that the reason for his pensiveness was something other than the deprivation of Polesie peasants. I discovered this reason a bit later. After an hour of looking at paintings and sculptures we sat down on a plush sofa to have a closer look at some portraits by Lenz. The Zacheta was empty, and we were able to talk in low voices. It soon became clear that during his vacation Wladek Sznej had made some new and important acquaintances.

As you may remember, I have mentioned a certain advantage I felt over him—both physical and spiritual, or at least extending to something more than physical. At this point, however, I feel I should add a few words of explanation. I see myself as a man motivated exclusively by his own principles. Putting it a bit less pompously: I am a closed circuit. I accept no criteria, and need no guarantees, other than those I myself consider valid and true. I have said "consider," although "feel" might be a better word, since the matters we are talking about are not exactly rational. I do not wish to go into details. I do not require any external sanction for my acts and thoughts and I care little whether they are in concordance—for example—with the course of civilization. It is as if I have an invisible witness. He resides inside me—not outside or above. And if I say he dictates my behavior, I can listen to him without straining my ears. My hearing is attuned to myself rather than to what surrounds me: the times, public opinion, the future, historic milestones, etc. I shall not try to identify my witness—he probably has his own genealogy. All I am concerned with now is the fact that he constitutes a kind of inner organ, one which functions as a plug or a stopper: he closes the circuit.

Now, after many years, I realize that the source of Wladek's intelligence was his profound uncertainty. He was lacking the plug, his circuit was broken and open to changes in the surrounding reality. He received any thought, idea, or concept that came to him from the world as though it were better, more valuable than himself. At least he seemed to subconsciously admit such a possibility. Perhaps he believed he could ally himself with a truth that was larger, more righteous, or more powerful than his own—a truth whose value could be confirmed in the future. I think the future was for him a constant source of anxiety. He was afraid he would not be included in the truth— that the truth would fulfill itself without him. When he finally started to tell me in the Zacheta about the people he had met, it took me some time to realize I was listening to a man under a spell. I hope you understand me well: an organized body, a marching community can often cast a spell on individualists. There are people who torment themselves to death if there is a party in town and they are not invited. Wladek Sznej was different. He was tormented by the thought that he was not invited to the new epoch. He felt a poignancy at the thought of a young radical group readying for action without him. I do not wish to libel him. I am far from making any accusations. What I am saying here simply seems to be a psychological diagnosis of a certain relationship—or, better, an affair—between an individual and reality. Today one rather says: between an individual and history. I must point out, however, that in the Zacheta I was very far from my present conclusions, which were formed in my older, therefore more naïve, years. Old age, in my opinion, is far less experienced than youth. What alerted me, though, during the conversation was Wladek's mention of my beating in the university courtyard. His knowledge of the incident could have been explained in many ways. But the fact that he learned about it from his new friends seemed to me amazing. How could they know and remember me, how did they track me down in the first place, why would they want to talk about me? Of course, I posed some of these questions directly. Not everything in Wladek's explanations was clear to me, but one thing appeared certain: they beat me because my looks seemed suspicious to them. Therefore I repeated my questions and demanded a reply.

Please do not suspect me of a lack of common sense. I could easily anticipate the answer. The problem, of course, was the color of my hair. Those gentlemen in riding boots probably did not like redheads. It was both simple and silly—very simple and very silly. When we were children we were told the story of Judas, and I happen to have the hair of the biblical traitor. We all know, however, that people also do not like the left-handed, or dissimilarity of any kind (the cross-eyed, homosexuals, albinos). Society creates its own separate minority, a tribe treated with suspicious curiosity. No arguments, in fact, are necessary. The healthy majority needs no justification precisely because it is the healthy majority.

Those were my deliberations at the time. Wladek, on the other hand, gave me some hard facts. It seems that on his kayak trip he met the young activists who had bashed me on the head. I was known by my looks even before the incident. Somebody remembered that I had been seen with Wladek Sznej—I was not easy to confuse with anybody else. It all led to a conversation about my person. The activists declared that my beating was a misunderstanding. What is more, they wanted to meet me, and for some reason it seemed to them very important. Why? I did not have to be Sherlock Holmes to solve the mystery. Of course Wladek had told them about my *filiation*. I could swear he had told it also to Tola before our evening at the Savoy. But let us stick to the facts. The Zacheta, as I said, was empty and we could talk freely. In front of us there was "Strike" by Lenz, behind us probably "The Storks" by Chelmonski and "A Village Funeral" by Witkiewicz (the father). I see no use explaining here the ideological foundations and the program of the group as explained to me by Wladek. It was a program of a typical radical nationalist organization of that time. I could not care less. Programs were always abstractions to me and I reacted to them with stubborn resistance. I was quite comfortable with my democratic, moderate worldview. Still, I was interested in natural phenomena, and on that day in the Zacheta I had the eerie sensation that Wladek had transformed himself over the summer like some plant or fish. I simply could not get rid of the image. I had never seen him like that: he spoke slowly in a voice muffled by reflection; he smiled occasionally as he searched for the right words and his smile seemed pregnant, almost painful. From time to time he lifted his hands from his knees as if weighing in them some newly ripened fruit. It all evoked the idea of conception and pregnancy, which was supposed to transform the whole species. To understand this fairy-tale weirdness one might imagine a friend changed into an owl, a friend with the head of a fox or a horse, and one should know him as well as I knew Wladek: since out first year in high school. While listening I watched his leg—thin like a rooster's, with a protuberant ankle. I remembered this leg from the school playground. He was a good short-distance runner. Though his legs resembled sticks, his calves were muscular. But now it suddenly occurred to me that it was not his leg anymore. An absurd thought. I stared at his gray sock as though it hid a different leg, belonging to somebody else. I listened as he spoke about unemployment and the commerce being taken over by strangers. His voice resounded with a metallic tone and I noticed the inert gleam in his eye. Again I thought they were no longer his eyes, no longer his voice. Like a laboratory animal, Wladek must have undergone some surgery over the summer. There was something private in this transformation, something deforming and embarrassing at the same time. I was afraid to speak, because I felt witness to a biological transmutation—as if

Wladek's person received the seed of some energetic organism, as if it had permitted itself to be penetrated and now was swelling with its meaning, assuming the proper potency and shape. The sight of such pupation is deeply disturbing and arouses many impure feelings. When I looked at his leg in the gray sock, I kept thinking about a young woman I had seen in my childhood at my grandmother's home. People said she had been raped by soldiers. She had black eyes and thin legs. She came to clean the house, and sometimes I spied on her when she knelt, cloth in hand, staring at the floor. "She hasn't been the same since then," my grandmother used to say. It filled me with fear and a sweet, nauseating shame. I remember her white calves and her raised hem, and the strange pensiveness of humiliation. Such episodes from early childhood can engrave themselves in memory. I am not trying to say that Wladek Sznej resembled this woman after his return from his vacation. With his tanned neck and jutting jaw he looked more masculine than ever, and more in control of his movements. Yet I kept thinking about that woman and I felt the same unchaste numbness, as when the sight of her bare legs brought to mind the image of panting infantrymen and the murmur of the river (she was raped in the bushes on a riverbank). And I imagined Wladek Sznej listening with wistfulness to the metallic voices of the new warriors, who possessed him through his consent. On a riverbank, in a tent. I do not know why it had to be in a tent . . . but yes, in a tent, at night. If you are curious about the outcome of our conversation, please note that I declined to meet the leader of the young activists, who apparently took a personal interest in me. I accepted, though, Wladek's second proposition. He decided to leave his job at the theater. He had been offered the position of literary editor on a new weekly publication. He asked me whether I would like to fill in for him as an extra. After a moment's thought I agreed.

For the third time I must appeal to your patience: please

read on! I assure you that I am not straying from the facts discussed by Professor Janota as far as it may seem. Despite all appearances I am sticking to my subject, and my rambling—as you shall see—is quite to the point. I would like to return, though, to my work at the theater. As I said, there was neither madness nor extravagance in my decision. The offer came at the right time also for purely practical reasons. I do not remember whether I mentioned the Krakow Fund. After my grandmother's death we sold our house in the suburbs of Krakow. The transaction provided us with a rather large sum of money. Since that time, however, the fund had been severely depleted. I had reason to believe that father covered my tuition out of his salary. In that situation any measure of independence would give me great comfort.

My relations with Wladek Sznej remained more or less unchanged. His job on the weekly involved quite a bit of work, however, and after our meeting in the Zacheta we saw each other rather seldom. I should also mention a significant fact connected with our meeting, or—to be more precise—with the following night. That night I lost my confidence. My life's foundations had been shaken, so to speak. I had lost my earlier conviction that as a man I was in the right. That night I could not sleep. Having rejected everything that in Wladek's new creed seemed to me unjust, blind, and vulgar, I still felt that in the larger social context my life amounted to no more than indifference—that is, selfishness. It was a painful realization, one that deprived me of my sleep. Until that time I had never felt involved with the country's problems, whether foreign or domestic. I considered them the concern of the rulers—that is, the professionals. Now my tidy consciousness suddenly turned against me. It was a very painful and humiliating sensation. Wladek Sznej's words started to press upon me and to undermine what until recently seemed quite obvious. If that which was obvious—the everyday course of events—evoked such a violent reaction, if the mundane, common existence of the people called for such iron hatred, for impassioned fury, if matters had gone so far, it meant I had a part in some enormous error. That night I was no longer sure of anything—myself, my convictions, the honesty of my father, my upbringing, memory, tradition . . . Something had snapped inside me. I felt as if a hole had opened and some ugly nightmare had started to flow in. Uncertainty about whether our life is not based on self-deception or misunderstanding, about whether the truth is not the opposite of what we take it for, the opposite of what we learned from our earliest childhood, uncertainty about whether bread, water, and air are not something else, some-thing entirely different from the bread, the water, and the air we ate, drank, and breathed—such uncertainty has an ominous, demonic quality which can easily ruin one's soul. If you have not known such moments I must congratulate you. At the end I found myself engulfed by an enormous confusion: in the dark-ness everything seemed possible and unreal at the same time, complex and horribly simple. I believed and rejected every-thing—everything mixed with everything else. Finally I fell asleep. I dreamed about my mother, who was brushing her downy hair the color of fresh rust. I woke up around noon per-fectly rested—a decent, whole man. My closed circuit had repaired itself in my sleep.

I have been describing various psychological states not to entertain you with psychoanalysis or to blame anybody for his past. I want to make this perfectly clear. I do not count Wladek Sznej among people of bad or little faith. I do not consider him a cynic. He was simply a good conductor. He conducted the currents of the times, and he overheated from them, burned, and faded. I was neither a better nor a worse man. I was only a worse conductor. Not everybody has the ability to conduct time. I am one of those who cannot. But if everybody was capa-ble of everything, nothing would exist. And if nobody desired anything, I am quite sure that everything would die out. The rapists, the seduced, the river . . . the hypocrites, the virtuous, and the exploited . . . the soldiers, the sky, and the boot . . . in my opinion all these things are attributes of this world, which is also a circuit. For us, the mortal ones, it is a closed circuit, yet with a hidden, mysterious gap we know nothing about. Therefore for us—a closed circuit.

Please understand me well.

Let us return to the facts. Despite the change in my life (rehearsals, performances), my studies did not suffer. I only stopped attending lectures, which were not obligatory. It was enough to appear once in a trimester to obtain the professor's signature in the register. Besides, I was sure that with my iron constitution and exceptionally good memory I needed only about six weeks of strenuous work to pass all my exams. Therefore I had at least six months, until spring, entirely to myself.

At first I used to spend my free mornings at the university. I avoided, however, the highly politicized Department of Law, with its endless boycotts, fights, and rallies. I went to the library, where I browsed among books on the history of the theater, or I attended the lectures of prominent professors of the humanities—Witwicki or Tatarkiewicz. I remember a lecture on Plato in an old, high-ceilinged room packed mostly with girls in blue dresses; I remember also an interesting discussion on historical materialism in Professor Kotarbinski's seminar. I did not participate in the discussions, yet I was curious about human types, vocabularies, faces. October was warm and people often went out without overcoats.

The end of the month witnessed some new events. Perhaps this expression is a bit too strong, but there were some significant new developments. *The Dove* was ending its run. Like an old, tired carrier pigeon, it was finishing its victorious flight and folding its wings in the theater storerooms. Halberds and greaves, costumes, decorations, galleries, the prison cell, the jug and Jorgens's hood, and the bloodstained gown of little Uth—all were moved behind the stage. For the first time, on Saturday, October 27, I shot Tola Mohoczy. When I pressed the trigger she was laughing like a harlot and spitting out profanities. There were eight of us. We were standing in a broken file aiming at her with our Mannlichers. We were wearing spiked helmets covered with oilcloth. It all happened during the rehearsal of *The Iron Maiden* by Marcenat. But I must return again to some earlier events.

From the day I started playing my walk-on parts our acquaintance ceased to exist (I speak, of course, about me and her), at least on the surface. I was deprived of even a passing acknowledgment. Anyone else in my position would feel hurt. Meeting or leaving the theater together was absolutely ruled out. She left after the second act, and I rushed onto the stage only toward the very end of the play. Ambition, principles—I tightened these screws quite fast in order to accept this maltreatment with a poker face. It was quite exhausting, and I really suffered. One can repeat hundreds of times that everybody has to live through such ordeals, but it is like telling somebody devoured by wolves that we all must die after all. And yet I knew I stuck in her consciousness.

Through her behavior she was teaching me a lesson, then and forever, that things are as they are—exactly as they are supposed to be—and they are going to remain that way. I wasn't, therefore, totally inconsequential. A didactic intent indicates at least minimal attention, or a less than perfect indifference. I wish to share with you a certain observation. I did not detect in her behavior any anger or repulsion. One could say she had no reason to harbor any of these emotions, but that doesn't really mean anything. Women have the habit of trampling men who do not know how to leave. Besides, she had changed. If I had to describe this metamorphosis in just three words, I would say: sadness, pensiveness, resignation. After the second act she left the stage in her bloodstained silk gown, and I was usually standing in the corridor behind set decorations. I started smoking a pipe, which helped me to control my hands and my face and gave my silence an air of stolid composure. Yet as soon as she passed me I experienced total exhaustion, my temples started to sweat, and I had to use all my strength to prevent myself from grabbing her hand. Only in order to ask what was wrong with her, if she needed me, and if I could be of any help. That, of course, would be a devastating foolishness.

Career, achievement, success—I never cared enough to even think about it. In my whole life I did not achieve anything in particular, and I did not try to. One could call me a failure—a man who squandered his life's potential. I never even got married. And yet I feel no bitterness and I do not think I've wasted my life. I did not spend a single day worrying how I could pursue a career, or wondering whether people who had made it were really happy. All that was too remote, and, as I said, I had no taste for abstractions. But if Tola Mohoczy was not happy that fall, even though she was cast in the role of Michele in Marcenat's *The Iron Maiden*—the title role in a play that was being put on all over Europe—what could possibly be the reason? Couldn't fame and success be understood as the ultimate fulfillment of one's dreams, as spiritual self-satisfaction? There isn't really much to talk about, unless we talk about the dreams of the audience. It seems that the audience, by granting somebody fame, projects upon this person their own dreams of fame, and crowns him as their representative—somebody who is supposed to be happy in their stead. I must say I would not feel very comfortable in that role.

But please imagine my surprise when one evening, just as I was leaving the theater after a performance, I saw a taxicab stop suddenly at the curb. The driver of the old Minerva told me to get in. I thought it was a misunderstanding, and I hesitated for a moment. I saw her angry, translucent eyes looking at me from inside. I got in. It was rather dark, and for some time we did not speak to each other. In the execution scene, when she was standing in front of the yellow wall, I noticed how thin she had become in the last few days. Now, when the car was taking a sharp turn, my arm pressed against her hard, thin ribs. I was not blessed with a lack of sensibility, and I knew the reason for her change. When half an hour ago I was aiming at her with my Mannlicher, she looked—in her black prison sweater and with cropped hair—like a hungry, screaming bird. It flashed through my mind that there was a real fury and hatred simmering in her thinness, and in the curses coming from her contorted lips. I told her this in the cab, when after driving around for three-quarters of an hour I understood that I should not listen to her any longer in silence. I interrupted her in the middle of a word and told her I knew what it was all about.

At first I was calm, although the situation seemed disgraceful and even ridiculous. A kidnapping—American style! I saw the driver cocking his ears. When she ordered the driver to keep driving around until she told him otherwise, I began to sense what we were up to, although I could not anticipate the final outcome. She passed him a bank note. That quiet rustling must have cost her ten dinners at a restaurant. I nodded my head and waited for events to follow their course. She could not find her matches. I gave her a light, but we both kept silent. I did not wish to start the conversation. Our Minerva was turning laboriously into Nowy Swiat. I saw the moving Chinese doll in the window of Meinl's store, and, for a moment, a movie marquee illumined the interior of the cab. Tola's stare was fixed on my face. She started talking only when we were rolling down Tamka Street toward the river. I helped her by reaching for my pipe. She asked what the pipe was for and why I started smoking it. I do not remember if I answered her at all. She told me it was totally idiotic, and that an extra should not smoke a pipe. The driver listened with visible curiosity. We were going under the Poniatowski Bridge. I put the pipe back in my pocket. "Why? What kind of an idea is this? You, working in the theater? You are no use there!" "Why?" I asked. "I had the impression the director was quite pleased with me." "Because a walk-on should never stand out."

Her bony elbow was piercing my side. She moved closer, repeating again and again that everything between us was finished, that there hadn't even been a beginning, that I was forbidden to count on anything, that I was forbidden to show my face in the theater again. I told her I was not going there for my own fancy. I was working, I was being paid. But I would not believe any of this myself. We were climbing Ksiazeca Street, and the driver asked whether he could take us to the Countess, a bar in Wilanow. She refused. Again, I heard the rustling of a bank note. That night they paid us our back wages. When I tried to stop her, she pulled my sleeve with such force I was afraid she was seized by a paroxysm. Later, when we were driving around St. Alexander's Church, I had to listen to some of her less orthodox opinions about myself. She told me I had the face of an honest boxer and the manner of a man from a good family. I heard that when she saw me for the first time in front of the theater, she definitely liked me, because such a combination is quite attractive, but now I have ruined everything with my perverse behavior. "I cannot bear it any longer. You in the corridor, with your pipe! In a spiked helmet! Who gave you permission to stare at me like that in the execution scene. An extra is forbidden to look at an actress in such a way!"

I was sitting stiffly, with my eyes fixed on the driver's neck. I took my pipe out. We were driving through some unknown, treeless streets, probably in Czerniakow. Low houses with dark windows, a lonely streetcar, few people. I knew it was time to speak. I filled my pipe and lighted it slowly, until the tobacco started to glow. I think she was sorry. The car rattled across cobblestones. Our knees bumped together. "Tom, please, don't think I am a monster. I only want . . ." "I know, you want to marry Jorgens and run the theater with him."

If I had understood earlier that our conversation in the cab would be so important, if I had tried to speak with clever irony, trying to show myself to be a generous partner, if I had tried to win her respect, her warm feminine feelings, or her kindness, I would lose definitively, and there would be nothing more to talk about. But because I did not care, and I was ready to back down, to accede to her every wish, and even to quit the theater—as the absurdity and hopelessness of my persistence were becoming more and more evident, and I was feeling really discouraged—because of my indifference and torpor, I behaved like an expert player. Unwittingly, of course! One has to remember, though, that she was very clever, and almost pathologically suspicious of any falsity or lie. I do not remember meeting anybody with her ear for natural, human truth—someone able to pick up any artificiality of tone, the discord of hypocrisy, triviality, or shallowness . . . She reacted to them with a nauseous repulsion (as some people react to the smell of mice) and treated them with manic contempt, disregarding common sense or tact. I have mentioned elsewhere—and I am writing these words from the experience of time that has passed—her spiritual strength from which she derived this abundant contempt. She must have treated her lovers with scorn. She did not belong to the class of women who are conquered "with the stream," by playing to their own self-deception and duplicity. Her courage and self-confidence could easily do without such guarantors. People constantly pretend and lie—to themselves and others—usually for no good reason. Most of the people I know resemble ill-tuned instruments. They do it for a variety of reasons and with different aims in mind, but also quite gratuitously. No wonder that insincerity is the subject of a rather extensive body of literature: scholarly dissertations, plays, novels, etc. But living with her perfect pitch amidst the cacophony of falsity must have been a real torture. That night in the cab she expected me to pretend, and hated me for it in advance. I managed to surprise her—first with my silence, and then with what I said.

When I said she wanted to marry Jorgens in order to run the theater, I realized I was saying something she did not know herself, and I immediately fell silent again. For a while the only sound we heard was the grinding of gears. We were speeding among gardens and suburban villas in God knows what part of the city. I put my pipe out.

"Why do you call him that?" I did not understand her question. "Why do you call him Jorgens?" "All right, then, Cezar," I corrected myself. "'I'm sorry." I gave her another light. She was thinking about something intensely. "It's nonsense. I don't want to be with anybody." I found a new, more stable ground, and from that time on I started to think more soberly. I was talking under my breath, so that the driver would not hear us.

Choosing my words carefully, I brought up what I had noticed in the theater during my couple of weeks there. I did not tell her everything. I did not say, for example, that I saw her suffering as obsessive pride and ambition, closer to sickness than love. I did not mention the door, although it was obvious to me that she started to lose weight when the adjacent dressing rooms of the Jorgenses were joined (supposedly on *his* request) by an interior door. I preferred to spare her that. Yet I told her everything I thought about her new role. It was a useful pretext. While talking about dramatic situations, I talked about the three of them. A small comment: I often use pseudonyms here, because for many years that is how I used to refer to certain people in private or confidential conversations.

The years of the occupation had a way of strengthening such habits. As you have certainly guessed, "Jorgens's wife" is Iza Rajewska. It is by no means a secret code. These matters ceased to be secret long ago, if they ever were. They were discussed publicly, though mostly inaccurately, after the war. I only wish to present my part in these events, which I will do a bit later, in a more appropriate place.

As far as I remember, our Minerva was circling a silent square, probably in Zoliborz near the Citadel. Everything around us was asleep, the moon was shining. I asked her whether she was cold. The driver said he had a blanket in the trunk, but she demanded that I keep on talking. While we sped on, rattling over cobblestones, I said that in my opinion she was best in the execution scene, because at that moment she could be so exquisitely hateful. She was hating not only the Prussians but also von Bockvitz's sister, played by Rajewska. Nobody remembers Jean-Claude Marcenat's play today, but at that time I knew it by heart. I also mentioned that she should never forget, not even for a moment, Michele Walter: a waitress from an Alsatian bierhaus who runs away to Paris in search of a great adventure and ends up in some "Chat Noire" in Montmartre, where she sings *chansons* and is incidentally spotted by French intelligence. A peasant girl from Alsace, a singer in a *café chantant*, and a spy—that's what she remains to the very end. I also said that in the reception scene, after slapping von Bockvitz's invalid daughter, she should look, not at Bockvitz, but at his sister, Rajewska. "You do not lose to German counterintelligence," I said, "but to a rival, who suspects you from the very beginning. In that scene you already know you have lost."

I could have dwelled on the subject longer, but I refrained from further remarks. I felt pity for her, probably because she was listening with such keen attention. I started filling my pipe again. While lighting the humid tobacco I cast her a look over my match. I noticed her knitted brows, which she used to shave or darken by turns. She asked whether in the reception scene she was less good. I considered what to say. In fact, in that scene Rajewska came out best.

"No," I said. "You are wonderful. But you've been given too many words to say. For me, at least, your laughter after the slapping would suffice."

I was sure my remarks were accurate. In the university library I had read the most important reviews of *The Iron Maiden* after its performances in Paris and Vienna: a handsome Prussian officer and a young widower, his demonic sister who brings up his paralyzed twelve-year-old daughter; a woman spy in the luxurious villa on Unter den Linden, where she receives tributes from the Kronprinz himself, while in love with a man from whom she steals secret documents; a Prussian staff major who confesses his torments and suspicions to his sister . . . love, espionage, aristocracy, Verdun, paralysis, incest, sacrifice, and death before a firing squad . . . isn't it a bit much for good taste?

These objections were not totally unfounded, yet Marcenat's play was conquering audiences throughout Europe, for the most part, it seems to me, thanks to the character of Michele, played at that time by the most famous actresses. As someone who has been associated with theater for many years, I know that sometimes—or even in most cases—fame can be won through roles in weak plays. Yet they have to be plays in which the author combines a knowledge of common psychology with vividness of character and the so-called stage instinct. Jean-Claude Marcenat possessed that ability. He did not even hesitate to make use of a scene in which a crippled child is slapped. One has to admit that it was, in a sense, a master move, which in his drama played a triple role of salvation, sacrifice, and revenge.

"By hitting that child you make him hate you in order to

save him, and at the same time you take revenge on his sister, who hates you."

She nodded. "I know. She is a scoundrel."

Our driver was listening intently and asked where he could see this play. I wish to remark that for some time our quarrel had turned into a professional discussion. I had to answer her detailed questions concerning gestures, inflections, makeup, and to assure her that her laughter in Act III was really remarkable and that her bow to the Kronprinz in Act II was not excessively courtly; I had to convince her that her death was faultless and that her curses in front of the firing squad really duplicated the scream of a street girl. She was carefully watching my intonation and she interrupted me only to voice some doubts, which she had already expressed at least three times. I dispelled them patiently for the fourth time. During that insane, frenzied night in a cab, I started to realize two things— both very important—from which I drew certain conclusions.

But all that came to my mind later, when we were lying, exhausted, in my sublet in Zurawia Street. She turned away from me to face the wall. I listened to her breathing, without feeling like a conqueror. Even though she had asked me to take her to my room. The janitor was opening the door when she jumped from the cab. I knew that what had happened had nothing to do with victory. Half asleep, I reached behind my bed and found her bra hanging on the chair. It was then that the double law of our relationship appeared to me. I sat up in the bed and lit my last pipe. I understood two things: always, everywhere, and despite all circumstances, I shall fulfill her every wish, and never, under any conditions, shall I really matter to her, although she may need me.

It was so simple. In the darkness, with a pipe in one hand and a bra dangling from the other, I had suddenly solved the puzzle: a role! There was never anything else in her life, and never would be. But there was the concluding dialogue in the car, which gave me a lot to think about. If I acted in a discreet, careful, and skillful manner, I had a chance of becoming the *second director* in her life.

What I am describing here is the introduction to the middle part of my biography, which has a crucial importance since all the key facts concerning the matter under discussion took place in this period, and I shall pass on to them shortly. Why do I dwell so long on the introduction? Because that is what I remember best. A couple of days, two nights, and several performances—all this has engraved itself in my memory with the pedantic, weighty precision of images from old costume movies. The rest is a tangle of time not fully experienced. From the two thousand days that remained to the outbreak of war I remember vividly only several hours: the death of the Marshal, the meeting with Nina Willman three years later at the university, a conversation with Cezar at the railway station in Kiwerce. Then there was the war—dreadfully condensed and abridged, like four or five years of high school taken in one hectic year without breaks or vacations. Dates, however, are insignificant—even those of historical importance. I divide my life into three parts: the technical, the natural, and the metaphoric. The technical one lasted until my meeting with Tola, when I was living like an intelligent, obedient, and civilized robot. The second—the middle one—resembled most the existence of nature: organism, instinct, struggle, fear, biology. It lasted ten years. I am living the third part of my life right now. I call it metaphoric because only in that period did I start to experience the secondary nature of my earthly existence—the things, the events, the feelings and shapes, as well as the various imaginary circumstances, constituting in fact a kind of metaphor—a projection of actual meaning or sense into a reflective realm more accessible to mind. Although today I hold a responsible, if only administrative, position as theater manager, and fulfill other, perhaps more difficult and delicate functions (I'll talk about them later), I can state in all earnestness that I am not really here in the literal sense. I am quite aware of my "derived existence"—to use my father's term. He considered man one of many forms of a universal being capable of incorporating itself into matter. He was quite an original, even for his own time.

I termed the middle period of my life a natural one. I would like to elaborate on it a little, since the following pages will concern precisely that part of my existence. It was a period richest in events, but also in fateful decisions and dramatic solutions. Besides—it was a period of selflessness. What I mean by that is my attitude toward myself and the world, which today often happens to be different. Then, it was a looser attitude, less informed about the general rules of life and free from the blackmail of acknowledged necessities. I was living more bravely and with a greater will to live. It seemed that I was picking something up with one hand and then discarding it with the other. I followed my instinct, my desire, my curiosity. I did not care about the structure of power, its mechanisms and standards, the style of my jacket, or the meaning of existence, about my position or even about my own death. I stuck to the rules—not the official and general ones, but my own. I was an animal, but not a predator. I did not chase or run away. I was following somebody who had already vanished, and it is possible that this somebody was myself. But since it seemed to me that nobody had trod my path before me, I felt free. Even if it wasn't true freedom, at least it was a true life. In comparison with my present existence I would say that I lived more "in nature." At that time people in general were less controlled by the two contemporary obsessions: the past and the future. Who in those days would think in terms of history or evoke the specter of progress! Life was lived on a slow wheel. Such wooden wheels with prizes attached to them were popular in provincial amusement parks. I remember them from summer excursions. There was one, for example, in Piotrkow.

No matter what point of view we take, my way of living at that time could not possibly seem like a sensible one. I wasn't preparing myself for a profession, I wasn't struggling for the improvement of social relations, I wasn't thinking about starting a family. I wasn't even a profligate or a carouser. Common sense would have dictated that I marry Nina Willman and start practicing law in her father's office. With her intelligence and charm nobody would suspect me of ulterior motives. In the meantime I was attending lectures no more than five times a year, and keeping my relationship with Nina on a purely friendly basis, I discussed the theater with her father. On the other hand, I worked out regularly at the YMCA's boxing club, I washed myself in cold water with a scrubbing brush and cheap Schicht soap, I fasted once a month, and twice a week I learned one page of a foreign text by heart.

The author of a certain novel—I do not remember its title—tried to portray a truly free man through a similar stereotype. My case, however, was somehow different. Everything I did was for me natural behavior in certain immutable circumstances. Today "freedom" as a postulated aim means for me the most precious kind of unawareness; the weaker the sense of our biological or metaphysical bondage, the stronger our need for social and individual freedom. But this is an utterly different subject. I was used to my bondage as one is used to the native landscape, which one doesn't want to change. Such attachment is very similar to freedom.

I have said I remember few details: I have forgotten not only dates and places but also their content. I am unable to describe any single month of my life or to recall what I was doing and thinking at that time, or to whom I was talking or the subject of our conversation. All I can remember are several sentences from a few important conversations; a whole long spring is represented by a bench and somebody's motionless profile with parted lips. One could ask whether this is normal. I think it is. A hero in a novel usually loses memory as the result of some psychological stress. In real life the opposite is true: the lack of memory is for me a sign of mental health. Perhaps if I tried really hard I could remember everything—week after week—dreams, conversations, meals, the rain and the sun. But this in fact would be sickness: the re-creation of past time is something abnormal. Besides, how much of what I would *remember* would be true? What does it mean to remember, after all? It is one thing to remember a telephone number. But to "remember" a November, a love, or a year in one's life? Such memory is either a disease or literature. I consider myself a thoroughly sane person, although Cezar told me at the station in Kiwerce, shortly before the war, that I was the only real madman he ever met, precisely because of my pathological normality. ("There is something of Buster Keaton in you. When all this shit is finally blown up, and the ashes start settling down, you will emerge from the rubble wearing a hat and shiny shoes.") He was quite drunk, though, and I almost had to carry him to his train.

Since we are talking about Cezar, let me refer to a passage in "A Chapter in the History of Struggle" where Professor Janota, without mentioning names, writes about "certain individuals who displayed clearly antisocial attitudes" and proceeds to list various measures the organization took against such people. Let me quote: "Irrespective of their position in public or cultural life before the war, we used the most severe sanctions, including the death sentence." Irrespective! Irrespective of the author's intelligence, before or after the war, let me say that if I did not know who we are discussing here, I would certainly think that only an idiot could be so simpleminded about a case (there were no other death sentences carried out by Rondo) of such tragic complexity. Yet the author

argues as above, not because he is a moron but because of a
certain cyclical quality to his polemic: clichés like this beget
articles of this kind, and such articles in turn produce clichés.
Thus, we create a new reality of words, in which all the secrets
of life are reduced to the configuration of printed signs. Such
expressions as "attitude," "culture," "individual," or "sanction," applied to the immense phenomenon of human weakness and beauty that was Karol Cezarewicz, tell us about the
man about as much as a toothpaste label tells us about a chalk
mountain. I am writing about a man whose name for many
years was mentioned with abhorrence. Not with fear or contempt, but with abhorrence. The most beastly crime fails to
evoke the blind horror of an unexpected debasement like his.
The old fairy tale about a knight who wakes up with a hare's
heart sewn into his chest is the most horrifying of tales. I used
to listen to it with a spasm in my throat. I really preferred King
Herod. It seems that the figures of slaughterers and henchmen
are something perennial and official in human imagination.
Their cruelty is a part of their job description. They appear
with license to sow misery and fear. But the sense of horror I
am talking about is a much more complex and overwhelming
feeling, because evil seems to come from nowhere. It does not
carry its usual insignia and does not sever heads. It is a familiar and intimate specter. Nobody has sent these specters upon
us—they are ourselves, as are the fallen and the humiliated
who have suffered the inexplicable. It is only then, through
this mysterious closeness, that we feel real horror—not fear,
but a stunning awareness of the strange stigma borne by the
people we know. We grow pale thinking about them and about
us, about what will continue to bind us to them, despite what
separates us. Cezar was called a traitor. Those were the years of
mental shortcuts, which is quite understandable. There was no
time for psychology. But he was never really feared. The fear he
evoked was not a fear *of* him. It was a thought about ourselves,

about a man and his human soul. One of us had failed to steer his soul in the right direction. Death penalty . . . As far as the circumstances of his death are concerned, very little is known today. Professor Janota recounts the testimony of witnesses— that is, the audience and his partners. That means nothing, or almost nothing. He has chosen to leave the rest untold.

I wish to come back to the point at which I interrupted my story. The night in my room after the taxi ride. Tola with her face turned to the wall and asleep. I, sitting in the darkness, with my sudden illumination and an unusual inner certainty. An intimate, sublime, and comic situation. I was subletting my room from a childless couple. Mr. Boguslaw Kummel, an electrical engineer, was my father's schoolmate. He and his wife resembled a gray-haired, smiling Japanese couple. They went to bed at nine and got up at seven. One hour after their departure a maid would come to clean the apartment. But it was Saturday night. On Sundays and holidays the day started later. Around nine Mr. Kummel would take his dog and go out to get a newspaper while his wife was busy in the kitchen. On Sunday mornings I used to lie in bed with my hands tucked under my head, listening to the calm Sunday noises and smelling the coffee and freshly waxed floors. At exactly half past nine the dog would thump with his nose at my door and deliver a copy of the *Morning Courier*. Soon Mrs. Kummel would bring me a cup of coffee with milk and home-baked cake. This was the routine every Sunday. I had to get Tola out after Kummel went out with the dog, hoping we would not be heard from the kitchen. Everything went more or less according to plan. I closed the door as quietly as I could, and we slipped quickly down the stairs. Then I saw tiny Mr. Kummel at the corner newsstand. His back was to us, but in a moment he would turn and see us. Luckily, we were behind a horse-cab stand. The dog barked, however, dropping the newspaper from his mouth in surprise.

We stopped at the intersection of Krucza and Piekna streets. I asked whether she wanted me to see her to her house, but she had other plans. She guessed that I wanted to go with her anyway, and looked at me seriously. "All right, Tom. If you wish." We walked along the empty pavement in the hazy autumn light, both absentminded, or preoccupied with ourselves. I think that after that night she must also have understood something. As we approached the Savior's Square, she stopped for a moment, and it seemed as if she wanted to tell me something. Instead she only raised her eyes, looked at me for an instant, and then suddenly ran the tips of her fingers across my cheek. When she started walking again, I froze for a moment—at the corner of Mokotowska Street—and watched her enter the church. I was bewildered by her gesture, which seemed neither a farewell nor a moment of tenderness, but simply an acknowledgment of what had happened between us—a half-sad and half-submissive acceptance. At the same time there was something very calm and very wise in it. If she had wanted me to leave, she could simply have said, "Go back now and leave me alone," and, of course, I would have done as she wished. But she said nothing, only made this unexpected gesture—quite meaningful in its own way—as if leaving me, or whatever was acting through me, with a choice of a future . . . I cannot find suitable words, it was a brief moment which contained, nevertheless, some condensed message and had the power of a dream. I knew that a lot would depend on my next move, though I could not say what or why. I circled the square and entered the church, taking a place near the door. After a moment I saw Tola kneeling in a pew next to a woman in a gray, crumpled head covering which resembled a man's hat.

I never was religious, at least not in the usual sense. In our home nobody made much fuss about religious rituals, prayer, or confession. My father did not like priests, but I would hesitate to call him an atheist. In Poland such people were considered freethinkers, although it was more of a critical attitude toward the clerical mentality than a rejection of the idea of a Supreme Being. My case was different. I was born later and did not have to liberate myself from anything. My parents did it for me during their Galician radical youth. Catholicism, the saints, liturgy and the sentiments it evoked, religious customs—all this seemed to belong to my family's tradition, but rather remotely. This tradition concerned the lives of my grandfathers and great-grandfathers. I saw it as a kind of natural folklore: it was hard to imagine a Polish town without a church, or a village road without a procession on Corpus Christi. And yet I did not identify these beautiful scenes with any deeper spiritual content. They belonged to the real, earthly domain—which I neither ignored nor permitted too close to my heart. This earthly domain existed outside the sphere of reflection, and was also quite obvious, like the order of things I inherited on the day of my birth. Such notions as school, church, the army, or the court of law seemed to me as enduring and indisputable a part of reality as rivers, bridges, forests, and buildings. There was nothing to meditate about, nothing to revere in the very fact of their existence.

I am saying all this in order to explain that my experience inside the Savior's Church during the morning mass had nothing to do with religious exaltation. It was similar to the experience I had two months earlier in the Turecka café, but much, much more powerful. I did not pray, and I wouldn't have known what to pray for. Throughout the mass I was standing far from the altar, near the door, and if I were to describe my psychological state, I would use such expressions as "relief" and "relaxation." Amid the singing and the tolling of the bells the whole outline of my future life started to appear to me more and more clearly. I saw Tola's head from a distance and I was sure that she also felt my presence. In the crowd of the devout, from time to time I saw her profile, her narrow forehead and her wide, open eyes. In these moments I felt a strange relief, a bond and a transformation, a sensation both rich and exhausting—not because of strain, but as in convalescence. Though it was a mystical experience, I wouldn't compare that moment with the act of entrusting myself to God. I was not entrusting anybody, least of all myself. It was I who had to make everything happen. It was only my will. I might even say that in a sense I was becoming God for myself, within my own modest capacity, although my resolution was anything but modest.

Let us consider what an average young man of today would feel in a similar situation. Probably he would begin to review the stages of his life: education, an apartment, the wedding, employment plus possible extras. If he weren't so totally average after all, he might also notice the larger context of his life in the universal system of values—the one that already exists, or the one that has not yet come into existence—an order in which he could find support now and in the future. Both in the first, average and barbarous instance and in the second, less average and more Christian one, we are faced with an attitude that makes man aware of his subordination. In my opinion contemporary people are religious in exactly that way— through piety toward the facts and expectations for the world. I did not feel anything of that sort. All I knew—and I knew it in the deepest possible sense, to the bitter end—was that I would not back off under any circumstances, that I would create a life—my own, hers, which were one and the same—in defiance of any conceivable obstacles, and that I had really nothing else to do. And that is what I did. Today I may say that I was successful. Let me add, though, that I was successful in a manner different from what I anticipated. It's obvious, however, that accident is a part of every human endeavor.

If you have read this far, I trust you will go on reading. It gets intriguing. A question arises: What is it all about? Nothing much, really, apart from one small detail: someone (myself in particular) has invented the sense of existence. Please give it some thought. I was not a tramp, a prophet, or an artist. I did not run a circus. I did not hunt rhinoceroses. I did not sail around the globe. I was one of many. Such biographies seem ready-made. People like me live in every epoch and constitute its gray material, the most common substance. Such people are called society, the masses, the nation, or the statistical average. Their lives are spoken about in an impersonal tone, as if they belonged to nobody in particular, but rather to the epoch itself. For me there is something humiliating in this approach. No wonder the gray material reacts with excessive anger and fury . . . which immediately falls prey to new columns of numbers. In reality I could blame myself for many things, but not for being *typical*.

I left the church before the end of the mass. It all took no more than fifteen minutes. When the crowd was repeating "And pray for us . . ." the woman in the man's hat, who sat next to Tola, turned and seemed to notice me behind the kneeling crowd. I recognized her. She was our prompter, Miss Lala Ubycz. I was a little surprised. There were rumors that Miss Lala belonged to a sect condemned by the Catholic Church. Did she and Tola have an appointment here, or did they meet by accident? I considered it on my way back, when the streets were filling with the Sunday crowds. The nature of their relationship was revealed to me only years later. At this time only Cezar might have guessed something. At least I think so. Even if he did not know the truth, he knew the regions where the truth was hidden. During our conversation at the station bar in Kiwerce he said several times that I would need Lala. I remember his words well: "I know her sort. She is straight from Shakespeare: a royal nurse. She keeps silent and wipes up the stains. Never underestimate secondary characters!"

In the eyes of poor psychologists such people seem inconsequential; one often appears irrelevant through another's shortsightedness.

To avoid unnecessary secrets, let me say that the person of whom I speak has shared my life for many years, and as I write these words she is separated from me only by the wall in our apartment. I am absolutely sure that without her keen presence and superhuman endurance, everything I wished to achieve, and everything I have achieved, would be lost many times over. I wouldn't be sitting at my desk now and writing to you, and I would have nothing to desire or to expect. I wouldn't exist today were it not for Miss Ubycz.

We are waiting together, living side by side. There are less than three months left until Tola's return. I should be able to finish by then. I have been writing for two weeks now. Two weeks ago I took Tola to the station. The day before yesterday I received the first postcard: a view of the snow-covered Alps. It means that they are together, and everything is all right. Two weeks ago, when I returned home by taxi, I did not feel too well—probably because of the weather and the prospect of a long separation. Low pressure seemed to drive the city underground, into dark, slimy gutters steaming with humidity. I had no time to search for suitable words. I do not like farewells. Besides, on that very day I read the article in your review, which I found at the theater in a bundle of periodicals and other mail. I was quite irritated and I kept recalling, God knows why, the scene in front of a commemorative plaque near the taxi stand. A man was repeatedly making a sign of the cross in the air with his hat, until he suddenly fell to the wet pavement. At the same moment a taxi pulled up I got in, since I was next in line. On my way I thought by turns about this scene and about the article. I never had any need to publish my memoirs. The war returns to me only in dreams (a dream is the best homage to the past), but the article I read seemed to be based on such a raw distortion that I could not get over a sense of embarrassment. In the hallway I took off my coat, my scarf and gloves, and extinguished my pipe. Behind the door I heard the sound of trumpets, in E minor, which subsided after a few movements. When I entered the room she was sitting on the floor and rewinding the tape. I had given her a tape recorder as a present on her saint's day a year ago. In the next room Miss Lala was packing the last small things into her suitcase. We had to go to the station in an hour. When I sat on the birch-wood sofa, resting my back on the crumpled velvet pillows, she asked—still rewinding the tape—whether I had slept well (we had not met that day at breakfast). I told her I dreamt about my father. With my mind on the article and on her departure, I casually described my dream. It turned out that my father did not die during the war, but has been hiding out all these years with a woman. I found him emaciated but in good spirits, and it was clear that since his death he had kept well informed about my life. When I was telling my dream, I saw Tola from behind, hunched over the tape recorder, and I was not sure whether she was listening to me at all. I wanted to remark lightly that it was easier for her to part with me than with Bach, or the ballad "Sunday at the Railway Station" (although I was not in a light mood at all). She lifted her head and said, laughing, that nothing ever changed with me and that even my dream about my father repeated itself at regular monthly intervals. I also smiled. She was wearing a red scarf tied very tightly at the back of her head. I felt a bit uneasy—was she trying to hide her hair? In order to break the silence I told her about the drunk who had fallen in front of the commemorative plaque. I used the expression "eerie inappropriateness," and I added that he was lying athwart the pavement, probably in the same position as the people who had been executed there, but that the pathetic ostentation with which he crossed himself just before falling was a hundred times more shocking.

I wanted to say something more on the subject and I got up from the sofa, but at that moment a red-haired, strongly built man in dark glasses appeared in front of me. Behind him was Tola's portrait sketched by Witkacy in Zakopane. Her green-ish hair, resembling a tangle of seaweed, was visible above the man's head, and they were both looking at me.

The sight of the man in the mirror was always surprising. I was astonished both by my looks and by my presence. It is unbelievable that one can change that much and yet remain the same person, the continuation of the young man from the provinces who came to Warsaw in order to . . . Why did he come to Warsaw in the first place? In order to realize his first person singular. Tola recorded a fragment of our Christmas conversation and perhaps a couple of days from now they will be listening to my voice together in some Alpine town. Yes, my fate must have been something radically different from the facts, something utterly resilient to change, one which has wiped several worlds from the face of the earth. With manic persistence my fate has managed to stay the same course through so many cyclones. It probably was a part of some other plot programmed within me, and its stubborn necessity, more logical than the laws of history, has given me the tran-quility of a madman who imagines himself to be a stone cast into a river.

Later I had coffee. I already knew that I would write to you, and the thought gave me some comfort. I decided to sit down to the task as soon as I returned from the station, I felt relieved. I spilled some sugar. Brushing it off the tablecloth and laugh-ing at my clumsiness, I searched for the large silver ashtray, which should have been within my reach. I noticed it on the floor among the tapes. With sugar in my hand I rose from the sofa and met again the two faces that looked at me: my own and Tola's. My face was concealed behind dark glasses whereas hers examined me with bright, narrowly set eyes, one brow slightly higher than the other, as if she were listening with incredulous attention to my tale about the American ballet performed in Warsaw not long before and to my insincere speculations about having caught a cold during that perform-ance in the Congress Hall and to my plan to go to bed imme-diately after returning from the station. The likeness of the portrait unnerved me: Tola in my memory and in my percep-tion had the face from the portrait. In Zakopane, Witkacy had painted it in a single day. She told me that while she was sitting for him, he taught her English words—all invented by him, as it turned out later. Thus he eternalized her for me.

We left around one in the afternoon. Once in the cab, I made some general remarks about the ballet. I claimed to be quite insensitive to that form of art because it rested on the mute harmony of movement, which made it somehow too abstract for my taste. In nature, movement is always noisy. Only suffering is voiceless, and it seems that ballet is like a shadow stolen from the theater and planted within music—or something of that kind. I remember Cezar talking about it some years ago. Later we stood on the railway platform. There was a long car and familiar-looking young people with flowers. When the train started to move I managed to give her the tape recorder she almost forgot to take with her. She shouted to me, "We shall return together. I am certain of that!" I nodded my head. Since Marcenat's death I see this prospect as possible and imminent.

When Clemenceau died, a week later the French press printed an announcement according to his wishes: "Monsieur Georges Clemenceau died last Wednesday, and was buried." I do not know whether this anecdote is true. Apparently Boy told it to someone during the premiere of *The Iron Maiden*. In any case, the old man must have hated funerals. Presumably not only funerals but all occasions requiring communal silence, mimicry, and gestures, when the air under the trees stands still

in an allegorical pause. I doubt if after my death I would care
much who came to my funeral. And yet I feel irritated at the
thought of the people marching behind my coffin. I see myself
prostrate, and them—marching triumphantly behind my body.
Unfortunately, I have not yet reached the longing for this well-
deserved rest. Perhaps because matters have not reached their
conclusion yet. I admit that during my walk through the Saski
Garden (despite bad weather I decided to walk home from the
station) I was visited several times by the image of the author
of "A Chapter in the History of Struggle" delivering a speech
over my freshly dug grave. The vision filled me with such irritation that I could not suppress a groan, fortunately drowned
out by the noise of the streetcars. Wreaths, solemn silence, and
words meant to cover over all traces of me, which I am unable
to deny: that was a truly unbearable image! Upon returning
home I sat, without much further thought, at my typewriter,
and wrote the first four pages you have here.

I think I owed you that digression. Or perhaps I owed it to
myself. Most of all I want to be clearly understood. This is all
about preserving a fragment of truth. My fragment—the one I
created myself.

The years 1934-39 were the period of my growing involvement with the theater. I did not think much about what was
going on in the country or in the world. Only occasionally did
I pick up the din of distant coups, annexations, strikes, and
wars echoed in the newspaper headlines: the Civil War in
Spain, the colonial war in Abyssinia . . . I went to rehearsals, I
made friends with actors, I listened to backstage anecdotes, I
played pool with an old comic actor, Wiaremko, who apparently remembered Modrzejewska. The extras and the less
prominent actors used to pass the time in a small café not far
from the theater, frequented also by old pensioners and bet-
tors. I enjoyed there a certain popularity reserved for well-

mannered eccentrics, patient listeners, and people free of fervent ambitions. I had a quite distinctive appearance, which—combined with my reticence—cut a rather memorable figure. I became a "character," one of those individuals who hung around certain theaters and cabarets of that time. Some of them have survived until today—like faded insects in a collector's box. Of course, I was also something else, but I preferred to keep my difference a secret. All that was known about me was that I was studying law (in May I disappeared from the café) and that I was a reserve officer. In 1936 I had to excuse myself from rehearsals of *The Wedding* because I was called up for winter exercises. Nevertheless, I still managed to appear as a farmhand dressed in a russet coat and brandishing a scythe.

This mode of existence had its attractive side since the theater, even in its everyday, mundane life, is always somehow less prosaic than reality. A certain atmosphere of illusion and fantasy lingers behind the stage, in the corridors, dressing rooms, and foyers, and is perceived also by ushers and cloakroom attendants. Today much has been lost of that carnival atmosphere, the carpenter's shop, the boudoir, the sanctuary of art that smells of powder, glue, paint, wood, and wigs. The fairy tale is over: today there is more administration and bureaucracy than sweat and cold-blooded stage fright. One has to imagine the prewar theater, where props, costumes, and stage sets still possessed the naïve illusionism of a circus. During performances, especially in small towns, actors often spoke their monologues while gnawing on real chicken drumsticks.

Besides, I liked actors. One often hears about their infidelities, their buffoonery or lack of seriousness. That was exactly what I liked about them: their deliberate, self-conscious lack of seriousness. I was curious about their pranks, their acrobatic skills, their compulsive lying. No doubt about it—they were dying to have some fun and they would sell their souls for a good joke! But there was one area where they were true—

more true than other people. Everything there was to know about them was visible on the surface. They were a closed, obnoxious society, and despite the fact that pretense was their profession, they pretended less than the so-called serious people. They played rulers, gods, women of debauchery, condottieri, and kindhearted uncles, but while impersonating such a variety of characters, they familiarized themselves with the multiple and paradoxical qualities of human nature: they imitated human sins and virtues, they changed their faces, voices, and actions, until they reached a border beyond which there is nothing and everything at the same time—where everything is true and nothing is false, or everything is false and nothing is true. That border obliterated shame. They were free from the shame of existence, like the rest of the natural world—beyond man. I watched them as one watches flowers or birds. I studied these gestures and mimicry which reflected a deformed yet authentic essence of tragedy, or tragicomedy, they neither perceived nor cared about. Toward the end of the German occupation, when Cezar's life had already deteriorated, he once drove up in a rickshaw to the Wild Hare bar just as I was leaving. He was paying the driver with crumpled bills of occupation money when he spotted me and was overcome by terror: he covered both eyes, his fingers clamped tightly together. I had to help him get out. In those days he was never sober. He looked into my face and said with a wink, "Ignominy gives the jester his security . . ." He grabbed my arm. He was swollen and heavy. I remember this line well—probably from Shakespeare, since Cezar never quoted anybody else. There was something pliable and helpless in it, something sorrowful and funny, and desperately proud. Such a sentence could have been written only by an actor.

I was living in the shadows. These years before the war were not easy for me. I was waiting. For what? Sometimes it occurred to me that things were going too fast, faster than I expected. First of all Tola's career. I never imagined her success would be so sudden and spectacular. She became famous as Michele Walter, and other roles soon followed. In my opinion these were less important, and I even worried a bit, because her acting had already begun to reveal a certain mannerism, which is exceptionally dangerous in young actresses. But I was gravely mistaken, since these roles really seduced the audiences. What seemed to me extravagant and overdone—the nonchalance with which she mutilated the text, her uneven intonation and pace, the unexpected pauses—all this drew protests but also left audiences overcome and stunned. Now and then one would hear a voice of misgiving or warning— other actresses predicted disaster, old Wiaremko giggled over the pool table—but it was too late. Her fame gained force like a hurricane that sweeps up dry leaves and bends the trees. After her appearance as Eliza in *Pygmalion* she was showered with praise. Rave reviews were blossoming everywhere, and from that time on I could occasionally see Tola in Swiatowid or Ace peep shows. In one of the photographs she was standing among laughing men, some in riding outfits and top hats, others in cavalry uniforms. The photographer captured a casual moment during the opening ceremony at an equestrian event in the Agricola sports complex. She was half turned away from the camera and wore a distracted, impatient, angry look, as if searching for a face in the audience. She had a miniature top hat on her head. I was moved by that photo. I couldn't help thinking she was looking for me among the spectators in that dotted, blurred background.

Yes, we continued to see each other. We did not meet regularly, but occasionally each of us initiated visits. She found my real name uninteresting, and in more tender moments she still whispered, "Tom, Tom . . ." I am sure that for a long time no one in the theater, except Cezar, suspected our relationship. Only Lala Ubycz knew about it directly. During those five years I had not betrayed myself with a single gesture. You have to know the perceptiveness of actors, especially in that particular domain, to appreciate my discipline and self-control. It was quite a good exercise in conspiracy. I required presence of mind not only in the theater but also with my landlords. I thought I pulled it off perfectly well, for I did not notice any cooling off in the kind and almost parental attitude of the Kummels. However, during the war, when I no longer lived with them, I met Mr. Kummel on a streetcar in Nowy Zjazd. I was shocked when he asked me with unexpectedly youthful curiosity, "And how is your charming lady? Please give her our regards. You know, my wife was very moved. And that messenger . . ." The messenger's name was Karmanski. He had a faded red cap, a face of a similar hue, and a gray mustache. During the day he stood in front of the Brothers Jablkowski department store or sat there on a little canvas stool that folded into a cane. He used to come to my home in Zurawia Street in the afternoons, between the rehearsal and the evening performance. While climbing the stairs he coughed so loudly that I could have the door open well before he had time to knock. He used to bring me hastily scribbled notes: "Tonight, after the performance." I waited in a passage near the streetcar stop at Nowy Swiat and Warecka Street. I usually left the theater early, sometimes after the first or the second act, especially when we were putting on *Pygmalion*; I was one of the pedestrians in the first scene. We stole into the apartment without turning on the lights. Later we would talk in bed until early morning.

Her egocentrism had nothing narcissistic about it, although it seemed almost pathological. I soon realized, however, that the source of it was her fear of an insufficient awareness of reality. She concentrated on herself as the most accessible and familiar aspect of experience, although her questions and doubts aimed much higher. I had the impression that she expected me to tell her what the world was all about, to explain God and the meaning of life, to help her solve the tormenting puzzle of who she was and the nature of her rights. I knew that she was constantly measuring herself against something and that her rebellion and suffering proceeded from the fact that she was measuring herself against the unknown. I was unable to help her, because her demands were unrealistic and insatiable. She would be satisfied only if I could prove beyond any doubt that she was truly evil or truly good. Although it wasn't possible, I understood something extremely important: the real meaning of the theater in her eyes. I had previously used the term "a role." The theater was for her a sequence of characters she played, each delivering her from uncertainty. The theater was her explicated world. That is what I guessed and one night I told her so. "You torment yourself because you don't know you real role," or something like that. I do not recall the exact words, but that was their sense. In the darkness, she turned and looked at me for a long time. I do not know whether we understood each other.

In any case, certain things had happened, and I was not only her lover. When I say "we talked," I mean something more than just talking. I mean a certain spiritual alliance—a psychological state for two. Perhaps I was a better listener than I was a lover, but even so, our relationship wasn't really based on my ability to listen, or on the fact that she could always tell me everything about herself. What was important was that in the darkness I became the recipient of a certain transfer. Please forgive me the monetary term. I do not wish to use psychological jargon, which has become so popular today. I am sure, however, that a woman who reveals to a man her internal life unites with him in a deeper and closer way than through a sexual act. I am speaking about a process of revealing that should not be confused with the Freudian confession. It was—let me repeat—a mutual process extended in time, gradual and slow, which occasionally led to the complete liberation of feelings, reflexes, and thoughts: the liberation of the whole consciousness. This can happen through entrusting one's mind to another human being, who thus becomes its plenipotentiary and guarantor, and also, to a certain extent, its co-owner. One cedes one's psychological content to somebody else, thus creating an extremely durable, though mostly unilateral link: the involved parties do not exchange their assets. The transfer takes place only in one direction, and the recipient is obliged to pay perpetual interest. After a year she knew practically nothing about me, whereas I knew almost everything about her. The Romans used to call such relationships *societas leonina*. In that particular partnership I was the lion.

The myth of her tragic affair with Cezar hovered above us in the darkness . . . I considered it nonexistent—purely an invention. There was no affair with Cezar. Everybody had some affairs with Cezar, myself included. But I listened patiently. She was revealing her sins to me, and I wasn't always able to tell the real from the imaginary. She loved to present herself to me—with indulgence and exaggeration—in the worst possible light, as a doomed woman, a woman possessed by evil! She asked me whether I could imagine the torments of erotomania. I had no idea—but we had a whole night before us. She would torture me until dawn explaining how she was attracted to absolutely every man. She never tired of reminding me of that. For example, the evening at the Savoy, when the boy at the next table had become ill: she asked if I remembered it. Yes, I did. And did I remember the father of that boy? She started to describe down to the smallest details this man I had hardly noticed, and to whisper a list of his features: his chin, the shade of his beard, his lower lip. She shook me by the arm. "It is a sickness, an affliction! Try to understand. You are walking down the street, and suddenly you remember somebody's hairy thigh. Or a calf! And this calf starts to chase you, follow you. Oh, Tom . . ." She pulled the sheet over her eyes. I said nothing because I had nothing to say. I both believed and disbelieved her. That whole area of experience seemed to me ambiguous. I felt pity—but in an abstract way. Even my jealousy was abstract. All I really felt was a sad astonishment at my own lack of knowledge. I never suspected that such torments, such sources of suffering, existed. I had no expertise in these matters.

On the day the Marshal died the messenger brought me a note early in the morning. I was barely awake—I had studied international law until three in the morning. From the brevity of the note scribbled in pencil I guessed that something important must have happened. "You know, of course. Come immediately to my place." Apparently she wanted to give me her condolences. I was puzzled, since I had not had time to look at the morning paper. I never learned how she got hold of old Karmanski, who used to take up his station in front of the Jablkowskis' store much later. I suspect it was Lala Ubycz who took care of that. At the time I was hardly aware of her place in Tola's life. I didn't even know they were living together on Topolowa Street. On a streetcar, over somebody's shoulder, I noticed a huge obituary with a photo on the first page of the *Gazeta Polska*. I spent the whole morning with Tola. The day was sunny and we walked toward the center of the city. Government limousines were speeding between the Belvedere and the Royal Castle carrying silhouettes in black hats. Sometimes a general's insignia flashed through a car window. Apart from that, nothing had changed in the streets: a spring day—breezy and blue. We didn't say much to each other, but I felt she was trying to ply me with sisterly tenderness, which made my uneasy situation even worse. When we reached Saski Square she decided to drop in at a café. There was an exhibition of sculpture in the low pavilion-like building, and as soon as we entered somebody drew her into conversation. Later we moved into a small gravel yard with garden umbrellas, and several people waved to us from their tables. It occurred to me that I must have seen some of them before—a man in a beret, for example, who resembled a masculinized Indian woman, and several ladies. One of them, with a bleached Slavonic crew cut and a cigarette sticking out of a small holder, invited us, in a deep, low voice, to join her already crowded table. I chose to sit alone at a free table in the corner, waiting for Tola. I lit my pipe. After half an hour I left unnoticed. It seemed she simply forgot about me.

One could ask why I put up with all that, and I could answer: because I loved her. Such an explanation, however, does not suffice. If I were a character in a play, the director, in search of a deeper interpretation of the role, should ask me *why* I loved her. To point out that in matters of love such questions have no significance is a commonplace which has been run into the ground, most probably by women. In any case, it is rather questionable wisdom—at least in my case. My feelings have reasons. I am not one of those who love or hate without a cause. As one of the possible interpretations, the director could point to the *kindness of my heart* and add that even if I suffered humiliations, they were caused mostly by her absent-mindedness. I was almost always rewarded afterward by her remorse—her spontaneous repentance. (After I left the café she soon sent me a note: "Tom, why did you leave? I feel terrible! I'm such a monster!") But even that would not explain everything, and a good director should discover the real source of my infatuation and should describe it as "moral enchantment." In order to explain it properly, I would have to insert a lengthy digression, far beyond the scope of my already extensive scribbling. I would have to present my views on human nature and discuss the means, provided by nature itself, with which we keep human nature under control. But most of all I would have to analyze *fear*. Not its biological or metaphysical essence but its destructive role in every moral pursuit. It is only within this larger context and through these comparisons that I might be able to describe what I really admired in her: her internal richness. Among other things, it consisted of the absence of fear. Everyone I knew was afraid of something: the future, other people, poverty, imprisonment . . . She alone was afraid only of the devil.

I knew I could never possess her, but I also knew I would never really lose her, and for the same reason: my love for her was stronger than her feelings for me. But these are the most private of my private concerns. I keep asking myself, though: How and by what means did I manage to endure, and why, from the very beginning, was I sure I would?

When I ask myself this question today I immediately start thinking about the war. Not that I predicted its outbreak. No, life in those years was seemingly solid. Until the very end we were deceived by the accessories, decorations, and natural charm of that time. Shortly before the war Warsaw started to resemble an affluent city. Modern buildings with marble hall-ways replaced old tenements, there were more squares, gardens, residential districts with single-family houses, more buses, etc. Nothing in the everyday routine foretold a cataclysm—it came without warning. On the eve of the war, in the morning, people were waiting quietly at bus stops on their way to work, the day was sunny, and young women, still suntanned after the summer vacation, were wearing light, colorful dresses. That was a description of the morning of August 31, 1939, I read not long ago. The author remembered a lot of details— for example, a beautiful woman putting on lipstick on a streetcar. Reality was misleading us until the last moment, and then it crumbled to dust. The end of the present reality—I cannot think of different term. If you see wounded people on the floor of a milk bar where you used to drop in for a glass of yogurt, it means that a certain reality is lost forever. That's how it was.

Store windows covered with boards, ditches dug across the streets, people squeezing in gateways and basements, over-turned streetcars, a dead horse in front of a pastry shop—all these things were horrible enough in themselves, but they also revealed the rupture in time. I was stunned by the ease with which the order of days and years, the familiar shape of reality, can be halted. I realized once and for all that it takes just a few explosions and an electrical failure and the broken glass starts gritting under our feet. On the next day one thinks of one's previous existence as of a mirage. After one day one loses faith in any routine—every mundanity will appear as something entirely unreal, and if at some time, in spite of our experience, the actuality regains its power of illusion, one should see it as a benevolent paradox which saves humanity from nothingness.

I did not anticipate the explosion and the chaos. But I counted subconsciously on some indefinite change, on things developing in a way less logical than one could predict. In other words, I envisioned a future that would not be a mathematical result of the present—at least for myself. I repeat, however, that in those years I was not aware of the approaching end. The politicians weren't either. Only naïve historians quote the Visigoth king: "It's time now to end Antiquity and start the Middle Ages!" I never expected something would come to an end. It never crossed my mind that something would begin.

During numerous interrogations after 1950 I was forced to explain my attitudes and my way of thinking in the prewar years. A dozen or so times I was ordered to write my detailed biography and, after additional explications, to rewrite it again and again. The part concerning my prewar years always met with disbelief. I was suspected of concealment. The main issue was my political beliefs, though I was also expected to reveal all my affiliations and contacts. When I tried to contend that I had no political beliefs and I did not maintain contacts, the reaction was most unfriendly, and my insistence on this point was to no avail.

I do not rule out the possibility of a similar reaction on your part. Immediately after the war my political and social indifference seemed incredible even to myself. But it seemed the sort of blindness typical of the intelligentsia. I had talked about it for several nights with Wladek Sznej, who thought the victory of communism was dialectically correct: the result of historical logic. Among the rubble, by candlelight, I looked back into the past with a sense of gloom, as if being flayed. It was the second time such a feeling had visited me: you probably remember the night after our conversation in the Zacheta? . . . It may seem peculiar that both instances had something to do with Wladek Sznej. In fact, there was nothing surprising about it, since he possessed a quality that was completely missing in me: an immediate response to theories which systematized reality, a gift, almost a talent, for understanding history and identifying with it instantly. These conversations influenced my attitude toward the social foundations of the new political system. I accepted them as a correction in our development meant to eliminate our backwardness and the inequality in the distribution of wealth. During our discussions (fuel was in short supply and we shivered from cold in our overcoats and earmuffs), Wladek Sznej was extreme in his intellectual fury, and with uncompromising, obstinate cruelty, he dismantled our whole past. I conducted in silence a similar operation on my own person, the mouthpiece of my pipe clamped between my teeth. At a certain point he attempted to prove that from our earliest youth we were being prepared for life in a society of exploitation. "We were corrupted even in our high school days," he said. I felt myself reddening. "Well, not really," I said. "We were still innocent back then." I had stopped listening to him because I had become preoccupied with a recollection of my father—his bony figure and prominent nose. He paced between the lectern and the blackboard explaining in his dry, slightly ironic voice that the Greeks knew everything about life and the Romans everything about power. For a moment I was sitting again in the second row of benches near a window that looked out on the yard. On my left, there was a patch of sky dissected by maple branches, and in front of me, Wladek's eager face, his neatly cropped hair. "No," I repeated. "We were still innocent in high school." Something in the tone of my voice must have disturbed him, for he fell silent.

In the first years after the war I did not hold my present position. I assumed it only in 1958. At first, I worked in the box office. My salary was less than modest. We were living in Mokotow in a flat partly furnished with furniture that had survived on Topolowa Street. I was supporting three people, and my cultural life was limited to the occasional cup of coffee in an establishment set up among half-demolished houses in Jerozolimskie Avenue. I read mostly at night. It was a difficult period. After years of an unconstrained personal life I had to care for a totally helpless creature. I was at the beginning of a journey. Friends I met were wrecks, in both the literal and the metaphorical sense. Old streets were canyons of rubble; I went to my office in a truck packed with people. Everything had changed: newspapers, addresses, offices, names of institutions, streetcar lines. Nothing related to the past, and all was viewed in a reversed perspective, one which showed the things we used to take for absolute truths as perfidious lies. Everything was chaotic, hurried, and improvised—everything, except the principal idea that thundered above the ruins, about the coming of a new order and the final destruction of the old.

As I said, this period was a hard one. If I had heard the same slogans ten years earlier—if I were willing to hear them at all—I would have considered them utopian. Now, when nothing in the world remained in its place, those ideas—once subversive and seemingly at odds with life itself—transformed themselves into obtrusive reality. There was something stunning in this phenomenon. I have seen people carried away by enthusiasm, and people sinking into despair, who could not understand what had happened. Only a few were able to assess the facts in the right perspective: a hundred years of evolution.

One winter—I think it was in 1946—I went to Saska Kepa to say goodbye to Nina Willman. Six or seven years earlier, through money and contacts, her father managed to get her Mexican citizenship. There were rumors at that time that Nina's parents would leave soon, and their daughter would join them in Rome, I do not know the exact circumstances—perhaps Nina did not want to part with them—but in the end nobody left, and the Willmans were resettled in the ghetto. Yet she kept her Mexican papers, and now, after the war, the consulate recognized their validity. She took them out of her purse. "See, that's what my destiny looks like. It was sewn into my suspenders." I did not ask her why she decided to leave. She had strong views on everything, and at a certain point she started to explain her reasons herself. I saw the old Nina Willman again: the well-educated, bright young lady thoroughly versed in economics, history, and literature. I would not be able to reproduce today all her arguments. I remember only a few sentences: "The epoch may be new, but I am not. Society will change in a hundred years. I have only ten, well, perhaps fifteen years left, and I will not change in that time. Besides, I might begin to hate myself. That is exactly what I want to avoid." She smoothed her skirt as she spoke. I looked with pleasure at her dark, oval hands, her well-groomed nails—I noticed that her skirt was made of imported tweed. I do not know how she managed to maintain this expensive simplicity and elegance. At that time she was working as a translator for the press, but even in the fourth year of the war, when Tola and I were leading her out through a basement, she emerged on the other side of the ghetto wall in a spotless beige suit, while Tola and I were covered with coal dust. She looked as attractive as she did seven years earlier when I had first seen her at the university. I had gone there one day to get a professor's signature in my register, and I immediately noticed a girl who was passing through the gate at almost the same moment. It occurred to me that I had seen her before, and I tried to remember where it could have been. She was walking three steps ahead of me, and I remember that I liked the sure motion of her hips—they were rather wide and prominent under her short elegant coat. As we approached the lecture hall, she paused unexpectedly, as if trying to let me through, and briefly our eyes met. Once inside, we were separated by the crowd at the cloakroom. The lecture hall was almost full, but as soon as the professor appeared there was turmoil in the audience. Several students jumped to their feet and began talking simultaneously. They were pointing to several free rows of seats at the end of the room. At first I could not understand what the trouble was, but soon I realized that she was the reason for the commotion. She was standing in the passage near the door. Before I had time to think, I heard stomping of feet and shouts coming from several directions. I kept seeing the motionless silhouette of the girl visible against the background of the wall. When the racket subsided for a moment, the professor asked a question. It was directed to her. The room was silent as she replied calmly. She said she was going to stand during the lecture as a protest against the regulation assigning certain seats in the auditorium to certain people. She used the words "ghetto" and "racial discrimination." At that moment a bottle of ink smashed against the wall near her hair. When I got up from my seat, nobody paid any attention to me, because it seemed I was moving toward the door. In fact, I really wanted to leave. When I stopped for a moment beside her, there was an uneasy silence in the auditorium. The professor used it as an opportunity to start his lecture.

We did not speak that day. What struck me most was the composure with which she handled the whole scene. I sensed, however, that our perceptions of the incident were different. For me it was something stupid and vulgar, like the scenes I remembered from my early years of high school, when infantile sadism and sycophancy were the favorite games. "This behavior passes when their voices start to change." I shrugged my shoulders. We were standing in front of her house on Czacki Street, and I was about to take my leave. "Why did you act that way?" she asked suddenly. She was looking at me differently—with warm curiosity and incredulity. "Me?" My reaction was utterly silly, but nothing better came to my mind. I seemed to have amused her, because she laughed, and we parted with friendly words: she could be found at home each Wednesday at five.

I have already said that the day of the Marshal's death engraved itself upon my memory. But I did not mention that the night before the funeral I was standing in the long line of people in front of the cathedral where the body lay in state. Behind me a stocky, informally dressed gentleman spoke quietly with his grown-up daughter. At that time I noticed mainly his face, which was constantly jolted by a zigzagging, mocking twitch. When I first visited Nina Willman at her home on Czacki Street, she introduced me to her father. It was only then that I remembered them from that night on the eve of the funeral. The funeral itself is entwined in my memory with a letter I received that very day. My father rarely wrote to me. His letter, sent by express mail, reached me that morning. It was as brief as always, but contained a postscript: "I hope that on the day of the funeral you won't stand in the crowd of curious onlookers. It is your duty to follow the coffin." I joined the procession at the corner of Krolewska Street. Before that, however, I had a look at the cortege: the small casket was borne on a gun carriage and a tall horse was to be led by two officers. It was possible to recognize the faces of ministers, commanders, and prominent figures from abroad. Of those people, in black jackets or dress uniforms, one was later sentenced to death by hanging, one was executed by a firing squad, and one lost a war.

All that, however, happened much later, in the days I shall certainly write about further on. I am fully aware that my original intention (a corrective!) expands from page to page. Yesterday, when looking through the typescript, I realized I have been writing my own *vie romancée*. I have been doing it for my own sake. It doesn't mean, however, I have given up on you as the addressee of my words. On the contrary, I still need you. Besides, I am far from sure I am really writing all this for my own private use. In any case, let me return to the events I was talking about.

During my farewell conversation with Nina Willman in her apartment in Saska Kepa (in 1946), three people were omitted entirely—two women and one man. The first of the women was Tola; the other one, Nina. The man we were not talking about was I. I am referring here, of course, to the most intimate matters that concerned each of us separately, but also, in a sense, concerned the three of us together. We were, after all, bound to one another, and divided at the same time, although the things which accomplished this binding and dividing were usually passed over in silence.

And yet we cannot avoid certain explanations. I am still speaking of the period before September 1939. They did not know each other then. In August, a year before the outbreak of the war, our theater troupe came to Gdynia with an English play, *The Talisman* (I played a servant), and I visited Nina, who was spending her vacation in Orlowo. I got on a bus right after the performance, and half an hour later we were walking along the beach and talking about contemporary literature, probably in connection with a recent stage adaptation of one of Nalkowska's novels. That night on the beach we unexpect-edly made love several times. We did it frantically, yet—how-ever strange it may sound—almost without interrupting our conversation. What changed, though, was the subject of the conversation. When we were lying on the sand Nina started asking me about the theater. She was curious about what made me take this job and why I did not go to a drama school. I pro-vided some half-mocking answers, but I carelessly dropped Tola's name while talking about our summer tour. I sensed some tension in her silence, and something warned me to be careful. In the morning she saw me to the bus. Just as I was about to get on she quickly swept her eyes over me and said, "You may not be all there, but you are all here, sir." "Sir?" I was a bit surprised. It was hard to guess what she was hinting at, and that's why I remembered her words. I also remembered her yellow pullover, which emphasized her tan. Later we con-tinued to see each other, but until the Willmans were forced to resettle behind the wall at Leszno, we maintained the formali-ties from before that night in Orlowo.

All these things are connected, and today I see some of these episodes more clearly than when I lived them, obsessed, as I was, by a single desire. In fact, there were certain situations and circumstances that totally escaped my attention. I remem-ber the Willmans' resettlement in the ghetto. When I visited them the day before they left, in their empty apartment on Czacki Street (the furniture and paintings were gone; they had stored them with some friends), while Nina was packing her books in her room, Willman suggested a game of chess. While pondering his next move, he suddenly said, his remarks punc-tuated by a zigzagging twitch, "Once I regretted you were not my son-in-law, but now I see you would only have been more trouble." I realized then—for the first time—that were it not for the war, I might actually have married Nina. At the same time I remembered that the Willmans' home was the only place

I heard, as early as a year and a half before September 1939, about the inevitability of war. As I said, I was so intoxicated by one obsessive idea that external events reached me like a parenthetical thought—without really penetrating my mind. The facts spoken of by foreign radio stations in Vienna or Prague, or Nina's talking about leaving for France, where the Willmans had close relatives—these had no immediate meaning for me. All I was thinking about was how to get Tola to meet me the next day, and whether she would spend the evening after *Twelfth Night* at the Café Club with satirical poets or at the Wrobel restaurant with a bunch of drunken painters.

I thought my near-insanity was invisible to the world, but I was gravely mistaken. Nina was too intelligent to believe I walked onstage with fake liqueur on a fake silver tray because that was my life's calling. In my naïveté I was afraid my voice would betray me one day; in fact, I was betrayed by my silence. Whenever, during a game of cards at the Willmans' or at a dinner, somebody mentioned Tola's new success, I kept silent and pretended indifference. I believed my disguise was impenetrable. What I overlooked, however, was a very simple possibility: that it might seem rather strange that I went against the natural order of my life only to appear for a couple of minutes onstage every evening. By "natural order" I mean the sum of my background, my studies, which I was just then concluding, and my apprenticeship in one of the better legal offices, where I was to work for one of the more popular lawyers, whose daughter had given herself to me on a beach. Thus, I rejected everything that was real and concrete for something that was made up, invented by myself. I was a student in love with a famous actress, I was fighting for a woman who did not love me, and instead of looking for a position, or spending summers in a sailboat, I appeared onstage with false whiskers, in a butler's uniform, at a local cinema as Puck. It was also quite possible, though, that I would cut an interesting figure with my existence turned upside down, in my absurd determination to exchange a life for a dream.

I have to point out, however, that I had a free rein and to the very end I never had to endure delicate situations or embarrassing questions. To the very end means until today. The questions in Nina Willman's letters today, from Mexico, concern my health and my work. But I remember that when I went to Czacki Street for the last time—I had arrived to help her pack her books—she asked, "And what are you going to do now?" I was shocked by her decision to address me by my first name, as if dismissing the two years of falsity between us on the very day when it seemed as though all the beaches in the world turned to stone in darkness and our memories were only dreams of a dead planet. Therefore I said nothing. Besides, I could not answer her question, because the day before I had received quite specific instructions as to my future tasks. I was to train a group of senior high school students in the use of machine guns and hand grenades. She must have guessed I would say nothing; without a word she presented me with two cloth-bound volumes of *The Magic Mountain*. We smiled simultaneously, since not long before she had introduced me to somebody as "a perfect combination of Martin Eden and Hans Castorp." "After the curfew you are going to analyze the soul of the last honest German"—that was the general meaning of what she said. I need not say how difficult it was for me to find words that wouldn't sound trivial. And *The Magic Mountain* got lost somewhere toward the end of the occupation—I don't remember exactly where or when. Maybe it was borrowed by Wladek Sznej, or perhaps I gave it to Tola before her illness.

In 1961 I was in Belgrade as a representative of our theater at an international congress of theater organizers and critics. On the last day of the sessions one of the speakers was a gray-haired Frenchman with the seared face of a sailor. He walked supporting himself on two canes. His oration was marked by the intellectually bombastic tone typical of the French and concerned the courage of man in the face of his present achievements, which he described as "breathtaking and awesome." He made an interesting comparison. In his student years he used to go climbing on the Swiss side of the Alps. On more difficult trips he was accompanied by a guide, a blond giant named Ringele. On steep walls he would often experience vertigo and cry out to his guide, "Ringele, my head is reeling!" To which the Swiss would answer, "So let it reel! *Schwindel' frei!*"—and he would pull him up on a rope. When we experience fear of the abyss that opens in front of us as we approach a summit, said the speaker, when our head starts to reel, and we feel the urge to turn back, we should repeat that call: "Let it reel! *Schwindel' frei!*" He left the lectern amidst general applause. His speech was exquisite. I had no intention of listening to the next ones, and I went out to smoke my pipe. As I was walking in the lobby I started to think about how this metaphor applied to me. Who was I, after all? A half-baked adventurer or a seasoned guide? I reached the conclusion that I was neither of them, but both at the same time. Especially during the war. If I compared those years to rocks and crags over the abyss, I could say that in my acrobatic feats I was both a visitor from the lowlands and a native highlander, and when fear took my breath away, I was telling myself from above, like Ringele, "So let it. Let it reel." Nina Willman was very perceptive. I had two people inside me. She was wrong only about their identity.

During the speech I did not catch the name of the gentleman with two canes, but on my flight back to Warsaw I found it among the leaflets and reports in the conference folder. He was a playwright, a prewar celebrity—Jean-Claude Marcenat. It is easy to imagine how I spent the rest of my flight in contemplation. Two years later a remark in one of Nina's letters made me aware of a certain situation unknown to me in Belgrade.

*

What I have written above does not include certain facts and circumstances of relative importance to my biography. Before I pass chronologically to the war years I feel obliged to mention these subjects.

I wish to speak of our summer tours. My duties during those travels did not consist only of playing walk-on roles. I was also entrusted with some administrative tasks, such as booking theaters, generating publicity, making hotel reservations, as well as the functions of a stage manager and a prop man. I didn't realize that I was preparing myself for my future profession, although the experience proved extremely useful after the war. I am not sure even now to what extent I owed those duties to Tola, but I am convinced she talked about me with Cezar. It is also possible that during these summer tours she needed me more than ever. We were usually playing small-cast comedies (three or four actors), and the main female role was always reserved for Iza Rajewska. The result was a dangerous triangle that threatened to explode at any moment. I think that Rajewska had already some suspicions about Tola, although, in my opinion, she hated everybody. I was assigned the role of neutral party. Thanks to my understanding of the whole arrangement I was usually able to defuse conflicts and to avert scandals at the last possible moment. Besides, I was a bit of an outsider—an anonymous person. It would be hard to suspect me of any personal ambitions. On top of that, Cezar began to like me.

For a long time I never suspected he even noticed my presence in the theater. When he directed a performance he always addressed me just like the other extras, shouting his instructions in a quick, hoarse voice: "Third soldier—keep your gun higher. Fifth soldier—straighten your helmet. Good." I could see him out of the corner of my eye above the half-visible rows in the orchestra. In order to see the whole stage he would stand

on one of the seats—erect and motionless, his hands outstretched in front of him. He seemed big and fat.

It seems he *noticed* me for the first time during a *Pygmalion*
rehearsal. He was playing Higgins. Tola was Eliza Doolittle.
The rehearsals started in early spring and the actors were not
wearing their overcoats to the theater. By noon the sun was
quite warm. But in the morning the theater was unpleasantly
chilly and everybody was cold. Cezar would walk onstage
wearing a hat and a blanket draped over his shoulder and greet
the troupe with his usual "Mornin', children." Then he would
sit down and stretch out one hand with clenched fingers. At
that signal my old pool mate, Wiaremko, would rush from the
wings and blow on the cold fingers. Both acted in a perfectly
serious, earnest way, enacting each day—for us and for themselves—the morning ritual of a master and his servant. To my
astonishment each time Cezar seemed equally amused, and the
cast got used to it, taking it for a signal to start the rehearsal.
One morning, however, Wiaremko was late, and when Cezar
stretched out his hand there was no one to blow on it. He
smiled and wriggled his fat white fingers, looking around
among the actors who were present. I was standing in a rub-
ber raincoat at the front of the stage. Cezar looked at me invitingly. His teeth glowed from behind his wide, full lips. He
smiled at me. Probably for the first time, he noticed the color
of my hair. I returned a cool, polite glance, and after a moment
he lowered his hand. When I was walking away from the theater after the rehearsal, he drew his cab to a halt at the corner of Jasna Street and invited me inside with a broad sweep
of his hand.

I shall never forget that ride. At first he said nothing. Later
he asked me where I lived and gave my address to the driver.
When we were on Swietokrzyska Street he suddenly turned in
my direction and declared that he was impotent. "In principle,
if we exclude some rare cases of men kicked by a horse," he

continued in a loud voice, "there are no real cases of impotence. It is an invention of women. When you hear that a man is impotent, you can be sure that that nonsense is being circulated by his own wife. Women do not want to understand that after five or ten years of marriage conversation is the only natural form of marital life. Yes, a conversation. . . . No, never! Then they take a lover, and in order to justify their infidelities they tell him in bed about this poor fellow, this tired fool, this pathetic man yearning for a fireside talk. . . . Impotent!" The cab was taking us along Nowy Swiat. It stopped from time to time to let people get on a streetcar. Cezar's face was recognized, and several times he answered somebody's salutations by tipping the rim of his light sombrero. The two of us redheads—one huge and sprawling on the seat of the cab, announcing that he was impotent, and the other sitting by dispassionately with a pipe in his teeth—we aroused curiosity. At the corner of Jerozolimskie Avenue we stopped for some time, and Cezar tried to persuade me in a loud voice—loud enough to be addressing the people at the stop—that he was the only real impotent in the whole of Poland. He nodded to somebody again, and sighed, "Please believe me."

He was making a spectacle of himself and of me. But at the same time I was shy only in a mild way, and for the first time I was filled with pride that somebody talked to me as a valued acquaintance, even a friend. I was touched, unsure of myself, but the situation occasioned a deep, though indefinite pleasure. Cezar was perfectly sober. At first I thought that he had managed to have a drink after the rehearsal. I was wrong. It was years later that I guessed why he chose to play this comedy in front of me. He wanted to assure me that there was nothing between him and Tola. I am fairly sure he knew about us— probably from Tola herself. But he could have guessed much earlier, during the rehearsals. Who knows how much he could see from the near-darkness of his seat. I also suspect he went to special lengths to make us even more uncertain of what he actually thought, what he knew (or pretended to know), and why he didn't want to know about some things. Perhaps he was an enigma even to himself. He never seemed know how he would finish a sentence he had just begun. Evidently he invited me into his cab in order to amend and clarify something. Maybe he realized the tactlessness of his behavior during the rehearsal, or maybe he wanted to dispel some bad blood, a vague sense of a mistake, and only later realized that we had really nothing to talk about. It is even possible that he forgot what he wanted to tell me. But then suddenly he remembered: an extra, from a good family, Tola Mohoczy told him about . . . He became concerned, yes, that I would humiliated, jealous! So he decided to put things right as soon as possible.

At that time I was not aware of Cezar's sensitivity, and his enormous reserve, which, in my opinion, was the result of a certain prejudice. He was possessed by a childish fear of words because he knew their dramatic power, and where other people's affairs were concerned he chose not to touch them with words at all. In the theater the mobility of words creates an immediacy: what is being said is what happens. And Cezar must have lost the distinction between the theater and life a long time ago. He would die of terror if he had to tell me he knew about my affair or if he had to assure me that Tola was not his lover. Such a declaration would seem unbearably ponderous: in the theater such words are spoken only on a deathbed. "Dangerous and vulgar," he used to say about excessive poignancy of speech, and this assessment was accompanied by an expression of real terror. He was afraid of the acoustics of things called by their name, just as some people are afraid of thunder. I guess that is why he invented such a subtle and original way to alleviate my suffering. Later he must have concluded that he had saved me from suicide, and thus immediately took a liking to me.

When we reached Zurawia Street and stopped in front of my home, Cezar spoke regretfully: "So that's it, so quickly? Unbelievable!" He pierced me with his eyes and muttered meaningfully, "Yes, the trip was most interesting . . ." He looked around, as if examining an unknown territory, and suddenly he noticed our newsstand. He smiled, evidently delighted by something. "Can you feel it? . . . We could save the color, the fragrance of the moment! . . . Well, then . . . two!" And realizing that I did not grasp his meaning, he squinted his eyes in displeasure. "There, at the newsstand. A woman with violets."

I chose two little bunches, and when I returned to the cab Cezar was asleep. He must have been very tired after the long rehearsal. I put a wet bunch of flowers on the seat and kept the other one for myself. I told the driver to take Cezar home. The whole scene was observed by Mr. Kummel, who had just returned from his office in the Ministry and was on his way, with his dog, to get the afternoon newspaper.

The next day, during the rehearsal, several times I sensed Tola's curious and uneasy glance upon me. Evidently somebody from the troupe had informed her about my ride with Cezar. She asked me for matches. When I gave her a light, she blew smoke at my match and squinted at me as she spoke. "I hear you are doing fine, Tom." "Quite fine," I replied. She was sitting onstage near a column. She was wearing Eliza's bright dress. A basket of violets sat beside her. The day before, she had shaved her brows again, and Cezar had interrupted her first line: "Anatomy, that's the least I demand. Who gave you the right to mutilate your face?" I told her not to take it too seriously. Cezar was often testy during the final rehearsals. "What did he say about me?" She was piercing me with her eyes. Her lids were painted black and green. "Calm down," I mumbled, and briefly described the scene with the violets. "The second bunch was for you." I had to leave her, because the artificial rain started to drum again, and I was supposed to hide behind the columns among a group of extras.

The second bunch was for her, but the first one—she must have known it well—was for Iza Rajewska, who was sick with pneumonia in Omega Hospital. Iza Rajewska! It is unbelievable that that woman *is still alive.* I often recall our first meeting in the dressing-room doorway when I was looking for Wladek Sznej. Thanks to her, I no longer equated beauty and virtue. But when I met her—during the first years of my studies—I still believed that a woman of such beauty must also possess a noble spirit. I imagined her soul to be infinitely harmonious and balanced, resembling a young dove. She was the only woman I could ever hate. Even now, after all these years, when I wake up in the middle of the night I am upset by the thought that Iza Rajewska is still among the living, and that our existences parallel each other. I see it as a discord, something that should never have been. Luckily, we do not live in the same town. After the war she moved to Szczecin. I have managed to avoid that city through all these years. How could I hate a person who turned out so common? It was a matter of instinct. I must have sensed she was a strong and dangerous species. A species with a future. Nothing is more demonic than mediocrity.

I have said that Iza Rajewska was the only woman I have ever hated. To be more precise, she *is* the only woman I hate. It seems that before the war she merely evoked my antipathy, but hatred . . . no, in those years that would have been too strong a word. Hatred, contempt . . . these terms were used with a certain caution. And when they were used at all, it was in a literary rather than a literal sense. Yet the case I am discussing has nothing to do with literary exaggeration or psychological license. My feeling has a simple and perfectly clear explanation. I hate her because she was the cause of death of someone I least of all wished to die. Still, complex psychological analyses are of little use. These are much later matters, connected with a later period of my life.

I do not cling to the chronological order of events, or to any other principle of composition. I find it especially difficult to pass on to the years of the occupation. I sense some inner barrier here, a tendency to postpone the moment as much as possible. I also notice that this abrupt, unceremonious leap violates the elementary principles of narration. One could describe it in the following way: one novel ends in September 1939, the other begins in October 1939, but each of them belongs to a different style, they speak about different matters, and they are united only by the characters. It might appear as if they were written by two different authors who have absolutely nothing in common. And yet—the most shocking thing of all—the author is the same. The first story has not been properly finished, as if the author became bored in midsentence, tore out the last page, and started a new work, quite at odds with the first in content, philosophy, and structure. And since he did not have the patience to invent new characters, he decided to keep the old ones and to transfer them to his new plot. I am not sure whether literature can tolerate such whim. It turns out, however, that in the real world the principles of art do not apply: everything can happen to our heroes, everything can be done with them. It is possible to cross out the whole work, after some blot in the middle of a sentence, and to start, right on the next line, a new version in which only the names remain the same. Someone once said that God is not a good artist, and one has to admit there is some truth to that, though it doesn't sound too congenial.

I remember people for whom the war meant the end of their youth or of a promising career. It also meant the end of a whole biography if it occurred between the fiftieth and the sixtieth year of life. Luckily, in my father's case things took a dif-

ferent turn. One morning someone rang the bell at my apartment on Zurawia Street, where I was still living with the
Kummels. After a moment I heard a muffled hum in the hallway and some strange sounds: footsteps, groans, whispers, the
wail of a dog. After that—a couple of words interrupted by a
familiar cough. My father, wearing a railwayman's cap, was sitting in the corridor on a suitcase tied with a piece of twine. He
was shaking Mr. Kummel's hand, saying, "Forgive me, Bogus,
but I thought I might drop by on my way from the station . . ."
I never learned why my father was wearing a railwayman's cap.
But it was that cap, with a pince-nez sitting askew under the
visor, combined with the diminutive name my father used for
his friend from high school, the cap that made my father look
so fearfully young, like a schoolboy just expelled—that cap
expressed the whole terror of a crumbling world.

We spent two weeks together in my sublet. His wife stayed
with her friends in Mokotow. She expected to get a job in a
hospital, but for a time it was difficult to find suitable accom-
modations for both of them. When I woke up in the morning
in my camp bed, I saw my father reading a book by the window. He would be already shaved and dressed, and, as usual,
he read with a red-and-blue pencil, neatly sharpened at both
ends, in his hand. While reading he would hold his book very
straight. His head was slightly pulled back and his brows
raised, which gave him an air of bemused surprise, as if he was
about to say, "So far so good. Let's see what comes next . . ." I
knew the expression well. Long ago, in my early childhood, I
identified it with humanity itself. I imagined the first human
being on earth seated in a chair, chin pulled back, an expression of irony upon his face, his slender hand holding a well-
sharpened pencil instead of a club. Now, as I watched him
from under half-closed eyelids, I was thinking what to do next.
I should provide him with decent living conditions, and not
only in the material sense. I should see to it that he could con-

tinue with his old-fashioned humanity and maintain this joyfully critical expression, which I admired in a slightly snobbish manner as one admires precious and elegant artifacts—precisely because they are useless. In such moments, when I tried to breathe regularly, pretending to be sound asleep, I wondered whether my father also was pretending to read. I was a very poor pretender and could go only as far as faking sleep. My father, however, continued for his own sake the gratuitous display of wise, skeptical humanity, and his playacting was certainly rooted in the desire to conceal nature, to cover the truth with a set of conventional gestures. I was sure I would never learn from him where he lost his hat and why he came to Warsaw in a railwayman's cap. It must have happened in some scandalous circumstance, which he decided to ignore. To my surprise, he kept the cap and wore it in Zoliborz, many months after his escape from the high school in Warthegau.

I rented a room in Zoliborz through Tola, but in fact I should be grateful to Lala Ubycz, who acted on Tola's behalf in such matters. After moving to his new quarters my father decided to express his gratitude personally, and one freezing morning he appeared with flowers in the Melpomena—a café on Przeskok where I worked as a cloakroom attendant. I don't know what he and Tola talked about. They sat together for almost an hour at a table in a corner of the room, which was almost empty at such an early hour. I was a bit embarrassed by their meeting, and kept myself busy vacuuming the carpet. It is unlikely, however, that I was the subject of their conversation. I did not ask any questions. At that time Tola and I exchanged just a few words during our working hours, and I visited my father only a week later. And yet that day lingered in my memory—not because it was an important date but because of its visual quality. An empty café, a winter morning light, a bald teacher clutching a railwayman's cap and ceremoniously bowing to kiss the hand of a famous actress wearing a waitress's apron. And me with a vacuum cleaner. It occurred to me at that time that we were playing in an utterly different drama now, with different costumes and sets, and we needed to accept our new roles, which were both bizarre and unknown. And yet I sensed that the real performance was yet to come. The costumes were only approximate, the house was empty, the lighting was not properly adjusted: the first stage rehearsal. I could congratulate myself. At least nothing had changed for me: after servants, armor-bearers, and passersby, I was playing a cloakroom attendant!

I don't know what they were talking about. Only later did Tola tell me one sentence she remembered from their conversation: "Of all the crusades against God"—my father said—"this is by far the most perfectly organized one." My father, on the other hand, never mentioned the meeting at all when I saw him a week later. The room in Zoliborz was big and well furnished. The owners were quiet and modest people: two spinsters with their deaf-mute brother. I could not say anything else about them in my testimonies after the war. But during the interrogations I was reminded that they belonged to the Jehovah's Witnesses.

I have skipped certain events related to the outbreak of the war, such as my early return from summer vacation (a night on the train from Kiwerce to Warsaw at the end of August 1939), the day of mobilization, and my part in the September campaign, which I ended as second-in-command of an artillery detachment during the siege of Warsaw (the Ochota sector). I would need a lot of space to write about these things, and it wouldn't contribute much to my story, apart from some merely journalistic details. The only exception could be the journey from Kiwerce, to which I shall return later. I have mentioned, however, my new occupation as a cloakroom attendant in the Melpomena café. It was opened on Przeskok Street during the first winter of the war. Right after the capitulation, some members of the troupe started working as waiters in the friendly café with a pool table near the theater. The theater itself was, of course, closed, but during the first weeks of the war people tended to hang around the old places, even if they were closed or bombed out. In such cases they would meet nearby. There was a reason for that. The old bonds were being reestablished, people could refer to their previous lives, rub shoulders— almost in a literal sense, to confirm their physical existence. Every familiar face brought some relief. I was even greeted with cheers when I appeared there the day after I took off my uniform.

I saw Tola carrying a tray with coffee. She did not see me at first. I stopped nearby and watched her with a sense of numb, heavy calm. Her hair was smoothly combed, and she was paler than before, as if a moment ago she had washed herself with hot water and cheap soap, and I thought that really she must have been very pure. She noticed me only when I came up to greet her, but my appearance was so unexpected that all the blood ran from her face. She dropped the tray and stared at me, squinting with surprise. Suddenly she clutched her head like a peasant woman: "Jesus Christ. He's here. He came back." I was smiling at her, still feeling the same strange calm we experience shortly before waking, when we already know that all the furniture is the right place. "Lala survived!" she told me a bit later at the bar. "I'll tell you everything in a moment. Tom, sit down. You must be wounded!"

Tola told me about the plans to open a café on Przeskok Street. It was Wiaremko who took the matter into his hands. I was surprised. Old Wiaremko, who year after year repeated the same anecdotes about Modrzejewska and Rapacki, suddenly revealed a skill for organizing. He was expediting important papers through the bureaucracy. He found a site for a new café? . . . After some time I stopped being surprised. There was an abundance of similar cases. In those days quite a few people discovered physical or psychological qualities they had never used before, or even suspected. While working in the cloakroom I brushed against black-market lords who had once been lawyers, or scholars who became top secret agents. It was something to think about. With each passing day I was more and more convinced that in each person we know we are given only one of many possible versions of his or her humanity. Similarly, while living in a community, we know only its one revealed form. At the same time there exist other, hidden variants, shapes and forms we know nothing about. Perhaps everything that is imagination, yearning for beauty or freedom, issues from those hidden layers that remain inside or above us. No doubt Wiaremko was a wonderful comic actor, but maybe he was that simply because of what he might have been otherwise. Perhaps the potential organizer and entrepreneur in him secretly supported his acting talent. I tend to think that the real rank of a human being consists in such unfulfilled possibilities: the blend of psychological sediments, which—by choice or accident—are never used and which are activated only by the war. But there is also something unwholesome about the whole process, something akin to robbing one's own wine cellar. The wartime transformations were like a hasty emptying of bottles that ought to have rested undisturbed in the dark corners of our subconsciousness.

The new café was to open in a couple of weeks. Wiaremko found a backer, a landowner from Pomerania who started a factory in Warsaw that produced marmalade, or ersatz grease, and was also an art collector. The names of famous actors were to be the chief attraction of the new establishment, and Wiaremko had to promise to invite Cezar to be an honorary host. It was a condition presented in the form of a request. Capitalists sometimes want to compensate for their inborn complexes. I hadn't seen Cezar since the night trip from

Kiwerce. Wiaremko told me that he had already gone to see him. Rajewska answered the door. The curtains were drawn and somebody was snoring in the next room. Apparently Cezar slept during the day. "But she'll wake him up," Wiaremko assured me. "Maybe she has already done so." And he asked me whether I would consider a job as a cloakroom attendant. The salary wasn't much, but I would have free meals plus tips from the patrons. I accepted immediately. I spent the night with Tola.

It was at the beginning of the winter of 1939-40. The Kummels had gone to visit their relatives near Zamosc. Tola left in the morning, and I decided to stay the whole day in bed. I succumbed to a vague anxiety and torpor, as if my whole life had paused suddenly to ask: What for? It was the first time something like this had ever happened to me. For the next two weeks I hardly got out of bed. A dirty gray wall separated me from the world. Something in me had run its course. I could barely lift my hand from the coverlet. Stretched on my back, I would watch, hour after hour, the past float across my ceiling. Scenes, silhouettes, gestures passed in no discernible order. Among them was my own comically solemn face, asking again, "What for?" Each reason floundered among thoughts of suicide, and I envied the young commander of my detachment, who shot himself when surrendering our arms. It was probably a nervous breakdown of some kind. After a long period of activity my batteries were dangerously run down, and I reached a point where a wire inside me had blown.

After two weeks I awoke. The sun was shining. I was hungry and I had no money for dinner. While washing in my ice-cold bathroom I remembered Wiaremko's offer, and I was shocked by the thought that for two weeks I had not missed Tola. After the last night, when she had shown more affection than ever before, she did not even send me a note. Now I wanted to see her again, but I no longer missed her. For the first time I started to wonder whether I still loved her. That thought seemed more stunning and powerful than anything I had experienced before.

I did not find anybody in the café near the theater. Wiaremko left me a note saying the new café was opening in one week and enclosed an advance of two hundred zlotys. I had dinner in a restaurant at the corner of Tamka and Dobra. At the door I spotted a face from before the war—my boxing instructor from the YMCA.

In order to explain certain circumstances and psychological conditions I must occasionally comment on them from my present perspective. My original intention was to avoid such comments and to talk exclusively of my experiences as they actually were. For example, the moment when my feelings for Tola began to waver appeared to me as repulsive and base. I was frightened by the inner emptiness that was precipitated by my discovery. But today I see it differently. I did not stop loving her. My affection had passed the first test of time, and the flash of emptiness was a sign only of initial exhaustion. Fear and self-revulsion should have made me realize that the affair was planted deep in me, and was in fact the focus of everything I possessed: my sense of right and wrong, my faith and my conscience, everything that is known by the name of morality. But the momentary breakdown filled me with such terror that I was ready to do anything to avoid its happening again. This explains many of my apparently erratic decisions. In any case, it is possible to see it as a kind of breakthrough: after a certain point my affair with Tola became my affair with myself. It is necessary to keep this in mind in order to understand my acts to the very end—that is, until today.

I owe you a warning: the events I am going to talk about now, especially those pertaining to the formation and activities of Rondo, are largely unknown except for a legend based on speculation and rumor. The legend has absolutely nothing to do with reality, and Professor Janota's article "A Chapter in the History of Struggle" crowns this deception. I have reason to believe that the main source of those rumors was a man I was once closely associated with. The situation becomes even more distasteful if one remembers that after the war such rumors were often considered sufficient material for prosecution—which I was to learn myself. It is quite impossible for Professor Janota not to know the facts of that period, although he passes over them in silence.

Today I am hard pressed to provide the exact date, but Wladek Sznej appeared in the Melpomena a couple of months after it opened to the public. The last time I had seen him was in the spring of 1939—an accidental meeting in the street. After our conversation in the Zacheta we saw each other infrequently, and the new preoccupations of my life made our meetings even more so. Eventually our ways parted completely. Occasionally I heard the distant echo of his articles, whose extremism and aggressiveness provoked frequent polemics. Wladek Sznej was at the time the editor of the literary supplement to a periodical described as "radical nationalist" which represented, as far as I know, the most belligerent faction of a certain political movement. I remember, when we met six months before the outbreak of the war, that all he could talk about were the clashes and squabbles between the factions of the movement, and he seemed completely absorbed by obscure conflicts whose meaning he explained with great agitation despite my total lack of curiosity. I listened to him with difficulty. Once I got hold of an issue of his magazine featuring an article that approved of the burning of an orphanage near Warsaw. The anonymous author reported with gusto that children of non-Christian denomination were jumping from the burning building right into the snow. I remembered Wladek from our high school years when he was free of such sentiments, and I could not understand why he allowed an article so full of malice to appear in his magazine. But when I mentioned the incident, he turned to me in genuine surprise. "These things are hardly a matter of emotions." He looked at me with a kind of pity, and his deep eyes were even larger than usual behind his powerful glasses. I don't remember my answer. After a moment we had nothing to talk about.

Though less than a year had passed since that day, one should remember how much had happened. Blaming somebody for his past activities or views would be absurd. I sensed that Wladek Sznej dropped into the Melpomena because he knew he could find me there. Evidently he was looking for a conversation. He wanted to get something off his chest. He was a man in whom any strong experience evoked an irresistible need for locution. It was quite late in the evening. I had to tend to our patrons, who often left the café in an intoxicated and querulous condition. And then I had to lock up the establishment. Sometimes it took me past the curfew, and I had to spend the night in the cloakroom on a folding bed. I asked Wladek to wait at a table. I would soon be through with the last guest, and we would be able to talk all night. He decided to return half an hour later.

We sat in the kitchen downstairs until three in the morning. Wladek looked as if he hadn't had any sleep or food for several days, but when I offered him some leftover *bigos*, he refused. Apparently he wasn't hungry. He started questioning me passionately about my views on "all that," and showing no interest in my answers, he immediately volunteered his own opinions. I understood that though he may not have had much sleep or anything to eat for several days, he came to me only to express his concerns. He already had a theory. Never, even under the most tragic circumstances, was Wladek able to exist without a theory. He displayed an organic affinity for abstractions, and was able to transpose even his most intimate problems into larger, social or political issues. Quite possibly it was a kind of defense mechanism. This time he postulated that the cause of Poland's defeat was the spiritual emptiness of the prewar social relations, the fictitious character of a state suspended in a historical vacuum among grotesque slogans, petty ambitions, and selfish deals. Every creative thought was bound to suffocate in this stale atmosphere; everything was a parody of itself, a hideous shadow of the past. Of course, I am presenting his views in a condensed form. Besides, I wasn't listening very attentively, at least until he started talking about the Marshal. That was the most astonishing part of his statement. He claimed that the Marshal was the only person fully aware of the Polish "artificiality" and deliberately strove to give a real dimension to his country. Out of myths, anachronisms, and legends he created an illusion of power to substitute for the real material base the nation lacked and could not afford. He knew that the nation, burdened with complexes after years of bondage, had to be given the illusion of power, and the illusion had to be transformed into a state of mind, a national character that would replace the missing tissue and convert our backwardness into imagination. Wladek called the phenomenon a "reality of the unreal" and saw it as the only road open for Poland—a road that had been lost after the Marshal's death, because his successors were interested only in preserving their own power. Wladek was also convinced that the solution was still valid and all we could strive for was the rebirth of our psychological existence—a rebirth in our collective dreams, obsessions, and myths: in spirit rather than matter.

I wasn't sure about the exact meaning of that philosophy, but I was struck by two things. First, from what Wladek was saying it did not seem that he had changed his views. He only admitted that in prewar Poland these views were doomed to fail (as any "creative thought" would). He did not, however, disavow their basic legitimacy. I must admit I felt a bit discouraged. Besides, I realized he came to me to talk about the

Marshal, which seemed a profoundly tactless thing to do. It wasn't too hard to guess that I was sensitive about the issue, and I tried to avoid such conversations even in the theater. I was quite upset at the thought of someone taking an interest in me because of the rumors about my parentage. In that particular case it was a double offense. I had real reasons to be on my guard. Wladek Sznej singing the praises of the Marshal in my presence! It was a clear sign of callousness, or at least a serious lack of subtlety. On top of that I was troubled by the change in his appearance. He wasn't wearing his glasses, he was unshaven, and there was something generally unkempt about him. All that made an unpleasant, embarrassing impression.

I remember that I went to the bar and brought back an open bottle of Hungarian plum vodka. After the third glass Wladek suddenly started to laugh. I poured again. He leaned toward me across the table and said, "In the winter I was dealing in pork cuts. The era of pork cuts." We drank another round. He became amiable and effusive, as in the old days during history lessons, when he used to impress my father with his knowledge of Byzantine customs. I came to the conclusion there was really nothing mysterious about his appearance—perhaps a residue of one of his earlier incarnations, the business of "mixing with the common men," or something like that. Besides, the very situation imposed a new kind of fellowship. What was most amusing was the fact that we were meeting after a year in utterly new roles: he as a meat dealer and I as a cloakroom attendant. That night, in the hot, clean kitchen, we were at ease with each other. The well-lit underground space gave us a sense of security. Wladek thawed out and started to tell me about his political problems. The faction of the radical nationalist movement he was involved with before the war, or rather the faction of the faction, was involved in some underhanded dealings with the occupiers. The result was that they were about to set up a legal organization. Apparently they had already rented an office on Ujazdowskie Avenue. The project caused a sharp conflict between Wladek Sznej and his colleagues. He accused them of collaboration; they accused him of betraying their cause. He had to go into hiding to avoid reprisals. That was the reason, as he explained, he started dealing in meat. The era of pork cuts helped him survive the critical days.

I filled the glasses. "And what next?" He blinked his short-sighted eyes in a somehow helpless way. "I don't know . . . I am looking for new contacts . . ." "If you really need them, let me know," I said. "I can be reached here at the café."

We did not mention the matter again. He told me about his readings, probably of Dostoyevsky. He had a general idea for an essay. We slept together on a folding bed in the cloakroom. Wladek left before I woke up. I am sure he was being honest with me. Later I felt uneasy and reproached myself for my initial suspicions. I am convinced Wladek Sznej harbored no evil plans at that time nor wished to harm me in any way. And yet I made a mistake. At that time, in the spring of 1940, I could not anticipate that our conversation would be quoted back to me in great detail when I was in rather poor shape after a number of strenuous interrogations.

I mentioned earlier my chance meeting with my YMCA instructor. He asked me to work for an underground organization. He was a silent, composed man who looked like an army officer in civilian clothes. During our boxing lessons he used to issue his instructions in a quiet, calm voice. He almost never smiled. I liked him for the particular—one could say, professional—sadness with which he fulfilled his duties. His name was Rabczyn. From his reticent remarks (in a restaurant on Tamka in the winter of 1939-40) I guessed his organization had a military character, and that its activities were the continuation of the country's defense. As an officer on active duty during the September campaign I still considered myself answerable to the military command, as long as there was one, and as long as it continued the armed struggle. I gave my consent without asking for details. I wish to avoid unnecessary pathos. It was not a solemn act of sacrifice, and I did not count myself heir to any romantic conspiratorial tradition. The whole conversation took about an hour. I simply accepted my new assignment, or my continued participation in one, and memorized the address to which I was expected to report. My role in the organization, which later came under the High Command of the Home Army, was a minor one. I mention the above circumstances, however, since they help to illustrate the complexity of the situation that developed soon afterward.

I have to remark also that for a long time my conspiratorial functions were closely connected with my job in the café. The cloakroom in a busy establishment was a perfect drop for clandestine materials and a contact for carrying on regular business. Two or three times a week somebody would leave me a package, and on the same or the next day somebody else would pick it up. I did not know these people. Only pseudonyms were used, and sometimes simply code words. Every ten days, more or less, I was visited by Rabczyn ("Kajetan"). From his questions, posed in a sad, dull voice, I guessed he was interested in some of the Melpomena's patrons. I also gave him information about several actresses who worked as waitresses. The café was often full, but after some time I learned to distinguish the composition of the crowd. I was able to know at a glance who was sitting with whom at a table, and why. I could tell how many currency dealers, underground activists, refugees, society ladies, and agents provocateurs occupied the main room and the adjacent bar. I was a good information source and my superiors, as it turned out, appreciated my services.

At the time I was still living in my sublet with the Kummels on Zurawia Street. I had documents issued in my real name and an officially endorsed employment certificate. All my belongings were intact. I hadn't lost any of my relatives or my close friends. Every second Sunday I visited my father in Zoliborz. I usually found him bent over a pile of school note-books. He had returned to his profession, giving clandestine courses in literature and history. His wife, Wanda, worked as a senior nurse in the Red Cross hospital in Solec. I mention all these details to give an idea of my situation at that time, a situation that was, if not better than, quite similar to that of thousands of men who managed to stay out of prisons or camps. In objective terms my situation was more favorable and less eccentric than before the war. It was hard to call me a maverick when the whole world seemed to have gone astray—not to mention my job as cloakroom attendant in popular downtown café, which was comparable to a solidly middle-class position before the war.

Moreover, I regained my mental shape (as to my physical shape, I never had any reasons to complain) and, I would venture to say, I lived on a higher spiritual level. I experienced my own existence in far less selfish terms. It was, to be sure, a general phenomenon with deeper roots. The old world had collapsed, the new one had not yet emerged. The present was a transition from one form of existence into the other, and everyone must have endured this fact with enhanced awareness—that our presence in the world was both temporary and revocable. The caesura between the prior and the future era spawned a kind of gallows metaphysics during the occupation: every day was an anticipation of the End and the New Beginning. All this increased our anxiety, but also boosted vital energies. In those days I witnessed many tragedies, but much less neurosis than today.

In short, surrounded by universal breakdown, my personal status not only did not deteriorate but even reached the average, perhaps above average, level. The same, however, could not be said about my emotional life. For some time now I had had the impression that Tola was avoiding me. I soon had direct proof of this. I tried to explain the change in our relationship by attributing it to the conditions we lived in (our work in a crowded café, the curfew), but I also sensed that the real cause was something else. I decided to wait for the right moment. Tola sometimes bought cigarettes at the cloakroom, and on one such occasion, while giving her her change, I asked her to come to my room on Zurawia Street after work. She looked at me with deep revulsion and left immediately without a word, leaving me the change. I understood I could expect nothing. I saw three crumpled bank notes on the counter and I put them mechanically into my pocket: a *tip* from Tola. For a moment I seemed completely stunned, as if somebody had hit me over the head. Something was turning very slowly inside me, and I realized that true despair is similar to the nausea which precedes a fainting fit. Yes, everything was reversed. I stopped doubting my love for her and all I felt was a spinning awareness: if I lost her I had nothing to live for. That night I did not sleep at all. During my sleepless hours I conceived of all kinds of fantastic explanations, and in the morning I was almost sure something must have happened in Tola's life—and I had no idea what it was. Who would tell me the truth? Lala Ubycz? She wouldn't betray Tola's secrets even under threat of torture. Perhaps I should talk to Cezar?

I soon rejected that thought. Too much time had passed since our conversation in Kiwerce. Besides, were it not for that one conversation, it wouldn't even have occurred to me to think about him. I still remembered, though, his broken, chaotic sentences about Tola and me—especially his strange warning, which, at the time, I took for drunken gibberish: "Watch out, she's crazy."

I am not sure whether I have already explained how this conversation came about. In Kiwerce we were supposed to give five performances of *Man and Wife* by Fredro. We interrupted our tour at the news of the imminent war, more or less at the time when all coins suddenly went out of circulation. Some members of the troupe, Tola among them, left by train in the morning. Iza Rajewska was taken to Warsaw by some local dignitary. I was to leave the next day after taking care of some financial matters and shipping our costumes and stage sets. In all that commotion I did not even notice Cezar. I was sure he had left with Iza. I found him in the evening at the station bar. He was sitting at a table with an emaciated monocled man in a black suit. Cezar called him "Baron." Later I learned that twenty-five years earlier that silent elderly man was sentenced to life for the murder of his nephew. After the amnesty he buried himself in his relatives' country estate. I noticed that Cezar was positively charmed by this individual. When I sat at their table he leaned over and told me in an audible whisper, "He's a murderer! Can you imagine? An assassin!" The baron remained indifferent and sipped his vermouth. The night train to Warsaw (I think it was the Paris-Moscow express) would arrive in an hour and a half. I went to buy the tickets and learned that the train was almost empty. Then I returned to the table. From that moment until I managed to summon the last of my resources and dropped Cezar on the plush seat of the first-class car, I can recall very little, only a sentence here and there—most of all the atmosphere of half-conscious, almost loving intimacy between Cezar and me. I have forgotten, though, how it all started. I must have been quite drunk when Cezar started talking about Tola. I think he knew everything about us, and he must have known Tola much better than I. At that time, however, this thought was far from unpleasant. It seemed quite natural and familiar, like the fact that I was calling Cezar by his first name, that our table companion had murdered his nephew, and that war might break out the next day. I sensed with great clarity Cezar's desperation but also his strange faith in me—his certainty that I would survive him.

But we were both drunk, and nothing could really surprise me. Besides, I was equally confident I would survive the war unharmed. Later, however, when I recalled our conversation in a sober state, it suddenly made me anxious. I had the impression that, when talking about Tola, Cezar left some things unsaid. I couldn't have been mistaken: he was consigning her to my care but simultaneously warning me against her. And while doing this he was constantly turning to the baron, whom he called *monsieur l'assassin*, and taking him for his witness. I repeat, however, that this struck me as unusual only when I sobered up and tried to arrange Cezar's convoluted words into some logical whole. He was no more drunk than in the cab on Zurawia Street when he told me to buy violets, and yet I remember him embracing me and mumbling, "Listen, Buster Keaton, she is a dove, do you understand? Yes, Michele. Watch out, she's crazy. I swear, I never . . . nothing! But you . . . When those bastards come to close the theater, trust Lala Ubycz. People of simple heart are our salvation, *n'est-ce pas, monsieur l'assassin*? There will be no theater, Buster. Nevermore . . ."

I had drunk at least half a liter of rowanberry vodka. Cezar drank even more. I was swollen with pride at the invocation of the "great Buster" and as he spoke of my "insane normality" (as he had, too, in his cab on Zurawia) and claimed I possessed the philosopher's stone. At the same time he constantly took the baron for his witness. But here I lose track of events. Everything became mixed-up and blurred. I came to for a moment dragging my suitcase, and Cezar along with it, down a dark, empty platform. Cezar tried to crawl under the train, and roared "Nevermore!" as he did so, shaking his fists at heaven. Even inside the car he tried to break loose. I dropped my suitcase and pushed him into a compartment. Then the train began to pick up speed. Suddenly Cezar collapsed. I put his legs on the seat and loosened his tie. He was sweating. A bright red curl had stuck to his forehead. "I cannot wish the fact undone, the issue of it being so . . . attractive?" He closed his eyes. "*Lear*," he explained, and fell asleep.

That night left me with confused feelings. Rapture, admiration, pity—how hollow these words sound. Of course, Cezar evoked admiration, and not only in me. How did he do it? Certainly through his talent and his strong personality and through the perfection in him. In the acting profession perfection is a physical quality. It is a radiance of the body, and Cezar often declared that an actor is a "charm of the anatomy." Yes, but if a body that commands limitless control over itself—a body subjected to the elusive ideal of harmony, a body shaped by years of training—if such a body is vulnerable in even one area, the admiration and joy it evokes may yield to pity. I have mentioned that everybody had some contact with Cezar. Each of us existed in relation to him somehow. I see it as a sort of private debt, the penetrating fear and anxiety about ourselves experienced in the presence of somebody's weakness, especially when the weakness is so pure and subtle that it makes us feel paltry with our own trivial failures. I never heard anyone in the theater mention Cezar's marital humiliations or the difficult character of Iza Rajewska. Actors rarely hold anybody in contempt. Yet Iza Rajewska was an object of silent disdain, and I wouldn't hesitate to say there was something sublime in the solidarity this disdain produced. Nobody dared to say anything out loud, but I believe all of us felt the same. People bowed to her evil in unspoken hatred because Cezar bowed to it in humility. This constant, humble forgiveness of his spoke of compassion beyond the reach of any of us—compassion for vice. It is possible, after all, to imagine such a thing. Baseness, pride, selfishness—I can picture someone seeing them as sadness, lack of grace, and craving. It is equally possible to see envy as a torture of fear, and desire as a pitiful farce. I guess in my case I had steered clear of debauchery because I knew how ridiculous it can be. I can also envision a man obsessed with a woman and obedient to her, not because of the dazzling beauty of her body but because of the monstrous ugliness of her soul. I think that goodness shocked by the spectacle of evil easily succumbs to pity. In such cases all escape routes are closed.

I am writing all this to explain things that are hard to explain, and I am doing so with little hope of actually explaining anything. To this day I am not sure whether I have understood anything even when I try to analyze things in the most impassioned way. Why wasn't I jealous of Cezar? Why am I not jealous of Cezar now? Yesterday, when I received a postcard from Milan ("The Last Supper." A trip to Italy, then. Later Spain . . .), I looked for a long time at the two identical signatures, and I was startled to realize that one of these signatures might not exist at all, were it not for Cezar. The thought caused me no pain: in fact, it resembled gratitude.

But why was I not jealous of Cezar back then? I had grounds for bitter suspicions. In Kiwerce he talked about Tola and me. I wasn't drunk enough, however, to fail to notice that in fact he was talking about Tola and himself. Even a quite unperceptive listener would have guessed from his rambling that something must have happened between them, though perhaps a long time ago. And yet—I wasn't jealous. Maybe I am simply not the jealous type. In any case, I definitely wasn't jealous of Cezar. That is why I thought of asking him for advice when I noticed that Tola was avoiding me in the café. First of all, I trusted him. Besides, I couldn't talk about her with anybody else. Finally, Cezar himself encouraged me by speaking about her, even though in a drunken state. But this advice never came to be, because I backed off. I was simply afraid that in his present condition Cezar wouldn't remember a thing.

Rabczyn, who from time to time spent an hour at the corner table in the Melpomena (he was evidently charged by some agency to make special observations), started asking me for an introduction to Cezar. It seemed absurd, but Rabczyn stubbornly returned to the subject with his usual drawl: "We are looking for such people." I believe it was a matter of personal ambition. I tried to stall as much as possible, but when I ran out of excuses I firmly announced that I wanted to hear no more. "What do you mean by that?" asked Rabczyn quietly. "In a simple, human way, can't you see he is a broken man?" I replied. Rabczyn looked at me with something glazed and blue suspended in his eyes. "Yes," he whispered. "The Poles have suffered most. Yes . . ." I must admit I was quite astonished. I had had something very different in mind. I judged, however, that it was best to respect the misunderstanding.

When I came to know Rabczyn better I was struck by one particular feature of his character—a feature that was often a stumbling block in our acquaintance. It also never ceased to amaze me despite my deep respect for him. Rabczyn's view of the world—I mean not only his opinions but his general mode of perception—was limited to the idea of the nation, and it totally excluded two other notions: that of the individual and that of humanity. It was quite astounding to see this rather intelligent man interpret the war as an exclusively Polish national tragedy. Whenever I started to talk about the suffering of other peoples—the Jews, the Russians, or the Dutch, for example—he simply remained silent. Similarly, he became silent and distracted whenever I touched upon the subject of individual human emotion. He seemed not to believe in its existence. For Rabczyn both God and Man were probably Poles, and everything divine as well as human flourished on Polish soil. Beyond this there stretched the unhealthy country of psychology and philosophy. Perhaps for that reason, despite my respect for Rabczyn's upright character, I never dared to explain to him what kind of man Cezar was. He wouldn't have understood, and I would only have saddened him. I liked Rabczyn too much to expose him to such unpleasant surprises.

One day I was thinking about him while trimming my mustache. I don't know why I started to grow a mustache. My reasons, I guess, were different from those that made so many men at that time grow beards. In 1942 I did not try to change my appearance. In fact, I find it rather hard to pin down the purpose of the reddish mustache I wore in the English fashion. I remember, however, that I was trimming it one day in front of a mirror and when I looked into my face I became immediately and absolutely sure I had to act without delay. I wouldn't be able to tell where that inner certainty came from and what my mustache had to do with it. But it was my mustache that captured my attention in the first place and pushed me into deep contemplation. For a long time I sat motionless, scissors in my hand, in front of a mirror that was propped up against a book. I could not know at that time how important that quarter of an hour would prove to be in my life, and I could not know that in the strain of intuition and in the mental effort of those minutes the first germ of Rondo was born.

The conversation took place the next morning before the Melpomena was opened. We met in a small restaurant in Zlota Street, under the sign reading "Viennese Breakfast." We were alone in an empty room. I was talking in a low voice and I knew exactly what to say. When I finished, Lala Ubycz sat still for some time, as if continuing to listen. I waited in silence. I was impressed by the strength and earnestness of the eyes fixed on me. "I was expecting this," she whispered. She was still wearing the strangely rumpled man's hat she had on several years ago in the Savior's Church. "Do you trust me?" I asked. A flicker lit up in her eyes and then subsided. I felt uneasy and wondered whether she'd absorbed everything I'd said. She smiled dimly and asked if she might order a cheese pastry. "I like sweet cheese," she said with an enigmatic stress. Miss Lala always spoke in a whisper. After all these years of prompting, her every sentence sounded like a hint. "You've guessed everything correctly," she said, barely moving her lips. I did not turn my eyes away. I was calm now. In front of me sat a mysterious ally, one I had underestimated. I looked at my watch: half an hour. Before nine I had to open the doors on Przeskok, and at nine I had to be in my cloakroom. (Miss Lala worked in the back room and took down the orders.) I had just half an hour to fill in the facts and to gather some information about the persons involved. I ordered three pastries. "You and I are thinking along similar lines, and we love the same person," I said. "But this is not enough. For me to do anything, I have to know more."

At nine I got into a rickshaw with Miss Lala's words resounding in my head. Of course, she had used a metaphor: She is dying for the lack of acting. She'll accept any engagement from them . . . The day was sunny and warm. On both sides of Bracka Street people were walking without their overcoats. That day the Melpomena could do without a cloakroom attendant. It was May 13. I always associated that day with the Marshal.

I jumped into a rickshaw and shouted, "Quick! Hurry up!" I was a man who had made a decision and was determined to carry it out to the very end. That I was in a state of euphoria, however, cannot be dismissed, and my driver must have sensed that I was an unusual passenger. Yet this is not what I want to talk about. I am examining my psychological condition at the moment which irreversibly shaped the future and generated events unusual enough to attract attention years after the war. After all, the events that followed had no precedent during the whole occupation. In short, I wonder whether I was acting as a balanced person. I was either a lunatic with a manic imagination or a thoughtful man who acted upon real premises. Which?

It is an important question, closely related to another one I frequently heard between 1950 and 1953. "Do you take us for idiots, offering these fabrications?" But I was telling the truth. I was upset because my interlocutors—and I am sure they were being sincere—took my truth for a fantasy. If only a madman could believe my story, what did that make of the man who created it? Was he a madman too? I never felt madness in me, not even for a moment. Everything I did was a logical consequence of certain necessities. I can explain my every step and motive. The plan I undertook was not the invention of a madman. It was an act of routine clarity.

Only once was I called a madman. But that title came from Cezar, and Cezar's words should not be taken at face value. He spoke in a code. His thundering paradoxes resonated in the cellars of silence. He called me "a man of insane normality," and I suppose he meant what I've just said: my spiritual sanity. It must have amazed him. Perhaps Nina Willman noticed it too. I was not all there, I lacked a common sense of balance, but I was all here—I was capable of personal freedom. Nina Willman was a very intelligent girl. On the other hand, everything boils down to good metabolism. My usual spiritual condition resembles a physical calm. I have a very strong constitution.

Whoever reads my scribbling will probably stop to think at this point. Such stubborn insistence on normalcy usually calls for suspicion. Why does he keep repeating he is not a madman? If he weren't, he wouldn't have to convince us . . . In my opinion, however, things look somehow different. How should one judge the normalcy of somebody's life and actions? Would it be right to say that sanity and sickness, sobriety of mind and madness, are perceived in the same way by every person and in every place? According to my knowledge, various religions, political systems, and historical epochs are far from unanimous in this respect. In a changeable and heterogeneous world we are left with nothing but our own standards and rules. I do not think it possible to probe one's human core other than with one's own concept of humanity. Those who do not blindly follow the dictates of the time and place should embrace the cruelest doubts in order to judge themselves. One of these doubts is the question of *guilt*, followed, in a natural order, by the question of *awareness*. I doubt there is a single man who feels completely innocent. If I am right, at least once in a lifetime one has to doubt whether he was fully aware of his acts. I would be a madman if I never wondered whether I was really sane. Similarly, if I never questioned my innocence, I would certainly be guilty.

That is, more or less, what I have in mind when I write of the "cruelest doubts" visiting an independent man. These happen to be also legal questions. Each jury has to weigh them carefully when analyzing the issue of responsibility. Yes, but the jury uses standards that have been worked out by a community. I was thrown back on my own resources. Responsibility? To whom? It's not merely a figure of speech: I was responsible only to myself. Were it not for Lala Ubycz, who helped me preserve all that I have today, I would certainly have lost my mind toward the end of the war.

As I rode in the rickshaw through downtown Warsaw, the city had not yet lost its morning freshness. The streets, despite the scars of war, were almost pretty. I felt a surge of energy, as if my physical being had focused and was filling with a warm calm. Now and again I would strike up a conversation with my driver, who turned out to be a graduate from the Mickiewicz high school and claimed to know me by sight. He often got fares to the Melpomena and apparently I once changed a large bank note for him at my cloakroom. Of course, he took me for an actor. "Does the job pay well?" He was curious about my income. "How should I know?" I cast over my shoulder. "One manages to get by, from day to day. I guess you won't be driving a rickshaw after the war either!" "I'll be studying in the

Biology Department," he shouted over my head. "How about you?" I was caught off guard. I never thought about what I would do after the war. "I don't know," I answered, trying to outshout a screeching streetcar. "I haven't the slightest idea." The driver giggled. "Perhaps you'll take biology too?" "Perhaps. Come to think of it, why not?" The exchange amused both of us. We were driving along Lindley Street. I examined his face carefully. Blond hair under a brown net . . . The boy stopped smiling. He fell silent under my glance, which clearly embarrassed him. At that time it had no significance. I did not suspect I was recruiting my first liaison. Later, after breaking into Tola's apartment and during our quarrel, when with every word I was burning the last bridges behind me, the only real element in my improvisation was the rickshaw driver in a brown hair net. Whenever I said "we," I meant the two of us speeding in the sunshine along Lindley Street.

I opened the door with Lala's key. I knew Tola had the day off and would not be up before ten. If I knocked or rang the bell, she might not react at all. I took this possibility into account. Sometimes she would stay in bed and listen to the pounding at her door. She told me about it several times, and I could never figure out why it gave her such pleasure. But my key added an important element of surprise. If I had rung the bell, she might have opened the door but refused to let me in. I would have had to explain the purpose of my visit. Perhaps she wouldn't have wanted to listen to me at all. She could have fended me off with "Not now" or "Some other time." And that's exactly what I wanted to avoid: the situation of a petitioner. I explained everything to Miss Lala. Without saying a word she immediately took a Yale key from her purse and put it on the table beside my plate. I was to give it back in the Melpomena after my conversation with Tola. I asked her for confidentiality. Of course, I was being naïve, and I underestimated her intelligence.

I turned the key very gently. I found Tola asleep, her naked back turned to me, her hand stretched toward the wall across the tapestry which covered her daybed. The window was open. On the rug, beside her shoes, there was an ashtray full of cigarette butts stained with coffee. A crystal flowerpot on the table was also filled with butts. I sat in the corner of the birch-wood sofa and lit my pipe. The room was quite cool, and a light breeze rippled the curtain. I stared inertly at Tola's back.

"You climbed through the window like a thief," she said weakly, when she woke.

I laughed. "In broad daylight? From the street side? To the third floor without a balcony? Wake up."

She pulled the sheet over her breasts as she turned toward me. "You stole the key from Lala?" With a grimace of pain, she grabbed her head.

"I'll explain later."

I went to the bathroom and soaked a handkerchief. The sink was full of plates and glasses rimmed with lipstick.

"Put it on your forehead," I advised. "It'll help."

She watched me with a sullen expression.

"Why did you come here?"

"It's a long story," I said. "Right now, all I'm interested in are the people you were drinking with. Of course, I don't mean Iza and Cezar. Or Wiaremko and Rena Delatynska. I mean Mr. Kozlowiec and the younger gentleman in riding boots."

"You mean Cezar," she interrupted. "You always mean Cezar."

For a moment I said nothing. "I'm not jealous of Cezar. Besides, he assured me . . ."

"What do you know about Cezar and me?" Her eyes glittered. "Perhaps you asked him if we slept together? Even if you knew, you wouldn't understand a thing. Not a thing!"

"Tola . . ." I tried to interrupt her.

She looked at me in anger. "He isn't jealous of Cezar . . . People fight, people die, half of the city has been burned, and he has grown a mustache, and he is not jealous!"

She threw the wet handkerchief on the rug. For a moment I caught a glimpse of her small, firm breasts.

"What do you want from me? Tell me!"

I shrugged. "Nothing. You know that. I expect nothing. I ask for nothing. Was it ever otherwise?"

"Jesus . . ." she moaned, holding her head. And suddenly she cried, "So what do you need me for?!"

I was looking for an answer. I was a bit confused by the unexpected turn in our conversation.

"You are very intelligent, Tola," I explained, emptying my pipe. "I like talking to you."

You may call my answer quick-witted. I took advantage of her surprise to shift to the proper subject.

"I didn't come here on private business." I spoke slowly and seriously. "Perhaps I came here not only on my own behalf. You were chosen because we were looking for someone we could trust implicitly and under any circumstances. Of course, you have been watched for some time. This isn't the first time this key has been used. There are rules to the game: unusual situations require investigation."

"Somebody was here before?" she asked quietly.

I was playing with the key.

"All kinds of people visit the Melpomena," I continued. "And for all kinds of reasons. Even in a cloakroom one can do more than just give out tickets and sell cigarettes. For several weeks now the bar has been visited by certain gentlemen whose business is no secret to us. It isn't important that they have chosen you, as well as some other people, for their target. It isn't important that you've been drinking with them. All we are concerned with is how far they have managed to implicate you in their affairs. Political affairs, needless to say. There are also military affairs, but these gentlemen have precious little to do with the military struggle."

I paused to gauge the effect of my words. Tola seemed to grow pale from excitement. I felt I amazed her with every sentence.

"I need a cigarette," she said. "There may be some vodka left on the windowsill."

I found some alcohol in a glass behind the curtain. The cigarettes were lying on a chair among scattered stockings and underwear. Tola followed me with her eyes.

"You didn't tell me, Tom," she sighed. "Why? You have to be honest with me."

"You didn't seem particularly willing to talk," I said. "Besides, in such matters discretion is usually recommended. I should ask why you kept me at a distance. If you despised me because I was handling tickets in a cloakroom, you should have told me so. But now these matters are of little importance."

What was of importance was to learn whether Tola had allowed them to draw her into the organization. Not long ago Rabczyn had mentioned that the Melpomena was frequented by activists of a very dangerous political movement. At the time I paid no attention to the remark. I remembered, however, that Rabczyn's attention had been focused mostly on the bar. He asked me several times what I thought about that "merry company." From his guarded allusions I guessed it was a matter of professional concern. At first I couldn't figure out why these new customers bothered him so much, and I took his suspicions lightly. "You don't seem to realize that those guys can get us all into a lot of hot water," he muttered, and, seeing my surprise, added, "They walked out of the negotiations."

As I was looking at my mustache in the mirror, it suddenly occurred to me that Tola was in serious danger. There was no time to waste. I could imagine her frantic desires, and I knew her advantage over me: the advantage of a soul consumed by uncertainty and hungry for revelations. She was scared of her sins. She dreamed about redemption. About a *scene* of redemption. She must have despised me when I suggested a night together in my room on Zurawia. As if nothing had happened since our last night . . . Why did Cezar never use her real name when he talked about her in Kiwerce? Why did he keep calling her Michele? Yes, Cezar knew her well. But it was Lala Ubycz who made me aware of the truth. Was I blind not to realize that for her the war would become a stage, on which she'd want to play her greatest pathetic role?

Now I knew I had to act so that she could play it. But not to the end.

In the second half of May 1942, I left by a morning train for Nowe Miasto on the Pilica. Many changes had occurred in my situation, and during my journey I tried to figure out how I could manage to hold it all together in the new circumstances. First, I had lost my job as a cloakroom attendant in the Melpomena. After an unexplained absence Wiaremko asked to speak to me. He made it quite clear we should part company. But my absence was only a pretext. Wiaremko spoke in a low, serious voice, with his eyes fixed on the edge of a table. "You have to understand me," he kept repeating. He knew what I was involved with, besides attending the cloakroom, and he did not want me to endanger the rest of his staff. "You have to understand me. I am as good a Pole as they come." Several times he looked up at me with the eyes of a sad monkey and mentioned Rabczyn's visits. "You know, it's really not my own neck I'm worried about. I feel responsible for the people. Perhaps you will explain that later, to whomever it may concern."

I felt his anxiety. He wanted to fend off possible charges after the war, and he knew that his position would depend on the way I presented our conversation "to whomever it may concern." I did not wish to incriminate him. After one of his disclaimers I told him I understood. I asked only one favor: I would need, occasionally, some information about people visiting his establishment. "But of course!" He almost choked on his whisper, and his face smoothed out with relief. We exchanged a few pleasantries, and suddenly Wiaremko looked at me with a warm, though cunning smile. "I always liked you, you know . . . and I know who you are . . ." I reddened, yet I tried to control my irritation. That was the end of it. He paid me three months' severance. I repeated my conversation with Wiaremko to Rabczyn word for word. He was distressed. "You weren't careful enough." When I pointed out that I did not work alone, he sulked but didn't disagree. He questioned me at length about Wiaremko and his contacts. He wanted me to remember who in the café could have had an eye on me. He kept at me for over an hour. I tried not to feed his suspicions. The case came to a stalemate: the contact point was broken—there was no doubt about that. As for employment, I would start looking around. In two days I would report for instructions.

At that time I used to meet Rabczyn at an apartment belonging to an elderly woman who had a private lending library. Two days later I met him there to learn about my new assignment, which I accepted without enthusiasm, because it called for my leaving the city—which at that time was inconvenient—and also because the job was not congruent with my character. It concerned a partisan detachment which reportedly conducted an irresponsible operation in a village near Nowe Miasto. There were illegal seizures of property and executions of alleged collaborators. The whole affair looked rather sordid. I was required to establish private contacts and conduct a secret investigation. The only person who knew about my arrival was a local landowner. I was to be presented as his cousin from Warsaw. Rabczyn asked me whether I played bridge. When I said yes, he told me it might come in handy.

It all happened unexpectedly. The order to leave town, on a day's notice, was quite inconvenient, though it also had its good sides. Travel by train favors meditation, and there was no lack of things to consider. The second half of May was unusually hot. The windows and seats radiated heat; parts of my car burned at the touch. My eyes fixed on the socks of a gentleman opposite dozing off, I tried to figure out how to handle my affairs with Tola. Only a week earlier we spent an afternoon on her bed, and with every minute I was more and more convinced that I had arrived at the right moment. On that very day, at six in the evening, she was to be sworn into a political organization. I listened to her with both horror and relief: the name of the organization had a familiar ring. It was the same group that had collaborated with the occupier during the first spring of the war. When its overtures were rejected, followed by arrests and internal fighting, the organization re-formed and started to operate in the underground as Thought and Action. It included people who, eight years earlier, beat me up in the university courtyard.

But that was not important. My beating was merely a nasty coincidence which, after all, gave me strong arguments in my conversation with Tola. I was alarmed, however, by something else: the lightning results of my intervention, the ease with which she believed me! I saw it as a pathological readiness on her part, an insatiable desire to sacrifice. This hysterical longing for auto-da-fé made it certain that Tola would perish no matter what organization she joined.

As I have said, I was trimming my mustache when I started to see the first, sketchy outline of my plan. At that time, however, I was still counting on several possibilities. I thought it would be enough to talk to Rabczyn, to tell him about Tola, to save her from more dangerous involvements. But as I rode in the rickshaw to Topolowa Street, I did not anticipate that I would take a decisive step in the opposite direction. Probably I wasn't able, then, to outline my plan clearly enough. I say "probably" because I can hardly re-create my state of mind, much less the state of my subconsciousness on that particular day. In any case, I had already spoken the words and could not take them back. When I said them I was lying on a daybed with Tola's eyes fixed upon me. She had been watching me like that for some time. She was so excited that I started to worry. Something had shifted inside me and I suddenly saw the danger: forget about talking to Rabczyn, rely only on yourself . . . *isolate her.* "Tom, would you please tell me what you need me for?" she asked me quickly, almost short of breath. "You'll be a courier," I said in a low and manly voice. I said it mechanically and I can only guess it was the memory of my mother that made me say it. She was a courier for the First Legionary Brigade.

There were times when I often regretted these involuntary words. I saw them, naïvely, as the cause of all that followed. As if words could really be a logical beginning of anything. We often blame the jests of fate, not on the elements, on nature, or on the depths of life, but on rational crumbs, on trivial errors or irregularities that are supposed to explain our destiny. My grandfather, paralyzed after a stroke, kept repeating almost until his death: "It's because I had too much to eat . . ." This explanation seemed to give him relief and provide nourishment for various hypotheses that muffled the irrevocability of his condition. He really used to eat a lot, and the stroke came after a heavy dinner. But it wasn't that dinner that knocked him off. His insatiable hunger had been killing him for years.

My case wasn't much different when I tried to imagine the course my life could have taken if, in May 1942, I hadn't spoken these words to Tola. And I was wrong. With the most strenuous analysis of these past events, I always reached a conclusion that could not be debated: the real issue was somewhere else. Even if my words were spoken hastily, they were the echo of a more general idea that guided my whole life. I am not too far removed from believing that each human life is an expression of some anterior concept it must fulfill in order to attain its own meaning. In my case, I suppose, it was a journey from the rudimentary, practical aspect of existence into the realm of subtle, more imaginative, and—one could say—allegorical needs. It is quite possible that my feelings for Tola Mohoczy, the irrational strivings and inner compulsion which characterized them, were the manifestation of such an anterior idea.

To put it simply, I do not believe my words were an accident, or mere lightheartedness. All had been waiting, ready, inside me. My association with the theater was also far from accidental, although at the beginning it seemed comical and useless. Perhaps I was craving fiction, looking for something higher than the everyday life, for a more complete composition and more harmonious rhyme. Existence was not significant enough for me, and my sober, practical mind did not speak the whole truth about my person. Tola would never have guessed it on her own. But Cezar understood it all, at least on those occasions when he remembered me. That is how it was on the day when I helped him from the horse cab in front of the restaurant on Dobra Street. His quote from Shakespeare will always ring as an epilogue, a coda to our unfinished relationship. At that time Cezar was already worried about Iza. He spoke obscurely about a "barter" as he looked into my eyes drunkenly. I had the feeling that he wanted to say something more. Later I realized that he actually did, in his own inscrutable way, by circling around, and touching upon a "certain person you know," and by refusing to mention her name. His eyes were perhaps more vocal than the rest of him. There was an acute tenderness to them, the hope of a perishing man who is the witness of his misfortune and who asks for forgiveness. If he chose me for his witness it must have had to do with his idea of me, my spiritual capacity or imaginative resources. In any case, he must have felt a kind of kinship between us, and during these moments he included me in his universe. For Tola I was, and would continue to be, a visitor from a strange world. (Later I heard a similar opinion from Selim.)

But I anticipate events and skew chronology. I discovered that memory does not respect the order of time and concentrates on certain areas of high density, like the fires of civilization scattered in a no-man's-land. But this irregularity is probably not accidental either. For example, the day I spent with Wladek Sznej in the country engraved itself upon my memory because of a conversation we had during our walk in the fields.

I came to the country estate near Nowe Miasto by carriage. The address Wladek sent me was only some twenty kilometers from where I was staying. Somebody mentioned the name of the neighboring parish during a game of bridge, and I realized that Wladek was living nearby. I decided to visit him.

He lived in a mill, or rather in a two-story home near a mill, with cows grazing in back, behind the flower garden. He had been living there since winter. He had found a job as private tutor for a wealthy miller's family. After our greeting he immediately suggested a stroll through the wet meadows nearby. He claimed his new way of life suited him fine. The Polish countryside is so backward, he explained, that even the occupation did not manage to degrade it. It would be quite impossible: what's made of straw and rags cannot be smashed with an ax. That's why it was better there than in the city.

I noticed he had gained some weight. He was wearing dusty sandals—a bit too large, so that his toes protruded somehow sideways. During our conversations I had always been a listener rather than a partner. That day too I hardly uttered a word. The landscape in that area was quintessentially rural: meadows, orchards, deep, rutty roads which led into the forests—a rolling terrain. Sometimes we had to slow down on a slope, and it struck me as we did so that the order of nature was something very heartening—its solid durability even in the trampled and defaced world of that time. Wladek's monologue, in which he explained Heidegger to me, did not disturb my peaceful contemplation of nature's harmony. Wladek never neglected his reading and each week he returned from Warsaw with a new bundle of books.

I walked lazily, inhaling with relish. Occasionally I acknowledged his remarks in a perfunctory manner, but in fact all I heard was his high-pitched, intelligent voice which flushed a flock of partridges several steps ahead of us. I had been living in a state that today would be described as "overtaxing one's vital reserves" and every moment of peace brought a great sense of calm. When I walked like that, with nothing to hurry to, without destination or instructions—as if completely relieved of my duties—I was engulfed by this relaxation.

But it should be pointed out that my collaboration with Rabczyn required constant vigilance—and not only in the physical sense. He was almost pathologically suspicious, and sometimes I had the impression that he deliberately tested my loyalty and my alertness. I'm quite sure he tested me in ways I knew nothing about. I had this feeling during my stay at the country estate near Nowe Miasto, where I impersonated the owner's relative, where I maintained my incognito even among the most reliable people. And yet I felt that somebody was secretly watching me, and that on my return to Warsaw to submit my report, Rabczyn would already know exactly what I did and whom I met. It was all quite exhausting.

I do not intend to provide a critical analysis of relations in the underground, in which I played an active role. I list my observations in order to point out that conspiracy as such inevitably leads to a certain perversion of human life because its very essence—secret activity in dangerous circumstances—

is profoundly antidemocratic. By definition it must be at odds with the basic tenets of an open, free society. Clandestine fighting organizations produce heroes more often than free thought and questioning minds. In a conspiracy even heroes are potential suspects. On the most general and theoretical level they are suspected of weaknesses that grow out of the human proclivity for reflection, hesitation, and fear. Every conspiratorial organization of some experience knows that the distance between heroism and betrayal is often minimal and every hero has to be *tested* on that account. An iron chain made of individual links has, first of all, to bind its links together. A truth one should remember. I did.

It would be hard to reproach me for lack of conscientiousness. I usually carried out every assignment. I could list various tasks I was entrusted with. I could still recognize the faces of the people I met at various "drops" or "contact points." I remember, for example, a certain store with homemade pastries where I met several times with a man whose pseudonym was frequently mentioned during the trial of the underground leaders a couple of years after the war. Rabczyn did not spare me, and if he sometimes decided not to use me in some operation, it was mostly because of my size and the color of my hair. Apparently I was too easy to remember. Rabczyn also fretted about my pipe. He sulked whenever I lit it in his presence. Once he told me, "Listen, Tom. A soldier does not smoke a pipe." I smiled, because his words reminded me of Tola, our quarrel in the cab, and her angry voice when she told me that an extra should never smoke a pipe. A student, an extra, a soldier . . . It was my fate, it seemed, to be an enlisted man, or at least to start as one at each stage of my life.

Apparently Rabczyn sensed there were unmapped regions within me, and he must have pondered about me quite frequently. Sometimes he would watch me in an uneasy silence. Each time I must have seemed too tall, improperly dressed, or perhaps improper in some different, deeper sense. Still, we liked each other a lot. Rabczyn treated me with obscure, but concerned, attention. I admired his unyielding character. In the spiritual sense he was one of the strongest people I ever met. Never before or since have I encountered such perfect fulfillment of the ideal personality: a fearless embodiment of the moral paragon. Perhaps only my father could provide an equal, though quite different example of an iron will to self-realization. They seemed to represent two sides—the civilian and the military—of the same phenomenon. Together they constituted a durable coin that was going out of circulation. Nina Willman once told me—it was during one of our lively after-curfew conversations over moonshine, after we had led her out of the ghetto—that the real similarities between people consist, not in their facial features or their characters, but in their common social environment and times. She used the term "cultural formation." As an example she pointed to a resemblance—even an external one—among three leaders of the French army between 1914 and 1918: Foch, Joffre, and Pétain. Rabczyn and my father were related in a different way—namely, Rabczyn was an extension of my father. I would classify them as the formation of the Polish Independence. When my father started his job as a teacher, his youngest pupils were Rabczyn's contemporaries. Had they worked together in the underground thirty years later, they would probably understand each other quite well despite the age difference and my father's tendency toward irony. It was no accident that the character of the Polish underground was shaped by these two generations. One important feature separated them from my generation, a feature exemplified by Wladek Sznej. Perhaps most of all by Wladek. Wladek Sznej belongs to my formation. (A different "mental sphere,"—as my father would say. Terminology also changes with the times and with the social environment.)

In high school my father gave Wladek the very best grades, and treated him, with some amusement, as the classroom know-it-all. He called him "our dear talkativus." I remember a trip to Gniezno: my father in a canvas hat and pince-nez with a group of students in front of the cathedral's portico, and Wladek in short pants asking him about some details from the history of the Church in Poland. The sole intention was to display his own perfect knowledge of the subject. I was slightly annoyed by his passion for collecting information on subjects which particularly impressed him. I saw it as a veneration of high-quality merchandise. I rarely rely on class definitions, but Wladek offended me with his petit bourgeois attitudes. I couldn't find another term for it. I had the impression that Wladek was unable to see the difference between real value and its price tag. Wladek's parents owned a men's apparel store. One used to buy coats and trousers "at Sznej's on Grodzka Street," and every couple of years my mother would take me there to get me a good cheviot winter coat.

I really don't know why I'm telling you all of this. It has nothing to do with my point. Besides, it is obvious that a son of a decent family can grow up a total cynic, and a shrewd merchant can beget a holy missionary. I may be wrong to guess that Wladek's home was to blame for the lack of spiritual values which were natural in my own family. I am talking about an inherited sense of spiritual decency which makes us ignore things that "sell" in the world, that quickly make a name or create popular demand. In my childhood I often heard my mother say that some people smacked of the "moral marketplace." My father avoided such descriptions and reacted with a frown, but I discerned his silent agreement.

Did Wladek also smack of the "moral marketplace"? Certainly not. He was simply a high-level "talkativus" and a superior intellect. Yet he also lacked something. His superior intellect was far removed from practical concerns, and it approached ideas in a mercenary way. It seemed that Wladek appraised all phenomena according to their current value in a highly complex market whose rules were totally alien to people like me. I am sure that having learned about my supposed origin, he instinctively calculated the objective price of the fact, and immediately invested in it. He probably wasn't aware of his motivations, just as he wasn't aware of the impulse that made him join the Communist Party after the war. Where and when does this propensity appear? I have no idea. Perhaps as early as in our fetal existence, in the formative proteins of our body? Or in the atmosphere of the times? With his highly tuned intelligence Wladek transformed his impulses into ideas and theses. But underneath, under his concepts and theorems, there were no absolute ideas.

One may point out that it is trivial to condemn an individual blemish while living next door to a slaughterhouse where hundreds of thousands are murdered. Yes, but what if that individual blemish in its ultimate intellectual form obscures the very notion of murder as an absolute evil? It is not a merely theoretical question. It is a question about the terminology that motivates a new epoch.

After the war, when the word "objectivization" entered the language, crimes were rationalized as a historical or political necessity. This was not the exclusive domain of theoreticians. Especially after the war. At that time I often met the people who were sometimes called the "tribe of middlemen." I am not speaking about their actual profession but rather of a proclivity for trafficking, publicity, and procurement. They acted as brokers between people and procured more than information. They served as mediators between truth and falsehood, honesty and fear, conscience and success. Most often, perhaps, they mediated between themselves and the "objective situation." Almost all these people shared one astonishing feature: flexibility of the line dividing the true from the false. They possessed a highly developed sense of relativity in every judgment (at that time it was called "dialectical thinking"), but in reality they lacked internal foundations. Their consciences were constantly on the lookout for endorsers. They compensated for this deficiency with all sorts of tricks. As a rule they avoided taking positions that required adherence to principles, positions that were not subject to constant fluctuations. By blurring the extremes and assimilating dichotomies they tried to identify life with their own psyche, where plus and minus signs had been obliterated. In fact, it was a matter of religious nature. As I said, they were a separate tribe. They made up quite a significant social stratum—a group of people totally unsure of themselves, people looking for safeguards and guarantees. And yet they practiced their religion without faith. Both the piety of a peasant and the enterprising spirit of a capitalist are founded on a deep conviction about the sense and purpose of life. The middleman lacks this certainty. It was not until after the war that the tribe of middlemen found its own world full of unexpected and limitless opportunities.

In my opinion Wladek belonged to this tribe, but he was a middleman of the highest level of initiation: he mediated between the weakness of the individual and the power of history. I wasn't absentminded enough to remain indifferent when during our walk in the fields he "objectivized," in his intelligent if screeching voice, the social causes of Nazism. We were sitting at the edge of a birch grove and he was shaking some sand out of his sandals. I filled my pipe. I asked him if he thought the Germans could win the war. He said he was sure they couldn't. It was too late for that. In his opinion Hitler made one unforgivable mistake: he started the war in the West and neglected the issue of national self-government in such conquered countries as Poland and Ukraine. When he analyzed that unforgivable mistake of Hitler, I was struck by a solemn, stern note of reproach in his voice, as if Hitler failed to confirm his unchallengeable thesis and his long-term prediction. "You see," he said, smiling, "I'm playing the devil's advocate."

That phrase "the devil's advocate" captured my attention. "Perhaps you're right," was all I said. "I never really thought about that."

My remark provoked further discourse. Wladek took off his glasses to wipe them with a handkerchief and looked up with his shrunken eyes. He spoke about the attitudes toward the Germans among the local peasants. His pupil, the fifteen-year-old son of the miller, wrote in his composition that after the war he would like to study at the Berlin Polytechnic. Wladek claimed that the agricultural areas prospered under the occupation and that the rural population was psychologically dominated by the Germans: "There is hatred, of course, but hatred induced by the sense of inferiority in the face of German technology and organization." Wladek went on to present, in a quite interesting way, his concept of a farm based on the American model: a way to transform the peasants into modern breeders and cultivators—that is, real agricultural producers. He said that as early as the fifteenth century some crowned heads toyed with similar ideas. Jan Olbracht, for example, wanted to create a class of farmers out of the less prosperous nobility and to base the Polish social structure on the strong and dynamic agrarian-industrial units. Wladek was convinced that were it not for Olbracht's premature death, the fate of Europe would be quite different and the partition of Poland would never have taken place.

I listened to this with considerable interest. Wladek was most likable when he tried to present some newly discovered theory. Often he became quite generous with his intelligence. He situated his listener on the same level as himself and assumed they both possessed the same education and knowledge of the subject. The more naïve of his acquaintances considered it flattering.

In any case, Wladek's monologue was really thought provoking. On our way back I tried to persuade him that he should commit his thoughts to paper. "You know, Wladek," I said, "you could write about the spirit and social relations in the countryside. It would be a valuable source of information." He became excited by the idea. After a moment he stopped and asked me whether I was authorized to make such a proposal. I was embarrassed, but did not deny it. "I understand," he said, and told me how pleased he was by our renewed contact.

Later we discussed other things. Wladek invited me home for a supper of ersatz coffee and kaiser rolls, and I had the opportunity to meet his future wife, the rather homely niece of the miller. She was probably several years his senior. It was getting dark when I finally climbed back into the carriage.

The date and place of this meeting were often mentioned during my interrogations. Each time I was asked to recall the minutest details of the fragment of our conversation which concerned the "recruitment for an intelligence-gathering mission." Since I categorically denied having ever recruited anybody, I was transported by my interrogators from Miedzeszyn to Koszykowa Street, where I was read Wladek's testimony. He presented our chat rather accurately. Only the language was incorrect. Wladek testified in writing that on the day mentioned he received instructions from me concerning reconnaissance and intelligence gathering in the Rondo unit, whose aims and name he learned only later, after his return to Warsaw. This last statement was true.

I had no witnesses to defend me, and thus my explanation sounded less than convincing. One can expose a lie, repel an accusation, but it is impossible to repudiate a falsity made up of true events and circumstances. Wladek's testimony about our conversation was not false. The distortion was in the shifting of nuances. Wladek testified that we exchanged views on current issues, "assessed pro-German sentiments among the population, and debated Hitler's chances for the ultimate victory." When I protested and said that no Pole in his right mind could wish for a Nazi victory, I was presented with a newspaper clipping. It was an article published in 1938 in a social and literary weekly. The author pointed to the role of national socialism in the moral rebirth of Germany and Europe. It was signed by Wladek, and its title was "Hitler's Great Chance."

I found myself at an impasse. I could not keep denying that I had asked for Wladek's "collaboration." All I could do was to call into question the credibility of certain particular phrases in his testimony. But this would amount to a deliberation on style—a quite ridiculous thing considering my situation. Besides, Wladek's testimony also contained the account of our earlier conversation in the Melpomena during the first wartime winter. We were supposed to have discussed—I quote from memory—"the political record of the Pilsudski camp and its future tactics under the occupation." That meeting was characterized by Wladek as the "initial contact."

It was a critical moment for me, and if it were not for the breakthrough that followed soon afterward, it is quite possible I wouldn't have been able to defend myself any longer. I mean my physical exhaustion and diminished psychological resistance after months spent in an isolation cell. I could hardly anticipate that Wladek's next statement would precipitate a surprising change in the interrogations. As for himself, he also could not expect that with a dozen or so lines of text he could adorn my dreary existence with a totally new element: a carton of Wawel cigarettes and Georgian brandy.

Of course, the few sentences we exchanged during our walk, which the interrogators considered an act of recruitment for the anticommunist underground, assumed in my imagination immense importance. Month after month I would fall asleep and wake up with these sentences on my mind. They accompanied me to the interrogations and lingered in my mind afterward. They were like a tune I could not clear from my head: sometimes I would jump up in the middle of the night hearing somebody utter them with my own voice. This was much later, though, during the postwar years. That night on my return journey and during my first days back in Warsaw, I hardly gave a thought to our meeting. My "proposal" was a polite compliment, and I did not consider it binding.

On our way home we talked about lighter, more personal matters—about the prewar days, about our studies and our work in the theater. Wladek wanted to know whether I still worked at the Melpomena and asked me about Tola. I remember his good-natured smile spreading under his glittering glasses. "Is she still madly in love with Cezar?" It was a surprise, and at first I did not know what to answer. "Well, yes," said Wladek. "She tried to kill herself twice because of that. And I imagined that loony loved me!" And he added some exculpatory remark: "Erotic escapades—a routine thing in every theater."

From the very beginning of my relationship with Tola I was aware of how little I knew about her. Sometimes it occurred to me that I knew literally nothing about her life before we met. "If I learned that the day before our meeting you were released from prison, I would have no right to be surprised," I joked once. "And who has the right to somebody else's past?" she grunted.

I have already explained that I didn't treat her "affair" with Cezar seriously. I would consider it rather indecent to learn about her life through gossip instead of getting to know her myself. I believe a man in love should seek to make his feelings complete in the cognitive sense as well, so that even his errors must issue from this one magnificent error of nature that we call love. I was therefore in the habit of cutting short every conversation in which Tola's name came up. I changed the subject as soon as a more confidential tone, or a warm glance, indicated that the speaker knew about our relationship. It happened several times with Wiaremko, who was a born gossip, and in cloakroom chats with Rena Delatynska, an actress and Iza's confidante. For the last couple of months people quite often talked about Tola in my presence. My behavior must have betrayed some anxiety. During the occupation quite a number of personal secrets had been revealed. Secrecy concerned a different domain.

During my conversation with Wladek I also preferred to keep silent. Wladek was not a perceptive observer—he was too preoccupied with his own thoughts. After a while he probably forgot all about it, and we moved on to something else.

The first thing I learned back in Warsaw was so depressing that it left me speechless. "Cezar? But that's impossible!" Rabczyn did not respond. His information was usually quite reliable, as I had the opportunity to learn several times. In the afternoon I had a meeting with Tola in a small restaurant, the Hare, at the corner of Dobra and Tamka. I came early and sat for forty-five minutes staring at the copy of "Prusian Homage" hanging above the entrance. The more elegant prewar restaurants were "Germans Only." There was a proliferation of new pubs and cafeterias run by the members of the intelligentsia. There remained, however, a number of old small restaurants situated mostly away from the main downtown routes, where it was still possible to find real, professional waiters and inexpensive food. These establishments maintained the illusion of continuity. Their banal decor, even their ugliness, when contrasted with the dilapidation of the downtown sections, emanated something warm and traditional. I don't know why, but I felt relatively safe in them. There was another reason why I came here earlier than necessary: I knew that at that time the establishment was frequented by Cezar.

The source of the information was, of course, Wiaremko. In the winter, when the restaurant was cold, Cezar sat there in his fox coat with his all-season sombrero pushed back on his head. He used to drink alone at a table in the corner under a trophy. Wiaremko told me that an old waiter who used to work at Simon and Stecki served Cezar in total silence, and in the winter he placed a pot with live coals at his feet. Before the war such scenes happened quite frequently. Everywhere Cezar went he had totally committed cabdrivers, barbers, janitors. He was worshipped by cloakroom attendants, and by a Jewish tailor, who made his suits for free and even invited him to his daughter's wedding at the synagogue on Tlomackie. "Simple folks love Cezar," someone told me once. It is important to note that the simple folks remained faithful to him even during the occupation. Actors were a different story.

While working at the Melpomena, I could observe the formation of a new hierarchy in the actors' world, a hierarchy that slowly replaced the old one, established before the war. Before the war there were theaters, roles, audiences, and reviewers; after September 1939 all that ceased to exist. Famous actors worked as waiters in several new cafés, were supported by their wives, or moved to the provinces and disappeared without a trace. It was not long before I realized that a shift was taking place in that uprooted world: a strange phenomenon, since it wasn't based on any clear criteria. Nobody played better or worse, since nobody played at all. And yet those years without premieres and reviews made several acting careers, while forcing others into oblivion. Before the war Wiaremko had a reputation as an actor who had lost his class and wasted his comic talent. During the war people started to speak of him as a genius. This opinion survived the occupation. In the postwar years Wiaremko played serious dramatic roles, and became a kind of living monument of the great, old-time acting. A born comedian and a shrewd businessman, around 1948 he commemorated his anniversary by playing the title role in *Kosciuszko's Oath* in one of Lodz's theaters. The show ran for 150 performances and was honored by high-ranking party officials and ministers, who came from Warsaw to see the aged Wiaremko perform in his russet coat and artificial retroussé nose.

It should be granted, however, that Wiaremko's moral position improved due to his good-naturedness and energy during the occupation. He helped people. Perhaps he did not do it for purely selfless reasons. Nevertheless, during these years many actors owed him their livelihoods. These reversals of fortune were far from uncommon. The caesura of the war reshuffled many lives and provided opportunities for some quite undistinguished people. It was the beginning of a process called, after the war, "the offensive of mediocrity." Each day of the occupation eroded the prewar social summit. At the time when Wiaremko was being elevated to the rank of outstanding actor, Cezar was spoken of as someone who "used to be a great artist."

I cannot imagine that anybody I knew hated the war more than Cezar. Perhaps I should say: hated it in a more terrifying and authentic manner. Cezar was incapable of the emotion commonly known as "hatred." To imagine Cezar plotting revenge, acting with premeditation against somebody, or being tormented by somebody's success would be a complete absurdity. But I am sure that nobody else saw the cruelties of war with more abhorrence and clarity. Cezar's hatred appeared in the form of fear and revulsion. I don't think he was afraid of air raids, but he shivered at the thought of the barbarity, the eruption of insane evil, which materialized for him in the global flood of foolishness and brutality of those years. "The mice will swim through," he told Tola the day after the fall of Paris.

I remember the day when Cezar showed up for the first time at the Melpomena in order to "play host," to use Wiaremko's phrase. He did not recognize or simply did not notice me. I doubt whether he recognized anybody. He was standing in the corner of the room under a plush drapery, and shook hands with the guests in a limp and absentminded way. I noticed he had lost a lot of weight, mostly above the waist. The collar of his shirt was too big and revealed a thin, almost feminine neck. His jacket bulged around his hips. The corners of his mouth were drooping, and his eyes were unusually bright and unseeing. His hair was cropped shorter than usual, and his face was shaven and powdered. I realized what struck me most about his appearance: he had been washed, trimmed, powdered—he was brought here powdered and perfumed. Cezar never paid any attention to onlookers. He did not acknowledge their presence, was unaware even of their existence. He allowed himself to be brought here to play host, but in fact he performed the ancient ritual of covering his head with dust. I admired him for the high-handed and merciless humiliation he inflicted upon himself and for his patient acceptance of the offense. Yes, most of all he must have felt *offended.*

Wiaremko told me that he brought him, together with Iza Rajewska, in a horse cab. Cezar did not say a word. He looked like a man who had been stabbed in the stomach. "And Iza?" "Iza"—Wiaremko paused for a second—"Iza was wearing a gray astrakhan."

I met Iza Rajewska, in gray astrakhan and earrings, in front of the Actors' Theater in October 1939, shortly after my escape from a prisoner-of-war convoy. Warsaw was still smoldering. People plundered stores for meat and cheese. Rice and broken glass still covered the pavements. I was wearing a cap, and instead of bowing, I put my fingers to the visor. Iza smiled. I remember the motion of her small, beautiful head when she answered my greeting, pointing me out to a companion who was walking with her. There was a good deal of contempt in her gesture. I must have appeared to her a laughable example of humiliated manhood, one of the fools who lost the war. Her astrakhan and earrings were there to prove to us fools that she did not lose. Yes, Iza brought Cezar—shaven and powdered—to show the fools that nothing had changed with her. And Cezar consented, allowed himself to be brought for display. For him everything was finished. He stood under the drapery, extended his hand to be shaken, and silently cried for God, who had been so cruelly compromised. It seemed that both Cezar and Iza, each in their own fashion, drew final conclusions from their situations. In that respect, at least, they were a perfect couple.

Everything that I say here about Cezar may sound like an apology, as though I search for special criteria to judge a man fallen so low. It isn't so. I guess Professor Janota would not hesitate to raise this objection, and it is easy to imagine his arguments. Yet I know who I am talking about. I am not justifying Cezar's acts. I am not trying to diminish his guilt. All I want, and need, to say is that in my opinion the sins of that man should not be judged apart from his talent. Cezar's sins were widely known: he never tried to conceal them. Sometimes he called himself "the master of all addictions," by which he must have meant not only alcohol and tobacco. Cezar's paradoxes, his aphorisms . . . "I don't like ugly women, but I never harmed any of them"—my God, how many similar sayings had he scattered around restaurants, in dressing rooms, or in his box at the racetrack!

I wouldn't dare to say that a man of talent has a right to sin, or that his talent redeems his wrongdoing. Besides, I am not sure whether anybody has managed yet to define talent, especially inclusive of its ethical and religious elements. For myself I stick to a theory that talent is a severe case of split personality, and this definition comes to my mind whenever I think about Cezar. Before the war a lot was written about his acting—but only about his acting, his roles, which is understandable. And yet Cezar onstage achieved something more; he reached beyond the limits of acting, and enriched it with an additional, unique value that escaped the reviewers. It is often said that an actor onstage reveals a part of himself, that he becomes one with himself or one of his selves. That may be true, I guess, but not in Cezar's case. Cezar did not play himself. After each role I was at a loss to identify who he really was, and I often asked myself which enemy he confronted in this way in his art. I sensed his pride: Cezar's acting resounded with the anger of a defiant mortal deprived of grace. It was really disquieting. And if God is the only audience, and if one day that audience fails to show up, then an actor like Cezar has no choice but to break his contract and accept an offer from the competition.

Having heard Rabczyn's story, I realized this was exactly what had happened, and I was terrified. I still harbored a frail hope: I hoped to meet him, to talk to him, and to learn whether the information was premature or untrue. I hoped to see him that day.

He did not come. Around four o'clock the restaurant suddenly grew dark. Through the window I saw papers tossing around in a cloud of dust. People ran through the street with their heads down. I heard their steps, voices, and then thunder. The door opened, ushering in the sound of a downpour. I saw Tola walking across the room, bumping against chairs and overturning glasses with the sleeves of her raincoat. Her face was wet, strands of hair stuck to her forehead. She was looking for me. She had lost her purse, and I ran outside to pay the rickshaw driver for her. When I sat down she was staring blankly ahead with glassy eyes. "Tom," she said, "that's the end of him. He'll never pull himself up."

That day it became known that Iza and Cezar accepted an offer from the Warschauer Stadttheater, established by the German occupying authorities. If I was shocked by the news, it was easy to imagine its effect on the other actors. Years after the war the "Rajewska case" was still a sensation. The verdict given by her fellow actors as early as 1945 was swift. What should we say, therefore, about the reaction the day after the fact? Older actors still claim that the news struck their circle like lightning. Soon afterward posters appeared in the city announcing the performance of *A Lady from Pest*. Before the premiere Iza came to the Melpomena with a terrier. The dog was thirsty, and Wiaremko apparently brought him a bowl of water.

On Sunday I went to Zoliborz to visit my father, who lived in the Teachers' Housing Cooperative not far from Wilson Square. Unlike most of the city, Zoliborz changed very little in those years. As soon as I stepped off the streetcar, I felt I had traveled five years back in time. Everything here was as it was before: well-kept streets, unpretentious houses, trees, and silence. Even the pedestrians looked tidier. It seemed at first that by some kind of miracle the war had left that part of the city intact. In reality Zoliborz was seething with underground activity. The cooperative apartment buildings and the individual houses on the side streets often sheltered headquarters of various clandestine organizations. It was mostly the result of the social composition of the district. A large segment of the population was made up of prewar intelligentsia with leftist leanings, and in the late 1920s several buildings were erected there to house military officers and their families.

It was my tenth year in Warsaw. The university, loneliness, the theater, love—everything took place in Warsaw. After ten years the city in which I once felt so estranged became the natural landscape for my life. After the war I wasn't eager to move, and I usually returned from my trips abroad earlier than planned. It must have had something to do with my deep disbelief in the possibility of changing one's life or escaping one's destiny. On several occasions I decided to stay put even when

common sense told me to run. In 1944, after a shooting incident on a streetcar, I preferred to dye my hair rather than disappear from Warsaw. It wasn't bravura—far from it. I'd rather
call it a psychological *terrae adscriptio*. I would compare myself
to the patient who rejects medicine to recover on his own,
because it is the only recovery he considers real.

I'm getting ahead of myself. It was only the spring of 1942.
I had not seen my father for several weeks, and he received
me with his usual caustic cordiality. His wife, Wanda, immediately spotted a dangling button on my jacket. She helped me
out of it and left us alone. We spoke about the military situation, and my father listened with reserve to my strategic projec-
tions (I claimed that the Western powers would launch a landing operation in a matter of weeks); then he asked some matter-of-fact questions about my life and my occupation, I did
not tell him everything, but he must have guessed the nature of
my job. I knew the flicker of light in his pince-nez masked a
penetrating glance. While I talked, my father was slowly turning a red-and-blue pencil in his fingers. He did not ask any
more questions. He simply reached for a box that sat on his
desk near a pile of notebooks. It contained tobacco and a cigarette roller. He smoked. I never saw him smoking before, but
I remembered his taunting tolerance for high school smokers.
The only thing he did not allow them to do was leave the classroom in the middle of a lesson. He noticed my curiosity and
explained that two weeks earlier he woke his wife in the middle of the night to ask her for a cigarette. From that time on he
smoked about fifteen a day.

We remarked on the effects of nicotine, but I had a feeling
that the real subject hadn't been mentioned yet. My father was
a man of conventions, and his polite remarks were the courtesy
of an elderly gentleman who waits for the right moment to
touch upon the real issues. When I asked him whether he still
forbade his students to leave the classroom to have a cigarette,

he ignored my joke. He aimed that convex pince-nez straight at me: "My students are young soldiers. Everything here ends up in the military. Always the military. Always."

In silence I watched his slender fingers turning the pencil. So that's what he wanted to talk about . . . Father's views often differed from mine, and frequently they made me aware that I did not, in fact, have any views on some things. His observations were well thought out, and when he spoke, he knew exactly what he was going to say. We talked for over an hour and I still remember most of the conversation. What worried him most (he kept returning to the subject) was the increasingly military character of the Polish underground. All factions of the national resistance, no matter what their political orientation, tended toward the military model. My father was skeptical about the possibility of armed struggle under the occupation. In his opinion the military conspiracy could not affect the outcome of the war—at least not in the global sense. And yet militarism involved immense costs. New generations were joining the resistance, and my father claimed that right after his lessons they rushed to their military courses. "They are an army," he repeated, "and they have commanders. When there is an army and commanders, there must be a battle." He took off his glasses and squinted at me with his youthful eyes. He told me about recent arrests among his senior students. Apparently some of them had died under torture.

He seemed to wait for my reply. But what reply? For me the whole issue was beyond doubt or choice. It was not dependent on any "yes" or "no." Some time ago I had trained a group of high school students in the use of hand grenades and in guerrilla tactics, yet I never pondered why I was doing it or whether it had any purpose. It seemed, like my collaboration with Rabczyn, an obvious necessity, which had nothing to do with opinions or beliefs about the general direction of the resistance. It simply had to be done—by me or by somebody else.

In short, I could not think of an answer for my father and instead I started to talk about the war and about soldiers dying on various battlefields. Father did not interrupt. "Yes, of course," he said when I finished. He took one of the notebooks from his desk, marked it with his pencil, and put it back. "My students hate the Germans. But nobody teaches them to hate Nazism. I'm not educating heroes, only people."

I have mentioned the distance that existed between me and my father. He was meticulous about proper forms of thought and appeared to treat them as the Romans treated virtue. In his rigid discipline and self-control I detected a fear of disorderly reality. He must have seen it as a threat to his cultivated system of principles. We were more than a quarter century apart. He was one of those hardy old gentlemen who after World War I had organized Polish education, self-government, health care, and the judiciary, and during World War II supported civilian resistance and participated in clandestine education. He was sixty when he died in September 1944 while carrying wounded from the bank building Under the Eagles. When Wanda returned to Poland in 1956 she told me she was present at the exhumation of his remains. His old cap and a white-and-red armband were well preserved. I told her about our conversation in Zoliborz when she was sewing on my button. Father predicted the outbreak of the Uprising. He called it "the battle," and he was probably aware he would also take part in it.

I remember that morning well, although I visited my father many times later. It was the first time he revealed his opinion about me. His request at the end of our conversation made clear his picture of my character. He trusted me and he admired some of my human qualities, though he observed them from a distance. I remember that I wanted to say goodbye, and I got up from my chair to do so. Father pretended not to notice my intention, and pointed with his pencil at two notebooks he had placed separately on a chair. "These are my best students—exceptional talents in the humanities," he said with a frail smile. "Perhaps you'll meet them someday . . . on some occasion . . ." And then I understood I should stay a little longer. That's what my father wished.

He presented his request in a few succinct sentences. It concerned these two "best students." It was a strange request but one that proved quite consequential. Father obliged me to *take responsibility* for these two students. This is my own description. My father used more subtle, less common wording, but that is not very important in this case. What my father had in mind could be summarized as follows: "Any day these two boys will be recruited. In a month or so they will be throwing grenades at German positions. In a year or two they will be killed in some shootout. It would give me some peace of mind if they belonged to your organization. Talk to your people about it. Take care of them."

That was Sunday morning. On Monday I had a meeting with Rabczyn and I broached the matter. His reaction was positive. "It's a good idea. They can work with you, and maybe they will prove themselves." He said he would soon give me instructions about my new assignment. He was in good spirits. He set our next appointment for Friday, and on Wednesday he was dead. That very day I met both potential recruits in the Botanical Gardens for a preliminary talk. The news about Rabczyn's drowning at the armory on Wolska Street reached me in the evening. He hadn't had time to pass on the new instructions. My father's students were Andrzej and Jerzy Borowik. They were brothers. I admitted them to Rondo in the first days of July 1942.

At eleven o'clock I was returning from my meeting with the Borowiks. At the same time the German gendarmerie were opening the hydrants on Wolska. When my streetcar stopped

at the corner of Nowy Swiat and Foksal, the police were dragging a man by the armpits to a black car parked near the streetcar stop. It took only seconds. All I saw were the two men in
leather caps, their silver badges, and the gray, lifeless face of
the man they had seized. When my streetcar started to move,
it was overtaken by the black car, and I saw again the two sad-
dle-shaped caps and the man between them. I decided to ask
Rabczyn on Friday whether he knew who was arrested on the
corner of Foksal and Nowy Swiat on Wednesday at eleven.
Two weeks later, as I was lying in Tola's bed pretending to read,
I suddenly started swearing, because it occurred to me that I
had forgotten to talk to him. Only later did I realize the
absurdity of my thought. Rabczyn was dead. I must have dozed
off over my book.

The period after Rabczyn's death was exceptionally hard
for me. I felt empty. Everything seemed to fall apart both
inside and around me. It was also a time of broken contacts
and paralysis among the leadership of the underground. Such
periods usually followed major setbacks or arrests. For a long
time each of us was thrown back on his own resources and
with no idea what would happen next. A "long time" might
mean just five, six, or eight days, but in the underground such
periods are experienced like a physical illness.

I had to sleep in many different houses, and I often visited
Tola just to wash myself in her bathroom. She saved her days
off for me, and we were able to spend a lot of time together.
Miss Lala returned home rather late, usually just before the
curfew. Every two or thee days I dropped into a bakeshop in
Narutowicz Square that sold mocha cakes. There was no news
for me: that contact was also broken. At home I would stretch
out on the bed with a pillow under my head and my pipe
between my teeth. The pipe allowed me to conceal my depression. With a pipe in my mouth I looked reserved, like a man
working on elaborate plans.

Sometimes, however, I was seized by the need to move, to mingle with other people. Apparently I wasn't in very good health and in the evenings I often had a light fever. But I would leave the house anyway and drag Tola with me. We would walk arm in arm in long strides toward the Fregata on Mazowiecka Street, where prewar society ladies were waiting tables. The bar was frequented by Germans in civilian clothes. Under Tola's excited, searching glance I assumed the most composed expression I could muster. She was always certain I was watching somebody in the restaurant. In fact, all I wanted to do was to sit for an hour in the smoke-filled room and drink a glass of rowanberry vodka. On one occasion I told her, while filling our glasses, "It is going to be tiresome as well as dangerous. You can still back out." For a second her pupils became so wide that her eyes were completely black. I felt a stab of anxiety: why was I bringing up the subject? That evening, when we were returning along Marszalkowska Street, she spat on a German soldier, and we barely managed to get through a gateway which had a double exit. I noticed a change in her face: her lips were strangely contorted. I saw a similar spasm some years later, shortly before the first attack of her disease.

Since the middle of May there was a noticeable change in my relationship with Tola. Several times she went so far as to offer me flowers. Her attitude toward me was close to worship. My arguments and jokes were met with pious resistance. I was dealing with a deeply religious person. Yes, she finally came to love me. But not as a man. She brought me bunches of wildflowers as if they were offerings to a saint.

She started to talk about music often and to encourage me to take more interest in that discipline. Her own relationship with music was much deeper than mine. She told me once that as a child she had studied the violin. Until that time music had been a subject we avoided in conversations, and I never tried to conceal my lack of training. Tola, however, frequented the weekly concerts at the musical salon of the Rylski family, where, she told me, one could meet all sorts of interesting people. "They all would love to meet you," she insisted. She also claimed that I was in fact musical, and that she discovered in me (to quote her words) "a magical yearning for rhythm, as in dancing bears." Such judgments embarrassed me. Tola's affectations were often quite irritating. Nevertheless, I finally gave up and accompanied her to one of the Saturday concerts.

I could not point out today where the Rylskis' villa was situated. It was certainly on one of the streets between Filtrowa and Wawelska. Yet I remember well the mood of the evening. At first it seemed that nobody paid any attention to me. I noticed a couple of glances in my direction but nothing more. When we entered Tola urged me to introduce myself to the lady of the house, a tall, shortsighted brunette. Her long, almost confidential handshake surprised me. As if to forestall any explanation I might offer, Mrs. Rylski whispered, "Yes, I know," and exchanged glances with Tola. Before I was taken upstairs, Mrs. Rylski and I talked for a moment in the hallway. I was struck by a familiar smell to the house. There was a pair of skis standing under the stairs. An elderly gentleman with a beard was pointing them out to some guests and saying, "I haven't had them on since 1912, when I used to ski to Helsinki for the newspapers . . ." Somebody laughed. "Selim, tell the truth. Were they just newspapers, or was it Bolshevik propaganda?" The hallway was cluttered like a storage room in a country manor: old shoes, faded raincoats, a bucket of coal, a dismantled bicycle, a dog's mat in the corner. It was a collection of objects that nobody cared to clear away and that seemed to have accumulated from before the war. One could find such hallways in the old villas of Zakopane. Sometimes there were porches piled high with off-season equipment: skis or sledges in the summer, faded backpacks and walking sticks in the winter. I remembered that atmosphere of careless habitation, and the rich scent of pinewood in the mountains from the summer vacations spent with my grandmother near Krakow. The hallway at the Rylskis' also had pine panels.

I remember that I perspired throughout the evening. I suspect that my crisis might have been the result—among other things—of some physical ailment. Perhaps I was just beginning my convalescence. Such states are often marked by periods of sharpened perception, which may explain my emotional reaction during the second part of the concert. When I first sat down with Tola in the half-circle of chairs, I could hardly concentrate. The effort to feel at ease concerned me more than the music. I could not get rid of a feeling that time had slipped backward, that the war had not started yet and I was at the Willmans', in their large sitting room on Czacki Street. It was a strange coincidence: the announcement I heard during the intermission led me to Nina's house the next day.

I hadn't seen her for almost a year. After the ghetto was closed I traveled to Leszno twice to visit her. The first time I passed through the Judiciary Building; the second time I was shown a narrow passage through a coal yard. Later I had to sneak through a series of basements. Shortly after my visits I received a joking note from Nina. She informed me she was giving English lessons and asked for a copy of Oscar Wilde's *The Canterville Ghost* in the original. One sentence had been underlined: "Send it by mail. No need to deliver personally, please." The news about the death of counselor Willman reached me during the evening at the Rylskis' after the first portion of the concert.

It was on that occasion that I made my acquaintance with Professor Selim, the father of our hostess. He resembled a joyful Tartar, with a gray strand in his beard and a tan, bald head, and he'd been watching me throughout the concert. Now he approached me, leaving the company of the ladies he had been standing with. He asked me whether I used to play bridge at the Willmans' before the war. He remembered me from those occasions. He passed on the news in a sonorous, unexpectedly youthful voice while watching for my reaction. He spoke of Nina as "Ignacy's daughter." I learned that Willman had embarked upon negotiations with the Germans to halt deportations to the camps. After one session he didn't return home. He jumped from a window in one of the Leszno tenements. Some neighbors saw him fall. Professor Selim continued to watch me with curiosity, and mentioned Nina again. He told me that one of his friends, who had been called for consultation in the ghetto, talked to her recently. Selim squinted. "Yes, yes, one should take care of one's health!" he said, and walked away. The pianist was already sitting down at the keyboard.

I should have mentioned that Selim (it wasn't his real name, but a pseudonym from his revolutionary days, which his family and friends continued to use) had no direct connections with Rondo. I am indebted to him, though, because he took care of Tola when I was no longer able to help her. Our meeting at the Rylskis' was brief—a couple of minutes at most. When I got back to my seat, somebody behind me mentioned his name. It was the name of a man involved in the escape of a famous political prisoner from a Petersburg or Moscow jail, probably before 1905. I remember the details: faked insanity, woman's disguise, a Polish doctor who made out the certificate. I knew about that adventure—about the Marshal's past—from my mother. The mention of Professor Selim's name was followed by a remark about his former association with the Marshal, and it struck me that the words were probably meant for my ears. Suddenly I became aware of the interest I had aroused since my arrival: I was being watched with an attention that was meant to be discreet but did not conceal a deep curiosity. After the first part of the concert, when Selim came to talk to me, several people made a visible effort to move closer in order to hear our conversation. Tola was right when she told me that my visit at the Rylskis' was eagerly awaited. It may seem strange, but for the first time in my life that thought was not unpleasant.

The circumstances I am presenting here cannot be ignored in the discussion of the initial period of Rondo. Everything I say will prove essential for the reconstruction of my psychological condition. I cannot give a simple explanation of my motives as the founder of Rondo. I am, however, able to re-create the sequence of emotions and moods that passed through my mind at that time and that I observed in the larger world. Two months had passed between my ride in a rickshaw on May 13, 1942 (the proposed date of inception), and Wladek Sznej's return from the country in the middle of July. Within that period Rondo assumed its objective existence as well as its name.

Does it really have any significance? For me, at least, it does.

I sat with Tola at the back of the room. Twenty or thirty chairs made an irregular half-circle. Two young girls and a boy with a dog sat on a rug near the piano. Others occupied armchairs near the curtained windows. It was still bright outside, but the curtains had been drawn before the concert started, and the room was lit by candles. Things blurred in that low, soft light. I promised myself I would see Nina Willman the next day, and the thought brought some calm. I tried to concentrate on the piece by Chopin. The sweat dried on my temples and out of the corner of my eye I watched Tola's profile. Her chin rested on the curve of her hand. I do not know whether the music actually reached me, but under its influence I felt an internal tide of emotion, and in this tide I began to think. For the first time I asked myself *how to do it*.

I am sure that during the second part of the concert I made the final decision and conceived of the idea of Rondo. At the Rylskis' I worked out the general concept and the stage setting. One week later I was already dealing with hard facts.

I knew what I was taking upon myself. I knew it would not

be easy: it had to be not only well thought out but well carried out as well. While watching Tola's hand I was telling myself: If you manage to play out everything to the end, you will save the life of that hand, with its long, distinct fingers. Years earlier, during our dinner at the Savoy, when I looked at her for the first time, my concern with her began with the strange motions of her hands and the awkward way she held her fork. Now I felt absolutely sure that there was nothing more real in the world than this hand. When compared with this hand, all ideas become mere abstractions.

When the pianist played Chopin's sonata, I started to compose the text of my oath, which I decided to have her recite that very evening.

This part of my testimony typically aroused the most interest in the officers of Department X. At first my explanations were met with contemptuous incredulity, as if they were fairy tales concocted during the lonely hours between interrogations. But as I persisted in my story and stuck to the same facts and the same motivations, it gradually began to dawn on them that my story might not be a fabrication. It possessed its own internal logic, and over many interrogations I was never caught in a contradiction. At the beginning of the investigation I decided upon a simple method: tell everything as it was without concealment. When asked about the time and circumstances of my decision to establish Rondo, I replied that it was assumed to have been May 13, 1942, but in fact it happened in the summer of the same year during a concert in the Staszic colony when the pianist was performing Chopin's Sonata in B Minor. This news was met with a particularly unpleasant reaction. When I repeated the same story during my next interrogation, all I got in return was an ironic shrug of the shoulders.

After several such exchanges, however, my examiners decided to accept my explanations as a working hypothesis. If everything was as I claimed, and if the formation of Rondo was for purely personal reasons, then the alleged activities of the organization, which, according to my claims, did not exist, must have also had no ideological and political program.

I replied that I had never had anything to do with politics and that the idea of Rondo was based on my own individual perceptions, which had no programmatic character at all. I tried to demonstrate that my contacts with other organizations were limited to certain particular kinds of activities with which I was entrusted by the underground, which I had already described in detail. During the initial stage of the investigation I tried to establish my credibility: today I see it was the perfect way to undermine everything I had to say. I was charged with directing a secret intelligence and sabotage unit under the code name Rondo. My stubborn assurances that Rondo was a fiction met with an unpleasant silence followed by a sardonic observation: it was possible that such an idea could germinate in the mind of a decadent intellectual, but a person with my profile couldn't conceive of such an absurdity. A man who is actively involved in the military underground does not deal with fictions.

But that was the whole point, I reiterated. During my years in the theater I dealt only with fictions! Not to mention the fact that the military underground also had its share of them. An organization that operated within Poland under the occupation was called an "army," yet according to contemporary military definitions it wasn't an army at all. Its armament, equipment, and operational capabilities were substantially different from those of a regular army. What was it really? A requirement of the collective consciousness—and its fulfillment. The military operations conducted by the underground could not affect the situation at the military fronts. The underground did not defend any borders or protect the population. From the strategic point of view such operations—their effectiveness and rationale—were fictions. Such fictions, however, often have more significance for the collective psychology than technological advantage or superior firepower. One had to create an army—which was not an army—in order to fulfill the national need for armed struggle. By creating Rondo I hadn't done anything different, with one exception: my fiction was meant for only one person, and was supposed to function without losses.

It seems that the composure with which I delivered my message had a certain effect. I somehow managed to keep my self-control—probably thanks to my physical and psychological endurance. Everything I was left with in life was being looked after by Lala Ubycz, which was a great comfort to me in those days. As for my own fate, it had already been decided, and the thought helped me to gain perspective on my situation. My revelations must have been quite astonishing, because the investigation was temporarily suspended. After several weeks I was given a statement to sign. I was expected to testify that I founded Rondo as a protest against the "opportunistic tactics of the reactionary group of *alleged resistance* known as the Home Army." Of course, I could not sign that declaration.

During my lengthy interrogation I was examined by a number of officers. In 1952 I was taken several times by car to the suburbs, to a building surrounded by a tall fence, where I was at the mercy of a woman with burning eyes. She wore a tie. Comrade Rita.

She was a legendary figure—the heroine of a famous trial in the 1930s and sentenced to death for "attempting to overthrow the state by military force and depriving it of a part of its territory." Through the intervention of the Marshal's wife the sentence was commuted to fifteen years in prison. It was said that Comrade Rita's father, the owner of several oil wells, used to finance some of the Marshal's clandestine activities.

The purpose of these sessions was ideological. Comrade Rita tried to convince me that in "objective terms" I was an enemy of the working class and that my past consisted of nothing but parasitism on the sufferings of the toiling masses. She pierced me with her burning black eyes and showered me with quotations from Marx and Engels, for which I had hardly a reply. Perhaps that was the most difficult part. When confronted with her Marxist perspective, I experienced spiritual paralysis and began to doubt my innocence. There was a selflessness in this elderly activist who looked more like a radical student from the previous century. She was struggling for my soul: "Just think of it, Tom! How can you resist it? Do you know the extent of human deprivation needed to produce just one tank for the struggle with fascism? These tanks brought you freedom!" In a single moment she could move from girlish languor to fanatical hatred. Never in my life had I seen anything like it. In silence I stared at her tie. There was nothing but simmering emptiness in my head. After each interrogation my value seemed to dwindle. I seemed to be drained of my inner content, just as in the Zacheta after my conversation with Wladek Sznej. Only after a night's sleep in my cell could I recover some sense of myself.

My interrogators tried a variety of approaches. The purpose was to make me reveal the names of Rondo's members.

The most gruesome situations had their comic moments. During one interrogation I was confronted with a strange, emaciated man who kept silent and avoided my eyes. Then he declared that he had met me at a concert at the Rylskis' in the summer of 1942. "I was sitting behind you," he said. "Perhaps you remember. For an encore the pianist played Chopin's 'Rondo.'"

The meeting did not help the investigation, but that night, back in my cell, I started to laugh aloud. But of course! At the very end of the evening, when the pianist performed an encore, somebody behind me mentioned the title of the piece: "Rondo." All those years I could not figure out where I got that name.

The reality of the German occupation became my normal, everyday life. It involved certain tasks and duties, as well as contacts with people I had never seen before the war. An accidental meeting in the street or a casual greeting on a streetcar often resulted in a renewed friendship. One made acquaintances more easily than in the prewar times because everything became more casual. Life in general was more youthful, less bourgeois. Sometimes it was even bohemian. For several weeks I spent nights in a studio belonging to a forgotten friend from the military college. I met him in Narutowicz Square in front of the bakeshop. He let me use his daybed and moved downstairs to his neighbors' apartment. Before the war he had been a legal apprentice. People would drop by unannounced, and there would be talking and drinking until the small hours, or endless games of bridge. On one occasion I spent a week with a merry young couple, both of them artists. Before leaving in the morning I would make scrambled eggs with bacon for them.

At that time Nina Willman was staying with Tola. After the evening at the Rylskis' I crossed to the other side of the wall early one morning. For almost an hour I couldn't find the right address. On the previous day Nina had moved somewhere with her mother. Finally I was directed to a tenement house at the corner of Leszno. I found her with her mother in a dark, unfurnished room in an empty apartment. They were both busy making sacks out of red pillowcases. The floor was almost covered with down. At first Nina wouldn't consider leaving the ghetto. She said her mother could not stay alone. I knew that Nina's mother was a helpless woman with a gift—her only one, it would seem—for flower arrangements. I remember that after my first arguments Nina calmly stuck her needle into a

velvet pincushion and said, "Please, let's not talk about it anymore." Her appearance had not changed since my visits to
Czacki Street. She was as composed and relaxed, and even
more beautiful than before. Two vertical worry lines had
appeared on her brow—which I used to call "Character" and
"Intelligence"—and these gave her face a distinct and more
severe look. When she was seeing me to the door she removed
a feather from my sleeve and looked briefly into my eyes.
"You've grown a mustache." Her father's death wasn't mentioned even once. There wasn't any talk, either, about the furniture in her room: a sofa, a folding bed, and nothing more.

Two days later I came back with Tola. My friend from the
military college worked for a trucking company that still did
some business with the "other side." He promised to arrange
to smuggle Nina's mother and her belongings out in a truck,
under German shipping papers. For the time being both ladies
could stay at Topolowa Street, said Tola, and there would be
no need to worry about what would come next. Lala would
take care of everything. I had two armbands with the Star of
David in my pocket. We put them on in a basement, though
incorrectly: they were to be worn on the right arm. Outside,
the streets were so crowded we had to walk in the road.

At the intersection of Leszno and Ogrodowa a silent crowd
watched a horse that was lying on the ground. Two men were
pulling off its harness. We had to push through the crowd.
Tola grew pale, and I held her hand. For some time we had
been followed by a man who breathed with great difficulty,
probably from asthma. Unable to catch up with us, he called
after Tola, "Miss Mohoczy, I didn't know you were Jewish." I
walked faster, pulling Tola by the hand. She started to fight me
and shout that she had to talk to this man. I wouldn't let her
go. In front of a doorway we were surrounded by begging children. Tola pulled out her purse and emptied its contents into
the outstretched hands.

In one of her letters, shortly after her departure to Mexico, Nina Willman wrote: "Sometimes I listen to her voice, usually in the evening, and later at night I remember you two, when you came to take me away. How it all got tangled . . ." The letter was written in 1949, when Tola was working as a Polish announcer for Radio Madrid. At that time we corresponded fairly regularly. In 1950, when she moved to Venezuela, and I was unable to answer her letters, our contact was broken for several years.

Tola and Nina. . . . The two affairs were so separate and so different from each other that until that moment they met only inside me. The war joined them together. These two women would live side by side—they would talk about me. I never expected anything like it, and I was both moved and embarrassed. Nina suspected my relationship with Tola and, though we never touched on the subject in our conversations, I guess it was the reason behind the cooling off between us. She addressed me formally even after our night on the beach in Orlowo. Nina took my manic determination to go on working in the theater for insanity, but I think she intuitively understood its source. And Tola? Tola suspected nothing. She wasn't the suspicious type, and it would never occur to her to be jealous. That day in the ghetto she learned about Nina's existence for the first time. Nina was simply someone facing a disaster, therefore one had to get involved, to help—the sooner, the better! Tola insisted on going with me. She would do all the talking; she would explain everything. All I had to do was wait outside, in the street. I did not wait in the street, though. I went upstairs with Tola and I was present at their meeting. Tola broke Nina's resistance immediately. I have no idea how she did it. I remember than when we entered, she started to smile, squinting a little, and I could not fail to notice Nina's astonished and thoughtful look. I don't even know when they both started packing. I only heard Nina say, "Not worth it. You know, it's a fairly old blouse." And then one thing more. When we were going back through the basements full of coal, Tola stopped suddenly. "Take it off." She came up to Nina and tore off her armband with one strong tug.

Nina stayed on Topolowa, and one week later we moved Mrs. Roza Willman to Dantyszek Street, where she joined a childless couple who were friends of the Rylskis'. The owners of the apartment on Topolowa had left a year earlier. Tola and Lala Ubycz occupied two spacious rooms. The third one, with windows looking out on a side street—Sedziowska, if I remember rightly—was given to Nina. Whenever our conversations extended past curfew, I would sleep on a sofa in a kitchen alcove. It is hard to recall today what thoughts visited me as I was falling asleep on that sofa. I usually fell asleep quickly, on my right side. It certainly wouldn't have occurred to me that I was spending the night under one roof with the three women of my life (the fourth one hadn't been born yet). Such thoughts are possible only after many years, when the darkness of long-ago nights is no longer impenetrable. But if someone had told me then that the one woman offered me by fate would be Lala . . .

Before the war almost everything seemed to favor my marrying Nina Willman. During the war I was certain I would marry Tola. In both cases marriage would probably have ended in divorce. Nina was a woman of strong character and outstanding intelligence. She needed a man who would meet her demands; that meant a man also of character and intelligence, but of an intelligence a bit less outstanding and a character a bit less strong than Nina's. Nina would be able to gently subjugate such a man—only a bit less intelligent and strong than herself—without losing her respect for him. Such a man would gladly allow Nina to subjugate him, and would even become dependent on that subjugation to the end of his days, without losing self-respect. It is possible that Nina met such a man. In

Mexico she married a well-known architect, a Belgian. I was not *cultured* enough for her: a husband who has to be prodded to read a new book by an avant-garde writer! As to my character, I think Nina looked in vain for any intellectual handhold, because I belonged to an utterly different species: not a neighboring branch, but a distant tree.

During Tola's illness, after one of her sessions, Selim told me that I was the reason for her nervous breakdown. He gave me a lecture on the "psychological blood groups." It was only then that I began to understand Tola. I have already talked about her courage: she didn't know how to fear other people. All her terrors were immaterial. She was horrified by the evil in the world and in herself. She must have shivered at the thought of some dark, terrifying mystery which could be unraveled as a dark and terrifying event. But this fear of existence and nonexistence was counterbalanced by hope. I have never met anybody in whom hope was equally powerful and infinite—and equally exaggerated. Before the war I had a dog, a pointer, which was staying with my parents. Whenever I stepped lightly on its foot, it uttered an agonizing groan. It wasn't afraid of me or of the pain. I think it was afraid of *something* that could happen to it, something unimaginable, terrifying—the worst possible thing. The dog wouldn't be able to live with that constant fear were it not for its hope—equally mysterious and as enormous as the source of its fear. It was the hope for a miracle which the dog awaited, yelping, almost crying, whenever it saw me put on my jacket before leaving. It seems that Tola's fears and yearnings discharged themselves in a similar way; she was living in childish terror of the darkness and in undaunted hope for the redemptive light. And I, with my temperance, my abhorrence of all extremes and exaggerations, with my calm that covered in its depth my own splinter of insanity? I couldn't be a good partner for her. Only a man stretched between magnificent antinomies could really possess

Tola—a man who would surpass her in the fury of terror, in the arrogance of hope and contempt, and, most of all, in his ambition—the insane pride of the chosen, who claims a personal partnership with Being. Only Cezar.

After one of his sessions with Tola—it was in the spring of 1944—Selim made the following pronouncement: "*Les extrêmes* not always *se touchent*. There are also *extrêmes qui* actually *ne se touchent pas*! Just like her and you. From the very beginning you must have been her adversary."

I wasn't aware of that. And it seems I paid dearly for my unawareness. At first, however, I found it hard to agree with Selim's diagnosis. I was convinced that Tola managed to mislead him, and I reassured myself by saying that psychiatrists are often naïve in their straightforward and literal interpretation of their patients' confessions: they underestimate the role of a lie in mental diseases. After all, Tola and I had known long periods of total understanding: she was blindly devoted to me, and sometimes I was even shocked by the extent of her trust. I shall never forget our reconciliations, those periods when she truly wanted to belong to me. After the evening at the Rylskis' I accepted her oath. We faced each other in a room with blanketed windows. I remember her muffled voice repeating the last line of the oath: "I swear to God, to the people, and to myself." Later the text provoked some criticism from Wladek Sznej, who found it lacking in ideological precision. I am not going to quote it here. It's enough to say that Tola was deeply moved. While repeating the words she was holding her hand high, with two fingers pressed together, and her elbow was shaking. Later she came to me in the night. I was sleeping on the sofa in the kitchen alcove with my clothes on. I woke up under Tola's gaze. She was sitting on the bed in her nightshirt, looking at me. In a loud whisper she asked if I was asleep. No, not at all . . . She said things I did not fully understand. If I had listened to them more carefully they could have explained a lot. She wanted to know whether it is possible to hate God. "How's that?" I muttered. She was talking rapidly and gesturing in the darkness. Finally I started to make some sense of what she was trying to say. She wanted to know if one could love God so much that one began to hate Him for the spectacle of evil. "It's He who allows it." She poked my ribs with her finger. "Tom, please understand. Imagine that somebody was born good, but later discovered he was cheated, betrayed, offended—and then became bad, out of spite! In order to show Him: look what You've done, that's what You wanted, didn't You? . . . Tom, you don't understand, do you?"

After a moment she lay down beside me. She was waiting—perhaps for my reply. But I was sleepy, tired. I mumbled only: "On your way back, don't wake up Lala . . ." And I turned over on my right side.

I was making mistakes, and Nina was the first to warn me. She said that my reticence wasn't doing Tola any good: I should smile less and stop my "approval with a pipe between my teeth." She was worried by some of Tola's gestures. "You shouldn't be afraid of hurting her," she said. "Don't you know that people are destroyed by silence, by not hearing what people really think of them? That's how people are killed off—not with words that hurt, but with those that remain unspoken. Why, she doesn't know the first thing about herself . . . !"

I had my reasons for remaining silent. Every couple of months, at unpredictable and irregular intervals, I suffered from exhaustion and mild nausea: periods of emotional emptiness, as in September 1939, when I lay in torpor watching my passion dying. Now it wasn't any easier. Before the war I was afraid of losing Tola to somebody else; now I was afraid of losing her because of myself. I often caught myself trying to arouse my dwindling passion with memories of our short, tempestuous moments of rapture, and finally I reached a unique state of mind that might be called "jealousy of self." I was jealous of myself from the past, and for a time the sensation brought me relief.

Never, not even once, did she suspect my anguish, and her disarming lack of perceptiveness only deepened my qualms of conscience. I had proof of my love for her, and I had reasons for keeping silent. I don't have to say how exhausting it was. I felt guilty and lonely. Once, however, on one such day (Stalingrad had been encircled, and the streets of Warsaw were covered with announcements of executions), I came across one of Iza's minions, Rena Delatynska. "She is going crazy," she said about Tola. "She creates some kind of messianic salon for herself instead of playing in a normal theater. Please tell that idiot, from me and from Iza, she shouldn't allow herself to be swept into the hysteria of those buffoons and mythomaniacs who want to bring us all to a catastrophe. And between us, she is dying—with that amateurish pseudo-talent of hers—she is pissing in her pants to be able to play again!" I was furious, and I glared at her so sternly that she promptly left. But after a few minutes—still clenching my fists and swearing silently—I suddenly realized that anyone who can be so hurt by a remark about another cannot be really lonely. This was also some consolation.

In the middle of July, I started to send Tola out with the codes. I think that the only person who could see through my ploy was Lala Ubycz. It took me some time to realize how accurately she guessed my intentions, and how well she knew me—better than I could suspect.

The mistake of numerous men who tried to win Tola's favor was to ignore Lala's presence. At first I also thought her a colorful character, an eccentric, a slightly grotesque figure attached to Tola's life, swimming around her with an amusing pensiveness—in a man's hat that covered half of her unremarkable features. Before the war one could sometimes meet such people walking alone in the parks or feeding birds in an alley. My mother used to call them "queen dwarves," in spite of their stature. The moment of surprise came when she took off her hat. Not because she had her hair cut in stubble, but because of the flat, leonine cast of her face. I was often struck by Miss Lala's resemblance to two portraits of Mickiewicz. Her face was fuller and less rapacious than the poet's in the 1840s—as if someone had added the weight and meditative mood of the other portrait made in the 1850s, the one with a walking stick. One day I noticed her small, shapely hands, strangely at odds with her square body, and then, during our financial conversation (in August, shortly after my first contact with Straga), I was surprised by Miss Lala's smile. It was a joyful, intelligent expression that flashed as if caught in a spotlight. It turned out that Miss Lala was interested in people. She asked me about Nina, about the Willmans' place before the war. We also talked about her lengthy acquaintance with Selim and the Rylskis. The tone of her voice, or rather her whisper, since she always spoke quietly, struck me as something familiar: some kind of perceptive curiosity, or tender, melancholic indiscretion. I remembered the fall before my mother's death, when on Sundays we used to go for afternoon walks, and I wanted to tell her about my friends. My mother, at least in my memories, was preoccupied with herself, with her legionnaire past or her—sometimes imaginary—spiritual torments. She treated me in an absentminded manner. Yet toward the end, a month or several weeks before her death, she started to ask about our acquaintances, who until then had been treated by her with total indifference. The same note of kind and worried curiosity sounded in her hushed voice when she asked, for instance, about Wladek Sznej's parents, whether they were still doing well, or whether the geography teacher still came to school in his little three-wheel car. I amused her with tales about various high school scandals or the foibles of my teachers. She listened attentively, interrupting from time to time: "Well, well. I never knew . . . That's really fascinating." She was departing life amidst amazement and curiosity. I think she was curious to the very end, curious and surprised by life's proximity which she noticed so late.

In Miss Lala, however, that warm attachment to being seemed organic. It emanated from her health, whereas in my mother's case it was the result of her sickness and approaching death. For some time I took her devotion to Tola for an aberration. I was wrong. Her love had natural foundations. An excess of power must have resided in her gawky body. When I learned about Miss Lala's extensive business operations and her contacts with the black market, it was as if I woke up from a slumber. But of course! I had always been amazed by her competence and specialized knowledge in such areas as bootlegging and pharmacy, or the prices of paintings that were on the market . . . These activities of hers were well known in the actors' community. After the war Wiaremko amused me with anecdotes about Lala Ubycz. (Around 1946 we spent over two hours talking on a train from Lodz to Warsaw.) He remembered he often borrowed from her in order to pay the waitresses at the Melpomena. Toward the end of the war she supported the family of an old woman, a dresser from the Actors' Theater. Perhaps not so much a woman—Wiaremko snapped his fingers as he looked for the right word—as a hundred percent human being!

After Tola's second trip as Rondo's courier, Miss Lala told me, "This is going to cost us." She quickly calculated the amount on a piece of paper. Thus the first budget of Rondo was drawn up, and I had to face the problem of how to get the money. How was it possible that such a practical sense of life coexisted with a profound mysticism? Miss Lala was a Jehovah's Witness, and people in the theater talked about it even before the war. Yet when I learned after my release that

Miss Lala Ubycz became a member of the Party and an activist in the National Front, I wasn't really surprised. It was obvious that she rendered unto Caesar what belonged to God. After the war Lala Ubycz returned to the theater. In those years prompter's boxes were still onstage. Shortly after my arrest, in the summer of 1950, Lala was fired. During the interrogations I had to reveal who was bringing up my daughter. Besides, I was sure they knew it anyway. A year later, Miss Lala got a position as cloakroom attendant in one of the theaters in Praga. As an outstanding cloakroom attendant she was admitted to the Party after a period of candidacy that lasted almost three years. It was one year before my return, and one could feel a warming trend in the air. At approximately the same time Wladek Sznej became the literary director of the same theater in Praga, and he saw Miss Lala during the meetings of the theater party organization. Come to think of it, there was only one spectator who could really appreciate the scene, and that spectator was no longer present! The caprices of fortune are often quite subtle.

The years 1942-43 were for me a period of exhausting activity in several different areas. The underground, Rondo, and the art dealership—all this not only consumed my time but also split me into three quite separate personalities. I shall have to return later to those matters and those days when I had to be three men at the same time, and each of them was forbidden to know the other two. They often confused me, and I was never certain which was the real me. Only occasionally, during conversations with Nina Willman, did I return to my old self, perhaps because she always treated me as a complex phenomenon—a personality who only appears homogeneous. During our meetings some of my tension disappeared. Nina noticed the changes that were occurring in me. She told me she preferred my two earlier personae: Martin Eden and Hans Castorp. Apparently they both looked good on me. I started to laugh. "But I am neither!" "Yet you could be," she said. "It's a matter of self-creation." She looked at me with a slightly reproachful irony, and with pleasure I watched her smooth, velvet neck and her pink fingernails as she played with a string of small pearls. She forced me to admit that heroism was nothing but the fulfillment of one's self-image as hero, and that sometimes this could be achieved only at the stake. According to Nina, Joan of Arc burned for her self-creation. Self-creation? I had never heard the term before. "It's rather simple," explained Nina. Every human being has an image of himself, and his humanity depends on whether he can invest that image with real life. There are theories, I learned, that see the man as a function of society, a cluster of reflexes, notions, and behaviors absorbed from the environment. As an individual he is *nothing.* In Nina's opinion, however, a person could become an individual entity, a somebody, only if he was able to realize the personality he had chosen for himself, if he managed to fully identify with it. And this was one possible solution. "Solution of what?" I asked. With a cigarette in her hand she made a circle in the air. "Of that . . . of that." I had nothing to say on the subject. Was I really interested in myself, in who I was, or who I should be? These questions never really disturbed me. I considered myself a rather simple man, quite similar to other people, and I saw no reason to ask myself whether I was really myself or simply a function of the society. I smiled at Nina. "You know, this is all very interesting, but it seems to have nothing to do with me."

Today I think—perhaps I needed all those years to think things over—today I think I was probably wrong. I think so more and more often. Take my affair with Tola—my love, obsession, passion—whatever we shall call it. Wasn't it, all along, my self-creation? Sometimes it occurs to me that I invented the affair only to measure myself against it. Now it seems to be a parable which I created for my own private use in order to make myself unique (to become an individual human entity, as Nina would say) and to obscure my normality and similarity to others. I did it for the lack of passion, not so much for Tola as for myself, for my own life, and in spite of a regimen of earthly factors. My mistakes—that's where I probably should begin. At the very source. I don't know if I am making myself clear, or whether I will be understood. What I've said does not contradict my feelings for Tola. At least not when the last account has been squared.

Conversations with Nina usually ended with jokes. I promised to read some Freud and to think about myself. I liked talking to her, especially when Tola was not present.

There was also the home of the Rylskis, where we often spent our evenings. The Rylskis treated Tola as if she was their oldest daughter, but Lala knew them even longer. She met Professor Selim in 1918 when he was lecturing in a Vilno occult circle. Tola was a friend of the Rylskis' sons. After the September campaign the two older brothers crossed the border and joined the army in the West. The three younger siblings remained at home. From morning to evening their house was filled with music. An old chestnut upright piano in the hallway and a black Steinway upstairs competed in a constant dialogue. Somebody, without even sitting at the instrument, would play a couple of movements from Brahms, a passage was heard from upstairs, and then somebody would hum an aria from *Fidelio* while brushing his teeth in the bathroom. Tola told me that before the war the Rylskis received a number of famous pianists and violinists, who stayed in their house during their concerts in Warsaw. I don't remember all the names she mentioned, but Paderewski was among their guests. In that milieu I enjoyed the status of a convenient foreigner. It was known that I knew little about music, but music was discussed in my presence without embarrassment. Sometimes, during a heated debate about a certain interpretation of Gluck, for example, the participants would ask for my opinion, as if forgetting about my total ignorance. It was a natural courtesy, but also an expression of disbelief that somebody could actually live without a perfect ear.

Apart from music the house resounded with the past. The older people spoke in a broad, melodious accent. For me, their way of speaking had the aroma of something rich and ancient. At the Rylskis' one could hear stories about life in Petersburg and Vilno, about the castle that burned in the uprising of 1863 or the bomb thrown by somebody's cousin or aunt at the czarist chief of police in Kazan. At the first mention of Siberia the family burst out laughing: the barge on the Yenisei! Everybody would try to explain all at once that Mrs. Rylski was born on a barge on the Yenisei, where Selim had hidden out, disguised as a fisherman. There was something sedentary and rustic about Selim and the Rylskis, about the way they talked and the atmosphere of those evening meetings. No one would hurry to get up from the table. There was a lingering quality in the communal, slightly monotonous reminiscing and debating, an abundance of time, as in the novels of the previous century, where an author was never in the mood to rush things. It didn't take me long to realize, however, that Selim had infected his environment with something new, more politicized, and that these political involvements also ran in the family. His home had been a meeting place for people connected with the Marshal. His signed photograph used to hang upstairs in the sitting room. It was taken in Vilno, and it showed the Marshal seated on a veranda in an unbuttoned gray field jacket. It disappeared after the Bzesc trials and the campaign against opposition in the Parliament. At the same time Selim declined the office of Minister of Education and chose an academic career instead. He had been a constant target of attacks from both political extremes: the right criticized him as a freethinker with Masonic connections, and the left for his sympathies for the Marshal. One night he was attacked and beaten as he was leaving his seminar at the university. It happened after *The Worker* had published his article "The Opposition Is Funny." ("The opposition has no secretaries; the opposition has no entertainment expenses and does not travel by parlor cars; the opposition travels by streetcars; the opposition is funny and ugly—it elicits nothing but pity and repulsion—but the opposition speaks the truth . . .")

I learned this from Wladek Sznej when we met in Lazienki Park soon after my release. It was eleven years since Selim's death. He died on the eve of the Uprising in the summer of 1944. He was a member of the Government Delegacy. He was found among the old stables and dumps at the Warsaw racetrack. His hands had been tied behind him with barbed wire, the back of his head smashed, and his body stuffed into a barrel. He had been taken from his home in the night. The Rylskis thought it was the Germans in civilian clothes. Even during the first years after the war, people said that Selim was arrested by the Gestapo. Wladek told me it was a political murder. It was a time of settling accounts within the underground. The Eastern front was moving closer and the resistance was preparing to battle for power.

In 1955 Selim's name started to surface rather frequently in various memoirs and documents. I was released in the spring. But I did not read any newspapers. I fell asleep over books. The trees in the park were starting to bloom. It was our first meeting since my return. That morning (we met early, at nine o'clock), Wladek and I had a lot to tell each other. The alleys were empty, and we circled the pond for two hours. I listened to him with growing indifference. In my cell I had had time to analyze everything a hundred times. Everything was obvious and thoroughly understandable: he had no other choice, therefore he was right. At a certain point, I stopped listening to him altogether. I was thinking about something else.

Later, when we were sitting on a bench near the Orangery,

Wladek asked me about Selim. He wanted to know if I had read a letter about him published in the last issue of *Przekroj*. He summarized it for me. The intellectual distance from which he "objectivized" Selim's fate struck me as suspicious. Wladek claimed Selim's life was a symbolic illustration of the "decline of democracy," with its "childish belief in the law." I thought this was the stupidest thing one could say, and I looked at Wladek's sharp, still youthful profile: the frame of his glasses hugging his ears and his hair graying at the temples. He must have been surprised by my gaze, and he asked me whether I wanted to say something. I didn't. But I remarked that the people who murdered Selim probably did not believe in democracy, and especially not in immortality. They must have been convinced that our history begins and ends here, on earth. And isn't such a belief the most childish of all? I have long considered our time between birth and death a mere fragment of a larger, hidden whole.

Wladek seemed quite intrigued by my words. "Does that mean that you believe in life after death?" "Wladek," I said, laughing, "what else could I believe four years ago?" Four years ago Wladek's first testimony was read to me. I was sweating as if in the midst of a nightmare, and my mind was capable of only one thought: Luckily there is a border beyond which all this will come to an end. I shall wake up *somewhere else* . . .

Wladek didn't seem to hear my reply. He was pondering something, and after a moment he presented me with his own opinion on the immortality of the soul. "One cannot guarantee there is life after death," he said, "but one can create a kind of man who will need no such guarantees."

At that time Wladek was still seriously involved with Marxism. As for myself, I was quite satisfied with my state of intellectual apathy. And yet, I always allowed myself to get involved in these conversations with Wladek. This time, while we were sitting on the bench, I finally came to express some rather nebulous opinions on the immortality of the soul, as well as on a few similar issues. As I remember, I tried to explain my attitude toward the forces governing human life. I said that providence operated on two different levels: on the level of small gods and that of the Great God. Small gods rule everything that happens to us—they are in the events, facts, coincidences. They try to subjugate us to their dictatorial will. In my opinion, however, the real human fate consists not in what happens to man but in what he becomes. And this is the domain of the Great God, who demands that we show our will, imagination, and love. This God is mightier than the gods of facts, and he guarantees our immortality. I do not recall Wladek's reply. I remember only one of his remarks: My "structure of the divine" did not differ much from the structure of power in totalitarian regimes. We talked for some time about similar matters. There was something comical about the fact that after all those years we were sitting on a park bench discussing the immortality of the soul and life after death.

My father, who was a historian and who derived his views on life primarily from antiquity, was skeptical about all systems of thought that tried to interpret reality as a battle between good and evil. During one of my visits in Zoliborz he said, "Who conceived of the idea that good struggles with evil? Only evil can fight with evil. Good cannot fight. Maybe good is merely a trace of some primordial civilization that lost its battles millions of years ago . . ." He claimed that every attempt at a universal interpretation of existence in terms of the conflict between good and evil only created a new element in the struggle between various powers of evil. In his view, ancient cultures were aware of the complexity of things: they sacrificed animals—a symbolic tax paid to evil that has to exist. When I pointed out that the struggle to eradicate evil was taking place right in front of us, and when I reminded him that at the outset of the war he himself called the crimes of the dictators a "crusade against God," he listened to me with patience but did not change his opinion. "God is neither good nor evil," he said quietly. "He is our possibility of a good or evil choice. And they have abolished that possibility."

I recall all this not because I see any relation between Wladek Sznej's views and the ethical and historical opinions of my father. I have never met two people more unlike each other in their way of thinking. I have something else in mind. My father's hypothesis seems to reflect directly on one of Wladek's personal characteristics. Only evil fights with evil. Good is not a part of this struggle. It is rather a spirit, or a shadow both connected with existence and separated from it. As I said before, I never considered Wladek an evil man. I am convinced that apart from his intelligence he also possessed certain positive qualities of the heart. There is a kind of person who can be good to his parents, children, cats, who has all the right reflexes, but who lacks principles. Through his whole life Wladek was looking for intellectual arguments to justify not his evil but the weakness of his good element, which was not organized into principles and was unable to fight for itself. Such a deficiency—the sense of one's own wretchedness—can subvert ambition and weaken self-respect. Wladek was looking for an idea that would substitute for his self-respect.

I understood all this during our conversation in the park. When he saw me standing near the pond, he quickened his pace, and then immediately began to protest that he did not wish to and was unable to exculpate himself. This was not true. He both wished and was able to. For two hours he explained the role he played in my case, and proved he had taken the best, the most logical path. Yet he never asked whether *I* had any choice. I did not reproach him, I remained silent, almost indifferent. In fact, I felt rather embarrassed. Even today there are no conventional rules of conduct to be appealed to on such occasions for men with all experiences, and that is why our meeting in the park took such an uneasy course. Besides, Wladek had an equal right to hold a grudge against me: after all, it was I who implicated him in Rondo's activities, and my arrest was not his fault.

I was arrested by accident. The summer was hot and I sent Tola with Miss Lala to Bukovina. My own vacation was not to start until August. One Sunday in July I went to the beach on the Vistula. The beach was crowded, and after an hour of frying in the sun I decided to return to the city. On my way to the bus stop I realized that the two elderly ladies who rented to my father in Zoliborz (their house was later burned) lived less than a mile away. Two years earlier they had buried their deaf-mute brother. For a long time I had been planning to visit them. They were living in a rented room in a one-story house near the road to Miedzeszyn. As soon as I pressed the button at the front gate I heard a buzzing sound. The door to the house had been left ajar. When I stepped in, it closed behind me. As soon as I was inside, my documents were checked. It was a quarter to twelve. Fifty-five months later, I returned home at exactly the same hour.

During the first stage of the investigation I was accused of membership in an illegal religious sect. Rondo surfaced only later, during interrogations. The old ladies testified I was never a member of their association or a follower of their creed. They were trying to present me in the best possible light, and they went too far: they said that during the war I headed an underground organization that fought against the Germans. They must have mentioned the names of my friends quite early on, because questions about Wladek Sznej started to appear as early as the third interrogation. Wladek often accompanied me to Zoliborz, and in my father's absence we used his room for organizational meetings. Perhaps we talked too loud? The other rooms were usually completely silent. It seemed nobody was there.

I am not sure, therefore, who should blame whom. First of all, I am not sure whether the word "blame" is appropriate here.

Everything I say is factually correct. Of course, I have departed—quite far, that's true—from my initial intention. My polemic with Professor Janota has turned into a wordy autobiography. Perhaps the need to reminisce has been with me for a long time? I can assure you, though, that I am not trying to erect a monument to myself. All I am trying to do is to present a part of the truth about myself—the part that is accessible to me today. If I occasionally become too garrulous, you shouldn't blame it on my narrative style. I would rather stand accused of moral exhibitionism than restrain myself with an eye on the possible consequences of my loquacity. Wiaremko used to say, "A wise man knows what he says. A foolish man says what he knows." On these pages I am not trying to be a wise man. I say what I know. What is more, if I didn't say certain things, I would feel wrong. If I kept quiet about my infidelities with Nina, or Tola's night with Cezar, I would feel as dishonest as if I were trying to hide some shameful secret of public importance.

All this is quite crucial to me. If I decide to write about myself at all, the truths one usually conceals become twice as important. These truths are concealed especially today, and especially if they are related to the war. These years have petrified into monuments of martyrdom. A certain style of remembering has developed with respect to them, one that irritates me personally, and which is visible also in "A Chapter in the History of Struggle." Did Professor Janota spend the whole occupation as an activist in the resistance? Let's assume that he did. Apart from his military activities, however, he must have lived in his own psychological underground, his intimate life full of inborn imperfections such as selfishness, vanity, ambition. Was he really nothing but a warrior burning with the desire to fight? Didn't he ever break down, quarrel, suspect somebody? Dear God, I'd say I doubt . . .

After Rabczyn's death I was taken over by Straga. My colleague from the military college had eventually left me his studio in Madalinskiego Street and went to work as manager of a sugar mill in one of the industrialized country estates near Radomsko. One day Straga appeared at my door at seven in the morning just I was finishing shaving. As I was putting a jacket over my pajamas, I registered the fleeting glance with which he inspected my chest. He sat on my unmade bed and waited until I got dressed. The terms of our relationship had been established at that very first meeting. I think that Straga rated me as a thoroughbred bridge player. I, in turn, was sure I had before me a cold-blooded gambler. What was striking about Straga was, first of all, the calm, mocking expression in his eyes with which he scrutinized whoever he was talking to. He liked to bluff. On several occasions, I caught a glitter of willful bravura in his eyes—a cool, bright shining—and I was sure he would not accept me until he knew the limits of my psychological endurance.

First, he briefed me on technical and organizational matters. Some contact points had been lost, among them the mocha bakeshop. I had to memorize several new addresses and the pseudonyms of our new liaison as well as a password she used. All this took us about half an hour. Straga displayed the competence of an intelligent professional, but also the nonchalance of a man of the world. I must say I liked that. There was nothing solemn about him. He spoke lightly and without undue emphasis. He never repeated himself. I was also pleased by his style of dress: sport shoes, tie, loose tweed jacket—nothing that would smack of the military. Only the sinews in his calves and wrists betrayed a cavalryman. A staff officer, I guessed after a moment.

After half an hour Straga changed the subject and asked whether it was true that I used to act before the war. We spoke of the Melpomena: Did I think that Rabczyn might have been watched by somebody when he met me there? Did anybody from the staff live on Wolska Street at that time? Of course, I didn't have any precise answers, yet the direction of his questions made me think. Apparently there was a full investigation concerning Rabczyn's apartment. While reaching for his hat Straga smiled in a slightly impertinent way. "Still, I would never take you for an actor. An officer . . . maybe, but never an actor." "You are absolutely right," I said. "I'm not an actor, and before the war I was an officer of the reserve."

In September, Straga conducted a famous operation at the Cooperative Agrarian Credit Union. I took an active part in it, although my weapon remained in my pocket. The Union was on Kredytowa Street, not far from Malachowski Square. At eight o'clock in the morning Straga and three other men entered the cashier's department on the second floor. At that time of day there were usually only a few customers in that section. The whole operation took less than ten minutes, and the bank was relieved of seven million zlotys. At eight o'clock I saw Straga enter the building accompanied by a man in a German uniform. He was dressed in a long black leather coat and a Tyrolean hat. When I followed them, I was overtaken by two other men who ran up the stairs. One of them was wearing a greenish uniform with the SS insignia, if I remember rightly. Before entering the cashier's department Straga put his hand on the brass doorknob and looked at me in a joyful, slightly cocky manner. He nodded his head and gently pushed the door open. My task was to see that nobody left the floor during the operation. If somebody tried to come in, I was supposed to let him through and then poke my gun in his back. If I encountered any Germans I was to disarm them. I was allowed to shoot only as a last resort. Luckily nobody tried to leave or come in. I stood for several moments between an alabaster balustrade and the heavy oak door. Now and again I would look at my watch. I kept my right hand in the pocket of my wool jacket. (I had a round pin with a swastika in my lapel.) Finally Straga left the bank followed by the two uniformed men, who carried canvas bags with metal rims. The third man locked the door. As we climbed down the stairs Straga looked at me again, and snapped his silver cigarette case under my nose. He probably wanted to see if my hands were shaking. I thanked him and lit my pipe. There was a gray Volkswagen with Wehrmacht registration waiting outside the building. The uniformed men threw the bags inside. Straga took the front seat. I took off my pin and walked toward Marszalkowska Street.

I describe this in detail to illustrate one thing. During the operation I kept looking at my watch. The reason for my nervousness was the expected arrival of a Jadwiga riverboat that was about to dock at a landing on the Vistula. It was important for me to meet the boat and to see whether Tola had returned safely from her trip. I worried each time I sent her out with the codes because I could not anticipate her behavior in the case of a roundup or luggage search. Until that day she traveled by train, which was exhausting, and after each trip she looked haggard. Besides, the Germans had begun frequent roundups on the trains and in the station. They were looking for smugglers, both men and women. After the operation I was to report to an apartment on Lwowska Street and deposit my weapon. I was worried that the operation would last longer than planned, and I did not know whether I would be dismissed immediately so that I could be at the landing at ten. While I stood at the door in the bank I wasn't afraid of the danger. I was afraid of unexpected complications. That is why I kept looking at my watch.

At the beginning my obscure remarks did not pose any serious problems. I informed Tola that she would be working for an intelligence and reconnaissance unit, Rondo, which was subordinate only to the Supreme Command. Because of the importance of the organization's tasks, she would have to observe a strict code of secrecy. About two weeks after receiving her oath I started to send her out to the provinces—each time to a different town—with a suitcase full of old books. In Krakow or Lublin she would leave the suitcase in the checkroom, and mail the receipt poste restante to a nonexistent recipient. Having fulfilled her mission, she would take the next train home. I usually chose dates when she had a day off and did not have to go to the Melpomena. I hammered into her head the basic rules of conspiracy, including personal appearance. First of all, never stand out in a crowd. I forbade her to use makeup (from time to time she would still shave or blacken her brows) and warned her about casual acquaintances. I also gave her instructions in case of a luggage search: Say that the books are meant for sale. They were mostly detective stories in various languages. At the same time I hinted that they contained coded reports which could be revealed only by chemical methods. I let her guess the rest: the reports contained Rondo's intelligence, which would be transported by various routes to London. Thus I fulfilled Tola's deepest desires while at the same time maintaining perfect security. Still, I couldn't get enough suitcases. My friends, whom I repeatedly tricked out of their old cardboard pieces, were certain I was smuggling lard. Besides, Tola wasn't always absentminded. Sometimes she could be unusually perceptive. I had to be a careful stage director and maintain the illusion that my fictitious network really existed. At first the task didn't seem too difficult. The familiar rickshaw driver from Under the Eagles Square would bring a suitcase to my apartment in Madalinskiego Street. Tola usually came over a bit earlier. Everything took place in silence. We called it "delivery of the goods." Later I would send Tola with the suitcase to the station. She was accompanied—without knowing it—by one of the Borowik brothers, who were to serve as her bodyguards and, in case of a problem, act according to a prearranged plan.

After some time I realized that one suitcase would be quite enough. One of the Borowiks—Jerzy or Andrzej—would take it to city X, leave it in the station, and mail the receipt. Tola would later travel to the same city, report at poste restante, collect the suitcase, and bring it back to Warsaw. It was a closed circuit. Depending on the direction of the journey the suitcase would change its contents: old newspapers, *The Mystery of the Yellow Room*, *The Hound of the Baskervilles*. They would travel one way as Rondo's reports, and the other as materials sent by the Supreme Command.

I have mentioned the perfect security of the operation. Of course, in those days there was no such thing as perfect security. Sending a young woman with a suitcase by train could always entail the unexpected. In case of an arrest or confiscation of her luggage, I had instructed Tola to stay calm and never try to resist or escape. I explained that confiscation wouldn't be a great disaster. Discovering the codes hidden between the lines required complicated chemical reagents. The books looked quite innocent, and it was really hard to imagine the Germans testing them chemically.

She returned from her first trip radiant, almost euphoric. I remember the whole day well—until the very evening. It was in June. I was waiting for her at the station at noon. People were leaving the train burdened with luggage and hurrying directly to the exit. I saw her from a distance. I recognized her dark blue dress with white dots. Her summer coat was hanging over her arm. She was walking in her careless way, smoking a cigarette. When she noticed me at the end of the platform she started to wave, and during our greeting she sprinkled me with ash. Just as in October, after the capitulation, I was moved by the look of her face, washed with exhaustion, with-

out a trace of makeup. I stopped a cab to take her directly to
Topolowa. She hadn't had anything to eat since morning, and
I thought she must have been dreaming about a hot bath. But
no—she wanted to go to the Melpomena. I was a bit surprised:
this was the first time she wanted to go there with me, which
was like a public announcement that we were a couple. I did
not protest. We were driving along Szpitalna Street and Tola
was telling me about some screaming pigs she saw in a boxcar
at the station in Czestochowa. She claimed they knew where
they were going. She grabbed me by the sleeve. "Does it matter who is afraid? A pig or a man? There is only one fear!" She
wouldn't stop talking about those pigs, and then about a flood
she saw in her childhood, and cows lowing in terror. And I
heard the following sentence: "We were also terribly afraid,
only Lala was older . . ."

Obviously, the statement was quite unexpected, and I had
to give it some thought.

That summer Wiaremko opened a garden at the Melpomena.
There were some trees in the yard, and he made something
that could pass for flower beds around them. The ground was
covered with gravel. Only one table was free when we entered.
A company of some ten people were sitting right next to it in
the shade of the trees. The central place was occupied by
Cezar. Iza, with her terrier sprawled on the ground, sat beside
him. They were surrounded by a group of less famous actors.
I recognized only young Nalecz. There was also Wiaremko,
and, of course, Rena Delatynska. When we came in they did
not interrupt their conversation. All I noticed was Iza's vigilant, squinting glance. Rena waved to us from a distance and
canny Wiaremko pretended not to see us. I hesitated for a
moment, but Tola sat down without a second thought. She
turned her back to the company, and I took a place opposite
her, so that I had an unobstructed view of the next table. The
day was unusually hot, and the men had taken off their jackets.

Cezar was wearing a light blue suit and his sombrero with upturned brim. He looked bored, and he sat in silence. He looked around with a gloomy, slightly impatient absentmindedness. I never met his eyes—it is possible that he did not recognize me. I noticed, however, that he had gained some more weight. Tola and I did not talk, and I heard every word spoken at the next table. The conversation was about vacations; Iza was talking about a villa in Zakopane where she was planning to go with Cezar the following week. Rena Delatynska kept interrupting her with sycophantic admonitions: "You must rest, my darling!" Nobody paid any attention to us, and there was nothing unsettling about the whole situation. I don't remember when Tola ordered a bottle of rowanberry vodka, but soon I noticed she was drunk. After the remark about vacations she mumbled something to herself, her eyes burning. "What was that?" I asked. "You must rest, my darling!" she said in a coarse, loud voice, and started to choke. I should have taken her away immediately, since she started to look like trouble. No doubt her words could be heard at the next table. She certainly wanted to provoke a scene, and I had no idea how it might end. There was no way I could control Tola. In moments of strong emotion she was quite unyielding. I tried to move the bottle away from her, but she grabbed it with both hands and started to wrestle with me.

What happened next can be described as follows: For some time there had been rumors that the Warschauer Stadttheater was going to put on *Hamlet* (which actually never happened), and apparently the next table picked up on the subject. When Cezar started talking, Tola let go of the bottle. As Cezar spoke, he wiped his face with a white handkerchief he took from his pocket. It wasn't clear who he was talking to. I remember this method of address from his rehearsals: as if he was thinking aloud or talking to himself. I gathered he was trying to explain the scene at Yorick's grave: "Well, try to remember this . . .

there isn't really any doubt about that. 'Let Hercules himself do what he may, the cat will mew, and dog will have his day.' Do we need anything else? Isn't that enough? . . ." Cezar looked at the company in astonishment. At the same moment he spotted me. His face was in the sun, and the light was hurting his eyes. He smiled, as if seeing somebody who would finally understand him well. "But . . . but that's obvious! A simulation! Please imagine . . . He exits barking. He's gone mad! Bark, bark!" Cezar barked with his handkerchief between his teeth, looking at me all the time. It was a perfect imitation of an angry dog that backs off baring its teeth. Iza's terrier jumped to its feet.

Why am I describing that scene? Because I remember it as clearly and physically as if each detail had some special significance. Perhaps it had. It's strange, but some of the events were repeated later under different circumstances. Cezar's idea was a premonition of his last performance. It may sound odd, but some of my thoughts at that time also seemed to anticipate events that took place months later. The thought about poison, for example. At a certain point I realized why Tola wanted to come here directly from the station. She was enjoying the possibility of playing a role. She identified with her role of courier, a young woman working for the intelligence, who after an important mission blends in with the crowd, with the colorful common crowd, and drinks in a pub with her boss just like any other flirting girl. I am sure it gave her great pleasure. It was just what she wished for—something special and refined. For her, conspiracy was an aristocratic perversion. All she lacked was a hidden poison, and it occurred to me that if I really wanted to please her, I should offer her a ring filled with cyanide. As soon as I thought about it, I was seized by anxiety. Considering the events that took place later, my thoughts and my anxiety were almost a kind of psychic phenomenon.

We stayed in the garden for about an hour. Cezar was the

first to get up. During his monologue about Hamlet I could not help but notice Iza's indulgent smile and the way she surveyed the company. I was irritated for a moment. Her smile was an expression both of tolerance and of her power over Cezar— a confidential and triumphant half—smile that enabled all present to participate in Cezar's amusing peculiarity: "You see, one has to allow him certain things. He isn't normal. I give him theater as a harmless drug. Besides, he'll do everything I want." Iza Rajewska knew what she wanted. Not only did she know that but she was convinced that everybody wanted the same: money and influence. This did not include Cezar, and she knew that too. I still wonder whether she loved him. Was there any deviation from, any exception to her meanness? I reach the conclusion that she did love him. She loved him as a patient, as someone terminally ill. Perhaps it was the only inconsistency in her life.

Cezar stood up. Perhaps he was feeling lonely since no one had reacted to his deliberations and the company had begun to talk about other things. Wiaremko also rose from his chair, as if ready to help him, or see him off. Cezar suddenly stopped at our table. He forbade any greetings, in a friendly way—and then for a moment he simply stared at Tola. He seemed to be trying to remember something. "My child," he mumbled, "you didn't sit with us . . . How sad." Tola raised her head—all the blood had run from her face. Cezar stood there brooding. He suddenly leaned in my direction and put his hand on my shoulder. "Wonderful," he said. "Just wonderful."

It was hard to guess what he meant. The summer weather? My appearance? Me and Tola? Probably all that and more: life, war, theater . . . himself. We didn't stay long after his departure. An acquaintance came up to talk, we exchanged a few pleasantries, and then Tola whispered that she wanted to go home. We took a rickshaw and we didn't talk on the way. Only when we reached Nowowiejska Street did I venture to ask if I understood her story about the flood correctly, and whether she had really known Lala Ubycz that long. She shook her shoulders. "What do you mean? Don't you know Lala is my sister?"

I didn't. She had never told me.

What kind of man, one might ask, has no other problems in the fourth year of war than psychological complications with women! I accept the charge and I am fully aware of its seriousness. When compared with the universal plague of those years, with the amount of suffering, the number of victims, the anguish of millions, each individual problem becomes ludicrous and unimportant. Yet one has to remember that this exactly was my life, and in those days we defended ourselves primarily by living—I could even say by producing life in a personal, individual way. If one gave up the personal sphere of existence, the last barrier against insanity would fall. I have heard it said that a society that lives in slavery is populated by demented people. As they lose the awareness of their abnormalities, absorbed as they are by their everyday striving, their dementia deepens. In my opinion the opposite is true. If slavery is murder committed on life, then everything that constitutes life's personal aspect—each individual thought, will, motion—becomes an antidote for psychological death. What is life, after all, if not a process of overcoming slavery—the slavery of absurdity and death? National or social slavery is perhaps only the explicit and brutal demonstration of this truth. There is no other defense but solemn continuation of one's existence, even if it requires the assumption of a freedom and immortality which borders on the abnormal. Therefore I had in those days a kind of instinctive philosophy of self-confirmation, and this philosophy was forged together through small but powerful bonds with the existence of several other people. This was the source of my endurance: my laboriously built honeycomb. Everything that took place within its limits was my primary and most important reality; yes, even when bombs fell and people were killed. When I remember these years today I do not think about martyrdom and extinction, but about a few familiar faces: Tola, Nina, Wladek Sznej, Cezar, Lala Ubycz . . . And isn't such a collection of faces sufficient material for one's life?

I talked to Lala Ubycz the day before the operation at the Credit Union.

The previous day I had sent Tola with a suitcase to Lublin. She had to take a boat to Pulawy and catch a train there. She was to follow the same route on her way back. She was guarded by Andrzej Borowik, the younger of the brothers, a poet and a student of history. I was calm, but I realized that the operation at the bank was a rather risky business. There was a possibility I might not return. Just in case, I decided to inform Miss Lala. If anything went wrong she would be alone: Tola, Nina Willman, and her mother—she would have to take care of them all. I spoke in a measured way, trying to be as precise as possible. The conversation was short, but I had the impression that Miss Lala dozed off. Finally I stopped talking. Perhaps I had frightened her with the details. She looked like a bird hiding its head in its plumage. After a moment she lit a cigarette. "Nothing will happen to you." "Thank you," I replied, laughing, "but nobody can guarantee that. All kinds of things are possible. I've heard some people even die . . ." Miss Lala looked at me solemnly. "You will not die," she said, almost reproachfully, and I must admit I was quite astonished. "What do you mean? I'll never die?" Miss Lala shook her head. "I am not sure about that. You are going to live as long as is needed." I must have looked quite uncertain. I noticed a bright glimmer in Miss Lala's eyes. "You know very well," she said. "Everything is as you wanted it to be, and that's how it will be in the future."

What was that supposed to be, a prophecy . . . ? It was hard to make anything of her vague remarks, yet I felt they were based on a prolonged, analytic observation. I was embarrassed. "Yes, I am her sister," she added. "Did she tell you anything else?"

Anything else? About what?! It was all too confusing. I could not guess at that time that Miss Lala was speaking about someone close to me, who was just reentering my life.

I mentioned an acquaintance who had sat for a moment at our table, though I hadn't said his name. He was a man I didn't think about too much. His name was Kozlowiec— Witold Kozlowiec. I remembered him from my time at the Melpomena. He was one of the regulars. Before the war he worked as a journalist. Rabczyn informed me that Kozlowiec was a member of Thought and Action and he played a prominent role in one of its factional splits—quite a frequent occurrence in that organization. I suspect that he was the person who recruited Tola for his underground group. His company didn't give me much pleasure, and I was irritated by his affectation of a brooding idealism. Kozlowiec approached us in order to pass me a message from Wladek Sznej, who seemed to have been asking about me for some time. He had married and moved back to Warsaw. Kozlowiec gave me his address.

I saw Wladek a couple of days later. He had just moved into two unfurnished rooms in Swietojerska Street. When I came in, he and his janitor were moving a wardrobe with a warped door. Our greeting was cordial, and Wladek immediately brought up our conversation in the countryside six weeks earlier. He reached into a still unpacked bag full of honey jars and various junk, and produced a folder containing a manuscript. He explained that it was the promised report. It was meant for internal use, but he wanted me to read it right away. He warned me that his work had grown, both in length and in scope, far beyond the original intention, and asked me to pay special attention to his conclusions. However, Wladek Sznej wouldn't be himself if he didn't summarize right away the main idea of his report. As a result, I didn't need to read it at all.

It is important to say something about that study. First, however, I have to point out that I had never seen him so captivated, almost possessed by his own thoughts. His message, as well as the way he presented it, was truly impressive. He was pacing the room, from the window to the door, stopping in front of me only to provide a footnote whenever he was struck by some important digression. I was sitting on a package of books, and I never uttered so much as a single word. I felt Wladek did not expect any comments. He was totally consumed by his own thoughts. Of course, I will not be able to present his line of reasoning in detail. The best I can hope for is an approximate outline.

Wladek's main thesis rested on the assumption that the coming epoch—the postwar decades—would effect the triumph of the masses, especially peasants. These homogenized masses, aware of their power, would diminish the importance of the individual, with his old, humanistic notions. Wladek claimed there was absolutely no doubt on this point. The civilized mob—as he put it—would be the motor of history. Civilized, because after the war we were to get American loans and would buy American machines. The peasants were waiting for this. They had seen the young German *Bauern* on motorcycles and in tanks: the uniformed and mechanized mass, which also happened to be well fed. They knew that this was their future. Such problems as totalitarianism or democracy, the parliamentary or single-party system, these did not concern the peasants in the least. The peasants thought of and wished for only one thing—to become equal with the city. "Don't worry," Wladek reassured me, "it'll happen without an ax and a scythe. It is already happening . . ." He went on to demonstrate that the occupation, with its black market, illegal slaughter of livestock, and smuggling, gave the peasant masses a sense of their role as providers. Without their lard and pork, the cities would starve to death. After the war, in Wladek's opinion, the country would present its bill, and wouldn't permit itself to be sent off with just anything. The process of compensation would involve an objective identification of the social reality of the village with that of the whole nation. Such a process, inevitable as it was, would overturn prewar social relations. What, therefore, are our historical chances? Shall we allow ourselves to be cast overboard, or shall we prove able to join in? By "us" Wladek meant the spiritual elite of the country, the social group of greatest awareness, the Polish intelligentsia.

It is hard to imagine circumstances that Wladek would find inappropriate for the extensive presentation of his ideas. I liked him for that. My visit was obviously untimely, and he could have easily excused himself and invited me to return another day, but that was out of the question. Wladek was obviously glad about my visit. He did not feel embarrassed to be caught in torn shorts and with a windbreaker thrown over his naked chest, or by the fact that he did not even have a chair to put me in. Such details never really bothered him. He did not seem to notice them, absorbed as he was in the reality of his thought. I suspect he thought around the clock: while walking, eating, even in his sleep, not to mention during so simple a task as moving a wardrobe. When I came in, all he had to do was turn on his voice to engage his perpetual thought machine.

I stayed there for over an hour. Before I left I assured him his report would reach the appropriate persons and would be thoroughly analyzed. I advised him to sign it with a pseudonym. He did so and handed me the folder, which I passed to Straga on the first possible occasion. I did not see Wladek for several weeks, until the robbery at the Credit Union. I almost bumped into him as I was walking toward Marszalkowska, while Straga and his men were getting into the car. He must have seen us leaving the building. He said he was going to the Credit Union to ask about some payments on an equity loan held by his wife's family. It wouldn't take long, he insisted, and afterward we could go somewhere and have a cup of coffee. "Don't you think," he remarked, "they owe me an answer?" Without a word, I grabbed him by the arm and pushed him forward with all my strength. Wladek resisted, and we had something of a tussle. He took it as a joke, and giggled. "Leave me alone, I've no time for foolishness." Suddenly something dawned on him. "A roundup?" "Robbery," I hissed. "They're going to blockade the streets any moment now." Wladek stared. I convinced him to go home, and he quickly departed in the opposite direction.

I deposited my gun on Lwowska Street, and at ten o'clock I was at the landing. Tola and I spent the rest of the day playing cards with Nina. Straga visited me a week later, around seven in the morning as usual. For the first fifteen minutes he told me prewar cavalry jokes. Then he mentioned casually that the operation had been carried out without casualties. "By the way, Tom, do you know we are already legendary? People say the robbery was the work of a reserve organization for national defense and that the Marshal's son was involved. God knows who conceived such nonsense. Everybody knows the Marshal had no son, only two daughters. Both, by the way, are now in London . . ."

The day after Straga's visit was my father's name day. It was raining when I went to Zoliborz to give him my regards. As I was taking off my coat, I noticed a number of other coats, all soaking wet, hanging in the hallway. I left my umbrella open in the corner. Through the door I could hear Wladek's piercing voice. I didn't expect to find him there. A married couple—teachers, my father's friends—were also there. While Wanda was offering me some berry-flavored vodka, Wladek turned to my father to explain his criticism of the policy of the Polish government before 1939. He described it as "foolish incompetence."

My father was tired. I usually recognized it by a stillness in his eyes. When he was tired his neck and shoulders stiffened, and his pince-nez seemed to freeze and to lose its transparency. He seemed to be listening to Wladek attentively, but it was difficult to make out the expression around his eyes: his brows rose slightly above the rims, which meant he had resolved to keep his opinion to himself. I felt he was offended by some impropriety in Wladek's eloquence. Perhaps he thought this matter merited less assertiveness, a meditative tone rather than a lecturing one, if it were to be mentioned in a social situation at all. He spoke only once. When Wladek addressed him again with his usual "I hope you agree with me, Professor," my father answered in a subdued voice, "You are talking about serious matters, Mr. Sznej." But "talkativus" did not seem to take these words for a delicate reproach, and maybe even saw them as approval. But I was moved by the form in which my father addressed Wladek. I remembered that in the last year of high school, usually after the New Year, he would start to call each of us "Mr." At first we took it for irony, especially when he turned his glasses toward one of us at the blackboard and asked, "What could you tell us, Mr. Sznej, about November 11, 1918?" Such words provoked a giggle from the classroom. Later, however, we got used to the fact that my father called us "Mr." and that he was the first to tip his hat when he saw one of us in the street with a girlfriend. And he did it now to someone he had sent not long ago to the corner for "notorious talking in the classroom."

Nobody took up the subject with Wladek. After the married couple had left, we started to talk about acquaintances from before the war. I learned that Mr. Kummel had died a month ago. I had last seen him on a streetcar when I was going to Praga. "He joined the majority," my father said. He often stressed that there are always more dead than living and that compared with the crowd of the departed we are only a noisy minority.

The conversation was faltering. Wladek grew silent. I sensed we would have to leave together, though I'd rather have avoided the possibility. When we got on the streetcar I decided I wouldn't be the first to speak. The car was almost empty and I was standing on the back platform. Wladek immediately attacked me, demanding to be put in touch with the command. I said it was out of the question for the time being and advised him to be patient. He was far from satisfied. He was excited and began to reproach me loudly for being disloyal to him. He claimed I was trying to isolate him from the rest of the organization. I stiffened when he used the name Rondo. "I don't know what you are talking about," I managed to say. "You know very well," said Wladek. "Reserve Organization for National Defense. Rondo is an acronym. Who would know this better than yourself?"

I would be guilty of misrepresentation if I said I slept well that night.

Many years after the war Straga told me that as we worked together in the underground I always seemed somehow distracted. "As if you were thinking about something else." He was absolutely right. Working for the underground was only one-third of my existence. The other two-thirds were divided between art dealing and Rondo.

I had to pay all expenses out of my own pocket. Even if I limited myself to bare subsistence, I would not have enough money to finance the transfer of Rondo's reports (return tickets, meals, etc.). Besides I had to keep up appearances, as if the funds at my disposal exceeded my expenses. I couldn't allow myself to be caught scratching for the last penny to pay for my coffee.

I often had lunch at the Hare (on the corner of Tamka and Dobra), where one could get a decent and inexpensive meal. One day I was approached by a short, florid gentleman with greased hair who sat at my table and introduced himself: "Janski." He asked if I was interested in art. Before I was able to say anything, he dropped the name of Lala Ubycz. Ten minutes later we were riding a rickshaw to Natolinska Street. When we stopped in front of the doorway of an imposing house, he handed me a square object wrapped in paper and explained: "Ice Floe in Spring." When we reached the second floor he showed me a brass nameplate and muttered, "Ersatz honey."

Within half an hour we had sold a small landscape by Falat depicting a river in early spring. As we descended the stairs, Janski paid me a ten percent commission and asked me not to shave off my mustache.

From that day on we worked together. Before the war Janski had been a butler at the residence of a retired ambassador, a collector and connoisseur of art. After his death, Janski started dealing in paintings by Polish masters. During the occupation Warsaw had several galleries and a number of independent dealers. Some of them were prewar collectors. Janski was one of them. To be more precise, he tried to be one of them. Many social barriers fell during the war, but despite that fact, or perhaps because of it, the new customers attached great importance to the origin of the artifacts they purchased. An art object that was a cherished family heirloom, with a patina of tradition, possessed a double value. Producers of ersatz food who were buying landscapes by Falat or Chelmonski wanted to be sure that a week earlier the Chelmonski or Falat had adorned some wealthy estate in the Kutnow district. Janski's manners and appearance hardly met these expectations. He did not inspire much confidence even when he appeared in a bowler hat and a coat with a mink collar. His very features made people think of forgery. He must have been aware of that. A shrewd man, he realized after our first transaction that I might be useful after all.

I affected the demeanor of a young country gentleman come to Warsaw to sell a family treasure. Janski believed that my stature, my mustache, and my tweed jacket made just the right impression. He took care of the rest. My task was rather simple, and it agreed with my natural temperament. When a transaction was being finalized I hardly spoke a word. Only when a customer tried to get a better deal did I become involved. "I'm sorry, but I'm not in the habit of bargaining," I would say, and then I would empty my pipe and begin to leave. At that moment the customer usually gave in. Janski seemed to be impressed by my composure. In any case, he was pleased with my performance, and on one occasion he said, "If the late ambassador were alive, he would like you." Our partnership brought irregular but ever-improving income, and our mutual relations became somehow taken for granted. (After the attempt on my life, when I had to change my appearance, Janski gave me a jar of his black bandoline.)

Yet I could not appear in my new role too openly. It was, in a sense, the third level of my clandestine activities. I preferred not to imagine Straga's reaction had he learned that a day after an underground meeting I was riding a rickshaw with a strange-looking man with greased hair carrying a cloth-wrapped artifact. I remember that on October 3 I was in charge of security during a prolonged secret meeting in a safe house in Wisniowa Street and on the fourth of the same month I was riding in an open horse cab through the center of the city carrying Axentowicz's "Gypsy Woman." If someone from Straga's guard had spotted me then, there would have been no time for joking.

I never thought about such prospects, though. I needed money for Rondo and I was increasingly worried about Tola. I was worried she might have learned about my partnership with Janski. I could imagine her look and her voice: "Well, so you are a dealer, then . . . you buy, you sell." The very thought of such a discovery collapsed the little theater I had built for her out of marked cards. On a day's notice I would have to cancel all performances. "Why do you need these sunglasses? There is no sun today," wondered Janski. By coincidence it happened just the other way around. Tola did not see me with Janski and "Gypsy Woman." I saw Tola. She was getting on a streetcar on the corner of Krolewska and Krakowskie Przedmiescie accompanied by Wladek Sznej.

It was then, I guess, that I realized matters were taking a new turn. Shortly afterward—less than a month after my father's name day—Wladek was admitted to Rondo with my consent, although against my will. One could ask how that was possible if everything in fact depended on me. That, however, was only in appearance. In reality very little depended on me.

During his trial in 1951, Straga was asked by the prosecutor (he told me the story six years later) whether he ever heard about a unit called Reserve Organization for National Defense. "Yes, there was talk about something like that," he answered. "But I personally considered it bunk." The prosecutor insisted: "Therefore the accused confirms there were rumors that such an organization existed?" Straga tried to duck the question: "Well, there were. There were all kinds of interesting rumors at that time." "At that time" meant the fall of 1942. As early as September of that year I started to hear them myself from various sources and in several different variations, mostly in connection with the famous robbery at the Cooperative Agrarian Credit Union. On several occasions the alleged involvement of the "Marshal's son" was also mentioned.

For the first time I started to perceive the supposition about my origin as something out of control and dangerous. How many people did it reach over the years? How many people could remember it now and connect it with the wild stories afloat in the city? Gossip plagued me since my childhood, and yet it would be unfair to say it ruined my life. In fact, it saved my life at a time when I had already given up. How many people knew it? Twenty? A hundred? Two hundred? I counted on my fingers: schoolmates, actors . . . It was pointless to go on. Numbers had no significance. One person would be enough— someone who met me only once and overheard somebody whisper it to somebody else. Such a person could be found anywhere. It could be someone I knew or a total stranger. I remembered the musical evening at the Rylskis' and the discreet commotion I provoked there. Discreet—yet I was certainly the subject of many conversations, and not only on this one occasion. During each visit at the Rylskis' I sensed a special, subtle distinction surrounding my person: something like respect for my incognito with a touch of caution to keep me unaware of their awareness. Only Selim broke with the convention. On one occasion he invited me to his study downstairs and remarked without preamble, "And he once called me an ass! It happened during a tea in the Belvedere. I wasn't among those present, but the story reached me anyway. He was angry because I had turned down the portfolio. You know, all strong men are childishly sensitive about such things. Apparently he remembered that affront until his death! When he gave up running the country, and just sat day after day staring into the fire in his fireplace, his aide often heard him mutter my name followed by a highly disagreeable invective!"

Selim, who knew my mother before World War I, must have heard the gossip about my parentage. I took the whole story for a mere invention. But even if I had had proof, or certainty, which I didn't at that time (I learned the truth only in 1962, during my brief visit in Krakow), I wouldn't have been able to dispel the gossip. And even if such a desperate idea had visited my mind, I wouldn't have known where to begin. The legend lived outside me, it was breathing down my neck, and the only person ever to speak it to my face was Wladek Sznej. It was at school, during a recess, fifteen years before! . . . Since that time not a single word passed between us on that subject, and it was only my guess that he shared his "knowledge" with Tola before our dinner at the Savoy. In more secure times before the war, one could take such fame lightly—but now? All it took was a single denunciation.

All kinds of scenarios were going through my head, and I tried to put them together in a logical sequence: Wladek meets me in front of the Credit Union right after the operation, which, a day later, would be a subject of detailed descriptions floating around town. He sees me leave the building with the others. A week later Straga reports the gossip about the "Marshal's son." I meet Wladek again at my father's name-day party. On our way back he tells me on a streetcar about an underground unit, the name of which forms the acronym Rondo.

In all that confusion of real facts, made-up names, and non-existent figures, one thing was really puzzling: who leaked Rondo's name and how?

A streetcar was overtaking the cab Janski and I were riding in, and started to slow down at a stop. At the same time I noticed Tola and Wladek stepping down from the car. Our cab was also slowing down. I shifted the painting to cover my face. Within the few seconds that elapsed I managed, however, to take in the whole scene: the church of the Sisters of the Visitation, the small crowd of people getting on the second car, Tola's unexpected profile, Wladek's grizzly hat, and two German airmen jumping from the front platform. What struck me about the scene was the fact that the couple were walking hand in hand without a smile and without talking to each other—not as two acquaintances who met for the first time after many years, but as friends who have been meeting frequently and for a long time.

I could have asked her that very evening, or the next day, how long she had been seeing Wladek. Such a question, however, would only provoke an angry outburst: she would have scolded me for offending her with my lack of trust in her, or for depriving her of her freedom. In the end, I would have to apologize and explain myself. I decided to wait. I knew that sooner or later some circumstances would confirm or dispel my suspicions. I was quite right. It happened on the day when I came to Tola's place to discuss her next trip. I was increasingly worried about her strength. Some changes had to be made. The riverboats were extremely slow and irregular. Trains were much less of a problem, but I was disturbed by the reports I was getting from Andrzej Borowik. On some routes Tola was already well known and passengers recognized her. Borowik noticed several characters who were clearly interested in her, and he had to chase one of them away. I had to invent more intricate itineraries with more transfers and trains departing at different hours. Having studied the train schedule, I drew up a detailed plan to send her from Warsaw to Krakow and then to Lvov.

That evening I planned to leave early, but she insisted I stay for tea. She said she was expecting somebody. I assumed an expression of bland politeness, but she replied in a rather casual tone, "But he is a very good friend of yours, you'll be glad to meet him, you'll see . . ." She looked at me with her bright, owlish eyes. I thought I wasn't so sure I would be glad. Just then the bell rang, and Tola went to open the door.

What happened next was quite unexpected. I mean not only Wladek's behavior—he greeted me with total naturalness, as if we had seen each other the day before—but a surprising turn in our conversation which led me right into the trap. At first, however, I didn't see the pitfall. We talked about the slowing down of the German offensive in the East and about recent deportations to the concentration camps. Wladek was very attentive, and I had the impression he had forgotten about his grudges. While discussing the situation at the fronts he addressed his remarks mostly to me. But my attention was captivated by something else: the way Tola listened to him. She fixed on him with famished admiration, the way she had listened to me a couple of months earlier when we were lying on her bed and I was explaining her role as my courier. I couldn't help noticing. Resting on her elbows, she stared at Wladek from beneath her disordered bangs, which she kept brushing away from her forehead. Her lips moved silently, as if she was learning his every sentence by heart. Was it a role played for my benefit? The thought passed through my mind.

Before I had a chance to answer myself, Wladek said, "We have to think about new forms of activity." These words made me wary. But of course! Wladek was talking about Rondo! And he was talking about it as if he were a member. I realized it with full clarity when he tendered his project of "citizens' circles," which, he explained, could act as local chapters of Rondo. He withstood my gaze, and shifted his eyes to Tola: "Or at least as nuclei of such chapters."

I understood that I was faced with a fait accompli. Wladek was already a member of Rondo. If I rejected him now, I would have both of them against me, and Rondo would cease to exist, or would exist without me. I had a second to calculate my odds. Should I admit Rondo was a fiction? I would lose Tola. She would never forgive me. Should I tell Wladek the truth, but keep it a secret from her? Then I would have to put him in touch with Straga, and I'd never be certain what Straga would hear from him about my "private" underground. An investigation, at best demotion and discharge.

"Yes," I said. "It is a good idea. I shall pass it on to my superiors."

"Will you receive his oath?!" cried Tola.

I explained with a smile that just the day before I had already received authorization to do so.

*

A dental metaphor comes to my mind. Last month I noticed that one of my upper molars was loose, and I went to see my dentist. The prospects were rather grim. I would inevitably lose the tooth, because the opposite molar in my lower jaw had been missing for quite a long time. "This one will have to go too," said my bespectacled lady dentist. "It lacks an adversary."

I keep thinking that Wladek Sznej's role in my life was that of necessary antagonist. I came to know many features of my character, and even my general attitude toward life, through constant struggle against the assault of his intelligence. This struggle did not always take the form of a discussion or quarrel. My reactions were usually delayed. My critical position surfaced after a period of anxiety. That's how it often was. Who knows, perhaps Wladek's intellectual onslaught provoked my healthy resistance. Now this salutary antinomy entered the ranks of Rondo.

If I remember correctly, I have already remarked here that there are always people who change much more easily than we do, and this phenomenon accounts for the major difference between us and them. We see a sudden change in somebody's outlook as treasonous, but after a time our views change too. It often turns out in the end that we cover a route similar to those whose inconstancy we had condemned only a year ago. And yet we are convinced this one year represents something more than a simple shift in time. Doesn't it mean that if we change more slowly, we also change with more difficulty, at a greater expense, and that the change in our views is even somehow painful? It involves not only intellectual but also spiritual transformations.

Wladek's metamorphoses often provoked my objections by their very facility. He was able to cross himself out without much effort, and this was something I never could learn to do.

Perhaps it is the reason why we finally came to a parting of the ways. As I have said, we met briefly during the years after my release. Once we met at the funeral of a famous poet in the Powazki Cemetery. I remember that funeral well: without a priest, with a guard of honor, with a medal borne upon a pillow. It must have been in the late fall or early winter. I went with Tola, my daughter, and Wladek caught up with us in one of the alleys. Tola was still in high school; she asked me to take her along because the deceased poet had had a reading in her school and she liked some of his poems. I also remember that Wladek, who was standing with us in the crowd, whispered something about the end of the pathetic era, and kept moving closer to me, saying that the ending was in fact quite interesting in itself. I could not figure out what he was talking about, and all I could see in front of me were the same bare heads, the same faces. Later, on a streetcar, he buttonholed me and presented his whole theory. In his opinion the departed poet closed a certain era, a period when the revolution still harked back to its romantic roots, the "blood and word" ethos, and from now on the intellectuals would be of little use to it. The intellectuals were attracted to the revolution by its social and moral postulates, the idea of social justice and the struggle against exploitation. But now these goals had been practically achieved. The coming years would witness the beginning of a new stage, which Wladek called the era of "peasant utilitarianism." In this new epoch the intellectuals would become a dispossessed class—that is, they would pay the bill for their revolutionary programs, their concepts and theories—for their utopia.

I didn't say a word. I didn't as much as open my mouth. Maybe I accepted Wladek's argument, though at the same time rejecting its value. Maybe my silence was a denial of anything that addressed me from the outside; of any truth that would encompass and define me no matter if it agreed with my inner truth, no matter if it threatened to reduce my inner truth to nothingness. At that time I was already indifferent to everything historically right, everything that strove to convince me intellectually, that had its source not inside me but somewhere else. My interest in sociopolitical trends and the evolution of civilization, which, after all, were determining my life, had substantially diminished. Apart from nature, in which I still lived, I did not have the sense of belonging to any larger whole, something more important than myself. But nature spoke in long sentences, and I understood only fragments of those words or separate sounds. Perhaps this is the reason why I become silent as I grow older.

In any case, I did not speak to Wladek on our way back from Powazki. What could I have told him? If we were heroes of a nineteenth-century novel, I would have embraced him and begged him to start believing in himself, in his own individual value, in the existence of individual human laws. "Wladek, can it really be that for you a law will always mean only a force governing human society?" I would criticize him for joining Rondo for the same reasons that made him, ten years later, join the Party: in order not to be left out of the game he called History. I would remind him that twice he spoke of an upheaval . . . And so on.

But since we were not fictitious characters from the nineteenth century, or even from ten years ago, and because his last testimony probably saved my life, because he was my father's pupil, I decided to say nothing. I am just as silent today when I meet Straga to play bridge.

Please remember, however, that on that evening at Tola's the time I am talking about was still twenty years off, and my consciousness was far less advanced. And yet I realized that events were getting out of my control. I was also hurt by Tola's comportment. On the next day, when I tried to sound her out, I met with a fierce, almost hostile reaction. She was incensed:

"Are you crazy? What do you suspect him of? What do you have against him? That he wants to be with us?" "You should have told me first," I answered calmly. She started to stammer in rage: "To t-tell you? It was you who t-told him everything. About the robbery . . ." "About the robbery?" It gave me pause. We were walking along a dark, empty street not far from her home. The pavement was covered with layers of dry leaves. "That you robbed the bank!" "Not so loud, please." I took her by the arm. After a moment I asked, "And you also told him Rondo's code name?" Her eyes became large. I noticed how surprised she was, and I started to feel sorry for her. "Well, of course"—I smiled—"you thought he already knew it, since I told him so much . . ."

I understood even more. She must have told him that Rondo answered directly to the Supreme Headquarters for National Defense in London. This piece of information must have excited him the most. He guessed the first two letters must mean Reserve Organization, and the puzzle was solved.

She came to me in the night. I reassured her that there was nothing wrong but that she should be more careful in the future. She sighed after a long silence. "You are right, Tom. I should hang myself. Why does a monster like me walk on this earth?" She was speaking in an already sleepy voice. "There is a young guy who always travels with me on the train . . . And he looks at me in such a funny way . . . And once . . ."

I bent over her. She was sound asleep.

At approximately that time I took certain steps which proved to be quite damaging later on. I am thinking about my conversation with Nina Willman. I should add right away that it was a thoroughly inappropriate and compromising conversation.

On the day Wladek Sznej appeared on Topolowa, Nina was not there. She was spending a week with her mother, who was down with the flu. Wladek and I left the apartment together, and since we still had some time before the curfew, we stood for a while at the streetcar stop and talked. Wladek tried to ease my suspicions and claimed he had no sexual interest in Tola whatsoever. Before the war, he told me, when, after only a week's acquaintance, he asked Tola to make love to him, she stared at him and said, "Isn't it enough, sir, that I give myself to you every day in my soul?" "Sir!" Wladek burst out laughing. "Can you feel the style of the epoch? Young ladies giving themselves to somebody in their souls! But in these matters I am not particularly fond of the church language: blood and flesh is blood and flesh! Eventually it came to nothing. We became just friends."

I listened abstractedly but with growing irritation. I saw my project turning into an idiocy. The whole situation was starting to get on my nerves. At that time—at least so it seems—it occurred to me I had better talk to Nina.

l did not have any plan. In a moment of self-doubt I simply needed the support of someone who knew me well and who wouldn't suspect me of wicked intentions. Nina was the person I could tell everything to. Why, then, did it all turn sour? Probably because of my own tactlessness.

She received me dressed in a light quilted gown that opened at her breasts. "You have a problem?" I felt a wave of fragrant warmth, and a strange anxiety, a different kind of pain. I suddenly lost all desire to confess and, clenching my jaws, I looked at Nina's tan décolletage which contrasted with the willow green of her gown. "Nina," I said, "I have to know everything that happens in this house." She looked at me with curiosity. "I'm asking you a favor," I said, sitting beside her on the bed. "I have to have information about people who come here."

"You mean the people who visit her?" she asked. She rose to pick up a hairbrush from a table, then sat down. "If I understand you correctly," she said while brushing her thick hair, "you conceived of the idea of my becoming your spy in the house I am hiding in—just to do you a favor? I am supposed to inform you about the acquaintances of your friend, who risked her life for me . . . Well, my congratulations. To you, and to myself." She smiled. "Your trust in me seems really unbounded."

It was strange, but I did not feel humiliated. Perhaps it was because of her voice, which sounded more hurt than contemptuous, and perhaps because of her gown, which revealed a bare knee. Only later did I scold myself silently for this unnecessary conversation.

On top of everything I had to ask myself how it was all going to end. Sometimes I had the impression I was running a scam in which I was also a victim, in which disaster was the likely outcome. If disaster threatened only myself, the thought would be less terrifying. But later, when Selim took Tola to his clinic, he proved that this was not the case. "Didn't you do something caddish to her? Well, let's put it in quotation marks and say: something that upset her too much. If you want my diagnosis, she seems unable to snap out of some profound state of astonishment." At that time Selim spared me nothing.

I am talking now about the period that came one year later, after 1943.

That year was the turning point of the war, the worst time during the whole occupation. I used to listen to the broadcasts about the Allied forces in a safe house on Lwowska Street. It was a two-room apartment that belonged to an old doctor. It had a radio receiver hidden in a double door of a kitchen cabinet. With a map spread on the floor and earphones on my head, I made notes I later passed on to Straga. The convoluted Eastern front was shaking and splitting under the blows of armored divisions. I took down the names of cities lost and won. The Allied air forces were smashing the industrial centers of the Reich. There was general anticipation of the great invasion by the Allied forces across the English Channel. After the monitoring session, the doctor, who happened to be a lady, and I drank vodka and snacked on black pudding. Later, when I was walking along Polna toward Union Square, I felt hot, and I opened my jacket despite the biting frost. I was living like a tightly wound spring. I slept soundly but not for long, I washed in cold water, and I brushed my chest and my thighs with a scrubbing brush just as I did in my student days. Every couple of days our courier, Aneta, brought me instructions from Straga. I would jump into a crowded streetcar. With each stop the car took on cold and sleepy passengers. Yellow announcements with the names of executed hostages flashed on every corner, and loudspeakers blasted arias from Viennese operettas, which I happened to know quite well—my mother used to hum them frequently in my childhood.

My whole organism, my nerves, my brain, became used to a permanent tension. I never came down with a cold or the flu, and as for boredom . . . I simply forgot such a thing existed. But loneliness . . . yes, in the evenings, after curfew, I often read books. I borrowed them from the Borowik brothers—always polite and serious fellows who treated my literary tastes with a benevolent interest, yet also with a measure of amusement. Once, with a book by Rimbaud in my pocket, and Aneta at my side, I followed an athletic man, an officer from the Arbeitsamt. Straga told us to trail him for half a day. Later I had to go with Janski to Mysliwiecka Street and wait for a customer in a sitting room full of paintings by the Kossak brothers. The host was late, and I had time to read *Le Bateau Ivre*. Janski glanced at me with surprise and mumbled something about the late ambassador: "Yes, you two would have had something to talk about, but you'll never get rich." In the evening Tola and I visited the Rylskis. I had already learned the Rimbaud poem by heart, and at tea, during a conversation about Norwid and the translations of Miriam, I suddenly recited it aloud. Everybody fell silent. Only Selim giggled and looked at me with devilish enjoyment. "It's strange," said Tola, when we were going back to her house. "In fact, I know practically nothing about you . . ." I assured her I was, and always had been, a man with no secrets. It had been a month since I assumed the identity of a low-level manager in the Typhoid Institute. It was an ironclad *Ausweis* provided me by Straga— really solid identification papers that guaranteed safety even in the case of a street roundup. Thanks to that piece of paper I managed to smuggle out a group of Jews from the ghetto during the final stage of deportations when our unit received orders to cooperate with the Council of Assistance to the Jews. In the winter of 1943 it was more difficult to get to the other side of the wall, more so even than six months earlier when we brought out Nina and her mother.

In the spring I decided to suspend the transfer of codes and give Tola a different assignment. The day after her last trip to Lvov, I found her covered with a blanket, with her neck wrapped in a thick woolen scarf and a sketchbook in her hands. Her throat was sore. She had caught a chill on the train. That day the city was in the grip of freezing winds and snow, and despite the early hour Tola had a small lamp turned on at her table. I sat down and started leafing through the books that were lying on her bed. After a moment I heard Tola mutter the words of a poem: "A man covered with blood sleeps with his wound nested against a strange footprint . . ." I was struck by something familiar about that line, and I remembered that my father once showed me true a notebook with poems by Andrzej Borowik. But of course: ". . . he listens to hear if the tread of human feet, while saving Europe, will trample him to the ground, his arms outstretched in the sign of the cross . . ."

They had become acquainted, then, and he was reading her his poems. I wasn't jealous. I didn't try to find out how often she saw the author, but I decided not to allow any more trips.

From that time on, both Borowiks were at my exclusive disposal. I made them responsible for security. Whenever I had an appointment with Wladek at my father's apartment, the brothers would go there an hour earlier to check the grounds.

Did I ever ponder the moral side of my enterprise? Did I have a ready answer to the question these boys might ask after the war?

First of all, I counted on their intelligence. Those muscular, dark twins with their asymmetrical faces, who apparently read everything there was to read in world literature, would certainly understand my motives. I trusted both their seriousness and their sense of irony, their awareness of the paradoxes of existence stripped by the war of any semblance of logic and virtue. I relied on their instinctive grasp of the relationships between imagination, deception, form, idea, and truth—all those changeable combinations of life that merged in one common current . . . Those boys would understand me well . . . I could depend on that. I used both ideas and lies in order to create my theater of illusion and to build a structure of deception identical with real life, and I did it to fend off death, to save life. In fact, my actions resembled fate, though they were neither blind nor accidental. I knew who I wanted to save and perhaps, subconsciously, I also knew why. Because I was involved in the killing. Maybe that was the reason.

I mentioned my contacts with Wladek Sznej and our meetings in Zoliborz. We established a certain form of coexistence, and we kept it on an even keel. I did not hide my opinions about his organizational talents. I did not consider him a man of action. One has to distinguish between people who fulfill themselves in action and those whose domain is ideas and speculation. For a man of action, for example, life is not an immutable condition. Life is a set of tasks to be accomplished, and fate refers only to success, or failure, at those tasks. For a real activist even prison and death are forms of action, as are his relationships with other people, his conversations, correspondence, etc. Wladek was always a man of ideas and intellectual concepts. For this kind of person external activity often results in catastrophe. Other people have to do all the work for them. It would be difficult to imagine Wladek in prison. He wasn't a coward, but he would regard imprisonment as a senseless mishap, because he lived in the world of his thoughts and did not understand that even thoughts— when communicated to others—become acts. After the war he avoided arrest by volunteering his testimony, and he found support in a new association of Christian communists, a splinter of the old Thought and Action. He was only trying to protect himself.

I want to talk, however, about earlier times—the year 1943 in Zoliborz. I would have considered my accounts with Wladek settled if only he had kept his promise.

I tried to maintain my one-man leadership of Rondo and to divide responsibilities in such a way as to minimize the possibility of any contacts behind my back. Apart from myself Rondo consisted of five members. Our courier, the rickshaw driver, was sworn in in February 1943. I could achieve maximum security only if no member knew about the others. This, of course, was impossible, but I tried to limit internal contacts. I gave Tola intelligence-gathering missions which kept her apart from the rest of the team. Wladek was placed in charge of ideology and social issues. After many discussions in my father's room in Zoliborz (Wanda would leave me her keys), Wladek finally agreed to put his project of "citizens' circles" on ice, and to prepare, instead, a monthly report on the living conditions, social structure, and morale among the population of the General Gouvernement. I in turn offered to pass his studies to Rondo's command. These exhaustive reports, copies of which were buried by Wladek in a basement on Swietojerska, became a valuable item in the archives of the underground, and several fragments of them appeared after 1956 in military and historical magazines.

After Easter, Tola stayed in bed for a week suffering from severe depression. She watched the shelling of the ghetto from one of the doorways in Bonifraterska. She returned covered with soot. In the evening she went there again. On the next day she did not get up. She turned her face to the wall and didn't even touch the food that Nina cooked for her. This state of affairs lasted the whole week, and it was apparently Nina who finally persuaded her to wash her hair. When I went there on a Sunday morning I found them both in the bathroom. They were washing their hair, and the apartment was filled with the smell of chamomile. Nina said, "Put your head down, here's the towel . . ." There were no more explosions. It was a quiet spring day. I brought her some of the fudge cakes she liked so much and I put them the kitchen. I saw an unfinished game of solitaire on the table among empty teacups. I sat down and drew some cards from the deck.

I spent the night on Topolowa. I was sound asleep when somebody started to pull on my arm in such a resolute and frantic way that I finally woke up. I recognized Tola in the darkness. She sat on my bed and pressed her knee against my calf.

"Don't sleep!"

"What happened?" I asked in a shaky voice.

She stared at me in the dark. She began talking in a whisper. She told me about Jewish children led by the Germans to the gas chambers. She described how they looked: pale, very thin girls with dark braids, pressing their dolls to their chests. She wanted me to picture myself as a little girl with a doll and a braid being pushed into a gas chamber among the crowd of screaming, naked mothers. She asked me whether I was able to imagine that—to become for a moment such a girl.

I remained silent.

"You brought me cakes," she said, "and then you went to bed. You were snoring."

I explained that this often happened to me in the spring. "I'm sorry," I said. "I'll try not to snore."

She didn't seem to hear my words. "So that's how it's going to be?" she said as if in amazement. "We eat our cakes, we say good night and go to bed. And as we fall asleep we know that mothers and children are burning in the ovens. You are not a bad man. Aren't you afraid it's going to haunt us till the end of our lives? Tom, Tom . . ." She dug her nails into my arm. "Just think of it. The smoke from those ovens is in the air we are breathing!"

I said nothing, yet I knew Tola was touching upon some very important issues buried deep within us, issues one rarely spoke of or thought about in those days. My heart grew heavy. I took Tola's hand.

"Tell me just one thing," she whispered. "Is there a God above us?"

I was lying on my back and holding her hand. The moment that passed was the longest in my whole life.

"Tola," I said in the darkness, "I cannot answer that question."

We talked for a long time. I held her close and tried to explain that we, after all, could meet the same end. We could also be killed one day, and we were certainly not guilty of the death of those people. She interrupted me, saying that everybody was guilty—everybody who managed to escape a similar fate. A Jew or not a Jew, no matter. She was shaking her head. "Everybody. Do you understand? Everybody who eats, who sleeps, when others are being murdered. But my brain was too small to understand that . . ."

She turned over onto her stomach and started to ponder, her fingers buried in her ruffled hair. After a moment she unexpectedly began to talk about the Heavenly Kingdom. I don't remember all the details. She probably meant the state of infinity after death where all our sufferings and deprivations will be compensated for. She described that fairyland Heaven full of happy children, birds, and little goats, and she predicted that the three of us—she and Cezar, and me—would live there happily together.

I could hardly believe my ears. I strained my eyes to see if she was talking in her sleep. It was hard to imagine she was telling me something like that while fully awake. But she was not sleeping. The darkness was breaking up, and I could see her smile as she wrapped her arm around my neck. It was then, I guess, that she whispered something about a monster that had to be slain. I had no idea what she was talking about. I did not contradict her, however. I was agreeing to something, and I felt her body pressing closer and closer to mine. Finally I must have made some promise, because she sighed with relief. "My dear, my dearest. I knew I would not be disappointed. You'll do it soon, won't you, Tom?" She knelt on the bed and her thighs embraced my hips. I heard her broken whisper and her moans about the Kingdom of Heaven, Cezar, and the Monster. I felt the pressure of my blood, and finally I stopped thinking about anything. We both started swaying rhythmically, and that's how it happened between us for the last time. In the morning I started to suspect, with embarrassment, that a moment before the climax I must have promised Tola that I'd kill Hitler.

I told her to keep an eye on a certain attorney, an elderly gentleman who frequented the Melpomena. He lived on Mokotowska Street. Two weeks earlier Janski and I sold a large canvas belonging to him, Okun's "A Lady with Rabbits," in a villa in Saska Kepa. I was sure he was perfectly harmless. He had a reputation as a pleasant sot. War did not stop him from pursuing life's little pleasures. After a month I knew his every step. Tola gave me the names of the people he met, informed me about the cases he worked on and his adventures with women. Once he gave her a lift home from the Melpomena. The next day he sent her a bunch of flowers. Her work was faultless. After six weeks of observation, I was certain the man had connections with the Directorate of Civil Resistance. I told her to withdraw immediately. Later on I had to reprimand her. Without my permission she went to his funeral. He had been found in an elevator. The cause of death could have been either a stroke or a heart attack. When she brought me the news, I could hardly conceal my surprise. She was shaking; she heard he looked as if he had been strangled. I tried to explain to her the symptoms of a stroke and angina pectoris, but she kept staring at me with a kind of fearful respect. She had no doubts I was a great actor.

All in all, I felt like an honest boxer from a good family. I had a difficult fight ahead of me, and I used all kinds of wily tricks, yet I kept my balance, obeyed my reflexes, and stuck to the rules. I was fighting calmly: I had a star of madness between my brows, yet I was careful and I trusted my luck. I was fighting, unaware of the outcome vigilant, hopeful—like whom? Like a man.

A certain very young actress once asked me about Cezar. It was quite recently. I dropped by our theater's cafeteria, and I sat at a table with two young actors. It is amazing, but Cezar's legend survived among the theater people into the present day, and that girl, dressed in a sweater and tight pants, born ten years after his death, talked about him with passionate curiosity, as if he had charmed her the day before with his new stage creation. Several weeks earlier *Theater Monthly* published several recollections about famous actors of the prewar era—among them a short profile of Cezar. The author concluded his presentation with the following statement: "For him theater was a compulsion to be onstage—always and under any circumstances."

After our meeting in the garden of the Melpomena I saw Cezar only once, as he was getting out of a horse cab at the corner of Tamka and Dobra (I think I've already mentioned this twice). Before that evening, however, he entered my life on one summer night. I learned about it in a rather unusual way.

On that day, at seven in the morning, acting on Straga's orders, I took part in the execution of a man sentenced to death by the underground. After my mission I had problems with regaining my equilibrium. I felt I had to spend the rest of the day with someone close. I went to see my father, but he had left for his classes. I sat for two hours in an empty café in the Square of the Invalids. Around ten o'clock I went to Topolowa hoping that Tola had the day off. But Nina was there alone. It seemed I had made a mistake, and Tola was busy at the Melpomena. When I entered the room Nina was pressing her skirt with a small electric iron. "Yes, yes, pray and iron," she said over her shoulder without turning in my direction. She was wearing the same green gown, and her hair was tied up above her neck. After all these months we were alone together again. I stopped right behind her. We exchanged some remarks and then fell silent. I could not lift my eyes from the nape of her neck. I should have left immediately, yet I was unable to move.

"If you have any qualms," she said, "I can certainly help you shake them off." Slowly she unplugged the iron. "Do you remember our last conversation? You wanted to know who visited her." She was now looking me right in the eyes. I watched her red lips. "Well, write it down in your little notebook that she had a man in her room last night. No, no . . . first write it down . . ."

After less than an hour I was lying in her bed. Her green gown covered us. The meaning of her words was finally clear to me.

After the war there were rumors in the theater crowd that

Cezar had been murdered by the Gestapo. In fact, there were two versions circulating after his death: that he was killed by the underground for collaboration with the Gestapo and that he was killed by the Gestapo for collaboration with the underground. There was no third version, and one could assume there was no third possibility. After a dozen or so years people started to talk and write about Cezar as if the circumstances of his death were insignificant. He became a welcome subject for critics and theater specialists. People wrote about his place in the prewar Polish theater, about his *Fantazy* and *Pygmalion*. As far as facts are concerned, nothing has been explained, and yet with the passage of time everything becomes clear. It all reminds me of the word puzzles in the old magazines: the magazines are still important for historians of culture, yet after fifty years nobody cares to solve the puzzles.

But if someone, like the author of "A Chapter in the History of Struggle," brings all this to light, and credits it to Rondo, I can hardly pretend total detachment. One thing should be made clear: by the time of Cezar's death Rondo was totally out of my control. It was run by a group of people who had formed the section called IR behind my back. This fact is essential for any judgment of my part in these events. It is also essential if we want to avoid a further mistake. According to the *cui bono* formula, it was easy to conclude that I was the only one with a real personal motive to wish Cezar's death. It all seems quite logical: I founded Rondo for love of a woman. When the woman betrayed me, I used Rondo as an execution squad to eliminate my rival. There is even a certain novelistic moral to this version. Life is a novel, that's a fact, but not always of the best quality. In this case the novel written by life lacked structural finesse.

It seems I am the kind of man nobody spares the truth. If Tola harbored any feelings for me, they had little to do with pity. She herself told me about her night with Cezar. She started talking about it during a conversation about something else entirely. I don't remember what. I recall we were sitting in a small café near her house. "Do you know who slept on your sofa last week?" She smiled to herself, and added under her breath: "Cezar . . ." I learned that Cezar left home during a party given by Iza for some German officers. He came to Topolowa after midnight, woke the janitor by pounding at the door, and asked to be taken upstairs.

It was a chaotic account, full of understatements, and yet perfectly clear on one point: for Tola it was a night of triumph and vindication. While listening to her, I began to wonder whether it would ever occur to her that I might be hurt. No, she would be profoundly shocked by the idea. Her infidelity was our common victory, a precious moment we had been awaiting for years. "I knew it would happen," she said. "It must have come to fulfillment." I do not know if she fully realized who she was talking to when she squeezed my hand and whispered, "Tom, you understand everything best . . ."

And yet she was right: I understood. In fact, I understood everything about her from the beginning, since our walk on Jerozolimskie Avenue when I felt her fingers squeezing my arm. After ten years we had returned to the point of departure. She was squeezing my arm and telling me about her love for Cezar. And I understood everything. Today I also understand that after his death, and after the birth of her child, she had to start hating me. This was the truth. And yet I have to add: an artistic, imaginary truth. This is why I never really believed in her love for Cezar or her hatred for me. I think she must have imagined both feelings, and I bet I'm right. Being right on such matters, however, does not amount to much. Even if we assume that her love and hatred were not entirely real, it would be hard to say whether there was anything inside her more real than this unreality. I remember my reaction to the revelation that she took care of paralyzed Jean-Claude Marcenat in France. Another exaltation—that was my first thought. But Tola did not exist beyond her exaltations. Her lies were her truths, but perhaps when she lands here in a couple of weeks equipped with her new, pathetic consciousness (a recovered mother returns with her recovered daughter), she will be the most real person to step down from the plane.

After our conversation in the Jeannette, I felt bankrupt. Although in purely external terms our relationship did not change in any visible way, I had no illusions: from now on she would be waiting for Cezar, and I had to learn to live without her. That sounds quite simple, but was I able to "live without her" if for ten years my life was built on her existence? The thought evoked a fear of emptiness and boredom. I was ready to accept any conditions, to forgive her any future trespasses, for one single sentence from her: I wanted her to say that for these ten years we needed each other and that nothing was going to change that. But of course this was a sentence she never uttered. She said some other things to which I never paid enough attention. At the end of our conversation, shortly before we left the café, she became pensive. "If only we helped him, he could leave all that behind . . ."

One has to know the theater world to understand what "being in the society" means for actors. Actors live exclusively "in their society" and matters outside that world have little importance to them. Everything that happens "in the theater" becomes their knowledge of life, which is, in many ways, more cruel than anywhere else. I often had the opportunity to listen to actors talking about themselves. What struck me most in those conversations was a compulsive need to dissect everybody's psychology. At first it seemed forbidding, and I did not understand how one can sip coffee and probe the most intimate motives of another's behavior, to discuss someone's shameful or terrifying truth. In my opinion those debates were scandalous from the moral point of view. After a time, though,

I understood that for actors "scandal" meant only something related to the stage. It was a scandal not to appear for a performance or to be drunk during a rehearsal. Only the theater was a serious matter. Life was an amateurish, thoroughly unprofessional kind of theater, and to a real actor a real man must have been something rather comical. It was this comical, amateurishly performed humanity which was the subject of their conversations backstage. Never in my life have I met people as knowledgeable about one another. I have heard it said that their peculiar code of ethics (sometimes held in contempt by the larger society) is nothing more than a means of protecting their trade guild. I think this theory is not totally unfounded. The theater is a trade, and a trade allowed only onstage. Private tinkering, therefore, was ruthlessly exposed like forged medical diplomas. The process of unmasking and pitiless indiscretion often led to unusual insights. I would never know the most important things about people if I didn't learn them from the actors.

Cezar ignored the opinion of this society: he was its sovereign ruler. During the occupation he did not pay much attention to what was being said about him. But the society not only talked. The actors also knew. Some things were never spoken aloud until the end of the war. In the winter of 1945, Wiaremko, whom I met in Praga, told me about the night Cezar escaped from the party given by Rajewska for the Germans. ("For Langewirth! Do you remember the lists of hostages signed with his name: Langewirth, General of the Police?") Apparently the next day the Melpomena knew everything. And yet nobody spoke of where Cezar spent the night. You can probably guess why . . .

It was known, yet it was never discussed. And though I knew more than the others, even I could not avert the course of events.

I was standing with Wiaremko in the corridor of the City

Hall in Praga. During the first weeks after the war it was a meeting place for people seeking professional contacts, accommodation, or simply a job. I found a small room in a partly burned house not far from my old studio, which had been smashed by an artillery shell. Every day I walked across the frozen river to the left bank. It was very cold and I wore a jacket made of blankets and a German army face mask. In the mornings I waited in the City Hall to be assigned to one of the working groups sent back to the right bank. The pontoon bridge was often closed, and in order to kill some time I would drop by a pastry shop in Zabkowska. One day I saw Rena Delatynska there. She was wearing a long, patched doublet and man's snowshoes. She was limping and her voice was hoarse. She sat at my table and started to tell me her story. She was waiting for a hearing at the Actors' Association. When I had heard enough I wanted to get up, but she suddenly whispered in my face, "He died because of her . . . I tell you, he would be alive today were it not for that crazy little megalomaniac . . ." She was seized by an abrupt, raucous coughing. She left soon afterward, frightened away by a familiar face. She was afraid she would be recognized. I stayed a bit longer.

I was deep in thought. It was all coming back. If Cezar had not escaped from the party . . . if he had not come to Tola . . . if . . . !

But it was perfectly clear he had to run away that night. He was running from his home, from himself. That night Cezar saw the monstrous face of his humiliation—and he became frightened. It was a scene he could not understand. Strange people in uniforms, noisy dialogue in a language he could not understand, drawn curtains that muffled the sound of life, because life itself was dead, because the world had ended—the world that loved Cezar, the world that Cezar repaid so generously. Because there was no audience, no welcoming murmur as he took the stage. There was nothing but humiliating, boring irrelevance, and a supporting role as the husband mooning around contemptuous stags in uniforms . . . So he ran away.

I am sure he had no idea where he was going to spend the rest of the night. After curfew the city looked dead: deserted streets, closed restaurants and railway bars. As he was walking down the empty streets, his horse cab clopping somewhere behind him, Cezar was terrified and mad, half conscious and hungry for compassion—and he remembered Tola.

Cezar always noticed those who loved him. He knew how to recognize them and how to cling to their memory. He rejected Tola's love long ago, but he certainly remembered it. During all these years he knew something I could not understand: she was waiting for him. When he became frightened by his lone-liness he dreamed of someone's generosity. He wanted to spend the night with someone who had been waiting for him for years, and who asked nothing in return—somebody far away, who remained faithful and pure. Tola told me in the Jeannette that he came to Topolowa in his old cab, with its huge gray horse. He left before dawn. Apparently the driver had a night pass arranged for by the theater. Each evening he waited for hours in front of Cezar's home. Cezar paid him a weekly salary. But during the last months of the occupation, the driver and his horse disappeared and Cezar had to pay for each ride. Janski told me about that.

I am always stupefied by the thought that over a quarter of a century has elapsed since these events: the time between the destruction of the Bastille and St. Helena . . . Such a distance allows a dispassionate evaluation of my errors. But did I commit any?

Apparently there was no visible change in my situation. The relations between me and Tola continued as before. I visited her apartment on Topolowa, and the three of us played cards or drank vodka and discussed art, history, or the theater; I also liked to watch Miss Lala at her solitaire. From time to time I would spend a night in the kitchen alcove. I thought it would go on like that. I got used to the everyday reality of the occupation, to small problems mixed with mortal dangers, to concerts at the Rylskis' and occult séances followed by Selim's lectures, to briefings with the Borowik brothers in the Botanical Gardens, to doing business with Janski, and to the indoctrinating dialectics of Wladek Sznej, whom I met in Zoliborz or in his apartment on Swietojerska. This was my life—intense, meaningful, sometimes even monumental in its stony grayness. I was regaining balance. Weeks, months would pass and each day would bring her closer to me again. Cezar would never leave Iza, and time would do its job. In a year she would forget about him. She would have to forget. For a long time now we had lived like a married couple. What, after all, was our relationship if not a marriage, a marriage past its initial stage of infatuation, in which we simply fulfilled our common fate? "You are in love with her," Nina once remarked, "and I can understand why. Because, despite her immense shortcomings, she is a magnificent person. You wouldn't be able to exist without her. I even like that about you—that romantic trap you've fallen into . . ."

I often visited Nina in the mornings (four short rings of the bell and two taps at the door), although our relationship returned to its normal course. The green nightgown was replaced by gray or brownish sweaters and blouses high at the neck. Her room was always aired and emanated an intelligent symmetry and order, which was striking, especially when compared with the usual chaos of scattered things in Tola's room. We talked about life and attitudes toward death. Nina professed a philosophy of "decency," a word she used as the equivalent of honor, courage, or sacrifice. Instead of "honesty," she would say "moral hygiene." She avoided lofty expressions, too large, in her opinion, for everyday use. "I don't like humanity on stilts. I prefer sport shoes with sturdy soles." I watched her calm, measured gestures, I appreciated her lack of affectation, but I sensed something strange in that sober spiritual order; I was more attracted to Tola's exaggerated, lavish dreams. We talked about her too. We talked about everything except what she had told me not so long ago. She only mentioned it once: "I knew you'd learn about it anyway—from her." I wasn't surprised. I guessed Nina must have been privy to Tola's spiritual torments. She must have heard her story about Cezar more than once. But was it only about Cezar? I am sure she talked also about me. It was Nina who told me first to keep Tola at a distance from my important affairs. "You know what I am talking about . . ." She shook her head. "I warn you, I warn you." I remembered Cezar's words in the railway station in Kiwerce. He also warned me about something.

Well, I kept Tola away from my important affairs. Nobody except me knew that Rondo was not a serious affair (though it was more serious than I thought), but for some time I tried not to get her too involved even with Rondo. After the unpleasant incident of the lawyer in the elevator, I asked her to gather information about the actors' community. I hinted enigmatically that the quick delivery of her reports to London was a matter of special importance, which made her think it was just a small segment of a broad plan devised by the intelligence organs of the Allied forces. I explained that her mission required unique guile and perceptiveness and that I was authorized to entrust her with this task by the Supreme Command. The remark had an immediate effect. She became very excited: she listened with pursed lips, while winding a strand of hair around her finger. I had to congratulate myself on this perfect idea: she would be bringing me gossip from the Melpomena and I'd be free from the nightmare of having to invent new fictitious instructions, free from suitcases filled with codes, from bodyguards and train schedules. My inven-

tion was like Columbus's egg: a simple and safe solution to all
my problems.

This was my first mistake. It didn't take me long to learn
most of the actors' secrets: social and more-than-social contacts with the Germans, clandestine connections with the
underground, Wiaremko's sentimental liaison with a young
beau from the Warschauer Stadttheater, Zbyszek Nalecz. I
learned that Rena Delatynska, through her contacts with
Kripo, the criminal police, helped those who were arrested,
but took money for these services from their families. I also
became aware of a transfer of an armored SS Waffen unit to
the banks of the Wieprz. After three weeks, however, she
returned from her shift electrified. She told me there was a
possibility that Rondo would form a branch in the
Stadttheater. She offered to recruit Cezar.

The best thing for me to do was to drown the proposal in
diplomatic silence. In any case, I didn't show much enthusiasm
for her idea. But a couple of days later Tola asked me directly
for a decision, because, as she said, the issue could not be post-
poned indefinitely. She tried to break through my silence with
a shower of arguments: Was there anything to worry about? It
was such a perfect idea—an intelligence post right under the
Germans' noses, not to mention the moral significance of having Cezar on our side. We had to start doing something! The
Monster was still alive—not a hair on his head was touched—
he still devoured people, and we were growing accustomed to
his crimes . . . She pierced me with her gaze: Give me an
answer!

I was inscrutable. I explained I hadn't obtained formal
authorization, and I happened to know there were some mis-
givings at the top about overextending Rondo's network. The
direct channel to the Supreme Command must be especially
well protected. "But that's . . . that's hermeticism," she said. I
wondered where she had learned the word. It was not part of

her vocabulary. She became embarrassed and quickly started to talk about Cezar. Why was it so hard for me to understand that it could be his salvation? He was waiting for our extended hand, for a gesture of confidence, he . . . "He isn't waiting for anything," I interrupted. "He simply wants to sleep through the war." And I described briefly a scene during a roundup at the intersection of Nowy Swiat and Jerozolimskie Avenue, as related to me by Janski. People were being arrested on the sidewalks, pulled from streetcars, and pushed toward the BGK building, where gendarmes were shoving them into trucks. All four exits had been blocked off by soldiers with dogs. The streets became deserted. The officer in command was standing alone in the middle of the intersection. Finally the shouts and patter of feet died out. The prisoners were all packed under the tarpaulins. Suddenly there was a clapping of hooves and a cab with a gray horse appeared from Nowy Swiat. Cezar, his head resting on the back of the seat and his crumpled sombrero pushed back on his head, was sound asleep. Frightened, the driver tried to turn the horse around. The gendarmes rushed to drag Cezar out, but the officer of the SS shouted something and called them back with a motion of his baton: *"Lassen sie weiterfahren! Das ist Herr Graf von Budapest!"* He saluted with his baton and let the cab through. Cezar did not so much as stir. The German must have seen him in *A Lady from Pest.* An artist who was among those arrested, but who was released later in Skaryszewska, told Janski the whole story.

Tola was touched by it. She seemed to be trying to restrain her tears. After that we stopped talking about Cezar. I didn't see her for a week, maybe longer. I was busy carrying out a rather unpleasant operation known as Jacob's Square.

Straga seemed to be playing with me, testing my nerves through a series of experiments that were becoming increasingly imaginative. As I have already mentioned, on one occasion he wanted to see how I would comport myself during an execution. He ordered me to carry out a death sentence on an informer who betrayed several of our people. It was supposed to take place downtown, near a commuter-train stop. "You don't have to do anything, so to speak, with your own hands," explained Straga, glancing at me with his unsettling blue eyes. "The guy will be dispatched with a needle: we have a specialist for that. It is a matter of supervision—well, let's say, a temporary cover." When we were waiting for the train I provided rearguard protection for the specialist, whose needle was actually a very long, thin stiletto. As we mixed with the crowd, the specialist plunged his instrument under the scapula of a man in a dungaree coat. Nobody noticed anything. The man sank to the ground, and it looked as if he fainted. Someone rushed to call an ambulance, and the specialist ran with him. I bent over the man: he was dead. When I reported to Straga, he looked at me with benevolent curiosity. "Not bad for a reservist," he said. "By the way, do you know that our specialist has an erection each time? At least that's what he says. What do you think about that, Lieutenant?" He offered me a cigarette. When I refused and reached for my pipe, he pulled out his lighter. Two streams of smoke passed through his nostrils. I listened again to bawdy anecdotes about cavalry sergeants and their mares.

And yet I liked something about the man. There was a cool fire in his dandy contempt for death (or perhaps for life?). He earned respect with his professional exactness. I was never able to catch him in even the smallest negligence. He had a perfect memory: he never forgot anything. Besides all this he was a charmer. I doubt if I'd ever encountered such natural elegance, such easy strength emanating from his every motion and gesture or the modulation of his voice. He was a nice devil, no doubt about it. At that time, in the late fall of 1943, we used to meet in a little park surrounding the Holy Infant

Hospital (today it belongs to the Academy of Medical Sciences). When I arrived there Straga was already waiting for me. Our courier, Aneta, was sitting a couple of benches away. It was a perfect meeting place. The park was full of patients in their hospital gowns. Friends and relatives, grouped under the trees and on park benches, were waiting for visiting hours. It took me several weeks to settle matters with the Jacob's Square. Straga brought me an order from the High Command to eliminate a gang of *schmaltzovniks*, Polish policemen and Kripo informers, who prowled the area several blocks behind St. Jacob's Church, between Sekocinska and Barska Street. Quite a number of people who escaped from the ghetto were hiding in that area, and there were frequent reports of blackmail and arrests; there was one shooting. Barska was also the site of a clandestine print shop used by the underground press office. But the area was crawling with provocateurs and informers, and one of them might accidentally discover our post. It was necessary to identify these people and their meeting places. The plan called for a quick retaliatory strike. First, however, we had to find the hideouts, or the identification would be extremely difficult. It took me two weeks to become a regular visitor at a certain caretaker's lodge on Wegierska Street, which also happened to be a local moonshine den. One of our observers noticed that the spot was visited by policemen and civilians accompanied by prostitutes. Two days later I appeared there myself, unshaven and without a tie, to buy some moonshine from the caretaker. When I became a regular visitor I hinted that I was willing to fence some gold and I established relations with a number of the customers.

I do not intend to dwell on these subjects—the details are quite revolting. In the end, a policeman and two civilian informers were shot, but the area hardly became safer and we had to move the print shop elsewhere. Much later I learned that the policeman was killed by mistake: he was taken for somebody else.

I am writing about all this in connection with my frequent meetings with Straga at that time. Every couple of days I reported on the progress of our operation. I usually came to the hospital park directly from the den, unshaven and reeking of alcohol. I felt lousy and it seemed Straga was trying to make things a bit easier for me. After hearing my report he would change the subject and try to divert me with sociable conversation. He must have guessed I was at the end of my tether. At this time I had his full confidence. Many years after the war, when he became a collector of military items and married a dentist, he told me after a game of bridge that during the first months of our collaboration I was still being investigated in connection with the flooding of the armory and with Rabczyn's death. "Later, of course, I could vouch for you personally. Besides, they found a different track to follow . . . You know what I am talking about."

Of course I remembered. When I informed him about the conclusion of Jacob's Square as we were walking in front of the hospital, he suddenly asked me about Wladek Sznej. He remembered the study I had handed him a year before. "He's a bright fellow, that Janota. It's a pity our philosophers from the Propaganda Department shoved his report into some drawer. Do you see him often?" My answer was rather vague. "I've heard," continued Straga, "he has some contacts with a guy called Kozlowiec. Perhaps you know him, Lieutenant? His pseudonym is Bulat and he's apparently trying to arrange something, together with Janota, among the actors at the Stadttheater . . . But this Kozlowiec is a suspicious fellow. Janota should keep away from him. You understand me, Tom, don't you? Maybe you could give him a hint. Would you be so kind?" And he added something about the new clues in the Wolska affair.

Obviously, I was deeply worried. I went immediately to see Wladek. The door was answered by his skinny, silent wife. I heard some chatter in the other room. When Wladek finally appeared I asked if I could have a word with him. He wanted to know if the matter was urgent. He was busy right now; his wife's family had come to visit. "If possible," he said, "let's meet tomorrow. I'll explain everything to you . . ." He was clearly embarrassed: he must have guessed the reason for my visit and he was bothered by the prospect of my meeting his guests. We made an appointment for ten in the morning. "Where?" He thought for a moment. "I have some business in Mokotow. I'll wait for you in the Jeannette on Independence Avenue . . ."

The Jeannette? That made me wonder. It wasn't a very popular spot. It was frequented mainly by a local crowd. Wladek mentioned it automatically, as if he had been there before. Whom did he meet there? I was besieged by suspicions, especially when I remembered a séance on Topolowa. A month before, perhaps earlier, before I took over Jacob's Square, Tola improvised a séance in her kitchen. Nina, Miss Lala, and I sat at a small table that was brought in from the hallway. Tola turned off the lights, and we made a "circle" around the table. We waited for the table to start rattling out letters of the alphabet. We sat in the darkness but nothing happened. Despite our invocations the table did not even budge, and Nina started to laugh. By an accident, or maybe out of boredom, I knocked the table with my knee. "Tom, he's speaking to us," cried Tola. "Spirit, who are you?!" I knocked out the letter M, then A. I conceived the idea of presenting myself as "Marcel." For several weeks Tola had been devouring Proust. When I reached E, she screamed, "Marcenat! I dreamt about him two nights ago!" So I knocked out the three remaining letters. "Do you want to tell me something?" whispered Tola. I set my knee in motion again in an effort to spell: "I am waiting for you," but it was becoming a bit exhausting. Tola was surprised: "I waiting you . . . ?" "That spirit is a poor grammarian," explained Nina. What happened next was quite amazing: the table started to knock on its own. First, on Tola's request, it introduced itself: "Mother." Then it announced: "Avoid Jeannette." Nobody said anything—there was a dead silence. Nina turned on the lights. "Let's stop it. It's really foolish."

I am absolutely sure that someone present must have known about Tola's meetings in the Jeannette, and I am also sure that someone was Miss Lala. Apparently she had already learned about Kozlowiec and decided to use the table to let me know something was going on behind my back. At that time Tola was meeting Wladek and Kozlowiec in the Jeannette to discuss Rondo's activities. (Wladek told me about it himself during our first conversation after the war.) I suppose now that the IR section, soon to have a decisive impact on the whole organization, was formed in the course of these meetings.

When Wladek proposed to meet me in the Jeannette, I didn't suspect that matters had gone so far, but after his first words I realized the discussion was going to be not so much between me and Wladek as between two opposite *sides* and that I was definitely the weaker one, the least aware of the current situation. Wladek seemed neither embarrassed nor surprised when I reproached him for unauthorized contacts with third parties. He listened to me calmly and didn't even ask how I learned about it. "You have to understand"—he spoke in a quiet voice, stressing every word—"you have to understand we are past a certain stage, and the present moment demands a reassessment of our principles. I am sure you are aware of the fact that Poland is not an agency of the Supreme Command. There are social forces at work here and we cannot ignore them. Elitism and hermeticism may be necessary in military intelligence operations, but they can also prove fatal from the point of view of general political action. We have to depressurize ourselves, to open up, to let new people in. This is an issue of the highest priority. You are talking about third parties. We were just about to present you with certain solid proposals . . ."

I didn't want to hear any proposals. I was shocked by Wladek's behavior and by the way he addressed me. In whose name was he speaking after all? Who was hiding behind that first person plural: we were about to . . . we cannot? I felt as if my brain had turned to ice, and at the same time I was boiling with rage. Reason told me to control myself and I tried to hide how offended I was. "Please, watch what you're saying," I said. "You are talking to me like . . ." I was searching for a good comparison, and I should have said "like a chief of staff to his commander who doesn't understand the battle has been lost." Wladek remained calm. He looked at his watch. "I still have fifteen minutes," he said. "Listen to me." And he gave me a lecture about political spirit within the Polish émigré circles in London. The opposition was attacking the policies of the government-in-exile, there was talk of a possible coup or an indictment at the Tribunal of State. In Wladek's opinion it was all leading to a rearrangement of the political forces within the country, to a rejuvenation of the centers of power and to a replacement of the old guard with people connected directly to the Polish underground. "It is time to give a straightforward answer to the straightforward question: Are we going to carry out the orders of some superannuated colonels of the Second Department on the Thames, or should we rather become an authentic social and national movement here on the Vistula? In our opinion there is only one answer to that question . . ." "In your opinion," I said, trying to control my rage, "who exactly do you have in mind? Yourself? Who else . . . Kozlowiec?" Wladek turned pale, but he wouldn't be caught off guard. "Yes, Kozlowiec. And people around him. You must excuse me now, I really have to go." Before he got up, however, he bent toward me and whispered in an angry voice, "For God's sake, we are friends, aren't we? Try to think about it objectively. Believe me, we don't want to give you up. For us Rondo is also the most important thing."

I spent the rest of the morning in town. I had two more meetings to attend. The first snow fell and started to melt right away. Downcast pedestrians shuffled along in the slush. The air was humid, with clouds low over the roofs. When I waited for a streetcar, and later, when I worked my way through the crowd, I felt as if I were carrying someone else's head on my shoulders. When I visited my father in the evening my cheeks were burning, as they did after a day of skiing.

I didn't stay long, and I do not remember what we talked about. I remember him at his desk, bent over a pile of notebooks, in the worn jacket he used to wear to school on the cool fall days when the classrooms were not yet heated. When Wanda gave me a glass of tea I couldn't hold it steady. My teeth rattled all the way home. It was a massive flu attack I had been cheating for a long time. Now it finally caught up with me and struck me down without much resistance on my part. I hardly managed to drag myself to the bed, where I tossed with fever for at least three days. I saw human and animal forms, and I conducted lengthy conversations with them. I cried when somebody pierced me with a thin, cold wire. A monstrous face with a snout looked at me from under the chair. My fever must have exceeded 104 degrees, for my visions were extremely clear; they stood in the doorway, they talked to me from the wardrobe or sat on my bed. One night I jumped up sputtering: Miss Lala Ubycz had said something very important and was about to leave, and I wanted to stop her by any means. I had to ask her something even more important, something decisive . . . She smiled at me and nodded mysteriously from the depths of my room. I heard her voice very clearly: "I shall take care of your child . . ." My sheets clung to me, soaked in sweat. I heard sirens sounding an air-raid warning. I had hallucinated through a whole Russian raid. Until morning I was wringing and drying my shirt, and later I ate a slice of stale bread. Then the hallucinations returned. They were interrupted by a loud pounding on my door. After a while, when the spirit did not give up, I stumbled to the door: the specter was standing in the hallway with a suitcase in his hand. It was my freezing friend from the military college, who had returned to Warsaw after arrests at his sugar factory and wanted to spend a night in his old studio. In the morning he called a doctor. I had pneumonia.

My illness became a kind of intermission: for several days I was separated from life by a curtain that stopped every sound. My friend had notified my father. Wanda brought me some food. Every second day I was visited by Aneta. I spent most of the day alone. I was still weak, but in a state of spiritual relief—almost detached from my physical body. I often slept, and when I woke up I was able to analyze my problems from a clear and neutral perspective. At such moments I often came to the conclusion that my illness had cured me of a chronic internal infection, and that after all these years I was really healthy for the first time. The nightmares visited me less frequently now; usually at dusk, when in half-sleep I felt the burden of the Rondo question. Again, something was staring at me from under the chair or from the wardrobe. During the day, however, my thoughts were clear, my attitude toward my own situation sober, and gradually I regained my ability to make logical decisions.

It became clear I was caught in a trap. Please understand me. It would be a serious breach of discipline if someone behaved like Wladek Sznej in a real underground organization. If it happened in my own unit, I would have to report such an incident to Straga straightaway. I think Wladek considered such an eventuality inevitable; after our conversation in the Jeannette he was waiting for something to happen, though he probably felt quite secure with Kozlowiec at his side. But nothing happened (who should I report him to?), and Wladek must have been surprised. After some time it must have occurred to him that I was merely a third-rate person, someone without significance who could be pushed aside with one hand. With that conclusion I practically ceased to exist as an activist and I found myself outside Rondo. But there was more. I lost all respect in Tola's eyes, and it all happened because of my reluctance to invite Cezar into the organization. She decided, and not for the first time, that I was really consumed by jealousy. There were sufficient grounds for her alliance with Kozlowiec and Wladek, and I was about to lose that game. What on earth could I do in a situation like this? Neither one way nor the other . . .

I read the note from Tola calmly. It consisted of a few words scribbled in pencil, with plenty of exclamation marks and spelling mistakes. She promised to visit someday soon. I smiled and thanked Miss Lala for the package of biscuits. She sat on a chair near my bed, her short, chubby fingers resting on her oilcloth bag.

"Many things have changed," she whispered after a moment. I closed my eyes. "You are tired."

She spoke in a secretive manner, almost without a sound, as if she was prompting from her box in the theater. I almost repeated after her: "You are tired."

"It seems," I said, "that everything I did was useless from the very beginning, Miss Lala. From the beginning."

"Does this mean you want to give up?"

She had posed a question, and she was waiting for an answer. When I turned toward her, I met her forceful gaze. It was like an X ray, and it occurred to me Miss Lala must have been examining my soul.

I shrugged—it was neither a confirmation nor a denial. "You don't want to see Miss Nina either?" Miss Lala knew about everything . . . I mumbled something about the futility of any activity—I really did not know who I was going to see, or not see, and what did it matter anyway? I continued for a while in a similar tone. Then Miss Lala vigorously changed the subject. She started to ask about my father's health. She was particularly interested in his marriage with Wanda: was it going well despite the difference in age? I became involved in the subject, telling her about my father's harmonious life. I said that Wanda's admiration for him could not be equaled. Miss Lala listened with great interest, and her face brightened. We offered each other biscuits. We smiled. "I was always convinced," she said, brushing crumbs off her fingers, "that old age does not have to be sad, but it has to be honest. This is not a joking matter, am I right?" And she suddenly announced that Tola had adopted a stray mongrel. "Very nice, kind of impish," she explained. "You'd like it." She munched at her biscuit like a squirrel. "It's name is Pikus."

I did not pick up the thread. Miss Lala became silent, yet I felt she was watching me attentively. She started to rummage in her purse, and took out an envelope. "Mr. Janski asked me to give this to you." She was about to get up, and I mumbled something in embarrassment, as if trying to apologize for something that remained unspoken. There was a moment of uneasy silence. Miss Lala did not move, perched on the chair, her head slightly tilted to one side. Again she resembled a sleepy bird.

"Please do not blame yourself," she whispered, "you haven't done anything wrong, and you shouldn't lose hope. You must not lose your hope."

I waved my hand. "Well, you know there isn't much left for me . . ."

"Dear sir," she said calmly, "an uncommon man should have uncommon expectations."

Her words really surprised me. "But why on earth should I be an uncommon man? What do I represent? No, you must be wrong."

I did not convince her. She claimed that if I could offer someone so much, I certainly was an uncommon man. "You offered yourself. Nobody can do more, I daresay, and that is quite sufficient. But one shouldn't expect anything in return. God writes everything down, but He does not pay. You are going through a difficult time, I know that. You feel you've been cheated. But you're certainly aware that we are limited in our projects, which are fulfilled somewhere else . . ."

"Somewhere else?!" I shouted. "Are you serious?"

"Didn't you know that? But that's impossible!" She started to shake with laughter. "That's simply impossible. Would you like life to be something other than a mystery? And what would we do with it, poor things, if we knew what would happen in the next hour? Just think about it. Would life be worth living if one were like a Swiss watch? . . . And isn't the unexpected the ultimate?! How can you be sure who is being born now?"

I looked at her in amazement, not knowing what to think about what she said, or how to respond. I was not aware that for the first time in my life I was hearing the words of true Christian consolation, clairvoyant words that embraced my whole future.

Before leaving, Miss Lala promised to run some errands for me. I explained who she was to talk to and what to say. She stood by the door in her soft shoes and man's hat, her purse dangling on her arm. Then she put on her woolen gloves and waved to me as if I were departing for a long journey in a sleeper car. In a joyful and meaningful tone she said, "I shall take care of your child."

I understood. I stared out the window until noon, and later I fell asleep. In my dream, which was unusually clear and visual, the sky was raining some black and sticky substance. Tola and I were driving in an open cab pulled by a white horse. We were meeting our neighbors, with whom we intended to drink through the whole night. We were greasy, soaked in the warm, sticky substance. We were laughing rapturously, we were finger-painting on each other's face and wiping away the dirty water that dripped from our hair. She was whispering into my ear, "Tom, Tom, Tom . . ." and I held her tight, feeling her drooping, boyish shoulders and her small breasts against my body. But there was no physical desire in that proximity, only a joyful emotion like that during a prayer or a blessing. Later, when a convoy of huge trucks appeared, all soiled with mud, and when they started to charge at us with sirens and yellow lights flashing in some large, empty intersection, when they were coming closer and closer, we were still happy, still certain that nothing would ever part us. I slept through half a day and the whole night. It was dusk when I woke up. Several hours later a friend told me the house had been surrounded by the Germans, who arrested everyone. I was so sound asleep that even their pounding at my door did not wake me. They must have thought the apartment was empty and left.

That was the most beautiful, the purest of all my dreams. It was not erased by time. It was the fulfillment of everything I ever felt for her, everything I wanted from her. All the lights of hope lighted up in that dream.

My convalescence did not last long. I cut it short to carry out a decision I made during my illness. I returned the money received from Janski to Miss Lala and asked her to pass it on to the Borowik brothers with an oral message: I had to leave town on urgent business. They should await further instructions upon my return. I also gave her the address of the rickshaw driver from the Eagles; she promised to give him the same message and some money, and never to mention my illness. Thanks to Janski's advance I could fulfill my final obligation before disbanding Rondo: to pay off my soldiers. After my conversation with Wladek Sznej it became clear I had lost control over my enterprise, or would lose it soon enough. I decided it would be better if I relinquished my command on my own. I only wanted to preserve appearances and to transfer my boys to a more responsible operation.

It was the beginning of 1944 when I reestablished my contact with Straga. The meeting was brief, and Straga assessed my condition in a single glance: "There seems to be a bit less of you, but what's left can still be useful." He hinted that the timing of my recovery was perfect, because something had just come up, and I seemed to be the right man for the job. He was in a hurry. At the end of our conversation, I asked him if it was possible to admit three new men, and he burst out laughing. "When did you manage to recruit them, in your delirium?" He promised to give me an answer soon. Aneta told me that during my illness some important decisions had been made, apparently at the very top, and the tension was rising. Things were hectic, and everybody was extremely careful with words. The Eastern front was approaching. For the first time since the outbreak of the war it occurred to me that it might be the last spring, and the thought made my head reel. Was it for real? Was it possible? Winter was still cold and snowy. Aneta was arrested in February. The Lwowska station was lost. Against better advice I spent the nights in my studio. Soon I received news that Aneta was dead. She was shot after a long period of torture. She betrayed nothing.

This was the most difficult period. I lived with clenched teeth, trying to survive my own failure. "One bout of flu . . . what it can do to a man," mused Janski when I told him I was leaving our partnership. I assured him in vain that the reasons were of a different nature. "I believe you"—he smacked his lips with skepticism—"but I can tell your reasons right away. You are an amateur. Nobody respects professions anymore. Artists become colonels, and colonels become ministers. Gentry! You'll always be an amateur. You'll drop everything to follow a shadow."

One listens to these kinds of lectures with little pleasure. "Perhaps you're right," I said. And I realized he had captured, after all, a true aspect of me, although in this particular case it was just the reverse: I was being abandoned by my shadow. I tasted more than failure. I was tormented by the shame of a fruitless effort and the humiliation of a life which suddenly revealed its hard, hidden skeleton. It was like an unexpected loss of freedom.

At the same time I was experiencing the standard disappointments of a beginner. I saw the shabbiness of my work and the pathetic awkwardness of my method. I was amazed I had managed to get away with things so easily for such a long time. How could they have been so naïve as to trust me for almost two years? They still suspected nothing. Nobody called my bluff—my fiction worked and was solidifying into a reality. It was an object of struggle: some people wanted to dispossess me of my own fabrication. And nobody—not even once—asked me if all this was true! Even Wladek with his probing intelligence. When we discussed Rondo he never doubted its existence. On the contrary, he saw it as a social movement and pointed to its national base. I did not anticipate anything of the kind. I allowed events to catch me unawares, to take me over. And Rondo continued to exist! How was it possible? A moment of meditation in front of a mirror, an idea born out of my anxiety, out of a sudden premonition or fear, had become so material and real as to attach itself, without my knowledge and against my will, to a faction within the London government, affecting the political situation in my country, pitting me against my friend, transcending my conscience, and finally dismissing me? No, that was something I could not comprehend, embrace, or penetrate. Sometimes I would wake up in the morning with a strange thought: how many such mirrors created history, the very history I had learned at school? And what if humanity was governed by a set of mirrors, a system that magnified endless reflections of a single thought or incident? Perhaps that's how it is. Perhaps thus, and no other way, reality is created; reality which we later interpret, shape through the categories of our mind, and reconstruct in reverse order—all according to our need for rational explanations, our desire for meaning. In this case life is just a tale spun by ourselves and about ourselves, a tale in which we find our origins and confirm ourselves, a tale which we continuously become and in which we willingly believe, because it alone can amuse us . . .

I think I was on the right trail. At least that's how it seems to me now. Just today I have reread "A Chapter in the History of Struggle," which is the first written account of Rondo's history. Everything in that account, even the name of its author, can be proven untrue. And yet, there is not, nor will there ever be, a more truthful account. This one will grow into reality and legend, it will slowly become the truth, and even I shall probably come to believe it sooner or later. There is hardly anything new in these revelations. But they were new to me in the years I am talking about, because I was discovering them for myself. No one is prepared for such discoveries: school textbooks usually keep silent about them.

Before spring I was back in my rut. There were new projects that required more frequent contacts with regional outposts. On several occasions I traveled out of town on business for the Warsaw regional command. I remember a forest covered with snow, a night in a ranger's cabin. I fell asleep to the bawling of dogs, and woke up to muffled sounds of conversation beneath my window and the harsh breathing of horses. Several hours of slumber on a train, and I was back in Warsaw—the dark, gray, cloudy city. Small groups of people were clustered at the streetcar stops. I dined in various pubs and visited the Hare only occasionally. The bar was usually full, and drunken guests in overcoats tried to shout each other down at vodka-spattered tables. After half an hour I left the heavy atmosphere with a sense of dizziness. On one occasion I asked the bald waiter if Cezar still frequented the establishment. He cleared his throat, swept some cigarette ash from my table, and didn't seem to hear me at all. But when I was paying my bill he hunched over me: "Mr. Cezar. Yes, he still comes here. One or two times a week we have to carry him out before closing time. Sometimes he is brought here already in a horizontal position. This is no longer a man, sir, this is nothing but alcohol and misery."

I remember Warsaw in those months as a dark place, as if drenched in the winter dusk. In the dim bluish light of street-lamps, not far from the station, I noticed a poster advertising *The Dove*. I stood there for a long time reading the freshly pasted billboard. The opening night was scheduled for March. Iza Rajewska and Cezar as the Jorgenses . . . I could not move from the spot. It was like a dream. A German patrol—five men in helmets and gorgets—was approaching through dry, hard snow. When they were passing me I heard one of them say, *"Wiener Burgtheater, das ist ein Theater . . . mein Gott!"* I had a map of a railway junction hidden in my shoe but I did not even think about the danger. At the moment all I cared about was whether Tola had also seen that poster.

I had not been to Topolowa for several weeks. I tried to be neither too frequent nor too rare a visitor. I just wanted to maintain an illusion of my presence there, a trace, or a shadow of presence, because I had quit her life for good. But the past—I kept telling myself—all those years and days cannot be dismissed in a single gesture. It is impossible to shake off one's memories like snow from one's shoulders. They have to be allowed to melt slowly. I believed that memory is a matter of dignity, that the passing of time deserves our respect because it remains a part of ourselves, and nobody starts his existence from scratch. It's simply a matter of human decency. Therefore I went there once a week, once in ten days, to talk, to play cards, and to pretend not to notice the changes in Tola's appearance. I brought her fudge cakes, which she loved, and when she grew pale and left for the bathroom I did not ask any questions. Her pregnancy was hardly noticeable and was visible more in her eyes than in the shape of her body. Tola was still slender and her posture was straight. But when I met her eyes, they seemed to be looking not at me but through me. It was not indifference, but a kind of engrossment with her own experience, a new, unknown kind of existence. She had an attitude of dreamy serenity and depth. She would smile at me. "Tom, do you like my dog?" She would put him carefully on her knees and whisper into his ear that he would be sure to survive the war (and yet he didn't). I counted in my mind: the fifth month. As I have said, there was no visible sign of rejection in her attitude toward me, no chilliness or estrangement. And yet I remembered our breakfast in the Turecka, when she assured me that one word on Cezar's part would be enough for her to cut off my head and sell it to the butcher.

We did not talk about Cezar. I was sure that she did not see him and that she constantly thought about him. She must have heard about the staging of *The Dove* even before the poster appeared. At that time she still worked in the Melpomena, where such news traveled fast. But we did not talk about that either. We talked about the dog, which she had found in front of the Jeannette. "The Jeannette?" I asked. "Well, that's a very nice café. Do you still go there?" She looked at me. "I'm sure you know." "Know what?" "Well, our unit is already operating in the Stadttheater. I meet Zbyszek Nalecz in the Jeannette. He has made up his mind. He'll talk to . . . to . . ." she stammered in excitement. "You'll see, you'll see it for yourself . . ." In a moment of panic I realized I had created the machine of fate: the evil I wanted to fend off by creating Rondo was now working through Rondo and was about to come to fruition. I told myself to stay calm. So there was clandestine activity in the

Stadttheater; there were open conversations with Nalecz, whom I often saw in the German army club on Szuch Avenue and in other German facilities. It could not turn out well. The theater had been infiltrated by the Germans; it was full of *Volksdeutsche*, informers, frightened collaborators . . . Whose idea was that?

But it was my idea! I had ordered Tola to watch the actors, and the operation in the Stadttheater was the next logical step. My speculations at that time were confirmed recently by the author of "A Chapter in the History of Struggle." Here is a quote from his article: "The aim of Rondo, or, to be more precise, of its specialized section for intelligence and reconnaissance (IR), was to intercept operational plans and information about the deployment of German units behind the lines. Among other means of intelligence gathering, we conducted a close survey of groups involved in collaboration. That included the actors from the Stadttheater, established in Warsaw by the Germans . . . In the course of the aforementioned operations an especially valuable contribution was made by a devoted member of Rondo, Tola Mohoczy."

It was all very logical. I underestimated my own ideas, but someone else saw their full potential. I was amazed by the facility with which these ideas turned into reality. There was something horrifying about it—the magic I unleashed suddenly turned against me and reduced me again to the role of an extra. There was nothing I could do. It seemed I had lost both my powers and my rights. I was strangely constrained even in the smallest gestures. I would light my pipe (an extra should not smoke a pipe) and then extinguish it after the second puff, telling myself that the smoke would be bad for Tola. Smoke . . . In a day, or perhaps in a week, she could share the fate of my courier, Aneta, who was finished off on a stretcher with a shot to the temple. All in all, I considered myself a doomed man.

And yet, if everything happened otherwise, if the events followed a different route, if unpredictable situations and facts germinated in situations and facts equally unpredictable, creating sequences of events different from those suggested by one's habitual causal thinking, if certain plots arranged themselves in such an original and uncommon pattern that today Lala Ubycz is the mother, and I the father, of the child of Tola and Cezar, if Wladek Sznej, who appears during university celebrations in an ermine robe and cap, has long since left the miller's skinny niece and married his assistant, a real princess in whose veins flows the blood of Jagellonians, Bourbons, and Hohenzollerns, if Straga, the owner of the largest private collection of Polish spurs, spends whole weeks in his slippers, if Mr. Witold Kozlowiec, Deputy to the Parliament and the president of Inco enterprises, the former leader of Rondo troops, is today an active member of the Association of Fighters for Freedom and Democracy, if General of the Police and SS commander Krystian Teobald von Langewirth is today an adviser to a black African government, if Iza Rajewska plays Mother Courage in the state theater in Szczecin, and if, finally, three days ago I received a letter from San Sebastián with a clipping from *Elle* saying that *"la grande comédienne polonaise en exil"* and a companion of Jean-Claude Marcenat during the last years of his life, according to well-informed sources, wishes to take monastic vows *"dans son pays natal"*— if things turned out this way, I believe these events should be regarded, in our epoch and in our stage of cultural development, as the phenomena of some still unmapped physics of fate, deserving, in my opinion, scientific research, or at least a public acknowledgment and an extensive analysis of their deepest social consequences.

Spiritually, Miss Lala was the person most suited to the task. Some secret reason, or biological instinct, allowed her to take the most whimsical games of providence with moderate composure and spontaneity. In the first months after the war, when our adventures during the Uprising became the subject of a radio play (two Warsaw survivors carried their child from the ruins), we were invited to visit the Committee on Nazi Crimes. Since we had nobody to leave Tola with, we took her along in her baby carriage. Miss Lala provided minute explanations while drawing upon her cigarette holder and quite resolutely trying to confirm our claim to parenthood. As for me, I said nothing. I rocked the carriage. I felt the aura of her intimacy with being, or even with providence, which must have been as obvious a matter for her as nature is for the others. "It's never easy to bring up a child," she stated solemnly after one of the more pointed questions from the Committee. Her moderation, her positive relationship with life, invoked the simplicity of freedom. I remember my father saying that the most important division among people is that which separates slaves, freedmen, and free men. He could recognize each of the three types immediately. When we spent holidays at my grandmother's house near Krakow, he taught me to see the difference between the peasants who sheepishly took off their caps, and those who did not hesitate to shake his hand. When his school hired a new administrator, and my mother asked my father at dinner whether he approved of the selection, he answered with a frown: "He is enterprising, ambitious, and without principles. He will be scheming, but we can count on his energy. He's a freedman." I am sure he would classify Miss Lala Ubycz as a free person.

It was already March when Straga agreed to accept my three recruits. I thought he had forgotten about the whole matter, but he finally brought it up himself, and in the most intriguing manner. It was shortly before my next trip to the Warka region, the operational area of a certain Lubon and his men. A couple or days earlier I reported to an apartment in Sadyba, where I received instructions (I shall return to them later) from a gentleman with the face of a kindhearted uncle.

He had a Vilno accent. We had left the meeting and were walking down an empty street when Straga said in a quiet voice, as if speaking to nobody in particular, "That's all right, Tom. You can take them along. Lubon is a country teacher, you know, a type from Zeromski . . . lectures, campfire debates. He's an idealist. And here? The summer will be hell." I did not quite understand him. "What do you mean?" I asked. Straga looked at me out of the corner of his eye. "The sun." he said. "It's going to be awfully hot. Take them away." Before we parted he added, "I did not train anybody for street combat."

I did consider transferring my people "to the forest." I had spoken to the Borowiks about such a possibility, and they had both nodded. Now they had to be ready for departure within three days. My father told me once that they had been brought up by their mother, a doctor. I asked them whether the news wouldn't upset her. They both smiled politely: "Our doctor is not easily upset. She's been working in an emergency room. And we've been working on her too."

But the rickshaw driver bowed out. He started to talk about spring examinations in organic chemistry, and blushed as he spoke. If it's an order, he certainly would . . . but personally . . . I explained it was not an order, and he could still be useful as a courier. I even released him from his oath. "No." He was frightened. "You misunderstand me. It's simply important for me not to leave Warsaw. Someday I'll try to explain everything . . ."

It was decided I would take three men on my trip: the Borowik brothers and the docent Zafir. I had heard about Zafir on several occasions at the Rylskis', even before my illness. I remember Selim talking about a surgeon from Lvov whose family was murdered in the ghetto and whom Selim tried to hide in the mental hospital in Tworki. After a week, however, he had to place him somewhere else.

"The word 'crazy' is strictly forbidden in a mental asylum," explained Selim. "But of all people, he seemed to provoke it more often than anybody else. Do you know why? He kept telling the staff that after the war all surviving European Jews would be given Polish citizenship and that the Polish Diet would pass legislation to that effect during a special ceremonial session. He quoted Mickiewicz: Israel is the older brother of Poland! Such things are considered pure madness, so we had to move him to a convent." Selim had no pity for people who thought Hitler deserved a monument for "solving the Jewish question" in Poland.

After some time Zafir started to send desperate messages via the nuns: boredom was killing him and he wanted to be useful in the underground. Through Zegota, the Council of Assistance to the Jews, the matter reached my unit. Partisans needed doctors. The day before my departure I made arrangements with one of the sisters who came from the Laski convent. At 4 P.M. I had dinner at the Hare. When I was leaving I noticed Cezar pulling up in his cab.

I return to this scene because it must have looked curious to whoever was watching me at that time (I am sure I had been watched ever since I left my apartment). I helped Cezar out of the cab and tried to hold him up. He wanted to pull me into the restaurant, and we struggled for a moment. I was too upset to listen to his mumbling, but today I am sure he was talking about Iza. He was worried about her, and had good reason to be. For over a year there had been talk about her affair with Langewirth. But people talked not only about the affair. There was a warrant for the arrest of two actors signed by Langewirth, and it was understood that it had been issued at Iza's insistence. (She was acquitted of that charge by a jury of her peers after the war.) What was most unusual, however, was that Cezar was afraid of me. At first I thought it must have had something to do with Tola. But he was afraid of something else—something he thought I might be involved in—and kept warning me about a "terrible mistake." He wanted me to influence somebody, to change someone's plans. "The person you know . . ." he mumbled, holding my arm. "You understand, don't you? The street is spattered with saliva . . . But considering the helplessness of some other people . . . as you know, the complete and painful helplessness. Now, let me ask you . . . is it, in fact? Well, well, that's it! Pyrotechnics!" He kept talking about things I could not understand, about Tolstoy's play "with a meaningful title, which will explain everything," and looked at me invitingly. My lack of understanding must have irritated him, because he moved away from me with clear disappointment. "My brave Horatio, didst thou perceive?" He sighed and closed his eyes. I wanted to leave, but he grasped me again. He was speaking quietly, his face so close to mine that I could feel his breath. "But maybe, still . . . just a spark? Morally I would be ready, and considering the physical usefulness . . . An intimate, personal proposition, but as for the effect! On the national scale, let's face it, just blinding! Purifying fire, am I right, baby boy? And the stairs to the roof. Do you remember? Yes, from the prop room. You don't doubt my feline agility, do you? Well then, shake? At night, of course. And only as a barter. Will you tell them?" He drilled me with his hopeful, imploring eyes, and for a moment I was terrified. Had he gone mad? That thought came to my mind. I wanted to say something, but when I began speaking Cezar grew apathetic. He looked at me with absentminded exhaustion, as if realizing that I had not understood anything. "Just joking," he muttered, lifting his brow. "We're just joking, aren't we?" He appeared to sober up and he seemed to want to be rid of me. And yet, as I started to leave, he called after me. Cezar seemed to ponder something. And then he suddenly gave me a bow. It was a deep bow with tilted head—the one actors give to their audience before the curtain goes down. That's how I remember him: his red curls and his light hat sweeping the pavement in a ceremonious, if clownish tribute.

Later, when I tried to reconstruct the details of our meeting, I was puzzled by Cezar's ability to predict an event nobody planned and nobody could anticipate. In light of future events his remark about a "terrible mistake" was an almost subliminal premonition. Today, however, it seems clear that Cezar was thinking only about a possible attempt on Iza's life. He did not think about or anticipate anything else, because nothing on earth concerned him any longer—apart from that one possibility. He must have panicked the moment he realized an underground organization was operating in the theater: "the underground" for him meant people who kill without trial. Who knows whether actors do not harbor the old fear of persecution preserved from the times they existed on the margin of society together with vagabonds and women of ill repute. They felt secure in front of the audience, but they still feared the mob. "A secret organization" was an arm of the mob with a stone hidden in its fist. Whom would the stone strike? Cezar could not have had any illusions: he must have been aware of the hatred surrounding Iza. And finally he conceived the idea of a barter . . . A barter!

Today I am able to explain all this. But at that time I did not understand much. As I was returning home along Tamka Street, I thought about some of the more elusive of Cezar's remarks—for example, Tolstoy's play. I tried to remember a title, and, to tell the truth, I wasn't even sure Tolstoy wrote for the theater. Besides, his words probably did not have much significance. I guess Cezar was thinking about *The Living Corpse* and tried to convey his own spiritual condition. In any case, as I was walking down Tamka Street I was so engrossed in my thoughts that against my instinct I did not pay much attention to the people who passed or followed me. On Kopernika Street somebody quickly walked past me and then waited for me to catch up. It was a rather remote acquaintance of mine, the son of a professor from the Warsaw Polytechnic, whose apartment on Foksal Street I used to visit with Janski. He greeted me and we walked for a while making casual conversation. After a moment, when I was just about to turn onto Ordynacka and proceed toward Nowy Swiat, I noticed that on my other side walked a stranger—a short, dark-haired man in a ski cap. He was smiling and holding his hand in the pocket of his coat. At that time I understood I was expected to keep walking. Where to? "Somebody is waiting for you," explained my acquaintance. We entered Foksal.

Until the last moment, I thought the incident might be connected with one of my business deals. Perhaps Janski was late with payments . . . But it was not Professor W. who was waiting for me in the apartment. When we came in, his son ushered me into a room that at first seemed completely empty. All I noticed was a fencing helmet on the floor, near a bookshelf, and a crucifix on the wall. When the door was closed, however, somebody rose from a chair near the window.

It was a grotesque situation. I was followed and kidnapped so that I could meet with Witold Kozlowiec, who could have asked me for a meeting in any café. I answered his greeting with a measure of irritation. Are we playing cops and robbers? Why this farce? And yet it wasn't hard to guess that the farce had a purpose. By ordering me brought in from the street Kozlowiec he defined our relationship: I wasn't asked for a meeting, I was brought to him by his men. I must give him credit for cutting right to the heart of the matter. He stated his demands right away. I was to reveal to the IR section Rondo's network of agents, the codes, and all the channels of communication with the Supreme Command. The demands were laid out in a few words, precisely and with the self-confidence of a man who knows what he wants and is sure to get it. He did not know, however, that in this particular case he couldn't get anything, because nothing he asked for existed. If I had been dealing with a different man, perhaps I would have assumed a different tone.

But Kozlowiec, with his pale, ascetic face and relentless eyes, always aroused my antipathy. He possessed all the attributes that were most alien to my own character: intolerance, lack of self-criticism, deafness to other people's arguments, and a preacherly stiffness totally incompatible with the complexities of life. All this prevented me from talking to him frankly and made me sound quite adamant. I flatly refused to acknowledge his demands. All I could do was call his activities by their proper name: subversion. Of course, there would be consequences. After these words I got up and walked to the door. It was locked. "You overestimate your influence," Kozlowiec said, and motioned me back to the chair I just got up from.

For an hour I rejected his demands, cursing silently the idiotic fortune that confronted me with this petty, ambitious chieftain. During that hour, however, I understood Kozlowiec's intentions. For some time I had been asking myself a question I finally posed to him directly: assuming that I met his demands, what would it all lead to? The liquidation of Rondo by the Supreme Command. "Just think about it for a moment. Your coup d'état sooner or later would sound an alarm in London . . ." "Yes," answered Kozlowiec coldly, "but not in Warsaw." I did not understand the remark, but something dawned on me when he announced that the existence of Rondo no longer depended on the Supreme Command. He said something about the "hypnosis of external centers" (in his opinion the Polish imagination was ruled by the myth of emigration, a government of souls radiating its influence from Paris or London), and he added that the opinion of the Supreme Command about Rondo's talks with the military High Command in Poland was of little concern to him. "And what does that mean?!" I exclaimed. "What are you talking about?!" I noticed something like a glimmer of surprise in Kozlowiec's alert eyes. "I thought Janota explained it to you some time ago."

I learned from him that I represented a minority within Rondo—a group known as the "hermeticists," who blindly followed the orders from London and tried to isolate the organization from both society and the rest of the underground. I also learned that the healthy majority had gathered around the IR command. On several occasions Kozlowiec called these people "dynamists" and described their program as a "strategy of realistic action." Of course, the talks with the High Command would be conducted by representatives of that group. Under these circumstances it was both obvious and necessary that I surrender my plenipotentiary powers to the new leadership as well as transfer all the contacts, information, and methods of operation. I learned that Rondo rejected its role as a specialized agency—the Reserve Organization for National Defense—and was becoming a group of great military and political capabilities based on growing support from territorial forces. There were grounds to believe the High Command would be receptive to proposals presented by the representatives of Rondo.

"So that's what you need my network and codes for!" I burst out laughing. "I am to provide the dowry for the bride!"

Kozlowiec nodded his head. "You could put it that way. But you are also a part of our dowry. You—personally."

I pretended not to hear this last statement, but I felt a hot pounding in my temples. I was a part of their dowry, I personally . . . or, to be more precise, my antecedence, my legend . . . I had no doubt what it was all about, and suddenly I was seized by fury. I got up from my chair. While looking Kozlowiec straight in the eyes, I measured my words carefully: "The High Command may not wish to talk to you. I am sure you know the case of the armory on Wolska Street. As far as I know, the investigation into that matter has not been closed yet."

I walked to the door. It was still locked, but when I pounded at it several times, somebody turned the key and opened it slowly. I pushed the door with all my strength. Nobody tried to stop me. A moment later I was on the staircase. As I was getting on a streetcar on the corner of Nowy Swiat, though, I felt a pang of anxiety and wondered whether I should have refrained from mentioning the armory.

On several occasions I have talked here about my imprisonment after the war, and yet I still have to explain the reasons for the favorable change in the course of the prosecution. That such a turn occurred was evidenced by the better treatment I received, after a time, from the prison and investigating authorities. Since 1953 I had the right to receive food parcels and to buy cigarettes in the prison canteen. After my written testimony I also received my pipe, which I filled with tobacco from cheap cigarettes. After the beginning of 1954, I could sometimes get hold of reading materials. I guessed about the death of Stalin from a column in the weekly *Theater*.

The change occurred when after a break of several months in the interrogations I was transported from my cell to Koszykowa Street. I was resigned. I expected a closed trial and a sentence. But I was led into a room where a major showed me to a chair positioned at an odd angle in front of the desk— the detail suggested I was in a study rather than an interrogation room. After a moment of silence broken only by the shuffling of papers, the major produced one of the documents piled in front of him, glanced at me as if surprised by my appearance, and expressed his astonishment that I had not, so far, revealed certain important circumstances of my life. After this introduction he read the document aloud. It was a deposition by Wladek Sznej, who explained that since the beginning of our acquaintance I was generally considered to be the natural son of the Marshal and that in my student years I was a frequent visitor at the Belvedere. In the last paragraph Wladek provided reasons why he had not disclosed the information earlier: he did not consider it important enough as far as the Rondo case was concerned. The document was signed: Dr. Wladyslaw Sznej. At that time Wladek was still using his prewar name. He changed it only in 1956.

When I protested, claiming that Rondo was a mere invention, the major, who listened to me attentively, reached into the right-hand drawer of his desk and produced a bottle of brandy, two glasses, and a carton of Wawel cigarettes. Within fifteen minutes I was made fully aware of what was expected from me.

The major provided some information about the impending trial of seven commanders of the Home Army. They were charged with collaboration with the German police in fighting the communist resistance and arresting escaped Soviet prisoners of war. I was to appear at that trial as one of the witnesses—a chief of a unit whose task was to spy on the democratic organizations within the underground. During my testimony the bench would ask me some questions concerning my prewar contacts with the Belvedere and my relation to the Marshal. All I was expected to do was to answer these questions in a matter-of-fact and positive way. My own case would then be closed and I would receive a light sentence.

These private talks continued for almost six months. If I had agreed to play my part, my testimony would certainly have provided perfect material for propaganda and for newspaper headlines ("Dictator's Son Heads Subversive Organization under Protection of Gestapo"). After four months the same proposal was presented to me in a somewhat modified form: during the trial I was only to confirm that such rumors about my origins had circulated since before the war. When I continued to refuse to cooperate, the pressure started to ease off. I was called to the meetings less frequently, and the trial was mentioned only in the conditional mode. Finally there was no more talk about my investigation. I was released without a sentence.

The reason was a shift in internal politics, which had been in the offing for some time. But in my particular case the change occurred earlier, and I have no doubt I would have been sentenced for activities hostile to the working class were it not for Wladek Sznej's latest testimony. As I have said, I was at the end of my tether in both the physical and the spiritual sense, and continued imprisonment with the same regimen would certainly have broken me.

I suppose it's not infrequent that gossip plays the role of fact. In my own life it happened at least twice. Twice gossip almost pushed me into the wheels of a dangerous machine. It is less important that in both cases I refused the offer. Each time the consequences were different, but equally grave and equally independent of my will. Both cases were based on pure nonsense. What is most striking, however, is that the vitality of this nonsense did not diminish with the passing of time. Even last year I received a letter from Montreal, dated March 19, which contained an unknown photo of the Marshal with his dog. The sender, whose name told me nothing, enclosed a few scribbled sentences along with it, the last of which said, "I hope you may find the enclosed photograph a valuable souvenir, yours sincerely . . ."

In the fall of 1962 I arranged a guest performance in Krakow for our theater. I spent over a week in the city I knew from my childhood, which I had not visited often since then. My stay was rich in observation, partly because of the special character of that city, in which Eastern socialism was mixed with the bourgeois and royalist past. One had the impression that among those Renaissance streets, among the Gothic and fin de siècle spirits of our forefathers, walked a crowd reduced to a common denominator, to one collective face. After several days, however, some familiar names and faces began to emerge from that anonymous mass, faces that evoked memories of my childhood: my father's retired colleagues, elderly ladies with tearful eyes, who remembered the secret meetings of the Rifleman organization and the departure of the First Legion. One of these women, almost eighty years old, was a friend of my mother's. They went to the same finishing school in the years before the first staging of *The Wedding*. She had a gift for me: seven bound notebooks filled with fine, still legible handwriting. It was a diary my mother kept from the time of her matriculation to the day of my birth. She left it with her friend on the eve of her departure from Krakow.

In the evening I started to leaf through the diary in my hotel room, and searched out—not without emotion—the fragments concerning the year 1913. The earliest entries contained remarks about her pregnancy: nausea, vomiting, and tender words about my father's concern. Later came a description of a summer in the mountain resort of Zakopane, notes from lectures on Krupowki, and short sketches of new acquaintances. Among them I found the following entry: "Yesterday at the S's I was finally introduced to the man I could up to now admire only from a distance. He was wearing a gray military jacket without insignia. He made me sit at his side and for the whole evening entertained me with conversation, which was later widely commented upon by some local ladies. I smile today when I remember his eyes and his lilting Lithuanian accent . . ."

The entry was dated July 17, 1913. I was born in October of the same year. I think scholars are wrong when they dismiss such personal notes, diaries, and appointment books as unreliable historical material. Sometimes even such scribbling can be of use.

Without much difficulty I moved the Borowik brothers and the docent Zafir to Lubon's unit, but unpleasant thoughts tormented me all the way from Warsaw. After the conversation on Foksal Street, I realized that the only function of Rondo was to facilitate Kozlowiec's political gambit. I was sure it was

Kozlowiec who put Wladek on my trail. He must have been manipulating him for some time and now he wanted access to an organization that operated independently of the High Command in Poland. After the split in Thought and Action, Bulat-Kozlowiec was left with about a hundred men and apparently found himself in total isolation. He learned about Rondo just in time to answer the call of his group. They lacked support and were waiting anxiously for their leader's word. After the operation at the Credit Union, he must have ordered Wladek to join the organization. The plans to take over Rondo were probably already in place. He achieved his goal more easily than he expected and he was ready now for the decisive step: talks with the High Command. What did he expect? Perhaps a place in the national leadership of the underground? In any case, my powers and my personal legend were to be the trump card he planned to use at the gaming table. Yet this card failed him. It was hard to guess what he would do now, after my rejection. I couldn't stop wondering whether it was prudent to rebuff him so bluntly, whether it was wise to burn all my bridges. Perhaps instead of my last harsh words I should have at least asked for some time to consider his offer. My anxiety grew as I moved farther and farther away from Warsaw: the theater! Why haven't I warned him about the amateurish conspiracy in the Stadttheater, about confiding in Nalecz, about Tola's heedless extravagances? I didn't even mention my meeting with Cezar, his fears and speculations, which showed that rumors were already circulating and that someone might report them at any time. Yes, I lost an opportunity to put Kozlowiec on the defensive. Instead of attacking me he would have had to respond to my charges. What is more important, my warning might really have put an end to their meddling, or at least made them more careful. But the thought that Tola was in danger was the only thing that really worried me.

Andrzej Borowik asked about her when we left the train

compartment to talk more freely. He used her pseudonym, Sea Gull. After my explanation be paused for a moment. He told me that the two of them spent half a day last winter walking around Krakow and visiting churches. It was after the incident with the drunken passenger, whom he chased off. When she came to thank him, they became friends. "Later I worried about her," said Borowik. "She disappeared so suddenly. She had had a premonition of death. When we were in Krakow she kept telling me she would certainly die."

I did not take up the subject. I only told him that Sea Gull was alive and well and that she had undertaken another important mission. But the conversation did not make me happy. I had some premonitions too . . .

We had to wait a day and a half in a peasant's cottage near Warka to contact Lubon. I slept most of the time. It was snowing and the feathery silence was narcotic. In the evening I woke up to the voice of the docent Zafir, who worried whether there were any surgical instruments in the forest. One of the Borowiks blew on the frozen windowpane; the other was memorizing English words from his notebook. I was lying with my clothes on. I wondered if, after my return to Warsaw, I should ask Straga to transfer me to a partisan unit too. I would feel better if I could stay with these boys through the end of the war. Of all the possible conclusions to the Rondo affair this one seemed most logical. But there was still one more possibility hinted at by Kozlowiec. I knew I could not hide from him, even "in the forest." That the possibility was quite real was confirmed during my meeting with Lubon. In the morning we were taken by sleighs to a cottage on the other side of the forest. Two armed country boys led us into a room where a man in an unbuttoned army jacket was shaving himself with a straight razor.

I had very specific instructions. Lubon was not carrying out his orders from the regional command. A complaint was sent to Warsaw, which Lubon ignored. The matter wasn't entirely clear, and I was asked to look into everything on the spot. I had to determine who was responsible and what was at issue. But first of all I had to make Lubon recognize the authority of the High Command. I was prepared for a difficult conversation. But Lubon, who had just finished shaving, did not resemble a rebellious warlord. He spoke in a low, muted voice, and something in his appearance resembled a singer, especially when he paced across the room and ruffled his mane of hair, which reached below his collar. The conflict with the command was caused by his refusal to merge with another unit, which had been decimated in a battle on the Pilica and was looking for support from a larger formation. People from that unit began to spread rumors about an impending change in the government-in-exile. They were recruiting peasants for a new organization headed by a certain Bulat. This was Lubon's version.

"You have come here to get me back in line, and I am telling you this: you can court-martial me if you want, but as long as I am here, I must know who is in these forests. I used to let in escaped prisoners of war, I used to let in Jews, even deserters from the Polish police, but I always knew who I was taking in. Who is this Bulat? What do I know about him? Maybe you gentlemen from Warsaw know something more, but for me Bulat is as familiar as the Himalayas. I used to play romantic heroes in a drama circle in Rawa Mazowiecka, but here, in the forest, I have to act just like any other boor."

Lubon did quite well at his boorishness. He definitely had a stage talent. Such people were not a rarity among provincial social activists.

He invited me to a partisan breakfast of eggs, sausage, and vodka. I still didn't know everything, but I could hardly be mistaken. I was almost sure that Rondo troops were operating on the Pilica. At breakfast Lubon confirmed my suspicions. It appeared that the first unit became operative during the prior fall. Between twenty and thirty partisans gathered at the local mill and marched through the village singing the anthem of the Warsaw underground. At that time Bulat and his men were apparently staying at the mill. One of his aides, married to the miller's niece, used to come here from Warsaw to organize the campaign "in a scientific manner." "And he did." Lubon laughed heartily as he poured another glass of vodka. "Later he returned to Warsaw. They sent a banner for the boys, a very beautiful banner. Many men went to serve under that banner."

It was all true. Jerzy Borowik told me about it after the war.

I'm not one of those who have visions. No internal or external voices warn me against oncoming disasters. Perhaps it is a sign of mental health. As I was returning to Warsaw I was carrying with me the frosty, white tranquility of the woods and the smell of campfires. Outside the train, fields lay covered with snow; when we stopped I could hear the calling of crows. It was as if we weren't moving at all: always the same flat, white landscape. When I reached Warsaw, however, it turned out the snow had melted. Everywhere there was the murmur of water gushing from the roofs. On my way from the station I unbuttoned my jacket. The sun was bright and at the second intersection I stopped to consider whether to take a streetcar or to walk home.

Please imagine a man standing on a street corner and breathing the first warm breeze, a man prolonging his moment of indecision; a man who left a winter camp in the morning and at noon arrives in a city awash in the spring thaw; a man who smiles to himself for no reason, and squints, his eyes tickled by sunlight; a man who is quite content to stand like that in an unbuttoned jacket on a street corner. The man does not know yet. It's God's mercy that he doesn't. If he knew, he wouldn't be standing there and experiencing this moment of serenity. He does not know what happened here after his departure to Warka and what will happen after his return.

I was bedazzled by the warmth and light, I felt like taking a long walk through the city. But I decided to go home first to shave and wash myself. I found a note tucked in my door. At first I thought it had been placed there by mistake. "T. is at R. Come immediately. Urgent. L." It took me some time to figure out the meaning of the initials.

After a moment I understood everything. It was not only a summons but also a warning. I must not go to Topolowa. For some reason Tola had to stay with the Rylskis. Who had been arrested? Nina? . . .

I rushed down the stairs. I was so upset that I wasted my last two matches trying to light my pipe. When I stopped at the newsstand a familiar newsman gave me a box of matches and a newspaper. I noticed an obituary in a black frame at the bottom of the first page. I had no time to read it, because at that moment a rickshaw pulled up. I had a chance to look at it only as I was on my way: *Karol Cezarewicz died at his artistic post.*

I was seized with terror: a shadow of a cataclysm, still remote and vague, passed over me; I was paralyzed, as if waiting, at any moment, to be crushed.

I entered through the main gate; the front door was open and the hallway was empty. I called, but the only answer was a yapping from Selim's room. When I opened the door, Tola's mongrel rushed toward me and danced around my legs. After a moment it sat still, as if chastised by my silence. Then I saw her, the newspaper still in my hand. Nothing came to my mind. "Is anybody home? Have they left?" I asked, and realized immediately how untimely my question was.

I must have frightened her. The soap slipped from her hand and fell on the carpet. She backed off into the room, her hand closing the open top of her pajamas. She was following me with her eyes, tracing my every move. "Why did you come here?" She grew terribly pale, and I wondered whether she was going to faint. As I moved closer and tried to lead her to the leather sofa where Selim used to sleep, she cried, "Don't come any closer!" She rested her head against the wall and closed her eyes. She asked me to go away, and I was almost ready to do as she wished. "As you wish . . ." I said, and buttoned my jacket. "I just came to help you." At these words she looked at me with such unmitigated hatred that I froze. I could not believe what she said.

She said I killed Cezar.

A man still shocked by the news of a death, who does not even know where it happened and under what circumstances, is suddenly accused of that death—what does he do?

It would have been best if I had left after these words. I should have left her alone and returned after several days. I should have given her some time. And yet that's not what I did. Astonishment paralyzed me completely, and I stared at her with my eyes wide open. So that's what it was? Cezar had been killed, and she suspected me of murdering him. In moments like this it is difficult to come up with the right reaction.

I still knew nothing about the cause of his death: I had only read the obituary. Later Wladek Sznej's wife provided me with some facts. But that was later. At the time, I could hardly ask for details, and I was so shocked it didn't even occur to me to ask. I told her again to sit down, and tried to explain, in a rather chaotic way, that for the last week I had been traveling outside Warsaw. I also tried to find out why she was staying at the Rylskis' and what had happened to Nina. Was she still at Topolowa? Was she in some kind of danger? One mistake followed the other. Finally I assured her that I felt responsible for the fate of her child. "I would be happy," I said, "if you would allow me to take care of it." Everything I said was leading in the worst possible direction, as if some evil spirit dictated each sentence.

And I didn't realize one crucial thing: everything I said would be used against me. I ought to have left immediately, rather than cause a catastrophe. I thought I was able to find some soothing words, but the words I used led straight to disaster. Selim explained it to me later: "I don't know what you told her, but you'd have done better to say nothing. Words, my dear friend, are a dangerous thing! And what did you achieve in the end? You have destroyed the very foundation of her psychological order. And just like that. The whole mental structure gave in! Only once in my career have I seen a similar crisis: a drunken man raped his own daughter and hacked her boyfriend to death. A quiet sort of man, a railway worker. He considered himself a good husband and father. Unfortunately, he did not know enough about himself. In your case, you have deprived her of her lies, which is worse than destroying somebody's truth."

Selim was certainly right. I should have kept quiet and left. I must have wounded her with every word. My very presence must have provoked her charges. I must admit I was not aware of her mental state, and because of that I feel guilty. Much could be said, though, in my defense. First of all, the fact that such a monstrous injustice literally petrified me, and that my first reaction was to come clean, to prove the absurdity of her suspicions. I started to explain how preposterous it was to accuse me of such a thing. I was looking for Miss Lala's note in my pocket, and swearing that I got off the train just that morning, that for the last week I was dozens of kilometers from Warsaw, that an hour ago I knew nothing about Cezar's death, that I still did not even know how he died. "Just think what you are accusing me of," I said. "You can't seriously believe that. For God's sake, tell me why!"

Then I met her eyes. She was looking at me with icy attention, as one looks at the most despicable liar. Finally I understood what she was trying to tell me. I killed Cezar *because he was the father of my child*. At that instant I lost my mind completely and showed her the newspaper, apparently trying to prove that I was absent from Warsaw and knew only what I had read. She stared like a lunatic at the obituary.

After a moment she raised her eyes from the paper and muttered, "You have been watching him for a long time. He caught you, and you roughed him up in the street. People saw that."

It should be evident how upset I was, because I did not even close the window. We spoke loudly, and anyone passing by might have taken an interest in our conversation. But I did not think about it at the time. I lost control of myself, I was too shocked to care about anything else. I remember a bad taste in my mouth, a burning in my eyes. I did not even have a chance to wash my hands after my journey.

People saw me struggling with Cezar. It wasn't hard to guess what people we were talking about: the same people who watched me on Kozlowiec's orders. And they told her. I suddenly felt the full weight of exhaustion. I thought I would never get out of that trap. I lost all desire to defend myself. I had just enough energy to mumble some denials. I lost another opportunity to leave. It must have been the last one, because minutes later I lost even the semblance of common sense and I spoke the desperate sentence that tormented me later at the most difficult moments. But when I realized that the "dynamists" from the present leadership of Rondo were determined to tread on my heels, I was seized with rage. Didn't she understand? I took her by the elbows and pulled her toward me. "Look at me. Tell me again I killed Cezar."

She turned her head away. I noticed her twisted mouth, just like two years ago when she spat on a Gennan soldier in Marszalkowska Street. She must have hated me very much and I still could not understand ii. A moment later I would let her go, but unfortunately she started to speak. She no longer tried to wrestle herself from my arms. She was breathing in my face. "And who was murdering all along? You! These poor people whom you made me follow and who were later found dead in elevators! You, with your boxer's jaw and your paws! You scum, you coward. You told me you'd kill Hitler, and instead you killed the best man in the world. First you watched him, then you murdered him. That network of yours, that damned hermetic network I allowed you to drag me into . . ."

"There was no network," I said. "There was nothing at all. Just some old suitcases and *The Hound of the Baskervilles.*"

I said it in an ordinary tone, with the satisfaction of a suicide who has just fastened the rope to a hook. I paced the room to collect my thoughts for the last time. Nothing could stop me now. All I had to resolve was the stylistic form of my epilogue. I decided to tell everything as it was, in chronological order and in the most ordinary way. I spoke under my breath as if describing events that occurred to one of our friends. I concealed nothing. One fact, however, should be noted: I turned over all my cards where the external side of my mystification was concerned, yet I suddenly lost my self-assurance when it came to my deeper motives. It was as if I stopped at the edge of a dark, unfathomed body of water and was afraid to take another step. "I did it because . . ." I started, and somehow could not find appropriate words. I wanted to say: I did it for you, for your own good. Yet I felt this explanation would fail to illuminate something much more complex, something unclear even to me.

It was a strange yet exemplary moment of imbalance. I stopped talking and looked out the window. After a moment I heard a muffled moaning behind me. Then somebody knocked at the door. The mongrel, who slept through our conversation, jumped up and started to bark. Tola, shaken by contortions, was lying on the floor. Someone was about to enter. I did something I cannot explain even today: I jumped through the window.

Cezar died onstage during a performance of *The Dove.* It was a violent death, and apparently the Gestapo set up camp in the Stadttheater to interrogate people. Wladek was not at home. He spent nights with his relatives in Kolo.

That much I learned from Wladek's wife on Swietojerska Street. Before letting me in she inspected me through a crack in the door. She would have told me nothing were it not for the fact that my throat was dry: I asked her for a glass of water. She opened the door and let me in. She sat on a chair and watched me as I drank the water greedily. My exhausted appearance must have moved her, for after a short conversation she gave me the address in Kolo. I drank another glass of water. It took me ten minutes to walk to Bank Square, where I caught a streetcar.

After my escape through the window I was in a state described in legal terminology as "diminished capability." It does not mean, however, that I was ready to commit an act of violence. What I felt was a compulsion, even an absolute need, to get all the explanations. A man trapped in darkness instinctively rushes toward a lamp. In this particular case only Wladek Sznej could be my source of illumination.

"A terrible botch," he said as soon as I entered the room. "They didn't expect he would drink it. I was against it. I warned them, but Bulat was stubborn. Can you believe it? That very night Lucyna went to the theater for the first time in her life. The next day she came running to tell me that he barked after drinking it. Isn't it bizarre? Jorgens drank the wine. I thought she made a mistake. You remember the scene, don't you? Yes, he drank it, and then went down on all fours and started to bark. Macabre."

Wladek was excited and kept pacing the room between a sewing machine and a double bed. Apparently I had interrupted his writing, for his fingers were stained with ink. Behind the wall there were voices. A child was cooing.

He sent his wife to the performance to get a firsthand account, while he, just in case, moved in with his relatives. For several months people had been talking about a death sentence for Rajewska, but he did not believe there would be an execution. He claimed he tried to prevent it by talking to Kozlowiec. The decision was sudden: he learned about it only the day before the event. He wondered what prompted the move.

"A sentence based on circumstantial evidence! I told him we had no right. Can you imagine his answer? He said the sentence was justified for political ends. To be absolutely honest, I have no idea what ends he was talking about . . ."

A prop man recruited into Rondo offered to add poison to the wine. It worked instantly. Wladek's wife said that Cezar was already stiff when the halberdiers tried to lift him up.

As I listened to these facts I began to understand their real meaning. I guessed that Kozlowiec had accelerated Rondo's activities in order to strengthen his position before the talks with the High Command. Since I had refused to reveal my "network," he needed some proof of Rondo's usefulness in the struggle against collaborators. Rajewska targeted! But on circumstantial evidence . . . When Straga warned me against Kozlowiec, he also made use of circumstantial evidence. Kozlowiec's role in the case of the armory on Wolska Street had not been proved. There was only circumstantial evidence. I used that evidence as a threat during our conversation on Foksal Street. Why should he defend himself otherwise? By using circumstantial evidence against somebody else be weakened the credibility of circumstantial evidence against himself. That was simple. Just an hour before I was accused of murder on circumstantial evidence. Rabczyn, Straga, I, Tola, Kozlowiec—we were all bound by an invisible circuit in which coincidence and chance often replaced proof of guilt. Kozlowiec knew how to defend himself. Cezar wanted to defend Iza. Two days before Cezar's death a night watchman put out a fire in the prop room and found a drunken Cezar sleeping under the stairs leading to the roof. The incident was covered up, but people talked about it around town. Cezar used to confide to other actors his plan to set the theater on fire. He believed a fire would save Iza's life.

Wladek waved his hand, as if pushing away issues of little importance, and began to talk about the differences of opinion that arose between him and Kozlowiec. "He lacks theoretical background. He believes only in action for the sake of action. I tried to persuade him to read the classics of Marxism."

Wladek maintained that the founders of Marxism had thoroughly analyzed the most important problems of society but forgot about metaphysics. "Add some transcendental symbols and you would have a ready-made religion. Yes, an opiate of the masses, but an opiate which confers on us a vision of the universe. There remains, however, the fundamental question of whether it can become a religion equal to Christianity or Islam. If communism today could conceive of a Red God, I swear it would conquer Europe and Asia without firing a single shot. If you have a moment . . ."

He pulled out a book marked with strips of paper. While reading he looked up, to observe my expression. I did not listen, though, absorbed as I was in a particular thought. When he interrupted his reading, I remarked that his conclusions were most interesting (which they probably were). Wladek smiled and squeezed my hand, saying we should see each other more often. He was relaxed. He saw me off to the hallway and watched me as I walked down the stairs.

I returned from the landing. "Did they warn her about it?" I asked.

Wladek was surprised and probably did not understand my question. "Wladek"—I lowered my voice—"did Tola know about the death sentence?"

Wladek was even more surprised. "We did not inform her about anything . . . considering her condition. And we were right!" He patted me kindly on the shoulder. "First of all, she has to give you a strong boy!"

I got off the streetcar halfway back to town and walked toward Swietokrzyska Street. I went to the Melpomena and discreetly asked the cloakroom attendant to call out Miss Lala. I was late: she had left half an hour ago. She had had an urgent phone call. I walked a couple of blocks. Thoughts about Cezar, Tola, and Nina were rushing through my head. When I passed the corner of Krucza and Hoza, I passed a bookstall and spotted an old bridge handbook there, tattered and bound up with a string. I started to leaf through it that night when I had trouble sleeping.

After the war, when Wiaremko entertained me with anecdotes on the train from Lodz to Warsaw, he told me all about Iza Rajewska's trial. It was held before a jury of the Actors' Association. According to Wiaremko, Rajewska appeared in a black costume—her hair smoothly combed, her face pale. "The best Mary Stuart I've ever seen! What composure, what cunning! Can you believe it? They couldn't prove a thing. She was sentenced only for accepting engagements during the occupation." Rajewska was barred from the stage for a period of five years and forbidden for life to act in the capital. During the interrogation she was asked about the circumstances of Cezar's death. Wiaremko imitated the voices of the members of the jury: "Did you know that the wine contained . . . well, yes . . . poison?" "If I knew about it I wouldn't have allowed him to drink it." Isn't that logical! And then: "How did you react when he grabbed the glass from your hands?" "I thought he was improvising. It happened before, even before the war." Most logical! Ah, and the room was decorated with a red banner that said: "Art in the service of socialism!" And when she was asked whether *he*, in her opinion, knew about the poison, she began to weep. So what do you think? An accident? A suicide?

My only explanation was: a moment of intuition. But I left Wiaremko's question unanswered. Yet I was chilled by the thought that Iza Rajewska was alive somewhere. I thought: Someday she'll die too, and she'll die in a rage because her death will be a humiliating proof that she also participated in our common fate. She'll never forgive the others, those who didn't die before her. But this was more of a pang, a shiver, than a thought. At the time, I tried not to recall the period of the occupation. A year and a half had passed since the end of the war. I had a job, my daughter could already speak, I was a member of a reconstruction committee in our apartment house. In a couple of years I would probably join the Party. Like many people I knew, I wanted to join, to become normal, and soon I would have been able to raise my hand at meetings to accept or reject somebody's self-criticism. I was a member of the intelligentsia, and the coming years were meant to invest people like me with an unprecedented capacity for self-negation. I would have undergone the collective process of self-renunciation, and today I might not have remembered my thoughts from that time. (That's rather understandable, because one's old, unwanted self is the easiest thing to forget.) Many people from the underground passed through this phase, which is described today in many different ways: sublimation of fear, opportunism, the result of moral manipulation. In my opinion it was often simply the need for social participation. I repeat, I was a member of the intelligentsia—that is, the kind of man who mixes morality with intellect and wants to be honest even in his imposed dishonesty. If he tries to adjust himself to the dishonesty, or the dishonesty to himself, he does so in order to remain honest—at least in his own eyes. The psychological conditions of these years, later described in newspapers as "the period of the cult of personality," "the period of errors and distortions," or simply "the period we have left behind," were multifarious—they extended both above—and underground. I was saved by my arrest. As a prisoner, I was a person whose infamy was a matter of self-definition; nobody expected me to improve myself, all I had to do was to acknowledge my ignominy and confirm it with my own signature. This circumstance saved me from other, more ambiguous experiences that were the fate of those of my kind who remained at large.

Excuse my digression, which has so little to do with my subject.

Now I would like to present several events that followed, in chronological order.

After returning to Warsaw, I was supposed to report immediately to Straga and to inform him about the results of my negotiations with Lubon. But Straga was hard to reach, and I could not get in touch with him for a whole week. The courier returned each time with the same answer: wait. After a week I went to Zoliborz to see my father. I felt obliged to inform him about the transfer of the Borowiks to a partisan unit. After all, he had committed them to my care. He had a visitor, an elderly woman who lived in the same apartment building, and I found them engaged in a discussion about prayer. For some weeks in the evenings the tenants had been gathering in the courtyard around a little shrine with an icon of Our Lady. It was not a new custom. Communal prayers in cellars and courtyards were also organized during the siege of 1939. Now, when the front was approaching from the East and there was talk about an organized resistance, people were turning again to Heaven for help. Communal prayers were held in almost all apartment buildings. My father's neighbor wanted to know why my father never joined them. "We see your wife quite frequently, but Professor is boycotting us. The neighbors often ask about you."

Father was in a good mood, and he glanced whimsically from Wanda to me. "You see," he said, turning his red-and-blue pencil in his hand, "I don't think God will take offense at my absence. He probably won't even notice it. And even if He does, would He visit a calamity on the whole house? It wouldn't be nice to wreak vengeance of all four floors because of the negligence of one neighbor. And you? Do you pray?" His looked my way with mock curiosity. I mumbled something unintelligible, and the neighbor blushed. "But, Professor, you are a teacher . . . an educator . . ." My father stopped smiling. "A teacher," he repeated after her. "Yes, I am a teacher." He put his pencil on his desk and interlaced his thin fingers. I knew he would say no more.

After the neighbor had left, Wanda brought me a cup of ersatz coffee. "You've lost weight," she worried, "and your face looks so tired." Bare twigs outside the window, sharp in the clear, deep air, intersected with thin veins of telephone lines, creating a black mesh against the glowing, silver sky. I remember the picture well.

Father cleared his throat. "I do not go to the shrine," he said, "but I listen to Holy Scripture. When the neighbors pray downstairs, those two spinsters who live next door read the Old Testament to their deaf-mute brother. They read very loud, probably hoping he'll somehow hear them. In fact, it is as if they are reading for me. I like those hours very much. I sit in the darkness and hear every word."

When I looked at my father I felt a vague pain, as if I were suddenly deprived of his past. He was a teacher, an educator, a man with a spotless record. He did not have to kill or cheat for his ideals and dreams. It seemed he appeared in this world with principles shaped by the previous century, and he remained faithful to them despite his eccentric views on some aspects of life. I did not inherit this legacy. Perhaps I too missed my own epoch, or at least its ideals and beliefs; for me it wasn't even "the time of contempt." Later I wanted to be an honest soldier, and I also happened to become a commander. It afforded me a double perspective: from below and from above. I would have preferred the obedient innocence of a soldier, but thanks to Rondo I came to know those who gave orders. I became scared when I realized it happened everywhere: every "top" has its struggle for power, its clash of human interests, ambitions, political maneuvering, and only an honest soldier shoots without knowing anything. But I knew. I could no longer be a naïve soldier, or a real boss; I forfeited my innocence and my clean record; finally I slipped down an ugly, slimy tunnel full of intrigues, traps, and murders. Is it always like this, I wondered, or is this only my own dark and treacherous time? . . . I was really tired.

When Wanda left us alone, I described my excursion with the Borowiks to the forests on the Pilica and assured my father they were in good hands. I also mentioned Lubon. It was true that there were adventurers among the partisan leaders, but this one seemed like a reasonable man. Before the war he was a village schoolteacher. "It may well prove," I said, "that they are in less danger there than they would be here in Warsaw." Father said nothing. He was sitting with his back to the window and I could not make out the expression on his face. When I was saying goodbye, he remained in his chair at the desk, slightly hunched over, his forehead resting on two of his thin fingers.

It was still early. From Zoliborz I went to the corner of Barbara and Emilia Plater Street. There was a contact point in the annex. Three days before, I left a message there for Straga. Nothing, no answer. I returned to Madalinskiego before curfew and fell asleep. The doorbell at six in the morning did not wake me up instantly—I stumbled to the door half asleep.

"No petty formalities, Tom," Straga greeted me. "You can slumber a bit. I, personally, like the rain." He threw his wet coat on a chair. There was the smell of cologne. He paced the room and listened to my report. "Well, yes," he said when I finished. "Do you know Lubon is dead? He was trapped in a fire—in a barn set ablaze with hand grenades. The news about his unit came yesterday. There was a battle in a village called Liwna. They were totally surrounded. Only a few managed to get through."

He thought for a moment, rubbing his smoothly shaven chin. "Yes, they cut through toward Opoczno and Konskie. What's most interesting, though, is that they got support from the very unit Lubon did not want to admit into his ranks. 'Rondo troops,' that's what they are called there. All the survivors have now joined up with them, but we are still waiting for figures and personal data. Maybe you know something about these troops, Lieutenant? . . . Are you looking for your pipe? Here it is."

I briefly repeated the information I got from Lubon. Straga toyed with his lighter. "That's absolutely true. They've been spreading rumors that the Marshal's son will soon take over the leadership of our government in London. Apparently he is supposed to be transferred from Poland. They were able to recruit a lot of young people because the Marshal is still revered in the country. His portrait is still hanging in many peasant cottages. The peasants respect him because he didn't get rich in office. All he left behind, they say, was a baton, a cap, and a horse . . . As soon as we get the report, I'll let you know who broke out of the encirclement."

The blows were coming one after the other. Five days earlier the news about Tola's illness, and now Lubon's death and the dispersal of his unit. I had no illusions. It would be a miracle if Andrzej and Jerzy had managed to escape. They were too inexperienced as soldiers. The summer before, I taught them what little they knew about guns and hand grenades. Never before had bleak thoughts besieged me with such fury. On a winter morning I had taken them to their deaths in a cold, rattling train. Otherwise they would be alive now. Only yesterday I assured my father they'd certainly survive. What could I expect? Some errant troops rampaging in the forests . . . the mirage of Rondo emerging from behind the trees? I could not believe it. So even the forest can be invented? The boundary separating reality from lie had blurred inside me. Things merged with their own shadows. I stopped believing in facts— I knew how they were fabricated. It seemed I wasn't certain of anything anymore. A month later, when Straga charged me, in the strictest secrecy, with the mission on the Titanic and hinted at a direct interest on the part of the Supreme Command in London, I stiffened in terror. I thought for a moment that Straga too had been recruited by Rondo. The blood drained from my face, and Straga, startled by my appearance, asked what was wrong.

For the first time in my life I saw myself as a man responsible for evil. I heard about Tola's illness from Miss Lala. The day after I missed her in the Melpomena, I found her on Topolowa Street. My visit did not surprise her at all. She was wearing a short man's coat, which served her as a nightgown, and an aviator's cap. She was just brewing her morning herbs. She said Tola was suffering from a mental disorder and was staying with the Rylskis. Nina moved in with her mother on Dantyszek Street (after the war I learned there was an underground print shop in the house). So far the apartment an Topolowa had not been disturbed, but an unexpected visit could not be ruled out. Nevertheless, Miss Lala had decided to stay.

"It all went wrong," she whispered. "You made a mistake." I sat on a kitchen stool and sipped herb tea in total silence. I had never seen her so depressed. "Does she suffer a lot?" "She doesn't speak to anybody," murmured Miss Lala. "Poor thing, she can neither sleep nor eat. Why did you frighten her?" "I had to tell her the truth"—I sighed heavily—"you should understand." Miss Lala looked at me with irritation. "The truth? What is easier than to tell the truth? The truth is the one thing people should be spared. The truth lives between us . . .

as it says in Scripture. An honest man does not speak the truth, he honors it in silence, just as he honors God. And you are not a godless person."

I could not find a reply to her words. She told me that Selim, who was taking care of Tola, said she shouldn't have any visitors yet. "But she isn't a schizophrenic," Miss Lala added quickly, "only a manic-depressive. These things pass . . ." She smiled mysteriously, as if leaving the passing of things to my imagination, as if this was a universal law. She handed me a little packet: herbs with a somnolent effect—I should take them both in the morning and in the evening. She also promised to keep me informed about Tola's health; we set up a schedule of meetings. As I left her, I felt a bit stronger.

Before the visit at my father's I met Miss Lala only three times. Tola's condition did not change. She spent whole days in bed, or huddled in an armchair wrapped in a blanket, unwashed and uncombed. She did not accept any food. On a few occasions Miss Lala managed to make her swallow a spoonful of sweetened water. Selim maintained she had undergone a very deep trauma, the result of which was a permanent depression of the kind once described as melancholy. When I asked Miss Lala to explain to her that Cezar died as a result of a tragic accident, that nobody should be blamed for it, she only shook her head. "I won't tell her anything, because she won't hear it. She is deep in her own thoughts. I don't even know whether she recognizes me or not . . ." She closed her eyes, puffing up like a sleepy sparrow. "Please be patient." After these meetings I usually went to Dantyszek Street to see Nina. With her intelligent, balanced mind she knew how to drive away the demons that besieged me.

I was to meet Miss Lala on Thursday. But after Straga's visit I was living in such fear and gloom I could hardly wait another day. It was as if I anticipated the worst that was still to come. I bumped into Miss Lala as she was leaving her home with a bag and some packages. She was on her way to the commuter station. The day before, Tola was moved to the mental hospital in Tworki. "Was there a relapse?" Miss Lala had red spots on her face, and she spoke in a strangely hissing voice, as if her mouth were a punctured balloon: there was a possibility of physical paralysis. "What are they going to do to her?" she squeaked. "Do you know anything about forced feeding? He said something about forced feeding and electric shocks."

The blood was pounding in my head. I offered to go with her to Tworki. "No," she insisted. "You must not. She cannot see you." And she gazed at me with her bright, severe eyes. "Now is the time you should pray."

When she left, I started to walk aimlessly. I was so stunned I seemed to lose all sense of time, for I cannot account for an hour or two of my peregrinations. Apparently I walked in the direction of Mokotow and sat on a bench in a treeless square bordered by tenement houses. Two bloodhounds were chasing each other, dragging their leashes, and in the middle of the square a troop of stocky, dark Georgians or Armenians in Wehrmacht caps, led by a one-handed sergeant, was practicing drills on the trampled grass and singing piercing, sad tunes. I got up and started along the side streets. It was warm after the rain, and my feet seemed to be made of lead. I returned to the square, but the soldiers were gone and my bench was occupied by two women with baby carriages. Somebody was beating a rug in one of the yards. I was struggling against the urge to lie down on the ground and go to asleep: to sleep through the whole tragedy. I do not think I have ever experienced an hour of such total loneliness in my life.

It must have been afternoon when I decided to take the train to Tworki. I felt I could pull myself together and regain my balance only by being close to Tola. I did not have to see her, but I could not remain in a place where she was absent. I wouldn't have been able to stand it. The moment I got on the train I felt better, as every minute took me closer to the station of my reassurance. When I finally saw the black sign announcing our arrival at Tworki, I sighed deeply as if I were returning to my own life.

Nobody paid any attention to me in the hospital. In the cloakroom I asked about Selim. I heard that after his rounds he had been summoned to Warsaw for a consultation. I went to the bathroom and splashed water on my face. For half an hour I sat quietly in the hallway and I got up only when I saw a young woman doctor. "Yes, we have a patient with that name," she said, "but she is strictly forbidden to have any visitors." She looked at me for a moment. "I'm sorry, but I can't help you." I explained I did not mean to interfere and wanted only to know her room number. I promised I wouldn't try to go there. She nodded her head and led me through a garden to another building. She took me to the second floor and showed me a corridor. Tola was in the third room on the left.

I paced the corridor for a long time, passing the tall yellow door which had no knob. Whenever someone from the staff approached I quickly turned around. Later I sat on a chair in a small waiting area near the stairs, and I must have lost all sense of time again, for the same young doctor asked me if I knew what time it was. "You may miss your last train," she said. "Shall I give the professor some message?" "No, thank you," I replied. "I'll come again tomorrow."

It was a crisp spring evening back in Warsaw. As I walked from the station to my home, I felt a familiar tingling behind me: somebody was following me again. I stopped and with a swift move I dropped a box of matches. When I bent down to pick it up, I noticed somebody stop several steps behind me. I walked some ten meters and quickly spun around. I saw two young men and immediately recognized one of them—a small dark fellow with an affable smile and a weak chin. Two weeks earlier, when he escorted me together with Professor W.'s son to Foksal

Street, he had been wearing a gray ski cap. This time he had on a cloth cap. I started walking in their direction. I was shaking with rage and trying to muffle the inarticulate growl that was escaping from my mouth. I stopped in front of them. The taller of the two hesitated under my glance and stepped back.

"Don't you dare follow me," I said quietly. "Stop sniffing around. Get lost. No more talks. Tell Bulat I don't negotiate with murderers." I was holding my hand in the pocket of my jacket. "And now buzz off," I snarled.

I walked on. As I was entering my house, I looked behind me out of the corner of my eye. The street was empty.

Selim did not want to blight my hopes. He thought it possible that she would improve after giving birth; the baby was expected in about two months. He maintained that labor might give her a salutary shock and restore her vitality; in the face of the oldest miracle of nature, he said, a doctor is more stupid than a peasant. However, he forbade me to hold my vigils in the corridor. The presence of a strange man often excited female patients. One of them might tell Tola about my visits, and that was something to be avoided by any means. From that time on, I waited in the hallway of the main building. After his morning rounds Selim was usually in a hurry. He ran toward the exit with his coat flying out behind him like a cape, but he always managed to pass me some news: for the time being there was no need for electric shock; there were the first signs of some communication with the environment; after a day and a half of artificial feeding she drank some broth. He stressed that Tola's illness had no endogenous character. The term was unfamiliar, but I sensed Selim used it as a farm of solace. He also mentioned "séances." When I asked him what he meant, he said they were a way of establishing spiritual contact between a patient and his doctor. It was a kind of trancelike confession, he explained. I remembered something I had heard about the treatment of mental illnesses through hypnosis. Selim must have guessed my anxiety, for he laughed heartily. "It's conversation, just conversation! And if you imagine we talk about you, I must disappoint you. We talk about God. Alas! I hope, nevertheless, we soon shall start talking about people. You see, in order to learn something about a human being, one has to see how he or she talks about other human beings. People, acquaintances! What we say about others reveals more about ourselves than about others. By the way, do you know that our patient has attacks of good and evil? At regular intervals! A most interesting thing. And please do not walk me to the train."

He said goodbye and rushed through the garden, his coat flapping. He had some business to see to in Warsaw. I suspected nothing, and at that time I would have been surprised to learn that for two years Selim had been in charge of the Education Department in the Government Delegacy. In certain situations his behavior revealed the discipline of a conspirator. For example, he never asked certain questions. He did not comment on the fact that I had shaved my mustache and dyed my hair. It would have given me something to think about, if I had been able to think about anything besides Tola's illness.

I must go back a little. I had promised to prepare a written report for "the Tower" (our name for the High Command) about my visit to the Warka region and about the information I received from Lubon. Straga told me to leave the material at the Barbara contact point. I worked on it the night after my first trip to Tworki. Before I went to bed I set the alarm clock for an early hour, in order to be able to deliver my report and then catch a train which would get me to the hospital just after morning rounds. Everything went more or less according to schedule on the day of which I am speaking, with one little exception.

I woke up to the rattle of the clock. I shaved and washed and drank a glass of hot milk. Then I folded and slipped my report into a narrow envelope. The morning was cool, so I wore my heavy jacket—the one with a hidden pocket under the lining. Before I went out I closed the opening with a few stitches. I was ready, and it looked like I would be on time. The streetcar was almost empty. As I jumped into the second car, I passed a woman with gray hair in one of the seats. I approached the woman conductor to buy my ticket. Then I saw the look of terror in her eyes as she looked over my shoulder toward the platform. Behind me I heard a sharp, breathless voice: "In the name of Fighting Poland!" I was about to turn around, but at the same moment I heard a shot and I fell to the floor between seats. "Don't stop!" I shouted when the streetcar started to slow down. There were footsteps on the road: the attackers were running away. The conductor pulled at the string and the streetcar started to gain speed. I crawled out from under the seats. I felt something burning under my right ear. "Blood!" moaned the conductor, her face turning green. I pulled up my collar. The lady with gray hair quietly offered me her handkerchief. I got off at the next stop and went to a pharmacy on Pulawska, where I bought a flask of hydrogen peroxide and an adhesive bandage. Then I went to a café near Union Square and dressed my wound in the restroom. I reached the corner of Wspolna without further adventure. As I walked toward Barbara, I stopped in front of a store window and examined my reflection. The bandage looked like it was covering a sore on my neck. Twenty minutes later I managed to catch the train departing from Nowogrodzka.

It may seem less than plausible, but when I was lying on the floor squeezed between two seats (it took only a few seconds), I realized with absolute clarity that Rondo was carrying out a death sentence on me. And during these few seconds I became aware of the real purpose of the attempt and had enough presence of mind to wonder whether Wladek Sznej knew about it. I cannot really explain it, but it was as if I acknowledged the bullet fired in my direction and at the same time was surprised that it could be fired with the consent of my old school friend. I managed to remain relatively calm during the whole incident, but in the restroom, when I was dressing my wound with the bandage and a wad of cotton wool, I was shaking all over and mumbling to myself, "Well, well, my dear Wladek . . ."

By the time I was on the train I had come to the conclusion that Bulat-Kozlowiec had aimed his guns correctly. It was not only revenge for my rejection and offense. My refusal to cooperate reshuffled all his cards and deprived him of his two trumps: the "network" and my own person. Right now he was holding two other cards: the anti-collaborator action in the Stadttheater and active Rondo troops in the countryside. In these circumstances, having twice expressed my adamant hostility, I became a dangerous ace of spades that could fall into the hands of his opponents. Now, since my definite break with him, Kozlowiec must have considered the possibility of my active opposition to his meeting with the underground authorities. But he did not know my hand; I could become useful, but only if I recognized his authority and kept quiet. Still, I do not know the role Kozlowiec played in the affair at the armory on Wolska. But Kozlowiec probably did not know, either, how much I knew. He must have taken my "network" seriously and he was afraid I might provoke a reaction from London on the eve of his negotiations with the Tower. His decision was logical. He had to eliminate me.

The episode left me safe in two ways. If during the talks with the High Command somebody mentioned my pseudonym, or my real name in connection with Rondo, it would be the end of me. No underground court could give credence to my explanations. I would share the fate of all provocateurs and I wouldn't even be able to blame anybody for that. After the attempt one thing became absolutely certain: my name would never be mentioned. All I had to do was make it seem that the attempt had been successful. This time, after my visit in Tworki, I did not go back to Madalinskiego Street. I went to the Satyr bar and called Janski.

My situation was pretty miserable, "beyond all criticism," as my mother would say, and my spirits were rather low. Janski appeared in the bar fifteen minutes after my call. He looked me over and said, "It would seem that that new business of yours didn't really work out . . ." I write this today from a perspective of many years, but how did I feel at that time? Awful. Everything I was experiencing seemed contrary to my character, my sense of duty and dignity. Everything seemed twisted and ridiculous. I shall never forget that choking voice behind my back, those words: "In the name of Fighting Poland!" I shall never forget the eyes of the elderly lady who passed me her handkerchief. As I was waiting for Janski in the bar on Marszalkowska, I felt I was hanging upside down, and I had the urge to leave my table immediately so that I would not attract attention of any kind. And yet . . . and yet . . .

How should I describe it? Somewhere deep inside me I felt, if not satisfaction, then at least a certainty that I was learning in the most succinct way truths that reach others only much later, or not at all, and that the degree and type of my initiation separated me from the crowd. I might try to express it in yet another way: I was never interested in ordinary human experiences such as career, power, debauchery—experiences leading only to the knowledge of the material shape of life. I was interested in life's formula, its hidden paradigm (or, as one would say today, "the code"), and perhaps I subconsciously knew it was not enough to live in order to break that code. One also had to challenge and provoke. It was not, as I have said, a fully conscious choice. If I said it was a "system" I lived by, I would be going too far. It was rather a direction followed by my instincts. Yet it became a system of facts following other facts. My part in this sequence was similar to that of a scientist who triggers a reaction and then observes its development.

I could resort to a commonplace: "Sometimes, when we accept an invitation to dinner, we are accepting an invitation from fate." But when I went to dinner at the Savoy, I already anticipated a meeting with fate, and it was by no means clear who invited whom. Do we choose our fate, or are we chosen by it? Honestly, I don't know. I cannot tell today whether I would have chosen a different fate, and this means our relationship was not purely accidental. In fact, I suspect myself of being free from the very beginning. I am not a pessimist who puts a yoke on his neck and claims that freedom does not exist.

Perhaps this is hypothesis, speculation, just another effort to interpret life from the perspective of years. Let's call it an effort to understand. If not every life is fate, and if only out self-aggrandizement raises it to the rank of fate, let's call these deliberations a bid to promote my own biography to that rank.

Witold Kozlowiec would be surprised to learn that I spent the first night after the attempt on my life under a Persian rug. I should have been in the morgue. Janski took me from the Satyr to his two-room apartment in a dilapidated four-story building on Wilcza Street near the corner of Krucza. I slept in the ambassador's pajamas among lacquered cabinets and Empire armchairs. There was a painting of a bear-hunting scene hanging over a recamier. Janski was a bachelor. "After the ambassador's death he never remarried," people used to say. He had only one coverlet, which I did not want to deprive him of. After much fussing I stretched out on the recamier and covered myself with a red-and-blue rug. "Do you take tea or coffee in the morning?" He looked at me inquisitively. "Milk," I said. "Good for your heart," he replied. He took his coverlet and left the room. It seemed he would gladly renew our partnership, but for now he displayed a tactful, somehow gloomy discretion. He did not know my plans.

I did not know them either. Deputy Kozlowiec would also be surprised at my limited activity at that time. I did nothing to ruin his political plans, to regain control of Rondo, or to warn the Supreme Command. Since I was alive I should have done all that. And Kozlowiec would certainly have suspected me of something of that sort, had he known I was alive. The High Command ignored his demands, and the negotiations never took place because of strong opposition from the Government Delegacy. Soon a new opposition emerged inside Rondo (Wladek Sznej told me about it shortly after the war), Kozlowiec found himself in the minority, and he left with a handful of men to organize partisan units on the Bug River. Shortly before the outbreak of the Uprising he was arrested by the Soviets. He returned to Poland in 1946 as an activist of the Christian Social Movement.

I stayed with Janski for over three weeks. It would have been better to disappear from the city. With my good relations with Straga, I could certainly have gotten a transfer to one of the districts outside Warsaw. There was a sabotage campaign being waged against the German transit lines used by divisions retreating from the East and the underground was looking for new men to do the job. And yet something in me resisted. I had a feeling that everything had to be decided in Warsaw, a place I came to regard as the natural setting for my life. Apparently I was not alone, since a million people decided to stay despite rumors of an imminent uprising. There was even something in the streets like the anticipation of a holiday. It reminded me of the end of the school year, when no one bothers to do homework anymore and everybody is waiting for the beginning of two months of freedom. It seemed there were more young people in the streets. The roundups had stopped and German patrols in the center of the city became uncommon, although when they did appear now, they consisted of larger units and carried their guns at the ready.

One afternoon, as I was walking down Marszalkowska Street, I noticed two young girls running hand in hand in high platform shoes. As we passed each other in a doorway, I met their joyful eyes. At that time I had already changed my appearance. I had shaved off my mustache and dyed my hair with Janski's bandoline. I wore horn-rimmed glasses and a bowler hat and carried a cane. My stage experience proved quite useful. Before leaving the house I would put a wad of tissue under my upper lip. I probably looked like an American mortician. In any case, Wiaremko did not recognize me when we passed each other on Marszalkowska. I used my full make-up only in the street. During my visits in Tworki I took off my glasses, removed the tissue, and left my hat in the cloakroom.

It was evident the end of the war was near. The traffic in the streets was heavier. The streetcars were packed; rickshaws were in high demand and some were now equipped with folding roofs to protect passengers from the rain. That spring there were more coffee bars and small restaurants, and an elegant café was opened right on the riverbank. The terror of five wartime winters was breaking up, and the old big-city charm was slipping back in through the cracks. There was still a quarter of an hour of dreary silence after curfew, after which the night quickly came. From a distance one could hear the murmur of trucks rolling toward Praga. People said there were practically no Germans in the city, and the underground newspapers reported the transfer of the last division to the Eastern front.

After the evening tea Janski would take out an atlas and a ruler to measure the distance from the front and to convert it into days. "In a month we'll open an antique store in Mazowiecka Street. I have an eye on a certain location. Just don't mention it to anybody yet." I laughed. Of course I was aware the war was coming to an end, but at the same time I had a sense of personal completion, of an abrupt finale to the main plots of my life. I tried to imagine a day when I would get up from my bed a free man. What then? I would leave the house. But where would I go? To meet Straga? To Topolowa Street? To Barbara? The postwar freedom was an empty horizon. Janski's antique store seemed more real than anything. If, before the war, I was accidentally in the theater, why on earth shouldn't I become an accidental antiquarian after the war? My future was characterized by a dreamy indifference. I would extinguish my pipe and go to the bathroom. Among the few books I came across in Janski's apartment were *Pan Tadeusz, or the Last Foray in Lithuania* and Casanova's *Memoirs*. I read them cover to cover.

I went to Tworki for the last time the day before the beginning of my new assignment. On that day I also appeared for the last time in my bowler hat, with a cane and with a pair of cream-colored gloves sticking out of my pocket. After waiting for Selim for half an hour I left the building. I started to walk around the women's annex and finally decided to go to the second floor. The corridor was empty. As I came closer I noticed that the door to Tola's room was wide open. The room was being aired. I saw a couple of beds, a cleaning lady with a broom, and patients in striped hospital gowns. Tola was not among them. I was horrified: either she was never there or she had been moved. Then I noticed a woman with unkempt hair. She must have known something about me, for she began to shout, trying to outdo the others: "She gave birth! This morning! A girl!" As I was running back to the main building, I bumped into the young doctor I knew. I doubt whether she recognized me, but she assured me both the mother and her daughter were fine. "The professor has a lecture now. Please come tomorrow." I knew I would not come. I could not wait for Selim any longer. The train was leaving in a quarter of an hour. At noon a man was to meet me in the Pomological

Garden. I was to recognize him by the jacket he carried over his shoulder and a newspaper in his hand. He would ask me about Pankiewicz Street. The next day I would be on the Titanic.

Titanic . . . I am not sure who invented that name. Was it Straga? It is quite possible. Black humor was definitely his style. I remember how he looked at my dyed hair. "What's that? Mourning? Was there a death in your family?" When I explained that I smelled something fishy and some suspicious types were hanging around my house, he thought for a moment. "And what would you say about a small disappearing act?" "From the city?" "No, from the earth." He said it was just the thing he wanted to talk to me about. He was brief, and he stressed the importance of the task (as I mentioned before). What was surprising, however, was his suggestion that I was free to say no. This was something quite unusual: in my clandestine work I received only orders. We were walking along the Kosciuszko Embankment not far from the Citadel. For a long time Straga was quiet. "This is for your ears only, Tom. You are one of two candidates. I could talk to the other guy, only . . ." When he saw that I did not quite understand him, he continued: "You will be isolated from any external contacts for an indefinite time. The post can be abandoned only after blowing it up." He laughed and pointed to the sky. I was never sure when he was serious and when he was just testing me.

On the appointed day, exactly at noon, I was overtaken by a courier who appeared in the Pomological Garden with a brown jacket thrown over his shoulder and a rolled newspaper in his hand. My appearance left no doubt: a bowler hat, a cane, a pair of gloves. When he asked me, "Which way to Pankiewicz Street?" I answered, "I really don't know. I'm from out of town." He led me through Poznanska and Koszykowa. I walked some fifty steps behind him. It seems we had a back-up. At the corner of Koszykowa my guide stopped to get a light from a cyclist standing in a doorway. A girl who was standing with him quickly crossed to the other side of the street. From that time on, the courier followed the girl, I followed him—still fifty steps behind him—followed in turn by the man with the bicycle. We passed the square in front of the Polytechnic and entered Polna Street. We walked along the old racetrack where Selim's body was later found. In the meantime I observed some other people from the backup team. In front of No. 40 my guide let me enter first. The girl who was leading the way was waiting for me in the hallway, and there was yet another man—high boots, his back against a window—waiting on the landing between the two flights of stairs. It was the first time I had encountered such stringent security measures. I suppose they were meant to protect one of the apartments used by the Tower.

The meeting, though, was not much different from other briefings. I was asked certain questions, and I gave certain answers. I familiarized myself with the general plan. My duties were spelled out in detail, point by point. In addition to me and my interlocutor, an elderly gentleman who looked like a prewar military commander, there was another man with a thick black mane of hair. He never spoke a word. The curtains were drawn and the room was warm. It was a doctor's office with an examination table and scales. It all took exactly forty-five minutes.

Outside, it looked as though an old riverboat had run aground and was rusting between the rotting remnants of a pier. A couple of planks led from the gangway to a slimy wooden landing. Next to the dock the body of the boat, its paint peeling, was covered with bird droppings. It was a deserted area: the ground along the river and under the bridge was littered with ruptured barrels, broken glass, and all kinds of trash. Further on, the sandbanks were overgrown with bushes. This was the Titanic and its immediate environment. In better days it must have been a small passenger boat. Only sections of the bridge remained. Under the deck, among all sorts of broken objects, I found a chipped washbasin with a tap, splinters of deck chairs, and an old lady's field glass.

Over eight weeks of idleness. I endured it quite well. I had been supplied with food: sugar, salt, marmalade. I boiled kasha and heated German canned goods on a small stove. I even acquired a taste for hardtack soaked in watch. I slept on a mattress under the deck, and on warm nights I took it outside. The sky was full of stars. In the morning I woke to the screams of birds in the rushes. I pulled on my sweater and watched the swarms of birds soaring into the sky. I shaved only during the first week. Later I grew a mustache and a beard. Once I looked in the mirror and saw a new growth of my red hair above my forehead. I cut it very short with my razor. From that time on, my head and my face were covered with the same red stubble.

My instructions were engraved on my mind. Never leave the post. A small lever hidden behind a fire extinguisher will cause an explosion. Leave the post only after receiving a coded message. These were the three basic instructions. I also had a score of others for every kind of situation. I was given new papers in the name of Roman Jesionek, master welder. The owner of the boat, Mr. Kraus, now on the Eastern front, had hired me to repair the hull.

I memorized everything, and yet I did not know one thing: why I was guarding the Titanic. At first I tried to solve the puzzle, but later I no longer thought about it. I was in good physical condition. I was living in a kind of healthy stupor. During the day I walked around in bathing trunks, and at night I exercised on the deck. One morning during the first week a courier appeared to receive my report. From that time on she came every week to supply me with food. Her pseudonym was Kinga. She was born near Nowy Sacz. During the war she abandoned the novitiate at the convent of St. Clare and started to work for the underground. When she unbraided her hair she was almost pretty. After a while she started to come in the evenings and leave in the mornings. My major daily occupation was watching the beach on the opposite bank through my field glass. The Sarabande café had been opened there in the spring. From the bridge I could see green, blue, and yellow umbrellas and moving silhouettes. On quiet afternoons I could hear the piano playing. I could spend hours looking through my field glass. I grew more and more attracted to the colorful, bright spectacle—the umbrellas, the beach, the sky, the movements of little figures on the grass. The scene never failed to arouse my curiosity. Long ago, when I was sitting in Lobzowianka and watching the crowd passing by, I had a feeling my life was passing me by too. Now, after all these years, it was as if I had come full circle and returned from far away, from the other side. Sometimes the sun hurt my eyes, but I kept watching, regretting every lost opportunity. I left the deck in the evening when the umbrellas were being folded. Then, from the right bank, I heard a rhythmical, hollow stomping. The front was approaching.

It was the end of July and the heat was intensifying. One day I asked Kinga to go to Topolowa. She returned one day later with the news that my wife was still living near Warsaw, my daughter was healthy and had red hair. Miss Lala sent me a prayer to ward off evil spirits. I was supposed to carry it on my person. The prayer contained a verse about the sea of blood that would cover the earth as high as the belly of a horse. For the next couple of days nobody visited me. One morning, after a night spent on the deck, I was awakened by the birds. Then there was silence. I sensed some anxiety. The front was silent too. All morning, since dawn, I lay on the deck with my field glass. In early afternoon the umbrellas were taken away, as if before a storm. The beach was deserted.

If I were to draw a diagram of my life, I would have to present two intersecting circles. In one of them I would write *fears*, in the other one *hopes*. The overlapping area of the two fields would be called *facts*. I would have to mark it as a special zone. For years my hopes and fears were projected into the future, until one particular fact would provoke a swift reaction—as if a gas were suddenly converted into a solid state. The outbreak of the war was one of these facts, as was the beginning of the Uprising and my excursion from the right bank into the city in September 1944. The soul seems to be a highly volatile thing when confronted with such facts, which tend to define our whole future.

I could say my hopes failed me and my fears did not come to pass. But the facts made them so insignificant I cannot even feel disappointment or relief. If I wanted to give my biography some meaning and continuity, I would have to decide first whether my life was a unified entity or whether perhaps I lived several different lives, each time amputating a useless part of my self. I am sure many people have asked themselves a similar question and in most cases must have arrived at a similar answer: a biography is not made of facts but of our attitudes toward the facts. Perhaps. In this sense, it is possible to argue that my own profile displayed some fundamental unity. Yet such a proposition does not explain everything. Perhaps the semblance of unity is my own creation: I erect bridges in order to fuse a multitude of disparate characters into one person: a student and a soldier, an impostor and a prisoner, a show boy in love and a loving father? I acted in a number of different plays, but today I wouldn't be able to repeat any of my roles. It is easy to surprise me with a question. Not because I cannot find an answer. The reason is different. Questions concerning my past force me to re-create my past role. On such occasions I feel ill at ease and my performance is less than convincing. The explanation is rather simple: I lack the old stage design, the setup. My partners have long since left the stage. The audience is different. This last element is perhaps the most important one: an audience that does not understand the plot of the play. How can I explain my epoch to someone who lives in a different time? Totally impossible. Reticence is the most reasonable solution. The fewer words, the better, almost complete silence, a mystery. I remember an evening after my daughter's return from her first stay with Tola in France. She brought back a stereo record player. That evening, when Miss Lala was playing patience in her room, we both listened to records. She asked me then what it meant "to pass through the Greenmarket." I replied that the Greenmarket was a square where the Germans rounded up the population of several districts during the Uprising. I spared her the details. She could have easily learned them from somebody else, and I am sure she did take care of that in advance. That question contained an accusation: Why weren't you with her? I started pacing across the room. I said the outbreak of the Uprising separated many couples and later it was difficult to find each other. As I was saying that, a strange thought came to my mind: I was lying to the same woman in the next generation. For a moment I felt like telling her I was not her father. It was only a moment, though.

When, shortly before the Uprising, I received the message that Tola was still in the hospital, I did not know what had happened before. I did not know she had been separated from her daughter. Two weeks after her birth they both returned to Warsaw and lived for a while on Topolowa. Soon, however, Tola had a relapse. It happened in the first days of July, when she accidentally heard about Selim's death. She stopped breast-feeding and, as before, would spend hours staring out the window. After several days Miss Lala brought her good news: Selim was alive. Tola allowed Lala to dress her. She was smiling on the train to Tworki. She believed Selim had escaped from the Gestapo and was hiding somewhere in the hospital. The child stayed with Miss Lala. I learned all these details only during the Uprising when the Powisle district had capitulated and I had moved to the center of the city with a group of Rondo fighters.

I shall have to move back in time again. During the first days of the Uprising I did not leave the Titanic. I waited, according to my instructions, for a specific order to abandon my post. I could hear shooting coming from the city; at night flares flashed over bridges—the sky was glowing in the west. In the darkness I heard people escaping through the rushes along the river nearby. I managed to stay put for five more days. I kept changing my mind and the hesitation was quite nerve-racking: should I stay or should I leave? In either case I would feel like a deserter. To wait out the Uprising on a rusty old boat or to disobey an order and leave my post? My instructions recommended that in "sudden and unpredictable circumstances" I should use my own judgment. This was something to consider. But were the circumstances—that is, the Uprising—really "sudden and unpredictable"? My head was bursting. I limited my rations, and moved my mattress under the fire extinguisher, so that if there was a German raid I could immediately blow myself up. During the day I watched the Poniatowski Bridge through my field glass: tanks were rolling into the city from the right bank. I swore aloud, because even through my small lady's field glass one could clearly see the German crosses on the turrets.

I left the Titanic the night before August 6. My food had run out. I still had no idea of the purpose of my sixty days in that old creaking boat. When I asked Straga after the war he speculated that the vessel might have been a kind of "empty safe." When in the spring of 1944 there was talk about the need to secure the archives of the High Command, the problem was resolved through a system of five different safes. There were five separate operations involving five different people. The instructions were given in five different locations. The archive was placed in one of the safes, and the other four were reserves in case the "full" safe was imperiled. In all five operations identical security measures were applied. Straga said the location of the archive was known only to two members of the Tower and the chief of staff in London. It was therefore possible there was literally nothing on the Titanic—neither the archive nor explosives. I base all this on the information provided to me by Straga.

I rarely wonder whether my life represented the fate of a generation, or how history will judge everything I did, alone or with the others. This is definitely not my interest. Such topics are the domain of Wladek Sznej, who likes to deliberate on them during our games of bridge at Straga's. We usually play every second Sunday. We sit at a table in the corner of a large room separated into halves by a screen. It divides the room into Straga's private space, full of display cases with historical spurs, and the reception room of his wife, the dentist, who also happens to treat Wladek. A few months ago a discussion ensued between hands. Of all people it was I who started it. Though I promised myself never to engage Wladek in philosophical debates, I asked, God knows why, whether the blood shed by our generation was really necessary, and how it could be justified from today's perspective. That, more or less, was what I said, and I was thinking mainly about the Uprising. Wladek's eyes immediately lit up. "The underground?" he said. "The underground is always a minority that believes in a struggle for ideals. But the majority of people never get involved in that struggle. The majority wants to survive in the physical sense. The majority does not believe in ideas. And the majority is right. You know, humanity is not a clash of ideas and values. It is a chaos . . ."

I noticed a cold glimmer in Straga's eyes.

"It is a highly structured chaos," continued Wladek. "It is a chaos we fill with meaning. We create legends and make ourselves believe in illusions. We, the people, use lies to bring some order into reality! There is no such thing as the truth of reality. All the testimonies and accounts are only interpretations."

"It seems I played diamonds, Professor," Straga said, and fixed his very light eyes on Wladek.

Wladek wiped his glasses.

"There is one mistake in our way of reasoning," he said. "It is a mistake about history seen as a struggle between right and wrong principles, or positive and negative factors . . . history interpreted through logical, aesthetic, and dialectical categories. This is simply a lie. Or, if you prefer, a lie about a lie . . ."

He laughed. "What is Man, my dear gentlemen? A creature that invests its existence with meaning. What is humanity? A community that reads meaning into its fate. You should know something about these matters, Comrade Rita!"

Miss Rita was dozing off with cards in her hand.

I forgot to add that Miss Rita was also a guest at our games. And not only at Straga's. After her departure from Marxism (she was expelled from the Party for ideological deviation) she frequented many houses and was always welcomed by people from whom, years ago, she was separated by ideas and—to say the least—contrary circumstances. She was also seen in churches during funerals. In March she was present at a mass dedicated to the Marshal by the Augustinian Brothers. She always dressed the same: a blouse and a tie. During games of bridge she would fall asleep during the bidding.

I left the Titanic during the Uprising. I left my bag with welder's tools, the mattress, and the washbasin. I took my shaving utensils. When I jumped down onto the shore that night, I heard a rustle behind a garbage heap there, and something like a moan. I stopped to listen. It could have been a wild cat. But after a moment something crawled out from that direction and grabbed me by my trousers. It was a man asking for help. He had been shot in the leg, and he kept assuring me we could get to the insurgents' positions. I lifted him up, and we stumbled a dozen or so steps. Then he collapsed, and as I was hoisting him up onto my back I noticed his deformed anatomy. I hadn't had anything to eat for a whole day and I was weaker than usual. Now I had to carry a hunchback. Even more, I did not know the territory, and I could not figure out how to bypass the German positions. They must have been quite close, and they certainly patrolled that part of the riverbank. Occasionally they rushed by on motorcycles shouting to each other. Now and again, we had to duck the spotlights that swept over the embankment. As we lay on the ground the hunchback seemed to be in the mood for conversation. Twice he asked me in a whisper where I was running from, and then declared a storm was brewing. It must have been fever, and I was worried. We had a clear starlit sky above us, and the night was cool. I took him on my back and ran for a couple of meters, only to fall to the ground again. The hunchback moaned quietly.

He must have been quite conscious, though, because when I took him piggyback he whispered authoritatively that I should get a good running start and climb over the embankment. From that time on he led me like a horse. I carried him through a sloping garden, through an empty factory yard, through several courtyards, and finally, jumping across some ditches, into a doorway full of sleeping people.

I don't have much time left. I'm pounding at the typewriter well into the night. To be honest, I have no idea what awaits me in a week's time, but whatever it is, I am not trying to anticipate it. The only thing I wonder about is whether I shall be able to act properly. Yesterday, for instance, as I was taking the keys out of my pocket, I suddenly became lost in thought. What if she steps off the plane wearing a frock? I was standing with the keys in my hand trying to imagine the welcoming scene at the airport. If it was true that after Marcenat's death she spent a year in a convent in the mountains, it was possible she had already taken her vows. They sent me an old clipping from *Elle* in order to prepare me for the worst, to spare me the shock. But if she comes in a frock, it will mean she has chosen to be a saint. And that will be the end of it. She'll demand beatification, and I'll allow myself to be pulled into that game. Who knows, perhaps I'll even manage to stage a miracle in order to convince her that God is in agreement with her.

She isn't here yet, and I am by no means certain she'll come at all, though I've already made various preparations. Last week I located Cezar's grave. I decided to go to the cemetery by myself to find the grave and to clean it up so that it wouldn't seem forgotten. At the cemetery gate I bought a wreath and a bunch of tulips. I think she'll be moved by these tokens of anonymous remembrance. And I am absolutely sure she'll come here the day after her arrival. I am also sure she'll try to conceal this visit from me. Yet it is important that everything hidden from me should work as smoothly as possible.

The woman who looks after the graves showed me the way. We walked quite a distance and she mumbled to herself as we went: she was mute. Finally, she gestured joyfully and showed me a black plate surrounded by pots of azaleas. The flowers were fresh and the plate had been polished. Seeing my surprise, the woman pointed toward the flowers and then to herself. Of course, somebody was paying her to care for the grave. She smiled—revealing her teeth, rotten to the gums. I thought Cezar would be frightened at the sight of his postmortem attendant. When she had left I stayed for a while to arrange the wreath and the flowers. As I was leaning over the plate, I realized that the tulips would die the next day and that I'd have to come again to buy fresh ones. Then I realized I would come every day, for as long as necessary, to buy fresh flowers. This willingness was free of hesitation. What surprised me most was that for all those years I never found time to come to Cezar's grave.

There were periods when I felt completely free from her. Sometimes, in moments of exhaustion, I couldn't even remember her face (more and more often I imagined her with the features from Witkacy's portrait). Her letters were rare and they did not contain photographs. Even her name was no longer uniquely hers: it was now the name of my daughter. Only once did I hear her voice. It was a week before my imprisonment. I was fiddling with radio dials one evening, and I accidentally picked up Radio Madrid. Through the interference I heard the words of a political commentary. When I switched on my amplifier—at that time we were living in a single room divided by a bookcase which sheltered my bed—the whole room was filled with her coarse voice. She oscillated between a whisper and a cry full of dramatic, accusatory vibrations. It seemed as if she whispered and shouted to me, to Lala, and to that sleeping redheaded child with four parents. I could have sworn she was drunk. I knew about her drinking problem from discreet hints in Nina Willman's letters. But even if she was drunk, the alcohol only strengthened her contempt and passion, the same religious, obsessive disagreement with life now focused in one direction—toward the East. She cursed! She cursed with the same fury as when she was standing in front of the execution squad in *The Iron Maiden* and I was aiming at her with my Mannlicher. Nobody in radio could match her voice. That voice became famous after the first broadcasts. She was described in the Warsaw press as "the croaking Egeria of political bankrupts," and the Polish newspapers in London lauded her as "our émigrée Pasionaria."

Her drinking bouts were followed by periods of depression. Apparently she was treated at the Red Cross's expense in a Swiss sanatorium. Nina mentioned this in one of her letters. In the first years after the war I found it difficult to imagine a Swiss sanatorium. It was a fantasy that recalled *The Magic Mountain*, which I borrowed from Nina before her resettlement in the ghetto. Snow-covered peaks, stone buildings, bearded doctors in white smocks. Sometimes I added a St. Bernard I remembered from a childhood photograph. Later, in prison, when I learned to live by imaginary events and could daydream without interruption for as long as two weeks, I created a whole "Swiss fantasy." Blue sky, mountain peaks covered with snow, a stone building with a red roof surrounded by evergreens, a terrace with a row of deck chairs. First I saw her on the balcony as she rested, wrapped in a thick white shawl. Then the image changed: she got up, walked around, spoke with people. I was one of the patients and she liked to talk to me the most. I taught her how to ski.

Such reveries may seem naïve, but I could certainly allow myself that diversion in my cell. I had more time and less prestige at stake than in real life. If I had been able to become that tolerant skier in my real life, if I had restrained myself during our conversation in Selim's room, perhaps she would not need the cure in that Swiss resort. The memory of that scene torments me to the present day. I left her on the floor—covering her ears with her hands, her body shaken by strange, hollow moans.

She escaped from the hospital one hour before the outbreak of the Uprising. She could not get into the apartment on Topolowa, because at four o'clock Miss Lala took the baby to a doctor on Mokotowska Street. We learned all this only after the war. When people from the Staszic colony were being rounded up by the Germans, she was seen with the Rylskis. In the winter of 1945 a person returning from the camps told me she was in the Greenmarket where men were being killed and women raped. In May we got a postcard from a DP camp near Frankfurt. It reached us through the Red Cross. An unsigned note: "I am alive. Please forget me."

From the legal point of view I had no rights to her child. Yet the birth certificate was issued by the Registry in Praga with my name as the father. I was not asked to present any documents: my oral statement was sufficient. When we had to identify her mother, Miss Lala and I declared she had been missing since the Uprising. I certified this with my signature and thought: Well, that's it. I was beginning a new period in my life and signing the document did not call for any philosophical reflections. It was simply one of the issues that needed to be taken care of. It was a matter of the past. A quite original past, one might say, but let us not exaggerate. The world and life involve more elements of fantasy than we usually admit. The period of time from the evening at the Savoy to the morning in the Registry was certainly not the most unusual in this world. The peculiarities of individual fates begin to fade as soon as we start to think about the miracle of life and the even more intriguing mystery of death. Therefore I say: Let us not exaggerate. What happened seems fantastic to me only because it happened to me.

The World published a photograph (the occasion, it seems, was the twentieth anniversary of the Uprising) showing a group of people posing in some courtyard. Several young men in German helmets, two girls with white-and-red armbands, and a group of civilians. Among them one could recognize Wladek Sznej and myself. Behind us, there were women seated on a little bench beside a cluster of graves with wooden crosses. I do not remember who took the photograph. What was striking about it was that we were all smiling and looking playfully into the lens, like a group on a picnic in some small town. The photograph impressed me even more because it must have been taken during the last days of the defense in Powisle. At that time I joined a Rondo unit retreating through the sewer from the Old Town, where it had been fighting since August 1.

Rondo troops joined the Home Army shortly before the Uprising, having incurred heavy losses in the Kampinos Forest, where Andrzej Borowik, a poet and a soldier, died a hero's death. I had been separated from my own unit, which was fighting in the Czerniakow fort. When I reported to the Powisle command and asked to send a message to the High Command, my pseudonym and rank were taken down and I was ordered to wait until the next day. I came every day for a week. Finally an officer in a beret told me that a messenger had been dispatched to the Titanic on the third day of the Uprising with a coded order: "prepare for the storm," which meant I could abandon my post. On the way he was wounded in the leg. He reported that I had carried him back to Powisle. There were no further instructions for me. During the next week we ran out of water, and the Germans started to bombard us with incendiary shells. I organized a fire brigade and helped carry sandbags to the roofs. I slept in doorways and staircases. The nights were still warm. On one of these warm nights two soldiers ran into our doorway and called for civilians to help them repair a damaged barricade. A couple of us went with them. There was a bustling in the darkness. Someone was tearing flagstones out of the pavement; someone was passing out picks and shovels. Everything was happening in the darkness and in a hurry. We had to be ready before daybreak. It was already getting light when a man passing me a concrete slab mentioned my name.

I had never seen Wladek Sznej in a similar state. He was a broken man—not so much in the spiritual as in the mental sense. He was unable to think, as if his brain had stopped communicating with him. One would need to know Wladek well to realize something was wrong when he started a conversation by saying that his wife, Lucyna, was safe in the country. He should have started with a historico-philosophical discourse and presented his assessment of the present situation. But he seemed indifferent to current events, and in moments of danger he displayed uncommon courage. When a shell from a heavy railway cannon was heard coming, everybody ran for cover, but Wladek never budged. He remained in place, leaning on his pick in the middle of the road. I pulled him into a doorway by force. After an hour the cannons went silent, and morning prayers began. When I woke from a short nap, I saw Wladek kneeling in front of a shrine among a group of soldiers and tenants. I waited until the end of the ceremony. Wladek returned and squatted beside me on a step. "I was praying for Lucyna," he said. He had left her in the country two weeks before the Uprising when he joined Rondo troops. He has been looking for me. He went to Madalinskiego and Topolowa. Later he heard some rumors about my death.

He took off his glasses—they were cracked—blinking and squinting. "I thought this country would become like all the others . . . that it would break its vicious circle of uprisings, prayers, and blood. But it's impossible. I'm telling you that it's useless to think here. One can only survive—like the peasants, like Lucyna."

There was another raid at noon. A group of civilians with shovels scampered around a dug-out grave. The tenants were sitting in basements and clustered in doorways. Wladek and I were standing at the wall of an annex next to the yard. "Wladek," I said, "let's move inside. That'll be safer."

Wladek did not react. His face was gray and he was staring at a brick lying on the ground a couple of steps from where we stood. He grew pale.

"I don't understand a thing," he muttered. "I'm not sure of anything anymore. What has happened to me . . . I do not comprehend."

Suddenly he lifted his head. He looked into the cloudless sky and shouted, in a high, shrill voice, "You! What do you want?! You want to play with me like a cat with a mouse? Speak! Say something! You! . . . You!"

He leaped forward, grabbed the brick and pushed it clumsily toward the sky. He was all red now, gasping.

I was frightened. At the same moment there was an explosion in the house next to us, and the sun was clouded by red dust. I was frightened by Wladek's words. "Listen," I whispered, "you shouldn't. You must not."

But a moment later it occurred to me that Wladek's intellectual constructions had entirely collapsed, and that he was in fact returning to God, whose name he never used before. It was a peculiar return, and a far from conclusive one, as it turned out.

My parenthood became a fact less than two weeks later. After thirty-six days of defense the Powisle command surrendered, and Wladek suggested that I accompany his little unit downtown, where the Uprising still continued. He arranged for a document stating that I was a member of Rondo, because military police during the Uprising did not allow people from other districts into the center of the city. We passed through several backyards to Foksal Street, and then we ran to Chmielna along a barricade dividing Nowy Swiat. From there we followed a tunnel dug under Jerozolimskie Avenue to Krucza Street. I was walking with Wladek. I was unarmed. I had a white-and-red Rondo armband, and I was followed by a young boy in a helmet with a white eagle painted on it. There was a long line of people waiting for water with buckets in their hands. Wladek turned around and smiled. "Didn't you live here somewhere before the war? On Zurawia Street?"

He was surprised by my lack of response. But I was rooted to the ground. Approaching from the opposite direction, Miss Lala was pushing a baby carriage. A small shaggy dog was tottering behind her, and the whole scene was bathed in the pink and golden glow of the sun setting behind the roofs.

It is difficult to grasp a moment when the impossible turns into reality. In any case, the moment when I bent over the carriage, when the child, red fluff on the top of her head, looked at me thoughtfully and grabbed my ear . . . well, I did not experience it as a turning point in my life, and after a couple of minutes it seemed to me quite natural that I was pushing a carriage toward Mokotow and listening to Miss Lala tell me how she was sitting in a doctor's waiting room when suddenly she heard shots and cries: "Make way for Fighting Poland!"

All I thought was that five years of military service had come to an end and I was joining the civilian population.

Finished?

It seems so. I have the impression I have written everything. Everything, that is, within my scope as the author of the story. I could just add some information about other people.

I could describe, for example, Tola's postwar life. Her marriage to an officer in the Royal Air Force, five years her junior, whom she left after two years. Her relationship with the lonely and paralyzed Jean-Claude Marcenat. Since 1958 she lived with him near Nice. They say it was thanks to her that he regained his ability to walk: with canes, but on his own two legs. His last, and fatal, stroke happened a year ago when they were driving along Via del Sole.

I could also say a lot about our daughter. Sometimes, for fun or out of tenderness, she also calls me Tom. I would be glad to record at least a couple of scenes—for example, her performance during a students' festival in 1964, when with red hair bouncing she banged a drum and shouted to two thousand twenty-year-olds: "It's a trap, trap, trap!" I must say I was very impressed. I could also describe our conversation on the eve of her breakup with a young literature graduate who failed to live up to her expectations. He reproached her for her prolonged visits to France. "It is because he is not like you, Tom," she said, among other things. It was a conversation that lasted several hours, during which she told me calmly that she knew the identity of her real father. She learned about it from Miss Lala before her second visit with her mother. The incident casts an interesting light on Miss Lala's views concerning telling, or not telling, the truth depending on circumstances. If I had more time I would gladly discuss the subject a bit further.

If I had more time I could also convey my opinions and thoughts about some strictly contemporary matters. I have the materials right here in my desk. In 1973, during the annual Congress of Theater Art in one of the old cities on the North Sea, I met a Harvard professor of Polish origin who invited me to participate in an international survey: thirty questions concerning the respondent's attitude toward himself, his country, and the world. For a whole week I spent each evening in my hotel room recording my answers. I changed the names of the people involved, their personal data, and the situations. I did it less out of fear than out of my natural disapproval of personal confessions, or perhaps . . . my conspirator's instinct. I made a copy of the tape and brought it back to Poland in the pocket of my coat. I keep it here, in my drawer, and if I had more time I could simply transcribe fragments of the texts and include them in my story.

But I don't have the time. Yesterday I got a letter from Paris, this time containing a photograph. It has been raining today since early morning. The photograph shows two women standing at a railing on some bridge, probably on the Seine. They are almost identical: long legs, elegantly styled hair. They are both wearing sunglasses that cover their faces like masks. I looked at the photograph for an hour, and were it not for a gesture of one of these women—a light, caring hand resting on the shoulder of the other—I wouldn't be able to tell which is the mother and which the daughter.

A telegram said: "Arriving 20th 1 P.M. Thursday." No signature. Thursday is tomorrow.

I have no doubt it means they are returning together. I know my daughter's codes: she sent me the photograph instead of signing the telegram. Tomorrow, therefore, I shall begin (how many times now?) a new chapter of my biography.

Before I finish I would like to close some accounts. Yes, Wladek. I owe you a couple of sentences by way of conclusion. Because your presence, your ideas, and you yourself have played an important role in my life. In both the good and bad senses. I am grateful to you for leading me twice to a place where love took total control of me. For many years. You were the involuntary arranger of these two meetings, which gave me a sense of existence. For that, I thank you, Wladek.

For many of my formative years you played the devil's advocate, provoking me to self-defense, or self-awareness. My resistance to you was somehow delayed (unfortunately I am a bit of a slow thinker); nevertheless, I opposed you with all my might and I am sure that without you, and my resistance, I would be a different man today. For that, too, I wish to thank you, Wladek.

I have only this one copy of my notes. I ask the person reading it after my death to deliver it to Professor Wladyslaw Janota-Sznej, who will certainly survive me. He'll do with it as he sees fit.

ABOUT THE AUTHOR

Kazimierz Brandys was born in Poland in 1916. He was awarded numerous prizes, including the Jurzykowski (1982), the Prato-Europa (1986), and the Ignazio Silone (1986). He was made a member of the French Order of Fine Arts and Literature in 1993. Bandys died in France in 2000.

Europa Editions publishes in the US and in the UK. Not all titles are available in both countries. Availability of individual titles is indicated in the following list.

Carmine Abate
Between Two Seas
"A moving portrayal of generational continuity."
—*Kirkus*
224 pp • $14.95 • 978-1-933372-40-2 • Territories: World

Salwa Al Neimi
The Proof of the Honey
"Al Neimi announces the end of a taboo in the Arab world: that of *sex!*"
—*Reuters*
144 pp • $15.00 • 978-1-933372-68-6 • Territories: World

Alberto Angela
A Day in the Life of Ancient Rome
"Fascinating and accessible."
—*Il Giornale*
392 pp • $16.00 • 978-1-933372-71-6 • Territories: USA & Canada

Muriel Barbery
The Elegance of the Hedgehog
"Gently satirical, exceptionally winning and inevitably bittersweet."
—Michael Dirda, *The Washington Post*
336 pp • $15.00 • 978-1-933372-60-0 • Territories: USA & Canada

Gourmet Rhapsody
"In the pages of this book, Barbery shows off her finest gift: lightness."
—*La Repubblica*
176 pp • $15.00 • 978-1-933372-95-2 • Territories: World (except UK, EU)

Stefano Benni
Margherita Dolce Vita
"A modern fable...hilarious social commentary."—*People*
240 pp • $14.95 • 978-1-933372-20-4 • Territories: World

Timeskipper
"Benni again unveils his Italian brand of magical realism."
—*Library Journal*
400 pp • $16.95 • 978-1-933372-44-0 • Territories: World

Romano Bilenchi
The Chill
120 pp • $15.00 • 978-1-933372-90-7 • Territories: World

Massimo Carlotto
The Goodbye Kiss
"A masterpiece of Italian noir."
—*Globe and Mail*
160 pp • $14.95 • 978-1-933372-05-1 • Territories: World

Death's Dark Abyss
"A remarkable study of corruption and redemption."
—*Kirkus* (starred review)
160 pp • $14.95 • 978-1-933372-18-1 • Territories: World

The Fugitive
"[Carlotto is] the reigning king of Mediterranean noir."
—*The Boston Phoenix*
176 pp • $14.95 • 978-1-933372-25-9 • Territories: World

(with Marco Videtta)
Poisonville
"The business world as described by Carlotto and Videtta
in *Poisonville* is frightening as hell."
—*La Repubblica*
224 pp • $15.00 • 978-1-933372-91-4 • Territories: World

Francisco Coloane
Tierra del Fuego
"Coloane is the Jack London of our times."—Alvaro Mutis
192 pp • $14.95 • 978-1-933372-63-1 • Territories: World

Giancarlo De Cataldo
The Father and the Foreigner
"A slim but touching noir novel from one of Italy's best writers
in the genre."—*Quaderni Noir*
144 pp • $15.00 • 978-1-933372-72-3 • Territories: World

Shashi Deshpande
The Dark Holds No Terrors
"[Deshpande is] an extremely talented storyteller."—*Hindustan Times*
272 pp • $15.00 • 978-1-933372-67-9 • Territories: USA

Helmut Dubiel
Deep in the Brain: Living with Parkinson's Disease
"A book that begs reflection."—*Die Zeit*
144 pp • $15.00 • 978-1-933372-70-9 • Territories: World

Steve Erickson
Zeroville
"A funny, disturbing, daring and demanding novel—Erickson's best."
—*The New York Times Book Review*
352 pp • $14.95 • 978-1-933372-39-6 • Territories: USA & Canada

Elena Ferrante
The Days of Abandonment
"The raging, torrential voice of [this] author is something rare."
—*The New York Times*
192 pp • $14.95 • 978-1-933372-00-6 • Territories: World

Troubling Love
"Ferrante's polished language belies the rawness of her imagery."
—*The New Yorker*
144 pp • $14.95 • 978-1-933372-16-7 • Territories: World

The Lost Daughter
"So refined, almost translucent."—*The Boston Globe*
144 pp • $14.95 • 978-1-933372-42-6 • Territories: World

Jane Gardam
Old Filth
"Old Filth belongs in the Dickensian pantheon of memorable characters."
—*The New York Times Book Review*
304 pp • $14.95 • 978-1-933372-13-6 • Territories: USA

The Queen of the Tambourine
"A truly superb and moving novel."—*The Boston Globe*
272 pp • $14.95 • 978-1-933372-36-5 • Territories: USA

The People on Privilege Hill
"Engrossing stories of hilarity and heartbreak."—*Seattle Times*
208 pp • $15.95 • 978-1-933372-56-3 • Territories: USA

The Man in the Wooden Hat
"Here is a writer who delivers the world we live in…with memorable and moving skill."—*The Boston Globe*
240 pp • $15.00 • 978-1-933372-89-1 • Territories: USA

Alicia Giménez-Bartlett
Dog Day
"Delicado and Garzón prove to be one of the more engaging sleuth teams to debut in a long time."—*The Washington Post*
320 pp • $14.95 • 978-1-933372-14-3 • Territories: USA & Canada

Prime Time Suspect
"A gripping police procedural."—*The Washington Post*
320 pp • $14.95 • 978-1-933372-31-0 • Territories: USA & Canada

Death Rites
"Petra is developing into a good cop, and her earnest efforts to assert her authority…are worth cheering."—*The New York Times*
304 pp • $16.95 • 978-1-933372-54-9 • Territories: USA & Canada

Katharina Hacker
The Have-Nots
"Hacker's prose soars."—*Publishers Weekly*
352 pp • $14.95 • 978-1-933372-41-9 • Territories: USA & Canada

www.europaeditions.com

Patrick Hamilton
Hangover Square
"Patrick Hamilton's novels are dark tunnels of misery, loneliness, deceit, and sexual obsession."—*New York Review of Books*
336 pp • $14.95 • 978-1-933372-06-8 • Territories: USA & Canada

James Hamilton-Paterson
Cooking with Fernet Branca
"Irresistible!"—*The Washington Post*
288 pp • $14.95 • 978-1-933372-01-3 • Territories: USA & Canada

Amazing Disgrace
"It's loads of fun, light and dazzling as a peacock feather."
—*New York Magazine*
352 pp • $14.95 • 978-1-933372-19-8 • Territories: USA & Canada

Rancid Pansies
"Campy comic saga about hack writer and self-styled 'culinary genius' Gerald Samper."—*Seattle Times*
288 pp • $15.95 • 978-1-933372-62-4 • Territories: USA & Canada

Seven-Tenths: The Sea and Its Thresholds
"The kind of book that, were he alive now, Shelley might have written."
—*Charles Spawson*
416 pp • $16.00 • 978-1-933372-69-3 • Territories: USA & Canada

Alfred Hayes
The Girl on the Via Flaminia
"Immensely readable."—*The New York Times*
164 pp • $14.95 • 978-1-933372-24-2 • Territories: World

Jean-Claude Izzo
Total Chaos
"Izzo's Marseilles is ravishing."—*Globe and Mail*
256 pp • $14.95 • 978-1-933372-04-4 • Territories: USA & Canada

Chourmo
"A bitter, sad and tender salute to a place equally impossible to love
or leave."—*Kirkus* (starred review)
256 pp • $14.95 • 978-1-933372-17-4 • Territories: USA & Canada

Solea
"[Izzo is] a talented writer who draws from the deep, dark well of noir."
—*The Washington Post*
208 pp • $14.95 • 978-1-933372-30-3 • Territories: USA & Canada

The Lost Sailors
"Izzo digs deep into what makes men weep."—*Time Out New York*
272 pp • $14.95 • 978-1-933372-35-8 • Territories: World

A Sun for the Dying
"Beautiful, like a black sun, tragic and desperate."—*Le Point*
224 pp • $15.00 • 978-1-933372-59-4 • Territories: World

Gail Jones
Sorry
"Jones's gift for conjuring place and mood rarely falters."
—*Times Literary Supplement*
240 pp • $15.95 • 978-1-933372-55-6 • Territories: USA & Canada

Matthew F. Jones
Boot Tracks
"A gritty action tale."—*The Philadelphia Inquirer*
208 pp • $14.95 • 978-1-933372-11-2 • Territories: USA & Canada

Ioanna Karystiani
The Jasmine Isle
"A modern Greek tragedy about love foredoomed and family life."
—*Kirkus*
288 pp • $14.95 • 978-1-933372-10-5 • Territories: World

Swell
"Karystiani movingly pays homage to the sea and those who live from it."
—*La Repubblica*
256 pp • $15.00 • 978-1-933372-98-3 • Territories: World

Gene Kerrigan
The Midnight Choir
"The lethal precision of his closing punches leave quite a lasting mark."
—*Entertainment Weekly*
368 pp • $14.95 • 978-1-933372-26-6 • Territories: USA & Canada

Little Criminals
"A great story…relentless and brilliant."—*Roddy Doyle*
352 pp • $16.95 • 978-1-933372-43-3 • Territories: USA & Canada

Peter Kocan
Fresh Fields
"A stark, harrowing, yet deeply courageous work of immense power and magnitude."—*Quadrant*
304 pp • $14.95 • 978-1-933372-29-7 • Territories: USA & Canada

The Treatment and the Cure
"Kocan tells this story with grace and humor."—*Publishers Weekly*
256 pp • $15.95 • 978-1-933372-45-7 • Territories: USA & Canada

Helmut Krausser
Eros
"Helmut Krausser has succeeded in writing a great German epochal novel."—*Focus*
352 pp • $16.95 • 978-1-933372-58-7 • Territories: World

Amara Lakhous
Clash of Civilizations Over an Elevator in Piazza Vittorio
"Do we have an Italian Camus on our hands? Just possibly."
—*The Philadelphia Inquirer*
144 pp • $14.95 • 978-1-933372-61-7 • Territories: World

Lia Levi
The Jewish Husband
"An exemplary tale of small lives engulfed in the vortex of history."
—*Il Messaggero*
224 pp • $15.00 • 978-1-933372-93-8 • Territories: World

Carlo Lucarelli
Carte Blanche
"Lucarelli proves that the dark and sinister are better evoked when one opts for unadulterated grit and grime."—*The San Diego Union-Tribune*
128 pp • $14.95 • 978-1-933372-15-0 • Territories: World

The Damned Season
"De Luca…is a man both pursuing and pursued. And that makes him one of the more interesting figures in crime fiction."
—*The Philadelphia Inquirer*
128 pp • $14.95 • 978-1-933372-27-3 • Territories: World

Via delle Oche
"Delivers a resolution true to the series' moral relativism."—*Publishers Weekly*
160 pp • $14.95 • 978-1-933372-53-2 • Territories: World

Edna Mazya
Love Burns
"Combines the suspense of a murder mystery with
the absurdity of a Woody Allen movie."—*Kirkus*
224 pp • $14.95 • 978-1-933372-08-2 • Territories: USA

Sélim Nassib
I Loved You for Your Voice
"Nassib spins a rhapsodic narrative out of the indissoluble
connection between two creative souls."—*Kirkus*
272 pp • $14.95 • 978-1-933372-07-5 • Territories: World

The Palestinian Lover
"A delicate, passionate novel in which history and life
are inextricably entwined."
—*RAI Books*
192 pp • $14.95 • 978-1-933372-23-5 • Territories: World

Amélie Nothomb
Tokyo Fiancée
"Intimate and ho   l romance."
—*Publishers Wee*
160 pp • $15.00   A & Canada

Valeria Parrella
For Grace Recei
"A voice that is   —*Rolling Stone* (Italy)
144 pp • $15.0   orld